"Trixie Lynn,"

. . . he said her name again.

The color drained from her face and her legs gave out at the same moment he reached her. Sam snaked an arm around her waist, holding her steady against him. The second he touched her, his senses sharpened. She smelled of watermelon shampoo and Ivory soap, a familiar scent that tugged at his memories. He had the fiercest urge to press his lips against her freckles to see if they really did taste like cinnamon.

Sam was transfixed. It was as if nothing had changed and they were jettisoned back to their freshman year in high school, so full of yearning. In that suspended second everything fell away and they were stripped bare of all defenses, all artifice. It was as if they'd never been apart. High school sweethearts. True loves. Soul mates.

Forever and always.

By Lori Wilde

THE TRUE LOVE QUILTING CLUB
THE SWEETHEARTS' KNITTING CLUB

LORI WILDE

THE *True Love*
QUILTING
CLUB

AVON
An Imprint of HarperCollins*Publishers*

AVON BOOKS
An Imprint of HarperCollins*Publishers*
10 East 53rd Street
New York, New York 10022-5299

Copyright © 2010 by Laurie Vanzura
ISBN 978-1-61664-152-8

Printed in the U.S.A.

This book is dedicated to my cousin, Tony Award-winning actress Judith Ivey. I might not have known you well growing up, but you'll never know how much your talent, courage, and dedication to your craft inspired the young writer in me. I humbly say "thank you" for showing me how to carve my own path in a competitive business.

ACKNOWLEDGMENTS

Many people think that writing is a solitary pursuit, but it's really a team effort. I want to thank my editor, Lucia Macro, and her assistant, Esi Sogah, for helping me produce the best work I'm capable of.

Thanks to the best agent in the world, Jenny Bent, who has never stopped believing in me.

On the level of research I must thank actress, writer, and award-winning audio-book narrator C.J. Critt, who graciously answered my endless questions about show business. C.J., you've got an amazing voice.

And to Linda Kelso Epstein, who so willingly gave of her time to help me research quilts. Thanks Linda, you're the best!

THE
True Love
QUILTING
CLUB

PROLOGUE

Twilight, Texas, 1994

A quilt is a quilt is a quilt.
—Trixie Lynn Parks, fourteen-year-old ragamuffin

It was turning out to be the second worst day of Trixie Lynn Parks's fourteen-year-old life.

Her father's hateful words pounded through her head like a migraine. The sound of her running feet slapping against the pavement echoed in her ears, compounded the pain.

For the most part, the streets of Twilight, Texas, stretched empty. Families were inside taking their evening meal. The stores on the town square had already closed. A few cars sat parked outside the diner; the smell of cooking oil slathered the air. A lone merchant swept the sidewalk in front of his mercantile. He raised a hand in greeting, but Trixie Lynn lowered her head and just kept running.

She'd come home from school to find her father

packing up their things just as he had so many times before. They'd never stayed in one town longer than a year. It was May and school was almost out. Two more days left. Everyone was looking forward to the last-day-of-school party on Friday and her father was packing.

The sight of him, with a roll of duct tape in his hand and cardboard boxes strewn around the living room, stoked something fierce inside her—anger, disappointment, hurt, betrayal. He'd promised her this time he'd stick with a job. The nuke plant in Glen Rose paid well. She loved Twilight, and for once, she was doing well in school. Why was he uprooting her again? She saw destruction in that flash of silver tape, felt it tear through her insides as effectively as a jagged-toothed saw.

He'd glanced up at her, a hard, determined expression sitting on his mouth and his graying dark hair sticking out in tufts from the side of his head. For as far back as she could remember, she'd never felt close to him. Not the way a girl should feel close to her father. He kept her at a distance with his tense, slope-shouldered posture and his faded, faraway brown eyes. There had always been a missing synapse, a gap between them, and no matter how hard Trixie tried, she had never been able to close it. When her mother ran off things only got worse. The mosaic of her fractured childhood pelted her.

"Dad, push me on the swings."

"You're a big girl, Trixie Lynn, push yourself."

"Can you help me with my homework, Dad?"

"Not now, I gotta mow the lawn."

"The boys at school are making fun of me 'cause I don't wear a bra. I need a bra."

"Here's twenty dollars, go buy one."
"I love you, Daddy."
"Stop talking with your mouth full."

She thought of how he'd failed to celebrate her birthdays ninety percent of the time. How he gave her the brush-off any time she'd tried to hug him. She'd thought it was because he blamed her for her mother leaving. If she'd been a good girl, if she'd just picked up her toys off the floor and eaten her vegetables and brushed her teeth like she was told, then her mother wouldn't have left and her father wouldn't hold her responsible.

All those years of feeling ignored and disregarded by her father converged into one big defiant lump in the pit of her stomach. Why not take a stand? He already hated her. What else did she have to lose?

"I'm not going," she'd said flatly before he ever said a word, and slung her schoolbooks onto the sofa.

Her father had said nothing, just kept throwing things into the cardboard box—a lamp made from a cowboy boot, a red lap blanket, a fistful of cassette tapes by George Jones, Marty Robbins, and Merle Haggard. "You're fourteen, you have no say in the matter."

She sank her hands on her hips. "You can't make me."

He'd rocked back on his heels, looked at her with the empty expression he so often threw her way. "I can and I will," he intoned.

"I'll run away," she threatened.

He blew out his breath. "Don't push me, Trixie Lynn."

She stalked across the room and pushed against his shoulder. "There, I'm pushing you. What are you going to do about it?"

He drew back a hand and she thought he was going to hit her. And for a bright second she felt a strange spark of joy. She'd caused a reaction in him. Even if he hit her, it meant he felt something. That he wasn't totally apathetic.

"Go to your room and start packing."

"No. I'm going to go find my mother and live with her."

He laughed, harsh and angry. "Good luck with that."

"I'll do it. Just watch me."

Slowly, he'd gotten to his feet, but he hadn't looked at her. He turned his head, jammed his hands in his pockets. "Go find your worthless mother. See if I care. I've tried to do right by you, Trixie Lynn. Take care of you after your mother left us. I've fed you and put a roof over your head. I bought you those purple sneakers you have on that cost sixty dollars, but none of it is good enough. You're always wanting more, expecting more."

"I don't care about all that stuff," she yelled. "All I've ever wanted was for you to love me. Why can't you love me?"

He spun around to face her, a balding, bland-faced dullard of a man who drank too much beer on the weekends and spent the majority of his spare time watching sports on television. "You want to know why?"

Mutely, she nodded. At last, to have the question answered. It wasn't her imagination. He didn't love her. He never had. Misery constricted her throat.

"You sure you really want to know why?"

"I do."

"Because," he said flatly, "you're not my daughter."

The words, once spoken, hung in the air between them, tight as a hangman's noose. She was not his daughter? How could that be? But some small part of her had always known. He was black-haired and brown-eyed. Her mother had been a brunette with hazel eyes. And here, she'd turned up with copper-colored hair and Irish green eyes.

"I've tried to love you," he said, "but I can't. I don't know how. You want too much. You suck the life right out of me."

His words hit her more sharply than a physical blow, the pain in her heart crippling. Her knees buckled, but she stiffened her spine, resolved not to show him how much he'd hurt her. "Whose daughter am I?"

"How the hell do I know? Your mama was a whore, and you're shaping up to be just like her."

She'd run away from him then, hurling herself out the front door, running as fast as her purple sneakers would carry her. She'd run until she couldn't breathe and a sharp pain cut a swath in her side. She sank down on the curb, not even knowing where she was, sank her head into her hands, and sobbed her heart out.

Only when a comforting hand touched her shoulder did she realize she had probably made a spectacle of herself.

"Are you okay?"

She'd turned her head and there he'd been, looking down at her with a worried expression on his face.

Sam. Her best friend in the whole world. Just when she needed him most.

"It's . . . I . . ." She hiccupped, then started crying fresh tears.

"Something's tearing you up inside."

She nodded.

"You need to talk?"

"Uh-huh." It was all she could manage.

"Let's find someplace quiet, out of the way of rubberneckers."

She looked up to see the curtain in the window across the street move, and on the porch next door, an old woman sat in a rocking chair eyeing them speculatively. "What are you doing here?" she asked.

"Mowing lawns for spending money." That was when she noticed the grass clinging to his jeans and the sweat stain ringing the neck of his T-shirt.

"Oh."

"How about you? Why are you on this side of town?"

"I ran away from home."

He held out his head. "Come on, let's go talk about it. I know the perfect place."

They'd walked down the street hand-in-hand, and it wasn't until they turned the corner that she realized they were on the block behind the town square. With his fingers linked through hers, he guided her to the side entrance of the Twilight Playhouse. He tried the handle. It was unlocked, and the door sprang open. Sam raised an index finger to his lips and drew her closer to his side.

They tiptoed into the darkened theater. The ghostly silence amplified the sound of their footsteps against the old wooden flooring. He guided her down the aisle of the auditorium and onto the stage. Simply stepping up on the stage immediately made her feel better as she imagined herself acting before a live audience. One day, she *was* going to be an actress. One way or the other, she was going to make it happen. Then everyone would love her and Rex Parks would deeply regret having treated her so badly and her mother would regret running off and leaving her.

"Where are we going?" she whispered.

"You'll see." He guided her around the velvet curtain.

It was dark as midnight back there, and her heart jerked with fear and excitement. As if sensing her mood, Sam wrapped a hand around her waist and from his pants pocket produced a tiny penlight. He shone it over the wall. The slender beam of light picked up the wooden ladder leading to the catwalk area that the stage crew used.

"Up you go," he whispered.

"I'm scared," she confessed.

"It's okay. I'm right here with you all the way."

In that moment she completely forgot about Rex Parks and what he'd revealed. She forgot that he was taking her away from Twilight, the only place she'd ever wanted to call home. She forgot everything except the fact that Sam Cheek was scaling the ladder behind her, his breath hot against the nape of her neck. In that moment all her teenage longing converged into one throbbing mass of desire lodged deep in her lower abdomen. She felt all shivery and breathless as she crawled out onto the platform and Sam came up beside her.

"Lie down on your back," he said.

"What?" Her pulse spiked through the roof. Was he thinking what she was thinking? But she was too young for this. Even though she wanted him, even though she was in love with him, she wasn't ready for lovemaking.

"Lie on your back," he repeated, and switched off the penlight.

With trembling limbs, she lay down on her back, and the second she saw the ceiling she understood his request. "Oh." She laughed. "So that's why you wanted me to lie down."

"What did you think?" he murmured, lying down beside her and cupping the back of his head in his palms.

"I thought . . ."

"That I'd lured you here to steal a kiss?"

"Yes," she admitted.

"I would never do that," he said, his tone deadly serious. "I would never take advantage of you."

They stared up at the ceiling dotted with hundreds of luminescent stick-on stars glowing an eerie white-green in the blackness. Amid the numerous smaller stars was one large one, brighter than the rest and positioned squarely in the middle.

"In my universe, that's you." Sam pointed. "The biggest star of all, outshining the rest." He reached down to take her hand.

Trixie's breath hung in her lungs. For the very first time in her life, she knew what it felt like to be utterly cherished. She lay there on the hard plywood floor of the stage loft, gazing at the stars, smelling his grassy scent, her hand warm in his, and for one sweet second, she forgot about her problems and drifted on the bliss.

"So what's got you so upset?" Sam said a few minutes later. "Why are you running away from home?"

She told him about Rex. How he wasn't her father. How he'd admitted he didn't love her, but was raising her because he felt a sense of duty. How he had quit his job at the nuke plant and they were moving on again. To a new job, a new town, one far away from Twilight. As she talked, she started to cry again. More softly this time, her tears weighted with inevitability. She knew she was going to have to go with Rex. She had nowhere else to turn. She had no grandparents that she knew of. No relatives to take her in. She was barely fourteen. Too young to get a job. And sad as it was that Rex didn't love her, he had taken good care of her, met her physical needs if not her emotional ones.

When she finished her tale, Sam sat up and looked down at her. The tracks of her tears had dried a salty rut across her temples into her hairline. She could barely make out his features in the dim illumination from the faux stars above.

He gazed at her with an expression that made her stomach flip. "I believe in you, Trixie Lynn. You're going to do great things, have a great life."

Joy, pure and sweet and powerful in the way only a fourteen-year-old in love for the first time can feel, poured over her with the rush of Niagara Falls. She sat up, not knowing what to do next, not knowing how to respond to the sensations shooting through her teenage body.

Then he'd leaned over and brushed his lips against hers.

Lightning. Trixie Lynn felt as if she'd been hammered by a white-hot bolt of lightning.

Sam must have felt it too because his eyes widened and he looked like someone who'd been through his first earthquake.

They'd kissed again, tenderly, slowly, exploring. It had lasted for what seemed like hours. Trixie Lynn dissected every nuance of the moment, every sound, smell, taste, touch. Her best friend, Sam, was kissing her, and it felt glorious.

"We better stop now," Sam said, pulling his lips from hers and threading his fingers through her hair. "My mom's gonna be looking for me."

Trixie Lynn sighed. She didn't want to go.

He got to his feet and held out his hand. She took it, and he pulled her up beside him.

In spite of all the kissing, she felt much worse. Now she knew exactly what she was leaving behind. She wanted to rage against the injustice of it all, but the look in Sam's calm eyes suddenly quelled her anger.

"It's going to be okay," he said. "You're going to grow up and be strong. You're going to get everything you want."

"I want you. I want to stay in Twilight."

"You can't stay in Twilight. But that's okay. You're destined for bigger things. You're gonna be a star. I feel it in my bones."

She peered at him in the darkness and saw the calm, steady light of certainty in his eyes. That look made her believe that anything was possible.

And just like that, the second worst day of Trixie Lynn's fourteen-year-old life became the best.

CHAPTER ONE

New York, New York, present day

Quilts are memories made visible.
—Nina Blakley, Broadway actress, owner of the
Twilight Playhouse, and founding member of the
True Love Quilting Club

Inside a cramped, dusty pawnshop on the Lower West Side of Manhattan, Emma Parks lined up behind a muscle-bound bald guy wearing Mr. Clean earrings, a stained peacoat, gray Dickies workpants, and scuffed Doc Martens boots. He smelled of powdered eggs, cod liver oil, and eucalyptus. He snarled at the woman behind the cage, demanding more than she wanted to give for the toothy orange chain saw he had slung over his shoulder.

A chain saw? In Manhattan?

From the forbidding look of the guy, Emma figured it was better not to ask, and closed her fingers around her most valuable possession. This was all she had left.

Over the years, she'd sold off her memories one by one—her grandmother's collection of Imperial Glass, her high school class ring, the Prada handbag she'd bought herself for graduation with money she earned playing summer stock at Six Flags.

The man slammed the chain saw down on the counter and turned away from the cage, a fistful of dollars crumpled between his hammy fingers. He glowered darkly. Emma took a step backward. He brushed past her mumbling, "Watch out, girlie," and stormed from the shop.

"Next," growled the woman behind the cage in a two-packs-a-day-Camels voice.

Emma stepped up to the counter.

"Whatcha got?" The woman had an oversized head on a near-anorexic body, a casaba melon face, and long, scraggly gray hair that tangled down her shoulders. Central casting would have been all over her for a cauldron role in *Macbeth*. On the other side of the bulletproof glass, she perched atop a hydraulic stool jacked up high. "Well? I ain't got all day. Show it or step off."

With a tug of wistful regret, Emma opened her hand, revealing the diamond-encrusted, star-shaped brooch resting in her palm.

The woman's eyes narrowed, and they took on a shiny yellow cast like a hungry feral cat who'd spotted a baby rabbit. "Stick it through the opening."

Reluctantly, Emma slid the brooch through the small opening cut into the barricade.

The woman pounced, snatching up the brooch, holding it up to the light. Then she opened the drawer in front of her and took out a jeweler's loupe. She studied it for a long moment. "I'll give you two hundred dollars."

Shock dropped Emma's mouth. "It's worth at least ten times that amount. It's white gold and there's a diamond on each point of the star."

"They're diamond chips of questionable quality."

"It was appraised at twenty-five hundred dollars over ten years ago," Emma argued past the nausea gathering in her stomach.

Two hundred dollars wouldn't begin to cover the thousand dollars she needed for the exclusive Master X's tutoring sessions. Master X was her last hope. She'd tried everything she knew to make it big, and after twelve years in the trenches, she'd hardly made a dent. So far, the most successful thing she'd done was a speaking role as the big toe in an antifungal ointment commercial. The residuals helped pay the bills, but every time that commercial aired, something inside her died a little. This was not great art. This was not what she suffered for.

Master X had grudgingly agreed to accept her as a student, *if* she came up with a thousand bucks by the end of the week. It was almost impossible to get accepted by Master X. He didn't advertise, didn't even have a Web site. You had to know somebody who knew somebody to get you into one of his classes. Jill Freeman, one of her old roommates, had taken his course last year, and a week later, she was cast as second understudy to Julia Roberts—who was, at her age, now playing M'Lynn—in a stage revival of *Steel Magnolias*.

After that, Jill's career had taken off. She'd moved to L.A. and snagged an ensemble role in a popular sitcom. Jill wouldn't tell her what she learned in the class. Master X swore his pupils to secrecy with a confidentiality clause. But she did put in a good word for

Emma. If Emma could just scrape up the money for his class, she believed Master X's techniques were the missing pieces of the puzzle that could shoot her over the top.

"Hey, times are tough all over. You shoulda sold it ten years ago." The caged woman glowered.

"I didn't need the money ten years ago."

"Two hundred dollars. Take it or leave it."

Sorrow-tinged disappointment swept through her. She bit down on her bottom lip to keep it from trembling. "Please," she whispered. "The brooch was the last thing my mother ever gave me."

The day stood out in her memory, clear and sharp. She'd come home from first grade to find her mother sitting on the couch, her secondhand, navy blue American Tourister rolling luggage at her feet with a dog-eared copy of Jack Kerouac's *On the Road* resting atop it. Her mother had been smoking, a snubbed-out Virginia Slims lay in a saucer, her eyes red-rimmed and her face blotchy as if she'd been crying. She'd smelled of wine and the Wind Song cologne Trixie Lynn and her dad had bought her for Mother's Day.

She'd never seen her mother smoke. Instantly, the hairs on her arms had lifted. "Mama? What's wrong?"

Mama had forced a smile, patted the sofa beside her. "Come, have a seat, Trixie Lynn."

She'd edged over, knowing something awful was about to happen. "Mama?"

"I gotta go, Trixie Lynn."

"Go?" she asked in a voice so small and tight it hurt her chest. Even now, just thinking about it, she felt that old pain, dead center of her heart. "Where are you going?"

"To follow my bliss."

She hadn't understood what that meant, but it didn't sound blissful to her.

"Listen." Her mother had taken both Trixie's hands in hers. "I can't do this anymore."

"Do what?"

"Stay here in Podunk, USA. Stay married to your father. I got sidetracked, derailed when I got pregnant with you. I'm almost thirty, Trixie Lynn. If I don't do it now, I never will."

She heard the whooshing of her own blood pounding in her ears. "Will what?"

"Make it big in Hollywood. I'm special. I'm destined to be a star. I can't keep living a lie."

"Can I go with you?"

"No honey. You gotta stay here. Stay in school. Take care of your daddy. He'll need you."

"Mama, please, please don't go."

"I gotta. You'll understand one day. Here. Put out your hand. I got a present for you."

Trixie Lynn had put out her hand, and her mother settled the brooch in it.

"It's worth a lot of money. A nice man bought it for me a long time ago, but more important than that, it's a symbol. You know what a symbol is?"

Trixie Lynn wasn't sure, but she nodded anyway.

"A star for a star. The man who gave it to me said, 'You're gonna be a star someday. You're destined for greatness.' So, Trixie Lynn, if you get to feeling lonely for me, you pull out that star and you hold it tight and you remember who your mother is."

"Okay." She ducked her head.

Her mother hooked two fingers under Trixie Lynn's chin and forced her face upward. "What does this brooch represent?"

"Stardom."

Her mother had beamed. "Good girl. Now give me a hug." She hugged Trixie Lynn so tight she couldn't breathe. Rocked her quietly in her lap. Rocked her and whispered, "You're gonna be a star, you're gonna be a star, you're gonna be a star."

Then a car horn had honked outside.

"That's my ride. I gotta go." Mama set her aside and stood up. Then she had walked out the door, strolled down the cracked sidewalk, and climbed into a shiny white Cadillac with a man Trixie Lynn didn't know sitting behind the wheel. They drove away, and Trixie Lynn never saw her mother again.

Following her mother's departure, Trixie Lynn had immediately gone in search of the perfect vehicle that would fly her to celebrity—ballet classes and soccer practice and art. But she was graceful as an egg, bruised like a week-old banana, and quickly discovered she had the artistic ability of a chimpanzee.

Finally, at fourteen, she found what she'd been searching for.

The minute she stepped onstage in the lead role in Twilight High School's production of *Annie*, she felt for the first time as if she'd finally found her way home. She'd been born for this, singing her heart out, sliding under the skin of a fictional character, letting her imagination flow, running away from the sad, empty life of Trixie Lynn Parks.

Once she embraced the stage, there was no turning back, never mind that her looks conspired against her ambitions. For one thing, she was skinny—all sharp elbows and knees, flat butt, even flatter chest. Not to mention her height (or lack thereof). She barely passed the five-foot mark. And then there was the matter of her copper-colored hair and the freckle-faced complexion that went with it.

No beauty, Trixie Lynn, no sirree. But she was whip-smart and possessed an iron will. When she made up her mind about something, it was a done deal, no matter how long it took. No matter what she had to endure.

She'd left home at eighteen. Not that there was much of a home to leave; she and her father had long since moved away from Twilight, the one place where she'd ever felt like she belonged. She legally changed her name to Emma and took off for New York City. For twelve years she waited tables, went to auditions, lived in cramped, cockroach-infested loft apartments with numerous roommates, and she never, ever stopped wishing and hoping and dreaming of her big break. She was going to be a star. Her mother had deemed it so.

She dated rarely and always casually. Love, she knew, could derail plans for fame faster than a stalled car on an Amtrak rail, and heaven forbid if she ever got pregnant. Unplanned pregnancies had ruined the careers of many an aspiring actress.

The only time she'd ever come close to losing her heart was at fourteen, back in Twilight. To the first boy she'd ever kissed, dark-eyed, black-haired, enigmatic Sam Cheek. His kiss had been a bottle rocket of sensation, and she'd never forgotten it. Mainly to remind herself of what she had to avoid. That kind of electric chemistry caused nothing but trouble for a girl with big plans.

Emma could still picture that beautiful boy. Once in a while she wondered what had become of Sam. Did he have a wife? Kids? What had he done with his life? He'd talked of becoming a veterinarian. Had he achieved his goal? But for the most part, she kept her thoughts where they belonged, on her goal of stardom.

"Two twenty-five and that's my final offer," said the woman behind the glass, snapping Emma back to the present.

"It's special," she whispered.

"There's no market for sentimentality."

"Please." Emma blinked. "I need at least three hundred."

The woman eyed her. "Let me guess. You came to New York with stars in your eyes. You were gonna make it big on Broadway. Am I close?"

Numbly, she nodded.

"You been here awhile. You been knocking on doors and knocking on doors and knocking on doors, and nobody's answering. Sure, you've landed a few parts, off, off, off Broadway that didn't pay a plug nickel. Or maybe you were even crazy enough to pay to be in some slipshod production. You've waited tables and worked as a receptionist and passed out flyers in Times Square. Anything to make a buck."

It was an Alice in Wonderland moment. How did the woman know this about her? Was she that obvious? That much of a cliché?

"Pipe dreams," the woman intoned.

"Pardon me?"

"You're never gonna make it. If you were, it would have happened by now. You're not pretty enough. Too short, too redheaded, too fair-skinned. You ain't connected."

"How do you know?" Emma glared, getting pissed off now.

"If you had connections, you wouldn't be here pawning sentimental crap."

"I could have a drug addiction," Emma argued.

"Do you?"

"No," she admitted.

"Pipe dreamer."

Her anger flared higher. "Stop saying that."

"Dreamer of pipes," the woman taunted.

Emma didn't have to put up with this, even though deep inside she feared the woman's estimate was far more than accurate. She stuck out her palm. "Just give me the brooch back."

"Tell you what," the crone said. "Because I feel sorry for you, I'll give you two eighty—"

"I don't need your pity, give me my damn brooch back, Hagzilla or I'm calling the cops."

An amused smile played over her thin, dry lips. "Three hundred, but only if you promise to give up on this stupid dream and use the money for bus fare back home, Cindy Lou Hoo."

"Why the hell do you care?" Emma snapped.

The woman's tight, hard eyes grew murky with an unexpected softness. "Because once upon a time, I was you."

Emma snorted.

"You think that's funny? You don't believe me?"

"No, not really."

"Hold on, I can prove it." Hagzilla dug around in a drawer, pulled out a yellowed, tattered playbill. *Death of a Salesman*, 1989. She flipped to the dog-eared page that listed the cast. "There." She pointed a grubby finger at a name on the list. "I played Miss Forsythe. *On* Broadway, and look where I ended up."

"Did you have a drug problem?" Emma asked hopefully.

The woman glared. "Three hundred *if* you give up this stupid dream and leave town."

"Yeah, okay, fine," she said. Three hundred bucks wasn't even a third of the way to her goal, but it was better than nothing. Still, that meant she had only five days left to come up with seven hundred dollars. In her situation it might as well be seven thousand. *Don't give up; you can't give up.*

"Say it."

"I'll give up this stupid dream and leave town," Emma parroted, not meaning a word of it.

The woman slid the money through the slot. "Leave town."

"Yeah, yeah." Stuffing the three hundred dollars into the pocket of her faded jeans (that had of late grown baggy), Emma left the pawnshop, left her star brooch in the gnarled paw of the failed actress reduced to working behind a cage and trying to chase people out of Manhattan.

She hustled down the street, carried along on the energy of the herd surrounding her, passing a collection of small, grimy storefront windows that today somehow felt ominous. The summer heat was heavy, oppressive, burning the smell of car exhaust into her nostrils. The air hummed with sounds; the sharp honking of taxi horns, the steady marching of feet, the mad mumbling of cell phone conversations. Dark clouds hung above the skyscrapers, sautéing the city in humidity. People bumped into her, glowered, growled. Her stomach grumbled, reminding her she hadn't eaten anything besides an apple and two Wasa crackers since the evening before.

Emma picked up her pace, almost running, pushing to escape fate.

Don't let the old crone rattle you. She's bitter. She's washed up. She's not like you. She's not special. She's not a star.

But the reassurance rang false. She could feel the lie of it deep inside her. She was the one who was bitter. She was washed up. She wasn't special. She wasn't a star. She'd been deceiving herself all along. Chasing a pipe dream. Trying to be something she had no hope of becoming. Her heart sank as all the old doubts collapsed, falling in on her like perfectly lined up dominoes.

Faster and faster she walked, breathless now, sweaty.

She passed a souvenir shop, heard Sinatra's rendition of "New York, New York" playing from a Wurlitzer, assuring her that if she could make it here, she could make it anywhere.

"But what if you can't make it here?" she muttered under her breath. "What happens then, Old Blue Eyes?" Sinatra had not sung a song about that eventuality. Great, now she was talking to herself. She was a shopping cart away from being homeless.

At her hip, her cell phone vibrated. Grateful to have a distraction, she whipped it off her waistband, flipped it open, saw the name on the caller ID. Hope muscled out despair. It was her agent, Myron Schmansky. Myron was seventy-five if he was a day, frequently forgot her name, and smelled of boiled cabbage and cheap cigars. But by God, he was an agent.

Then a terrifying thought occurred. What if he was dumping her?

Her spirits—which were already stuck to the bottom

of her sneakers—withered, turned brittle. Great, this was all she needed. Myron was going to add insult to injury. She didn't want to answer, but ignoring reality wasn't going to make it go away.

She caught her breath and pressed the phone to her ear. "Hello?"

"Anna," Myron said in his raspy, on-the-verge-of-throat-cancer voice.

"Emma," she corrected. "It's Emma."

"Emma, Anna, whatever your name is," Myron grunted. "This is it, babe."

"What's it?" Emma asked, a sudden fear stomping on the hope. Had he called to dump her?

"Your big break." Myron wheezed.

Her pulse slowed instantly, and she felt as if she was floating outside her body. The street shrank and Emma grew taller in some surreal Alice in Wonderland moment.

"You got an audition with Scott Miller at three P.M. this afternoon." He gave her the address. "He's casting for a supporting role in a new play, and he specifically asked for you. Said he caught your Munchkin role in *Oz* at the Half-Moon. Claimed you blew him out of the water. He raved about you. Wanted to know why someone else hadn't plucked you from obscurity years ago."

"Seriously?" Hope was back, dancing the hora inside her.

"Miller's got a thing for natural redheads, capitalize on it."

"Scott Miller? *The* Scott Miller?" Emma squeaked as all the air fled her lungs. She was so excited that she ignored the tiny little voice whispering at the back of her mind that Miller had a reputation as an aggressive hound dog. She wasn't much for gossip. Who knew if it was true or not?

"You know any other big-time Broadway producers named Scott Miller?"

Nausea beat out the glee surging through her. Oh God, what if she screwed this up? She couldn't screw this up. She'd been working twelve long years for this moment.

"Don't screw this up," Myron said. "If you haven't made it in this business by thirty, you might as well hang it up."

"What about Morgan Freeman? He didn't have a Broadway debut until he was in his thirties."

"Well, you aren't Morgan Freeman, are you?"

"No, but there's no reason I couldn't be."

"It's different for women and you know it."

Emma had just turned thirty. He was right, and she just didn't want to admit it. This was her last chance to become a star. "Thanks for the pep talk, Myron."

"Don't mention it. Go knock 'im into next week, kid."

It took Emma an hour to decide what to wear to the audition. Finally she settled on the artsy look, donning a short black skirt with turquoise tights and a matching turquoise blouse that hung off one shoulder. She layered the look with a black leather belt, black ankle boots, and bright pink bracelets.

She was still having trouble believing this was really happening. Oh, she'd fantasized about it plenty. Most nights she lulled herself to sleep with visions of seeing her name in lights on a Broadway marquee. Whenever she got the blues and feared she was just another cliché, she'd head down Forty-fourth to Sardi's and sit at the bar. She'd order an old-fashioned, because, hey, it was old-fashioned, and she would stare at the framed caricatures on the wall—Katharine Hepburn, Marilyn Monroe, Clark Gable. Yes, these days Sardi's was little more than a tourist hangout, but you could still feel the energy, and if you listened closely enough you could hear the ghosts from the past.

If she closed her eyes she could see the special watering hole the way it had been in its heyday. There sat Walter Winchell and his Cheese Club cronies at their table—joking, laughing, and telling newspaper stories. In that corner were Bette Davis and her friends, drinking highballs and trying to pretend they weren't anxious about the impending reviews. Across the room, Eddie Fisher canoodled with Elizabeth Taylor.

A trip to Sardi's never failed to snap Emma from her doldrums. After her audition she'd go there again, either to celebrate or to drown her sorrows, depending on how it went.

She arrived at the theater fifteen minutes early and was surprised to find no one else was there for the casting call. Surely she wasn't the first to arrive. Had the audition been canceled? Had she gotten the time wrong? A bored-looking assistant, years younger than Emma, sat at the front desk. She was enrapt in an e-book reader and barely glanced up.

"I'm here to see Scott Miller," Emma said, forcing a note of authority into her voice. "I'm auditioning for him at three."

Without looking up, the assistant waved toward the door at the back of the theater. "Go on, he's in his office."

"We're not auditioning in the theater?"

"You're the only one who's auditioning."

Her heart lurched, and a ripple of apprehension ran through her, but she tamped it down. This was good, right? She'd never been the only one at an audition before. She wasn't sure what it meant, but suddenly she felt like a fox in a trap. Mentally, she shoved aside the sensation and chanted the mantra she repeated in front of the mirror every single morning after she brushed her teeth.

You are a Broadway star, I am a Broadway star, Emma Parks is a Broadway star.

"Which way is his office?" she asked.

"Through the back corridor, past the black curtain, last door at the end of the hall."

"Thanks." Emma smiled, but it was for no one. The girl wasn't even looking at her. She shouldered her handbag and moved forward, gliding past the stage entrance. How many times had she come to see plays in this very theater, sat in the back-row, nosebleed-cheap seats, and imagined herself up on that stage? Dozens for sure, maybe even fifty or more.

This is it. This is it. This is it. All your dreams are about to come true.

She eased down the corridor, following the assistant's directions, and pushed back the dusty black velvet curtain. To Emma, the building smelled like years of stardom. Meryl Streep had performed here. She could almost feel Meryl walking with her toward the door at the end of the hall.

Not to put any pressure on you or anything, but don't blow this.

Damn that naysaying voice. Purposefully channeling Meryl, Emma strode forward, knocked boldly.

"Come in," rumbled a deep masculine voice.

Resisting the unexpected urge to run, Emma turned the knob and stepped inside.

The office was ordinary—desk, chairs, framed pictures on the wall. The man sitting on the burgundy leather couch was not. He was the most famed producer on Broadway, and he looked every inch the part.

Scott Miller styled his thick mane of gray hair combed back off his broad forehead and curling to his collar. It lent him a leonine mien. He wore a white button-down shirt with the top three buttons undone, revealing a mass of wiry gray hair, and he had the sleeves rolled up, showing off his muscular forearms. Even well into his sixties, he was in great physical shape. His wedding band was a wide chunk of gold interlaced with a sprinkling of small diamonds. He wore a Rolex at his left wrist and oozed an aura of pure money in spite of the faded black jeans with a tattered hole in one knee. He had on black loafers with no socks and a look of supreme ennui on his face. She resisted the urge to curtsy even as mental alarm bells went off.

His eyes lit on her. Miller sat up straighter and gave her a predatory smile. "Ah," he said. "The Munchkin. Come on in, shut the door and lock it so we won't be disturbed."

Emma's pulse pounded and her mouth went dry. Something inside her told her to run, but maybe it was simply because she was in the presence of greatness and she didn't know how to handle it. She felt humbled and thrilled beyond measure. She closed the door, locked it, and turned back around to see that he'd gotten to his feet. He was tall, at least six feet. Standing beside him, Emma felt like a redheaded toadstool.

"You're gorgeous," he said, moving quickly across the floor to close the gap between them.

Okay, she'd taken extra care with her makeup and clothing, but gorgeous was not the initial response she usually got from men. Perky, yes. Cute, uh-huh. Adorable, yep. Gorgeous, not so much.

"I knew the minute I saw you that you were perfect for Addie, except you're going to have to ditch the spiral perm." He reached out to finger her Nicole Kidman curls.

"It's not a perm. That's the way my hair grows."

"Then you'll have to have it professionally straightened."

"Okay," she said, even though she had no idea how she'd pay for that. It was perilously close to sounding like he was seriously considering her for the part. Did she dare hope?

He stood so close she could feel his hot breath on the nape of her neck, and it was no secret he'd had garlic for lunch. Cloves of it, apparently. *Dude, ever heard of Tic Tacs?* Unnerved and a tad nauseous, she stepped away from him to study the pictures on the wall of Miller with a pretty, much younger woman and three kids in their late teens.

"Is this your family?" she asked, and turned back around to face him. "Your wife is beautiful and—"

"Yeah, yeah, that's my wife and kids. Now take off your clothes."

"Pardon?" It wasn't that she hadn't heard him; it was just that she couldn't believe what she'd heard.

"Get naked."

Her mind grappled with the situation. Was this really happening? Oh God, were the rumors really true? Emma gulped. "My . . . Myron didn't tell me the play involved nudity. I don't do nude scenes."

"The play doesn't involve nudity."

"Then why do I have to get undressed?"

"Honey, do you want the lead in a Broadway play or not?"

Anxiety slammed into her. This wasn't happening. It couldn't be happening. The biggest producer on Broadway wanted to have sex with her? "I do."

"Then get those clothes off. I'm dying to see if the curtains match the carpet."

She wasn't naïve. She knew such things went on. She'd come up against a lot of sexual innuendo in this business, some inappropriate touching, and, yes, she'd even been propositioned. But nothing so blatant as "Give me sex and I'll give you a job."

"Come on," Miller said, closing the gap between them. "Schmansky said you'd do anything for a part. I gotta see that red hair. He said you're a natural."

Inside her chest her heart was an engine, revving hot and fast. Was this really what she was going to have to do to make her dreams come true? Humiliation tasted soggy and sour, like laundry left too long in the washing machine.

Do you want the part?

Not like this. Please God, not like this.

Miller's hands went to the snap of his jeans. His eyes were two lusty black dots. Spittle gleamed at the corner of his mouth. She realized he was standing between her and the door. Over his shoulder she could see the smiling face of his wife and kids. What a prince.

Emma straightened her spine, stitched together the scattered pieces of her courage. "I'm afraid there's been a misunderstanding."

"Yeah?" He slid his zipper down.

She knotted her fists. If she screamed, no one could hear her. She was five-foot-nothing and ninety pounds. Miller was over six feet and weighed at least two hundred. She didn't stand a chance of fighting him. She tried to look haughty. "You've been misinformed."

"How's that?" He came toward her.

She inched backward, her longing gaze caressing the door. "Myron misspoke. There's a lot of things I won't do for a part."

"Just a blow job then. Five minutes you're done, the part is yours." He stripped his pants to his ankles and stood there completely naked from the waist down, sporting a boner the size of Detroit. It made her hurt just looking at him.

"I . . . I . . ." She was so stunned she couldn't breathe, much less talk.

Miller snaked out a hand and grabbed her by the waist. "Here, let me help you with those clothes."

What happened next was pure reflex. She forgot he was big and she was small. Forgot he was the most famous producer on Broadway and she was a lowly struggling actress. Five years of Krav Maga training took over. She brought her knee to his crotch at the same time she jammed her fist up underneath his chin.

Miller's head snapped back. He let out a blood-chilling shriek, clutched his testicles with both hands, and sank like a sack of salt to the floor.

Emma turned, leaped over his prostrate body, and ran for the door. She fumbled at the lock as Miller cursed her with every colorful word in his extensive vocabulary. "You'll never work in this town again," he screamed.

Feeling like the utter cliché she was, Emma stumbled down the corridor, staggered past the assistant who no longer looked so bored, and tumbled out onto the street.

It was only as she ran, pushing her way through the cluster of humanity thronging Forty-second Street, that the enormity of what she'd done hit her.

She'd just clocked renowned Broadway producer Scott Miller squarely in the gonads.

It was official. Her long-cherished dream of stardom was over.

CHAPTER TWO

*Friends are like quilts, you can never have
too many.*
—Lieutenant Valerie Martin Cheek, R.N.,
late member of the True Love Quilting Club

The Rottweiler was a licker.

Every time Dr. Sam Cheek bent to place the stetho-scope on Satan's chest, the drooly black dog lavishly bathed his face with a thick pink tongue.

"He's giving you kisses," explained Satan's owner, a woman in her mid-forties who was dressed like an escapee from Cyndi Lauper's "Girls Just Wanna Have Fun" video. She wore her hair—streaked with various colors, the primary one being pink—pulled up into a high ponytail on the side of her head and pink leggings underneath a pink and black polka dot miniskirt. If Sam's older sister Jenny were here, she'd whisper, "What not to wear" into his ear.

But Sam didn't care about things like that. Clothes were clothes. Sam cared about three things—his family, his town, and animals, and not necessarily in that order. "Could you lean over here and let him kiss *you* so I can listen to his heart?"

"Oh sure, sure." The Cyndi Lauper wannabe puckered up and cooed, "How's my little Satan? Who's my good boy? Is it you? Is it you?"

The Rottweiler transferred his sloppy kisses to his owner's face, leaving Sam free to finish his examination. Ten minutes later, he straightened, shook his head. "Tell me about Satan's symptoms again," he said. "I'm not finding anything out of the ordinary and all his lab work is negative. I could do a CAT scan, but that's expensive and I don't like putting animals through unnecessary procedures."

The woman cocked a hand on her hip and her cheeks tinged pink. "Okay, I guess this is where I come clean."

Sam took a step backward, twisted up the stethoscope, and tucked it into the pocket of his lab jacket. A sheaf of hair fell over the right side of his face, but he didn't brush it aside. He let it hide the scar that made him feel self-conscious. He didn't say anything, just waited for her to confess whatever secret was making her blush.

"There's nothing wrong with Satan," she admitted.

Other than that hellacious name you gave him. Still, Sam did not speak. He was the fourth child out of six and he'd learned a long time ago that the best way to get to the truth was by keeping your mouth shut. Ninety percent of the time the other person would trip himself up if you just gave him a chance.

"I'm new in town." She batted her eyelashes. "And newly single."

Aw crap, not another one. Satan flicked out his tongue and licked Sam's hand. He scratched the dog behind the ears. It wasn't the pooch's fault he had a lovelorn owner.

"I heard you liked older women and—"

"Who told you that?"

She looked shamefaced. "Belinda Murphey."

Sam's mother's younger sister, Belinda, ran a local matchmaking service called the Sweetest Match. She'd been trying for months to get Sam to sign up, but he wasn't the least bit interested in dating again. It was too soon. Valerie had been gone just over a year, and between being the only small animal vet in Twilight and raising his son, Charlie, he had no time for distraction. His aunt Belinda had been surreptitiously sending women his way, and if it wasn't for keeping peace in the family, he'd have confronted her before now.

"I don't appreciate you using your dog as a matchmaking tool," he admonished.

"So you *don't* like older women? Belinda said your late wife was six years older than you and I—"

"I'm not ready to date again," he said curtly. "Now if you'll excuse me, I have patients to see."

"Yes, okay, sure. I didn't mean to offend you, Dr. Cheek."

He wasn't offended. He was just irritated. "No harm done," he eased his tone. The problem wasn't this woman, but rather his matchmaking Aunt Belinda.

"I'll pay for the exam," she offered.

"Never mind that," he said. "Just stop using your dog to pick up guys and we'll call it even."

"It's a deal." Her smile shone falsely bright and her perky pink ponytail seemed to sag a little.

She left the clinic with Satan through the side exit, and Sam went to the reception desk. "Don't charge the Rottweiler's owner for the visit—"

"Not another freebie," his receptionist, Delia, groaned. "You can't make a living if you keep giving away your services, Sam."

"I don't need a lecture," he said. "I've got a mother, two sisters, and a very nosy aunt for that. Just letting you know that I'm leaving the building for a few minutes."

"You have a poodle that got pecked in the eye by a rooster on the way in." Delia stamped "no charge" on Satan's bill.

"I'll be right back." He turned and went out the rear door.

The alley of the clinic ran parallel to the town square that was one block over. To get to the square he had to walk past the Twilight Playhouse, built in 1886. In the summers, the theater hosted touring companies performing Broadway musicals. In the winters, the town put on its own productions, including everything from cowboy poetry readings, to musical groups, to Christmas pageants.

Now that it was September and the kids had gone back to school, the playhouse would be gearing up for a new round of homespun programs. The sound of someone banging out a ragtime tune drifted through the open window of the sandstone building as he rounded the corner to the town square. The first time he'd ever kissed a girl, it had been in the upstairs stage loft.

He couldn't help thinking of Trixie Lynn. Even now, he could still remember her impish green eyes surrounded by a riot of burnished orange curls. He'd had a thing for redheads ever since. Valerie had been a redhead as well, although her hair had been darker, more brownish. Trixie Lynn had possessed corkscrew tresses as vibrant as oak leaves in autumn.

After the kiss he'd filched from her in that loft, he'd fallen madly in love with Trixie Lynn the way a guy only falls once. Never mind that he'd been only fifteen, he'd yearned for her completely and without reservation. He was embarrassed about it now, the way he'd been so overcome. Not just that, but he was embarrassed at how often he still remembered it. Almost every time he passed the Twilight Playhouse, he thought of her and wondered where she was. Had she married? Did she have kids? Had she ever achieved her dreams of being a star?

It was so long ago. So dumb to keep thinking about her, but if he closed his eyes, the memory came back sharp and fully in focus. He remembered all the little details: the way she'd smelled like watermelon shampoo and Ivory soap, the way her soft curls felt slipping between his fingers. The way the storage loft had been hot and airless, how sweat had trickled down his back, how no one knew they were up there together in the dark.

"I feel like I've cheated you," Valerie had said to him on their honeymoon. They'd gone to San Antonio and were strolling the river walk hand in hand. Cumin from a nearby Mexican restaurant had scented the air. In the distance, a mariachi band sang "El Paso" in Spanish. They'd just shared a kiss, and he could taste her mild milky flavor on his tongue. Her comment surprised him.

"Cheated me? How's that?"

"I had my one great love with Jeff. He was my soul mate. But you . . ." She'd stopped walking, dropped her hand, looked him in the eyes. "You'll never have that as long as you're married to me."

What Valerie hadn't known was that he'd already

had his one great love and lost her as surely as she'd lost Jeff. "What we've got," he'd told her and meant it, "is better than soul-mate love. It's safe and solid and secure."

She'd look at him so sadly that a cold shiver had shot down his spine in spite of the sultry July heat. She reached up, traced his chin with her finger, and whispered the name he knew everyone in town called him behind his back. "Oh my sweet Steady Sam."

His aunt's business, the Sweetest Match, sat on the opposite side of the courthouse. A pair of mockingbirds trilled from the wide-limbed mimosa across from the Funny Farm restaurant on the corner. The scent of sautéing onions and garlic wafted in the air. Sam's stomach grumbled, reminding him that he'd forgotten to eat lunch. Again. He often got so absorbed in his work he forgot to eat.

He cut across the courthouse lawn thick with heavily watered zoysia grass. At this hour on a Wednesday afternoon the streets were fairly empty. Not late enough to pick the kids up from school, but past the lunch hour. His boots made a scraping noise when he hit the pavement on the other side of the lawn, and he rehearsed in his head what he was going to say to his aunt to put a stop to her infernal matchmaking without hurting her feelings.

The cowbell over her door tinkled gaily when he opened it. All things romantic dominated his aunt Belinda's world. The walls were painted pastel pink and lined with framed pictures of all the couples she'd successfully matched. The lush pink carpet led to a private area where she ushered clients to fill out forms, be interviewed on camera, and pay their fees. Belinda specialized in hooking up people with their long-lost loves, and she seemed to have a real knack for knowing how to go about igniting those old embers into fresh flames. She made a nice living at it. Enough to support a family of seven after her husband, Harvey, got laid off when Delta Airlines pulled most of its flights out of DFW airport in 2005. Now Harvey worked for the local country club as a greenskeeper, and he kept Belinda supplied with a string of upper-crust gossip.

Belinda peeked her head in from the back room. "Hiya, Sam," she greeted him with a warmth that went around him as snuggly as a hug.

His aunt was an ebullient woman in her early forties. Everything about her screamed, "Mom." Just like his mother, she was helpful, kind, generous, loving, and more than a little meddlesome. Belinda wore her hair in a short, practical style and she favored blouses ubiquitously appliquéd with bunnies or ducks or puppies. She smelled like chocolate chip cookies. She had a round cheerful face and a full motherly bosom just right for little heads to rest against. She was the "fun" mom, full of games, laughter, stories, and art projects. Kids congregated at her house.

"Do you need someone to babysit Charlie?" Looking hopeful, she moved from the back room into the main shop, knitting needles and a half-knitted scarf in her hands.

"No."

"Are your folks leaving later than expected?"

"They left yesterday." Sam's father had recently retired at age sixty from Bell Helicopter with a pleasant pension, and he'd bought a recreational vehicle to celebrate. His parents had embarked on a two-month sightseeing odyssey from Labor Day to Halloween.

"Oh." Belinda sounded disappointed. "So no up-coming dates?"

"We need to talk," he said flatly.

Belinda set her knitting down on the counter. "Sure, sure. Would you like some iced tea? It's peach-flavored."

"No thanks."

"I'm getting the feeling this isn't a social call."

He cleared his throat. "Aunt Belinda—"

"Yes?" She smiled like she had the power of the sun behind her.

"You gotta stop sending women over to the clinic. It's my place of business."

"Oh dear," she said. "Who interrupted you at work? Was it Misty or JoAnna or Caroline? I clearly told them not to bother you—"

"Three of them?" He groaned. "You sicced three of them on me?"

"Well, I wasn't sure what type you liked. Misty is petite and dark-haired, about your age, and—"

He held up a hand to silence her. "I know you're just trying to help, but I can get my own dates, thank you."

Belinda pursed her lips. "No you can't."

"What?" Startled, he stared at her.

"Okay, maybe you can, but you won't. You haven't been on a single date since Valerie died. You're thirty years old, Sam, but you act like you're sixty. When was the last time you went out and had a good time?"

"That's my business, Belinda."

"This isn't all about you, you know," she said softly.

Sam's spine stiffened. "What do you mean?"

Belinda pressed her lips together and shifted her

eyes as if casting about for a gentle way to say what was on her mind. "You weren't the only one affected by Valerie's death."

He lowered his voice. "Don't you think I know that?"

"Charlie has lost so much. To be in the car with his father when they got T-boned and then just a scant eighteen months later to see his mother get on that army plane and fly away, only to come home in a casket. That's a lot for a six-year-old to absorb."

Sam clenched his jaw and bit down on the tip of his tongue to stay his anger. None of this was his aunt's concern. She had five kids of her own to fret over. He wanted to lash out at her, but he knew she really was worried about Charlie, so he said nothing, just stood there feeling the muscle at his temple jump.

"That boy needs a mother. Whenever he comes over for playdates with my kids he . . ." Aunt Belinda trailed off. "Well, as you say, it's none of my business."

"No, it's not."

"But it's not right, him not speaking a single word since Valerie died."

"I know," Sam said hoarsely. The pain he tried to keep at bay every time he looked at the boy he'd swiftly grown to love, as surely as if he'd been his biological child, squeezed his heart. "I've taken him to doctors, therapists. I've been patient. My folks help in every way they know how. I've tried everything I know."

"You haven't tried *everything*," Belinda braved.

He fisted his hands at his side, took a deep breath, and responded with as much measured control as he could muster. "He's not ready for someone to replace his mother."

She folded her arms over her chest and held his gaze. "Are you sure it's Charlie who's not ready?"

"I appreciate what you're trying to do, but please stop sending women over to meet me. When and if I decide to remarry it will be under my own power. I don't want or need a matchmaker mucking around in my love life. Got it?"

Belinda swallowed visibly. "I never meant any harm and I don't want to overstep my bounds, but Sam, have you thought about what it means for your boy if he never speaks again? What kind of future is he going to have?"

Sam had thought about it far more often than Belinda could imagine, but he'd decided that his approach to just give Charlie his space and not pressure him was the best one. The boy would talk eventually.

"And then there's this," Belinda said.

"What?"

She opened up a drawer and pulled out several sheets of notebook paper covered with drawings and pushed it across the counter toward him. "Charlie drew these on Saturday when he spent the night with his cousins."

Sam picked up the pictures and flipped through them. Page after page of crayon drawings featured a stick figure in a skirt being killed in various ways. In each picture her eyes were X's and her mouth was a wide open O of distress. There were bombs and knives and guns. Looking at the pictures his son had drawn weakened Sam's knees, made his stomach lurch drunkenly.

"I'm really worried about Charlie," Belinda murmured.

"All little boys draw images of war. I did. Ben and

Joe and Mac did too. Are you telling me your boys don't?"

"Exclusively?"

Sam blew out his breath.

"With women as the battle victims?"

He shook his head and suddenly realized Charlie was feeling as dead inside as he was. Sam had trouble talking about his thoughts and feelings, and his boy couldn't talk at all. Belinda was right. He'd been setting a terrible example for the child.

"So what am I supposed to do?" he asked.

His aunt drew in her breath. "It's time to find that boy a new mother."

"Valerie is irreplaceable."

"I know that, but it doesn't mean you both don't deserve some happiness in your lives. You need to feel normal again."

"And you think the aging Cyndi Lauper wannabe you sent to my office is the answer to my problems?"

"No, of course not. It's just time you tried again. Not just for your own sake but for your son. He needs to see how people move forward after a tragedy. Right now you're both in a holding pattern."

It was true. He didn't want to admit it because he didn't want to date, but it was true.

"Okay," he relented. "You can fix me up. But I'm only doing this for Charlie's sake."

"Oh yes." Belinda clapped. "Your mom is going to be so excited."

"Yeah, well, you and she are the only ones."

"We gotta talk."

Emma met the determined stares of her two roommates and knew they'd reached the end of their rope.

Two weeks had passed since that awful day in Scott Miller's office. Two weeks of being hounded by the tabloid media. Two weeks of being ridiculed on morning radio. Two weeks of eating too much chocolate and reading romance novels because it was the only thing that kept her mind off her dire straits. Yes, Miller had had it coming, but she couldn't help feeling bad about what she had done.

The nightmare of that day had not ended with her sprinting from the theater. Before she'd gone two blocks, she heard the wail of sirens, but it wasn't until a few hours later, when the paparazzi showed up on her doorstep, that she learned what had happened. It turned out Miller had a preexisting condition that caused his testicle to torque when she'd kicked him in the groin.

By the time they got him to the hospital it was too late to save the damaged testicle. She was feeling pretty damn guilty about that until Miller released a statement to the press claiming she'd assaulted him because he'd refused her advances when she'd tried to have sex with him in order to procure a part in his new play. After that bullshit, she let go of the guilt and daydreamed about hacking off his remaining testicle.

Her roommates, Cara and Lauren, circled her futon, their sleeves rolled up, looking like people who were about to stage an intervention or deprogram someone who'd been kidnapped by a cult. Emma swallowed the Tootsie Roll she'd been chewing and laid down Rachel Gibson's latest novel. Cara sat at Emma's feet. Lauren took the chair at the head of her bed.

"We're sorry, Em," Cara said, "but we just can't take this anymore."

"We can't step out of the apartment without stepping over the paparazzi. It was fun at first, until we realized they only want to take pictures of *you*." Lauren shook her head. "We don't like it."

Hey, she understood. She didn't want this kind of attention either, although Myron kept assuring her that any publicity was good publicity. It certainly didn't feel that way. Her stomach hurt whenever she peered out the window and saw reporters skulking on the street below, although their numbers had started to dwindle over the last few days as fresh news stories pulled them away to more gossip-worthy pastures. Her goal had been to outlast them. Stay holed up in the apartment until they got bored or a bigger celebrity did something more shocking. The plan had worked.

Until now.

Cara folded her hand on her hip and took a deep breath. "We have someone else who wants to move in with us."

"Someone who's got cash," Lauren added. "You gotta go."

Cara glared at Lauren. "She doesn't mean to be so blunt."

"Yes she does," Emma said, "and she's right. You have to do what you have to do. I appreciate you letting me hang on as long as you did."

"You're welcome."

"When do you need me gone?"

"Meg's moving in tomorrow." Lauren leaned one shoulder against the wall and crossed her arms over her chest, a look of bored patience on her patrician features. She was a fashion model, obligatorily tall, underweight, and petulant.

"You want me out *now*?" Emma cringed to hear

her voice come out high and reedy and desperate. God, she was pathetic.

Lauren and Cara nodded in unison.

"Okay, great." She forced a smile. "I'll get packing."

Cara hovered, wringing her hands, her lips pursed. "Do you have someplace to go?"

Emma almost preferred Lauren's blunt disinterest to Cara's false concern, but she wasn't going to play the victim, so she lied through her teeth. "Yes, sure, no problem. I've got lots of friends."

The real answer was no, she had nowhere else to go. The man she'd grown up thinking was her father now lived in Seattle with a new wife and ten-year-old daughter. They would not be happy to see her, even if she could scare up the money for a plane ticket—which she couldn't. She'd be lucky to afford a bed for the night at the YWCA. Most of her acquaintances were aspiring actresses living with multiple roommates in apartments as cramped as this one. She had no idea where her mother was or if she was even alive. She had no siblings. No grandparents. No boyfriends. No fallback plan. No soft place to land.

It's what happens when you spend your life chasing stardom instead of building relationships.

New York had a way of making people feel anonymous. It was not the best city for a girl bent on standing out and being special. Emma had been down. She'd been low. But she'd never been this up against it. Two hundred dollars in her bank account, another fifty in her wallet, a credit card that was rapidly approaching maxed-out status.

Feeling like her limbs were made of sticks, Emma swung her legs off the futon and got to her feet. She kept smiling idiotically and tamping down the hysteria pushing against her rib cage.

Don't break. You won't break. You're Scarlett O'Hara plucking that damn radish from the hard, dry soil. You're Ripley battling chest-ripping aliens. You're Dorothy in The Wizard of Oz.

Okay, maybe not Dorothy because Dorothy's theme was "There's no place like home" and Emma had no home, but she was strong. She could handle this. It was always darkest before the dawn, right? Can't go up until you've hit rock bottom. Well, if that was true, then, baby, she was primed to be a shooting star.

"You want us to help you pack?" Cara offered.

Emma drew on every ounce of pluck she possessed. "You know, why don't you guys go grab a cup of coffee at the Daily Grind, I'll be gone by the time you get back."

"Are you sure?" Cara knitted her brow.

"Absolutely."

Lauren already had hold of Cara's arm. "Come on, let's give her some space."

After the door shut behind them, Emma fought the urge to sink to her knees and burst into tears. Instead, she recited the names of every strong woman of film she could think of as she pulled her suitcase from the closet and tossed it on the futon. "Lara Croft, Ilsa Lund, Elizabeth Bennet, Buffy the Vampire Slayer."

She stuffed her clothes into the suitcase and switched to strong-minded actresses. "Susan Sarandon, Glenn Close, Bette Davis, Uma Thurman," she said, raising her voice against the undulating waves tightening her stomach with spasms of dread. "Barbara Stanwyck, Joan Collins, Demi Moore."

But even as she uttered the names of determined women who'd taken rejection and turned it into success, Emma feared that no matter what her mother had told her, she simply didn't have what it took to be a star. She didn't even have her mother's star brooch to wish upon. Her touchstone was gone. She had nothing to keep her grounded.

Once her bags were packed, she looked around the dingy apartment they'd tried so hard to spruce up— bringing in braided rugs to hide the deep gouges in the ugly hardwood floors, caulking and painting over a bullet hole in one wall, hanging festive curtains over a window that looked out over a debris-filled alley, but it had been like putting lipstick on a pig, and the attempt came off looking sad and desperate. Emma hitched in a breath. God, she was going to miss this place.

She stepped to the door, bracing herself for any media types who might still be camped out, ready to duck her head and let loose a string of "no comments." She unlocked the three deadbolts, and just as her hand touched the knob, a knock sounded.

Startled, she jumped back.

"NYPD, open up."

The police? Emma stood on tiptoes to peer out the peephole. Sure enough, there was an NYPD badge being held up to it.

She opened the door.

Two burly, dark-haired cops in uniform stared at her, expressions neutral. "You Emma Parks?" the taller one asked.

"I am."

"You're under arrest." The shorter cop dangled handcuffs. "Turn around and put your hands behind your back."

Alarm spread through her. What had she done? "What's this all about, Officer?"

"Sexual assault charges, ma'am, brought against you by one Scott Miller. Now if you'll turn around and put your hands behind your back."

Not knowing what else to do, she complied. A chill of fear squeezed her heart as he clamped the cold metal handcuffs around her wrists and intoned, "You have the right to remain silent. Anything you say can and will be used against you in a court of law. You have the right to have an attorney present during questioning. If you cannot afford an attorney, one will be appointed for you. Do you understand these rights?"

"I do," she whimpered.

They hauled her down the steps of the third-floor walkup, and when they hit the ground floor, the media converged on them at once, microphones thrust in her face, cameras rolling, dozens of people clamoring to speak to her.

And as the policemen stuffed her into the back of their squad car, Emma couldn't help thinking that this was the most attention she'd ever received.

"What do I look for in a woman?" Feeling put on the spot, Sam stared into the camera.

After promising his aunt he'd let her put him on the dating circuit, he'd dragged his feet for a week. Honestly, he didn't see how his dating was going to help Charlie stop drawing disturbing pictures and start talking again. But then Belinda got his mother in on the act and she started nagging him as well, calling from their campsite in Jackson Hole, Wyoming. Finally he'd thrown in the towel and set up an appointment. And now here he was sitting on a stool, with the background scene of Lake Twilight behind him, his hair freshly trimmed, wearing new Levi's and a red shirt. Belinda had picked out the shirt because she said the color made his eyes pop. To Sam's way of thinking, that wasn't a good thing. He felt like a giant dumbass.

Aunt Belinda stood behind the cameraman holding up the cue cards with the questions she wanted him to answer written on them. She had a big smile on her face and flashed him an enthusiastic thumbs-up. How he hated being the center of attention. He'd rather visit the dentist.

He paused, considering the question. Should he say what he really wanted? Or should he say what he thought women wanted to hear? Should he even consider his desires at all? Or should he be looking for the kind of woman best suited to be Charlie's new mother? What did he want in a woman?

Belinda gave him an exaggerated look that said, *Say something.*

"Um . . . well . . . I want someone who is traditional."

Belinda shook her head.

Sam frowned. "I want someone untraditional?"

"Cut!" Belinda exclaimed and bustled over to Sam.

"What?"

"Traditional isn't a good descriptor. With that you'll get women who tend to be rooted in their opinions."

"So what should I say?"

"What does traditional mean to you?"

He shrugged. "I dunno. Like Valerie I guess."

"Okay, then mention Valerie's appealing qualities."

"All right."

Belinda dodged out of the way of the camera. "Let's try it again. Let's take it from the top. And sit up straighter."

Forcing himself not to roll his eyes, Sam sat up straighter. "What am I looking for in a woman?" For some reason Trixie Lynn Parks popped into his head—captivating, artistic, soulful, dramatic, outrageous, intrepid, audacious, resilient, profound. A woman like that would be a lot to keep up with. "I'm looking for a woman who is calm and practical, with a lived-in look."

"Cut!"

"What now?"

"Lived-in look?"

"What's wrong with that?"

"You'll get unkempt women who've let themselves go."

"I mean that I don't want someone who is fussy about their appearance. None of those girly-girlies who act like the world has come to an end because they broke a nail."

"Let's change questions," Belinda said. "Tell us what you value most." She nodded at the cameraman, who started recording again.

"What do I value most?" Sam smiled. That was easy enough. "Being a father and a veterinarian. My family means a lot to me. I love animals, and I live in the greatest town on earth."

Belinda held up a new cue card.

"My hobbies include running my dog, Patches, in sheepherding trials, and gardening. I'm down-to-earth. With me, what you see is what you get. Except not this red shirt." He plucked at the shirt. "My aunt picked it out because she said it looks good on camera and makes my eyes pop, whatever that means. But the color is too showy for me."

He signaled for the cameraman to stop filming and stood up. "This is dumb."

"No it's not, you were doing great."

He raised his hands. "I'm done. No offense to what you do for a living, Aunt Belinda, but this just isn't the way I want to meet a potential wife."

"Why not?"

"It feels forced, artificial."

Belinda tapped her cameraman on the shoulder, shook her head, waved him out of the room. When the door had closed behind him, she turned back to Sam. "Matchmaking might feel a little forced, Sam, but you haven't been doing so well on your own. You need help moving on."

"That's because I haven't been looking."

"It's because you haven't let go of Valerie yet. All her clothes are still in your closet."

He winced. Aunt Belinda was right, but he couldn't seem to bring himself to throw her clothes away. The thought of it knotted his gut to the size of black charcoal. "She's only been gone thirteen months."

"Valerie's not coming back."

"I know that."

"I'll come over and clear her things for you if it would make it easier."

That would be the easy way out. Sam shook his head. "It's my chore. I'll do it in my own time."

"Just like Charlie will start talking in his own time?"

He glared at her. Aunt Belinda was round, sweet, and romantic, but she had a steely inner core that could move mountains. She met his glare with a chiding expression that made him feel like an ornery old goat. He knew what she was getting at. How could he expect Charlie to start talking if *he* couldn't move forward enough to give away Valerie's things?

"She'd want you to move on and you know it."

Belinda was right on that score. More than once, Valerie had told him, "If anything happens to me, I want you to marry again. Build a new family for Charlie. I trust you to take care of him. I trust you to make the right decisions."

"I'll handle it," he said gruffly.

"All right then." Belinda's eyes softened. "But if you need me, you know where to find me."

CHAPTER THREE

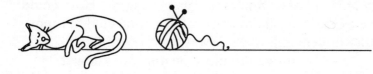

Quilters sew the past to the future.
—Belinda Murphey, matchmaker and member of the
True Love Quilting Club

The only thing that kept Emma from completely cracking up was her ability to detach from reality and slip inside the fantasy world of make-believe. All the time she was being stripped of her belt and her shoelaces, and relieved of the contents of her purse, she kept telling herself she was preparing for the role of a lifetime. As her fingerprints were pressed onto the ink pad and she looked hangdog for the camera, she pretended this was nothing more than extensive research.

But when the iron doors clanged behind her and she saw the other women eyeing her with unfriendly intent, caught the stench of unwashed bodies, her self-delusion wavered a bit. How had this happened? All she'd done was defend herself, and now she was behind bars. How fair was that?

They treated her to a bologna sandwich on white bread and a cup of rotgut coffee in a Styrofoam cup, no sugar, no cream. She didn't have a lawyer, and when she got her one phone call, the only person she knew to call was Myron.

"Anna," Myron wheezed, "this isn't all bad. You've been all over the evening news."

"Emma," she corrected. "I'm in jail charged with a sex crime and I've alienated one of the most powerful men on Broadway. How is being on the evening news going to benefit me?"

"Ya never know what twists and turns life will take, doll face," he said.

She almost asked him if "doll face" was considered a compliment or an insult, but the fact that the guard standing beside her was tapping the face of his watch told her it was time to wrap up the conversation. "Can you look into getting me out of here?"

"I'll do what I can."

"Hurry please, it's not a day at the spa."

"All grist for the mill."

"What?"

"Experience it. Channel it. Adversity will make you a better actor."

"Gee, thanks for that advice."

"Dontcha worry, doll face. I'm working on getting you sprung."

"Time's up," said the guard, and took the phone away from her.

Back in the cell, she curled up on a metal bench to sleep, but didn't dare close her eyes.

Then early the next morning, a miracle happened. The guard called her name. She leaped to her feet. He let her out of the cell.

"What's going on?" she asked.

"You're free to go."

She blinked. "What do you mean?"

"The charges have been dropped."

"Just like that?"

"Just like that."

She wasn't about to argue with him. She collected her belongings from the police desk and turned to go just as Myron came rushing into the station house. Well, as much as he could rush with his arthritic knees and respiratory condition.

"Doll face, you're free," he greeted her amid the ocean of blue uniforms coming and going.

"Yes, I don't know what you did to get the charges dropped, but thank you, thank you, thank—"

"It wasn't me."

"No?"

His withered old head rotated left and right.

"Then what happened?"

"Miller dropped the charges."

"All on his own?"

Myron shrugged. "I don't know what happened. Probably because he didn't have a case. Just don't look a gift horse in the mouth."

He had a point.

"But I'm here for another reason entirely," Myron said.

Emma cocked her head. Myron was almost as vertically challenged as she was. "What's that?"

"Job offer."

"Seriously?" She scarcely dared hope this could be something good.

"Yep. I told you being on the evening news was a good thing."

"I don't have to audition for this job?"

"No. It's yours."

She moistened her lips and her pulse quickened. Maybe it was true what they said. Maybe it really was always darkest before the dawn. "What is it?"

"Now don't get all excited. It's not a big deal. Not nearly as lucrative as a commercial spot. Still . . . after that mess with Miller, a job offer is a job offer."

She balled her hands into fists. "What is it?"

"You're gonna hafta travel out of town."

"That's fine." Right now escaping the city seemed like the perfect solution.

"The venue is small, but the pay's ten grand for two months' work and they're putting you up in a local B&B."

"Is it a movie role?" she asked hopefully.

Myron snorted a laugh.

Hey, was it so unbelievable that someone would offer her a movie role?

"It's regional theater. You'll be playing the lead role of one of the town founders."

"Sounds interesting. Where's it at?"

"Some dinky little town in Texas. Let me see." Myron pulled a piece of paper from his jacket pocket and lowered the reading glasses that sat perched on the top of his head. "Here we go. The place is called Twilight."

"Twilight?" she repeated, unable to believe it.

"You know the place?"

"I do."

In all the fifteen towns and cities where she'd lived, it was the only one that had ever felt like home. A blast from the past raised goose bumps over her arms as emotions peppered her. She thought about the kindly older ladies who'd often brought casseroles over to the house because they knew she didn't get decent home-cooked meals. She recalled Lake Twilight and how beautiful it looked at dusk with the setting sun slanting orange rays over a purple sky. But most of all, she remembered Sam Cheek. The only boy she'd ever loved.

"The woman who runs this theater, Nina Blakley, she used to be a big star back in the day. Won a Tony in the late sixties. She was part of the original cast of *Firelight* and one of the first stage actors to have it in her contract that she makes money every time the play's performed. She's gotten rich off those residuals. Anyway, now she runs this small regional theater that's got a pretty good rep. The best news is that she has a lot of connections in the business. Doing well for her could get you in with the right people."

She knew of Nina Blakley. Emma had been a kid when she lived in Twilight so she hadn't paid much attention to older people, but she was aware that Nina ran the Twilight Playhouse. Her heart jumped to think she'd be going back to Twilight. Part of her was eager, hopeful, but another part was filled with shame. Back when she was Trixie Lynn, she'd bragged how she was going to make it big as an actress, how she was cut out for better things. Now, she'd be returning with her tail between her legs. Suddenly, she realized that this was a pity offer, just like those casseroles had been. The town matriarchs had seen the news, read the tabloids, cruised some blogs, heard about what happened between her and Scott Miller. Nina was throwing her a life preserver all the way from Texas.

Pride had her wanting to tell him no way, but honestly, she couldn't afford pride. She had nowhere else to go. Besides, she couldn't help thinking about Sam.

She knew he still lived there. Sam would never leave Twilight.

Don't be ridiculous. He's probably married with a herd of kids. Stop being pathetic and dreaming of a love that never stood a chance.

"They want you there by Monday."

Emma hitched in her breath. Pity offer or not, she had no choice but to accept it. "Myron," she said, "can I borrow money for bus fare?"

The bus arrived in Twilight on Sunday afternoon. Emma couldn't believe how little the town had changed in sixteen years. Yes, new businesses had sprung up out on Highway 377 sprawling toward Fort Worth—a fourteen-theater cineplex, a miniature golf course adjacent to a water park, a bowling alley and a Super Wal-Mart. Around the lake, new condos and hotels had cropped up.

But the town square was exactly the same. Sure, some of the old businesses were gone and new ones had taken their place, but the architecture remained the same. From the looks of it, one of the buildings on the square had recently burned down, but the rest were renovated structures from the 1870s. Glancing around the square at the old white stone buildings and wooden sidewalks, she half expected to see Jesse James sauntering down the street, six-guns strapped to his hip.

Both a U.S. flag and a Texas flag flew proudly over the neatly manicured courthouse lawn. A clot of people clustered outside the Funny Farm restaurant.

On the south corner sat the Twilight Playhouse, the framed posters advertising an event that had already come and gone. As a gangly teenager she'd gotten her first kiss in that very theater. She smiled. In a shop window, she saw an intricately designed, peach and navy blue quilt displayed. Looking at it made her feel . . . What did she feel? Emma's stomach gave a happy little squeeze, and one word branded red-hot inside her head.

Home.

That was crazy. How could she feel such a flash of warmth for a place where she'd lived for little more than a year? The same place where she'd found out that her father wasn't really her father, that she had no anchor, belonged nowhere, to no one.

The bus rumbled on through the square to the makeshift bus depot several blocks away. She was the only one who got off. The driver unloaded her suitcase and left her standing beside a sheltered bench next to a convenience store that, according to the prominent signs, sold wine, beer, condoms, and lottery tickets, along with bus passes. Ah, the shadier side of small-town life.

Okay, she had directions to the B&B tucked inside her pocket. It was supposed to be on Topaz Street. If memory served, that was only a couple of blocks north.

She bent down to tug up the handle on her suitcase and that was when she saw him, staring coolly at her with icy blue eyes. She inhaled sharply and took a step backward. He came straight toward her, moving slowly, deliberately.

Panic struck her heart. Oh no!

Her knees trembled. All the air left her body in one hard gasp. She froze, unable to move. She was deathly afraid of dogs, and this one was looking at her like he wanted to eat her for dinner.

He dropped down low on his haunches, ears laid back against his head, his eyes never leaving her. He wasn't a huge dog, but neither was he small, and she had a feeling if he stood on his hind legs he'd be as tall as she. He was lean and wiry and looked like he'd move very fast. She couldn't decide if his coloring was white with black patches or black with white patches. Closer he crept, stalking her like prey.

Emma let out a little squeak of terror, and abandoning her suitcase in the parking lot, she started toward the convenience store, but the second she made a move, he was there, coming between her and the building, cutting her off.

She took a step backward.

He moved forward.

She tried to holler for help, but dread constricted her throat and she couldn't push out even a whimper.

Her fear of dogs had developed when in one of her many appearances as Annie, the producer had insisted on using a real dog instead of the prop variety. The mutt had taken an instant dislike to Emma and bit her every chance he got. While the nips were minor (he never broke the skin, but damn, it still hurt) the attacks were so sudden that she cringed whenever she got near the dog. The more she cringed, the more the ornery little beast lunged at her. She tried complaining to the director, but it was his pet. He told her to suck it up or he'd be happy to replace her. She'd needed the money, so she'd stayed in the play, but from that time on whenever she got near a dog, her old fear response kicked in.

The dog kept coming.

She took two more steps backward. She didn't dare turn her back on him. If she turned her back, she just knew he'd jump on her, knock her down, and rip her throat out. If he was going to attack, she wanted to see it coming.

Blood strummed through her ears, pounding loud and fast. All she could think about was his sharp white teeth sinking into the soft flesh of her ankle.

The dog never lost focus. His gaze never strayed. He herded her from the parking lot of the convenience store, maneuvering her onto a quiet side street lined with large oak trees and Craftsman-style houses with acre lots. For the most part, he maintained a five- to six-foot distance, and as long as she was walking straight down the street, he stayed in front of her. But when she tried to angle off to one side or the other, he'd move around her, forcing her back to the center of the street. She prayed someone would drive by, but no one did.

She attempted to fake him out. Feigning that she was moving in one direction but stepping to the opposite side. She didn't fool him for a second. He followed her movements, wrenching back control like a determined man waltzing with a hardheaded woman who kept trying to lead.

After what seemed like an eternity, but was probably only ten minutes or less, the dog picked up his pace, slinking closer.

The knot of fear, which tasted and felt like a slab of bacon in her throat, expanded. This was it. He was going to tear her to shreds.

He circled around to her left side, forcing her up onto the lawn in front of a white frame house with a wide, welcoming veranda.

She backed up the slope of the slight incline leading to the porch steps. The dog's nose twitched, his gaze glued on her feet as he continued to move toward her.

There was nowhere for her to go but up the steps. The dog was between her and the street.

Her heel hit the first step. Up she went.

The dog moved in.

She took another step and then another.

The dog was on the bottom step now and Emma was on the porch. If she whirled around, perhaps she could bang on the door and cry for help before the dog could do too much damage.

She didn't get the chance. The dog suddenly bounded up the steps, sending Emma quivering into the corner of the porch. She was trapped. No way out.

The dog stopped at her feet, looked her in the eyes, and barked.

Emma braced herself for the pain that never came.

From the open window, she heard a woman's voice call out, "Doc, better get out on the porch, your dog's herded home another one!"

"In the house, Patches," Sam commanded the Border collie, holding the screen door open with his left hand.

The dog lifted his ears and cocked his head at the cowering woman cornered on his front porch as if to say, *See what I brought home for you?* Great. Even his dog was trying to play matchmaker.

"House." He snapped his fingers.

Reluctantly, Patches trotted inside.

Sam let the screen door ease closed and turned his attention to the woman, meaning to apologize. But one look into her face and he felt as if he'd been smacked in the gut with a bowling ball. He blinked, certain his imagination was playing tricks on him.

It couldn't actually be she, could it? Back here in Twilight after all these years?

Her hair was the same shade of fiery copper, like the luxurious coat of an Irish setter. It looked as if she hadn't grown an inch in sixteen years. Still five-foot-nothing with the lean, tomboyish build he remembered. And she still had a dusting of freckles over her pert little nose. His mother used to tell her that the angels had sprinkled cinnamon on her, adding spice to the sweet. It never failed to produce a grin, which was why his mother said it. Lois Cheek had a penchant for children, and it tore at her heart when she saw one neglected.

Sam's gaze snagged hers. A rush of emotions he couldn't quite identify tangled around his heart. "Trixie Lynn?" he asked, his voice coming out strangely husky. "Is that you?"

Her gaze tracked his face, flicked up to his forehead.

Self-consciously, Sam's hand went up, pulling his hair forward to cover the scar. He hadn't possessed it when she'd known him before. Did it revolt her? His stomach pitched. Mostly, the people in Twilight let him forget about it. He didn't see wary distaste or morbid curiosity on their faces, but strangers seemed to fixate on it, as if Sam was nothing more than his wound. Suddenly, he was terrified Trixie Lynn would judge him harshly.

That's when he noticed she was trembling.

"Trixie Lynn," he said her name again.

The color drained from her face and her legs gave out at the same moment he reached her. He hated that she'd seen him looking scarred. It must have ruined the fantasy of him that she held in her mind. To him, she looked absolutely the same, but he knew the reverse could not be true.

Seeing you made her dizzy, you should step back, give her some space.

But he didn't back up. He snaked an arm around her waist, holding her steady against him. The second he touched her, his senses sharpened. She smelled of watermelon shampoo and Ivory soap, a familiar scent that tugged at his memories. A slant of sunshine, angling through the cottonwood tree beside the porch, dappled her hair in a fiery light. He had the fiercest urge to press his lips against her freckles to see if they really did taste like cinnamon.

Sam was transfixed. They stared into each other and time stuttered to a stop. They were ensnared, frozen in the moment. Her wide-eyed. Him winded, as if he'd just sprinted a hundred-yard dash like he used to do in high school.

It was as if nothing had changed and they were jettisoned back to their freshman year in high school, so full of yearning and teenage hormones. In that suspended second everything fell away and they were stripped bare of all defenses, all artifice. It was as if they'd never been apart. High school sweethearts. True loves. Soul mates.

Forever and always.

Bull crap.

He'd been living too long in Twilight, listening to silly legends about long-lost lovers reuniting. What in the hell was wrong with him? He was a respected veterinarian, a father now. He had no idea who Trixie Lynn was anymore.

He didn't want to feel what he was feeling. It was too complicated. Too messy. Too scary. Sam liked things simple and neat and predictable. Trixie Lynn had never been simple, neat, or predictable.

And yet his heart beat faster and his stomach churned with excitement and he wanted to ask her a million questions, which wasn't like him at all. Instead he asked her only one. "Are you all right?"

She nodded mutely. He was used to that. He didn't talk much, Charlie not at all. Even his housekeeper, Maddie, was quiet.

"I . . ." She swallowed. "I'm deathly afraid of dogs."

"Oh," he said, surprised by the relief pulsing through him. "That's why you're shaking." *Not because his scar horrified her.*

"Of course," she said, "what did you think?"

He felt sheepish. "You're back."

"I am." She smiled.

He realized that he was still holding her even though she was no longer trembling. Sam was not a particularly tall man, but even so, the top of Trixie Lynn's head barely reached his chin. He looked down at the lush pink lips he'd tasted only once and longed to taste again. What would she do if he followed his impulse and just kissed her right here, right now on his front porch, as if sixteen years had not come and gone?

You can't do that. For all you know, she's married.

He darted a quick glance to the ring finger of her left hand. It was bare.

Don't get excited. That doesn't mean anything.

She stepped back, breaking free of his embrace. The next moment was heavy, awkward. Had she somehow read his thoughts? Had she guessed he'd been thinking about kissing her?

Sam ducked his head, splayed a palm to the back of his neck. "It's good to see you again, Trixie Lynn."

"It's not Trixie Lynn anymore. It's Emma. Emma Parks."

"You've got a pseudonym."

"I had it legally changed."

"Emma," he tried out the word. "I like it. It suits you."

She looked pleased.

"What's brought you back to Twilight?"

"You haven't heard?" She blinked at him like an inquisitive little bird.

"Heard what?"

"I thought the grapevine would be buzzing about it."

He waved a hand. "I never listen to gossip."

"Still too engrossed in animals to have much time for people?"

"Yeah," he admitted with a grin. "I'm a vet now."

"Really?" The smile breaking across her face was genuine. "That's great. I'm so happy you made your dreams come true."

"I'm guessing you got what you wanted as well, since you changed your name and everything."

"Yeah, well." She took a deep breath, and he saw sadness flash in her eyes. "Not everyone's dreams get to come true."

"Doc?" Maddie asked from behind the screen door. "Is your guest staying for lunch? I made pot roast. We've got plenty."

"Would you like to stay for dinner?" he asked. "And meet my son?"

She looked at him oddly, and he realized he'd restlessly raked his hand through his hair and given her a better glimpse of his scar. An emotion passed over her face, half pity, half sadness. His anxiety mounted, and he immediately wanted to retract the invitation.

But it was too late.

"I'd love to," she said.

Chapter Four

Quilts are love made visible.
—Dotty Mae Densmore, oldest member of the
True Love Quilting Club

Sam stood on the porch looking just as Emma imagined he would look at thirty. Deeply handsome, with a shaggy sheaf of thick black hair and intelligent brown eyes that didn't miss a trick. Animals surrounded him, just as they always had. Hummingbirds darted at feeders full of red sugar water, suspended from the porch on hooks; a terrarium filled with turtles sat on a table behind the wicker patio couch where a plump calico cat lay curled in a ball on one of the cushions. An end-of-the-season butterfly flitted around his head, and then landed on his shoulder. And his dog, Patches, sat looking through the screen door, his gaze trained on Sam as if he were St. Francis of Assisi.

A day's growth of beard stubble sprouted on Sam's chin, and he was dressed in a short-sleeved, button-down cowboy shirt; faded blue jeans; and scuffed brown work boots.

His face was shadowed by the revolving blades of the ceiling fan circling slowly overhead. He had changed, but he was still the same as she remembered. Introspective, solemn, calm. Her polar opposite.

He has a son.

That meant the son had a mother.

Sam was married.

Disappointment tasted as sharp as expensive aged cheddar. It made her want to drink wine. Sam had a wife and a kid.

She'd expected it. Why not? He was good-looking, sexy, a veterinarian. Not to mention calm, reliable, and steady. Of course he was married. He was thirty. Most people were by their age. Fully adults.

But not her. She'd been holding on to her Peter Pan dreams for so long she'd forgotten to grow up.

Depressing, that thought.

He ran a hand across his forehead, shoving back a hank of hair from his eyes. The shifting of the sun through the cottonwood cast his face in a harsh light. That's when she saw it.

Emma had to dig her fingernails into her palms to keep from gasping, and she drew on her acting skills to stop shock from showing in her eyes. Something terrible had happened to him.

Four deep, long gouges dug into his flesh from the middle of his forehead to the side of his left temple, and the top of his ear was gone. The scars were silver-white with age. Empathy tightened her throat, twisted her heart.

Her own forehead throbbed, and it was all she could do not to reach up and run her fingers over his brow. She saw his body tense, his shoulders draw forward. He tossed his head, sending the long swatch of hair falling back over his forehead again. Now she knew why he wore it long. He hid behind it. Sorrow arrowed through her. He'd been badly hurt. Damaged.

His mouth set in a firm line, and she knew then she'd slipped for a second and let her pity show. He didn't say anything, but she could see the snap of anger in his narrowed eyes and the blotchy flush of embarrassment that rose to his cheeks. She started to regret agreeing to stay for lunch, but she didn't know how to get out of it without it seeming as if she was running away because of his scar. She wanted to run, yes, but because of the intensity of her feelings, not his wound. She hadn't expected to feel such sympathy, to ache to pull him into her arms and kiss those scars and tell him how sorry she was he'd suffered so.

Yeah, I'm sure his wife would appreciate that.

Another reason she wanted to run. Why had she accepted his invitation?

Because you're stranded and lonely and you found a friendly face.

Sam stepped to open the door. "Come on in."

Emma stayed on the porch, warily watching the dog.

"It's okay. Patches doesn't bite. He might snap at your heels to get you to go in the direction he wants you to go in, but that's all."

Emma went up on tiptoes as if it would protect her heels. "Why does he do that?"

"He's a Border collie. They're a herding breed. It's in his nature."

The dog sat looking at her, head cocked. Emma remained welded to the porch. "So to him I'm just a big sheep?"

A smile tipped Sam's lips. "That's it. But he's well trained. He'll leave you be since you're with me."

Emma didn't want to take a chance on it. She kept remembering the vicious little terrier that had repeatedly bitten the crap out of her.

"You really are scared of dogs."

She nodded.

"Patches," Sam said, "upstairs."

The dog turned and disappeared deeper into the house. Emma could hear his feet padding up a staircase she couldn't see from her vantage point on the porch.

He held out a hand to her.

Emma took it.

His fingers were calloused; his grip strong, yet gentle. Something twisted inside Emma's chest. An emotion that eluded definition, but she felt it all the same, curling up tight inside her. She held her breath, acutely aware of him. Her palm tingled beneath his. Oh, this was so stupid. She had no business feeling anything for him other than normal cordiality. So they'd kissed once when they were fourteen. Big deal. He was married now. With a kid.

She wondered if his wife was home. Would he call her outside? Would she come down the stairs and wrap her arms around him for a kiss and rest her head on his shoulder and call him by some cute pet name?

A brackish taste filled her mouth. She didn't want to see that.

They stepped over the threshold into the foyer and immediately were enveloped by the delicious smells of roasted meat, stewed vegetables, and robust herbs—onions, garlic, black pepper, bay leaf. Once upon a time, Emma had loved to cook, but she'd let all that go when she'd moved to Manhattan. No space to indulge her culinary skills in that tiny little apartment she'd shared with Cara and Lauren.

She didn't see the boy at first. Rather, Sam dropped her hand and moved away from her. No, not away from her, toward the child.

He was a skinny little thing. Pale freckled skin, black-framed Harry Potter glasses with thick lenses, hair as red as Emma's own. His eyes were green too, just like hers. He wore blue denim short pants and a white T-shirt with a blue biplane logo on the front. His knees were scraped, and a cowlick stuck straight up at the back of his head. He reminded her of bespectacled Opie from the old *Andy Griffith Show*. She guessed his age at five or six. He must look like his mother, because she didn't see a drop of Sam in him.

It struck her then that Sam had married a redhead, and a new set of emotions had a whack at her—curiosity, nostalgia, wistfulness. The boy could be hers if she'd stayed in Twilight. Married Sam. If she'd never dreamed of being a star. That was a lot of what-ifs and she'd never regretted pursuing her acting career, but now here she was seeing another possible path she could have gone down. A path she'd never before imagined.

"Trix—er, Emma," Sam said, "this is Charlie. Charlie, this is an old friend of mine. Her name is Emma. She's going to have lunch with us."

She'd never been particularly comfortable around children, perhaps because she'd been an only child. She never knew what to say to them, so she said nothing, just smiled and squatted down to his eye level.

The boy stood staring at her. He didn't say anything either.

Emma grinned wider, using her smile to battle back the uncertainty churning her stomach. Did the kid hate her at first sight? She felt the heat of Sam's gaze on her skin, and doubt assailed her. She didn't know what to do next. Should she stand up? Say something?

A second passed.

Charlie stepped toward her.

Emma didn't move.

He came closer, reached out a hand, and gently stroked her hair. His eyes softened and his bottom lip trembled.

"Charlie's mother had red hair," Sam murmured so quietly she almost didn't hear him.

Had.

Past tense. As in Charlie's mother was no longer around. Was she dead? Had she walked out on them? Her stomach lurched. Emma knew exactly what it felt like to be abandoned by your mother.

Charlie stared into her eyes and she could see his pain. Emma's heart clutched. Who was she kidding? She could *feel* it.

"Hi Charlie," she whispered.

Charlie said nothing.

"He's chosen not to speak," Sam said.

"Oh."

The boy kept stroking her hair like she was his long-lost mother returned. Emma battled the tears pushing against the backs of her eyelids. Her emotional nature might help her in acting, but in a situation like this, crying would be counterproductive. She blinked, widened her smile.

Charlie threw his arms around her neck and squeezed tight.

All the air rushed from Emma's lungs, and she fell instantly, madly in love.

"Lunch is ready." A middle-aged woman, with an

apron tied around her waist, appeared in the foyer. "Charlie, go wash up, please."

The boy let go of Emma's neck and scampered off down the hall.

"Hi," the woman said, and held out her hand. "I'm Maddie Gunnison, Sam's housekeeper."

Maddie carried a cautious aura about her, as if she didn't take well to strangers. She possessed sharp cheekbones, intense blue eyes, and a nose that was too long for her narrow face. Her brown hair, threaded through with gray, was worn in a single braid down her back. She spoke with the lazy drawl and marshmallowy lilt of the East Texas piney woods.

"Hello." Emma shook her hand. "I'm Emma Parks."

Maddie looked from Emma to Sam and back again. "I take it you know Sam."

"We're old friends."

"How fitting that Patches herded you home from the bus stop," Maddie said.

Was she being sarcastic? Emma couldn't tell. "How did you know that's what happened?"

Maddie waved a hand. "That dog herds home at least one person a month. I keep telling Sam that Patches belongs on a sheep farm, but he's too attached to the dog to ever give him up."

"Who knows, Maddie, maybe I'll buy a sheep farm one day," Sam said.

"When would you have time for a sheep farm? It's a miracle you haven't been called away on an emergency today. It happens almost every Sunday, your only day off."

"You have a point," he said.

Maddie inclined her head toward the room she'd emerged from. "Why don't we go into the kitchen?

Would you like something to drink, Emma? I've got a big pitcher of sweet tea made up."

"That sounds wonderful."

"Charlie." Maddie raised her voice. "Wash the backs of those hands too, little mister."

"Can I help with anything?" Emma asked as they walked into the kitchen.

"No, no, everything's ready. You just have a seat."

The kitchen table was set with napkins and silverware. Sam pulled out a chair, and Emma moved past him, going for the next chair.

"This is for you," he said.

Emma's cheeks heated. He'd held the chair out for her. When was the last time a man had done that? She couldn't remember. Had a man ever done that for her? "Um, thanks."

She sat down awkwardly, and Sam took the seat opposite her. Charlie came into the room, palms held out for Maddie's inspection. "Good job," she said. The boy took the chair next to Emma, reached for his napkin, and spread it out in his lap.

Maddie turned from the stove, two plates heaping with pot roast made with carrots and potatoes and a side of green beans in her hands. She slid one plate in front of Emma, the other in front of Sam, and then went back for two more plates for her and Charlie. Lastly, she deposited a wicker basket lined with a white linen napkin and filled with homemade yeast rolls in the middle of the table, along with a dish of butter. Then, finally, she sat down.

Emma picked up her fork, ready to dive into the food, when she noticed everyone else at the table had bowed his head. Maddie reached for Emma's hand on the right, Charlie's from the left.

She realized belatedly that they were saying grace. No one had ever said grace in her household, but she remembered the times she'd taken meals with Sam's family and they'd always bowed their heads, joined hands, and given thanks for their food.

Sam blessed the meal and then everyone echoed, "Amen."

In unison, movements so simultaneous it felt choreographed, they all tucked into the pot roast.

"Bread?" Sam asked, and held up the basket of rolls.

"Yes, thanks." She hadn't had a good meal in days so she figured the few extra carbs would be okay. An actress always had to be on guard against weight gain, but sometimes a girl just had to indulge herself a little.

Emma reached for the basket and her fingertips brushed his knuckles, provoking goose bumps. The look in his eyes told her he felt it too, and she quickly ducked her head.

"Sam grew the potatoes and carrots and onions and green beans himself," Maddie bragged. "In his backyard garden."

"Really?" Emma asked, impressed.

Sam shrugged. "Digging in the dirt relieves stress."

"You have a lot of stress?"

He said nothing, but she saw him dart a glance in Charlie's direction. She wondered how long it had been since the boy had spoken and if Sam had taken him to therapists. Probably so. The Sam Cheek she knew was nothing if not responsible.

When they were kids she'd been the one getting him into trouble. Like the time she dared him to climb the ancient pecan tree in the park off the town square and he'd fallen out and broken his arm. She'd felt so guilty, but when he'd returned from the hospital, his arm in a cast, he let her be the first one to sign it. And he told her he'd had so much fun the fall was worth it. That was when she'd decided he was her boyfriend and she was going to let him kiss her if he ever tried.

She smiled at the memory of her audacious fourteen-year-old self. She'd been so fearless back then. What had happened to her? She took a bite of carrot. Whether it was Sam's gardening skills or Maddie's culinary talent or just the simple honesty of fresh vegetables grown in Twilight soil, the tender, slightly sweet buttery carrot was the best she'd ever tasted. She didn't even realize she'd closed her eyes and murmured, "Mmm" until she heard Sam's laugh. Her eyes flew open.

"You've been away from country life too long if a carrot can make you moan like that."

Was there a hint of sexual innuendo in his tone or was she reading something more into an innocent comment? Emma slathered her roll with creamy yellow butter. "You might grow good carrots," she said, "but I'm a city girl through and through."

She bit into the heavy bread and almost moaned again at the succulent decadence of fresh butter. There were several local dairies in the area, and she had a feeling the butter must have come from one of them. Okay, so maybe food *did* taste better when you got it closer to the land.

Sam's gaze was on her face. She could feel the heat of his eyes drilling into her. "You never did tell me why you were back in Twilight."

"Didn't I?" She wondered if he'd heard about her troubles in New York. If he didn't already know, he would soon enough. Gossip spread like a forest blaze in Twilight.

"No."

"Nina Blakley hired me to play Rebekka Nash in the Founders' Day skit."

An odd expression crossed his face. "They skipped the skit last year, I thought . . ." He trailed off, not finishing the sentence.

"Valerie played Rebekka for the last five years before that," Maddie explained.

"Valerie?" Emma arched an eyebrow.

"My late wife," Sam said.

"Oh Sam, I didn't know. I'm sorry, I didn't realize I was taking her place, I . . ."

He gave a sharp jerk of his head in Charlie's direction. "No reason to apologize. I just hadn't realized Nina decided to reinstate the skit."

An awkward silence settled over the dinner table. Emma turned her head to see Charlie studying her as intently as his father. He might not resemble his father physically, but their mannerisms were the same, from the quiet quizzical looks, to their guarded body language. Both of these guys could use some lightening up.

"Nina must be paying you a lot to lure you away from Manhattan," Sam said.

Emma shrugged, not sure how many of the details she should get into at this juncture. "She gave me the opportunity to get out of the city for a few months. Her offer made me realize I hadn't left New York in over twelve years." That was true enough.

Sam drank his iced tea and leaned back in his seat, studying her with a level gaze. "See, even you realize you'd been in the city too long. Every so often you have to get back to nature, clear your head."

If he only knew the real reason she was here, that she was a failure and this was her dying dream's last gasp. Emma's stomach tightened, and misery rolled through her. During all these years of wishing and hoping and struggling to establish her acting career, she'd been kidding herself. She should have done what Scott Miller wanted. If she had, she'd be on Broadway now. Instead she let her foolish pride and misguided sense of morality ruin her best chance at stardom.

She felt out of place here. She no longer belonged. If, indeed, she ever had. Her childhood had been nomadic, her ties few. She concentrated on the pot roast, but she couldn't help slipping an occasional glance Sam's way. His long fingers curved around his fork. They were the hands of a veterinarian, a vegetable gardener. Large and square, the backs tanned and riddled with little nicks and scars, the nails clean and clipped short.

In her imagination, she could feel those fingertips on her skin, roughly calloused, yet amazingly gentle, and she had to bite the bottom of her lip to keep from shivering.

A knock sounded at the front door.

"Who could that be?" Maddie frowned. "Interrupting Sunday dinner?" She laid down her napkin and moved to get up.

Sam pressed his palm downward, pushed back his chair, and got to his feet. "You sit, Maddie. I'll get it."

Compelled by some unseen force, Emma tracked his movements. Something about the way he carried himself made her feel calm and comforted, and she had no explanation for it. Perhaps it was nostalgia. More likely it was simply because she found him dead sexy. He paused just before he left the room and turned to stare at her as if he could feel the heat of her gaze, his chocolate brown eyes cloaked, enigmatic.

The pulse at her throat fluttered.

His face remained unreadable. Sam disappeared into the hallway, and a second later she heard a feisty female voice say, "Your damn dog hijacked another one of my guests."

"Why, come on in, sis, it's great to see you too."

Emma tilted her head toward the sound of Sam's voice. She noticed Maddie and Charlie did the same.

A clattering noise—small wheels against a hardwood floor—echoed, and a slender woman appeared, dragging Emma's suitcase behind her. Her coloring was lighter than her brother's, and she wore her honey brown hair pulled up in a bouncy ponytail. She had on beige capri pants and a black V-neck T-shirt, with a frilly, full-length blue gingham apron tied over the ensemble.

"Hi!" She beamed at Emma. "I'm Jenny." Then she wiggled her fingers at Maddie and winked at Charlie. "Do you remember me? I kinda remember you from when you were a freshman in high school, but I was a senior and you know how self-absorbed seniors are. Plus that's the year I started going out with my husband . . . well, he wasn't my husband back then of course, but you know what I'm getting at."

"Emma, you remember my sister, Cyclone Jenny?" Sam came over to lean a shoulder against the wall of the entryway and folded his arms over his chest. He had a tolerant, brotherly smile on his face.

Emma got to her feet. She remembered Sam's older sister because she'd been in awe of her. Jenny had been the most popular girl in high school—cheerleader, prom queen, Miss Twilight, the works. She was as chatty as Sam was quiet. No wonder he didn't speak much. He'd grown up never being able to get a word in edgewise. "It's nice to see you again."

Jenny shook a finger. "Your name used to be something else. "Trixie Mae, was it?"

"Trixie Lynn," she said. The name felt rusty on her tongue.

"But you prefer Emma?"

"I had it legally changed."

"Then yes, of course you prefer it." She smacked her forehead with a palm. "Duh, blabbermouth Jenny."

Sam shook his head, grinned.

Jenny glanced at the remains of the pot roast. "I see they've already fed you. That's a shame. I made chicken and dumplings from scratch."

"For me?" Emma splayed a palm to her throat. She felt oddly pleased and flattered and yet distressed to think Jenny had gone to so much trouble and she'd already eaten.

"I'm sorry we fed her," Maddie said. "We didn't know she belonged to you."

"I came as soon as I could. If I'd known Patches was going to round her up from the bus stop, I would have just popped right over, but I had no idea she'd arrived until Rusty called from the Grab and Go and told me there was a suitcase sitting in the middle of his parking lot."

Confused, Emma frowned. "I'm not quite following this conversation."

"Ohhh." Jenny whacked her forehead again. "I didn't tell you. My husband, Dean, and I run the Merry Cherub, the bed-and-breakfast where you'll be staying. It's just around the corner. In fact, the back of the inn butts up against Sam's property." She gestured in the direction Emma supposed was her B&B. "Honestly, little brother, you should teach that dog of yours to herd the guests to *my* house. He could be the official escort service."

"The Merry Cherub?" Emma echoed.

"She collects angels," Sam explained. "Wait'll you see."

Jenny leaned over to lightly punch her brother on the upper arm. "Don't say it like that."

"Like what?" He smirked.

"Like you think my angels are silly."

"They're not silly, they're . . ." Sam paused as if trying to think of a polite way to phrase it. "Um . . . plentiful."

"They make me feel good."

"I'm sure they do."

As she watched their exchange, Emma experienced a sense of sad longing and wistful loneliness. How many times had she wished for a brother or sister of her own to squabble with good-naturedly?

"You could do with an angel or two in your house." Jenny eyed the kitchen.

Sam shot a glance at Charlie. "I have one."

Jenny smiled tenderly at her nephew. "Indeed."

Charlie looked at the adults as if he didn't understand why he was suddenly in the spotlight.

"She does have some very lovely angels," Maddie said to Emma.

"Thank you," Jenny said to Maddie. Then she held

out a hand to Emma. "Come on, let's get you over the Merry Cherub and get you settled. And, little brother, if you can't keep that dog from herding home my guests, lock him in the backyard."

Sam hadn't expected to feel so . . . What the hell did he feel? Seeing Trixie—er, Emma—again had him feeling like he'd drunk too much coffee. He resisted the urge to pace. He was accustomed to being in firm control of his emotions, and this detour was unexpected. He needed something to do. He could better make sense of things, more easily organize his thoughts when he had something to keep his hands busy.

"Hey, buddy," he said to Charlie. "Wanna go to the park and throw the baseball around?"

Charlie's eyes brightened, and a big grin spread across his face. He shot upstairs after his ball and mitt. Sam watched him go, the familiar sadness settling on his shoulders. Was the boy ever going to speak again? When he was feeling optimistic, he thought, yeah, sure, of course. But it had been over a year now, and the kid hadn't uttered a single syllable. Sam himself was quiet, pensive, and cautious. Maybe if he were more outgoing, it would help draw the boy out of his shell. Although the thought of changing his personality at this late date seemed daunting, he'd sure give it a try if he thought it would make a difference with his son.

He recalled the way Charlie had been with Emma. How he'd gone right up to her and stroked her hair. The boy was never so forthcoming with strangers. It had to be that her red hair and petite build reminded him of his mother.

Charlie clambered down the stairs, struggling to

carry Sam's mitt, his own, and the softball. Sam's instinct was to offer to help, but he knew he needed to let Charlie do things on his own. Sam opened the door, and Charlie followed him outside.

"You want me to take my mitt?"

Charlie nodded and handed it over. Side by side they walked the three blocks to the town square, and then cut catty-corner across the lawn, headed for Sweetheart Park.

Charlie was small for his age, and Sam couldn't help wondering if that was an element of his shyness. Even before Sam had married Valerie and legally adopted the boy, Charlie hadn't played with other kids much. He was more like Sam on that score as well, preferring to play alone or with animals. Charlie was who he was, and Sam was okay with that. He just hated to think that the boy was missing out by staying so much inside his own head.

Just like you.

"Stand over by the Sweetheart Tree," Sam instructed, and took up his position near the gazebo a few feet away.

The Sweetheart Tree was a two-hundred-year-old pecan thick with sheltering branches. In the past, hundreds of names and hearts had been carved into the trunk. The oldest names were those of the original sweethearts. *Jon loves Rebekka* had been carved in the center of the pecan, faded and weathered now, but the etched lines were still visible. Sometime in the 1960s a botanist had warned that if the name carving continued, it would kill the pecan, so a white picket fence had been constructed around the tree, along with a sign sternly admonishing: "Do Not Deface the Sweetheart Tree."

Sam smiled. He and Trixie Lynn . . . no, she was Emma now, he had to remember that. He and Emma had climbed that tree together once upon a time. Climbed high into the branches and carved their names with a pocket knife where no one could see. *Sam and Trixie Lynn were here.* He hadn't been bold enough to scratch: *Sam + Trixie Lynn,* but damn, he'd wanted to. Then he'd fallen out of the tree and broken his wrist. He'd had to stay calm to keep her from panicking, and he told her to run home to get his mother. Even though his mother thought Trixie Lynn was a bad influence, she'd let her come with them to the hospital. Trixie Lynn was the first one to write her name on his cast.

Hey, what was past was past. Forget about it.

Sam slipped his hand into the catcher's mitt and squatted down. "Let 'er rip, champ."

Looking far too serious for a game of catch, Charlie drew back his arm and slung the ball as best he could.

"Good job." Sam snagged the ball, pitched it back to him. Charlie wasn't interested in joining T-ball. Valerie had tried to sign him up, but he'd quit after one game. He didn't like the pressure of team sports. Sam couldn't blame him for that. He was the same way. Which was why he'd run track instead of playing football or basketball or baseball. But Charlie did enjoy tossing the softball with his dad.

His dad.

Never mind biology, he loved the little guy more than he'd ever thought possible. Charlie was the glue that held Sam's life together. He remembered the day Valerie and Charlie had come into his veterinarian office just after he'd first opened his practice, and not long after Valerie's first husband, Jeff, had died in a car crash. Charlie's cat, Speckles, was lethargic.

"Please," Valerie had pleaded with Sam in a whisper after drawing him aside in the exam room, while Charlie sat tenderly stroking the calico. "Don't let the cat die. I don't think he can handle losing the cat on top of losing his father."

"I'll do my best," he promised her. He'd gone on to discover that Speckles had a heart defect that could be corrected with surgery. He'd charged her only the cost of his supplies. Speckles had pulled through, thrived, and ironically had outlived Valerie.

They'd look so vulnerable, mother and son, that he'd taken to dropping by their place—the place where he and Charlie still lived—to check on them, mow the lawn, hang pictures, build shelves. A friendship had blossomed among the three of them, and when Valerie learned she'd been called up as a nurse in the Army reserves, he'd proposed. She'd had no family left. Although Jeff had parents, they were really old so she had no one to take care of Charlie while she was gone. By marrying her and adopting Charlie, Sam vowed to stay behind and look after her son, while she put her life on the line tending to America's soldiers in Iraq.

She'd been a hell of a woman. He'd admired and respected her. And he'd loved her, even if it had been more like a dear friend than a passionate lover.

Thinking of passion made him think of Emma again and how his pulse had sped up when he'd found her standing on his porch. How even after sixteen years she could still make his heart misfire. Maybe there was something to the town's sweetheart myth. Maybe there was nothing like your first love. But even if that was true, he had no business exploring these feelings.

She was only in town for a little while. It was best to steer clear of her, even if she was staying at his sister's house just around the corner. He had his work, he had Charlie.

It was enough.

CHAPTER FIVE

Quilts are permanent hugs of love.
—Jenny Cheek Cantrell, owner of the Merry Cherub and
member of the True Love Quilting Club

The Merry Cherub lived up to its name.

The house was a restored Victorian converted into
a homey bed-and-breakfast. The minute they stepped
through the door, Emma's nostrils were assailed with
charming aromas of vanilla, grapefruit, and lavender.
Underneath the initial potpourri fragrance she detected
fresh paint, new carpet, and polished wood. The comforting sound of Pachelbel slipped quietly through a
piped-in stereo system. But the intriguing scents and
the uplifting music weren't what took center stage at
the Merry Cherub. Rather it was the overabundance
of angels.

Everywhere she looked, Emma saw angels.

Angel wallpaper, thick and velvety-looking. She
traced a finger over the paper in the foyer; amazingly, it
felt like velvet. Angel mobiles dangled from the ceiling,
flying gently from the movement of the air-conditioning.

Angels were carved into the staircase and the impressive crown molding. Ceramic and porcelain angels sat on display inside a mahogany curio cabinet beside the front door. There was an angel umbrella stand and an angel coat rack and even an angel rocking chair.

The angels came in every conceivable style and color—round, cherubic angels that looked like babies; fun, playful cartoon angels; tall, thin angels with windblown hair and benevolent expressions.

She fought an overwhelming urge to burst into tears and she had no idea where the emotions were coming from, but they flowed over her, along with the baroque music. She felt at once incredibly inspired and sad all the way to the center of her bones.

Jenny reached over to pat her shoulder. "Don't worry. Sensitive, artistic people often have a strong emotional reaction to the Merry Cherub."

"Really?" Emma said.

"Glenn Close started crying when she walked through the door."

"Glenn Close stayed here?" Emma was impressed.

"Yes, she and Nina are good friends. She did a two-day run at the playhouse in *Tobacco Road*. She is the nicest person. I got my picture taken with her and she wrote a letter to the *Fort Worth Star-Telegram* praising the Merry Cherub. Business has been brisk ever since." Jenny picked up Emma's suitcase and started for the stairs.

"I can carry that."

"No, no, you're my guest. Come on." Jenny's eyes sparkled.

"Put the suitcase down, I'll take it upstairs," a male voice scolded. "How many times have I told you to leave the luggage for me?"

From a side room a handsome, blond-haired man appeared and took Emma's suitcase from Jenny. He was built like a lumberjack, with broad shoulders and bulked-up biceps. He had lively, garrulous brown eyes and a ready smile.

"Hi, I'm Dean. Jenny's husband. You must be Emma." He extended his hand. His handshake was warm and welcoming.

"Nice to meet you, Dean," she said.

"Patches herded her over to Sam's," Jenny explained.

"Just like we figured." He went up the staircase ahead of them.

"We're putting you in the pink room," Jenny said. "That's where I put all the VIPs."

"I'm not a VIP."

"Sure you are. Local girl does good on Broadway."

She wasn't really a local girl and she hadn't exactly done good, but Emma let it go and followed Jenny up to the landing that was carpeted in an angel-print rug.

The pink room was just as angelic as the rest of the place, except here all the angels were various shades of pink—mauve, salmon, magenta, rose, cherry blossom, fuchsia.

"Best room in the house. The mattress is a pillow-top Stearns & Foster and your bathroom has a pink spa tub," Dean said, setting her suitcase down at the end of the bed.

"Wow."

"I know, right?" Jenny grinned and hugged herself. "It still gives me goose bumps."

Or nightmares.

"Hard to believe this B&B is ours." Dean draped his arm around his wife's waist.

"So," Jenny said, handing Emma the room key. "Is this weird for you or what? Seeing your first love for the first time in what? Sixteen years, is it?"

"You mean Sam?"

"Of course I mean Sam."

"Sam's not my first love," Emma denied. At fourteen, they'd both been very shy about labeling their affection for each other as anything other than friendship, until that kiss in the theater. But then the day after that Emma had moved away for good.

"Don't be silly, of course he is." Jenny lightly punched her upper arm the way she'd punched Sam's earlier. "Everyone in my family knew it. He moped for *months* after you left town."

The punch on her arm was an intimate gesture. Something you'd do with a sibling or close friend, not to a woman you barely knew. It unsettled Emma. Not because she didn't like it, but rather because she did. She ran a hand over her arm.

"Did I hurt you? I'm so sorry." Jenny rubbed with her palm where she'd just punched. "I get carried away sometimes. Coming from a big, boisterous family with four brothers does have its downside."

"She doesn't know her own strength." Dean ruffled his wife's hair with a big hand.

"I'm fine," Emma said.

"Whew, good. Sam would kick my ass if I hurt you. He's always standing up for the underdog and taking in strays."

"He does seem to have grown into a very nice man."

"Out of all my brothers, he's the most tenderhearted. He was always quiet, but after he got mauled by the mountain lion he did turn a bit dark and broody." She clicked her tongue.

Shock seized Emma. "Sam was mauled by a mountain lion?"

"Junior year in high school, on a Boy Scout camping trip, he comes across a young male mountain lion in Big Bend National Park. The lion is sick, can't walk, but does my brother go for the game warden? Does he even go back for his scoutmaster?" Jenny shook her head. "Nooo. Sam tries to help it. And even when the rest of his troop came upon him, bleeding and almost unconscious, he wouldn't let them shoot it."

Emma hissed in her breath through gritted teeth. "That's how he got the scar on his forehead."

"Yeah. He's very self-conscious about it and he's worn his hair long in front ever since to cover it up. But, you know, women are crazy for the scar. I mean, come on, he's so handsome and the scar lends him a dangerous air, don't you think? Even though Sam's not the least bit risky."

I do. Emma said nothing.

"But that kind of attention makes him uncomfortable. I swear I think that's a large part of why he hooked up with Valerie. She was a nurse and she didn't make a big deal about his scar. She was neither impressed nor repulsed by it. She saw him for who he really was beneath it."

"He must have loved her a lot."

"She was good for him," Jenny hedged. "Brought him out of his shell a bit. But since she's been gone, he's reverted. Although he does take such good care of Charlie. It still amazes me."

"Why does that surprise you?" Emma asked. "He's Steady Sam, and Charlie *is* his son."

Jenny raised an eyebrow. "He didn't tell you?"

"Tell me what?"

"Charlie's not his. Not biologically anyway."

Emma pressed three fingers to her lips. "Are you saying his wife cheated on him?" Why she should suddenly feel an irresistible urge to kick a dead woman's ass, she didn't know, but she felt it all the same.

"Oh, no, no. Sam married Valerie after her first husband was killed in a car crash, and she got called up from the reserves to active duty. She didn't have any family to take care of Charlie. So Sam adopted him."

"It wasn't a love match then?" *Damn.* Why had she said that?

Jenny's eyes sparkled. "Not like you and Sam, but he and Valerie had a nice thing going. Of course he and Charlie both have been in a blue funk since she's been gone. That's why it's so cool you're here."

"What do you mean? What do I have to do with it?"

Jenny spread her arms wide, "Come on, Emma, you're in Twilight, the town that specializes in hooking up their childhood sweethearts with each other. Don't you remember the town myth?"

Emma shook her head.

"Rumor has it that if you throw pennies into the fountain in Sweetheart Park, you'll be reunited with your high school sweetheart. Many reunited lovers come to Twilight to get married under the Sweetheart Tree, and in fact, that's how Aunt Belinda got started as a matchmaker."

Emma shook her head. "That sounds pretty far-fetched."

"It worked for me," Dean said. "That's how I won Jenny back after we had a big blow-up after high school and broke up for a year. I bet I tossed a hundred dollars' worth of pennies into that fountain."

Jenny grinned at him and then said to Emma, "Okay, but don't say I didn't warn you. There's something about Twilight that brings old lovers back together."

"Well, see there. I have nothing to worry about. Sam and I were never lovers. We were just kids."

"You don't have to get physical to be in love," Jenny said sagely. "Now we're going to let you freshen up, and then in half an hour, I'm going to take you on over to the Methodist church on Holloway so you can meet Nina and the rest of the True Love Quilting Club."

Half an hour later, Emma walked into the community center of the Methodist church with Jenny, who was chattering like a cheerleader on amphetamines. Did the woman *ever* wind down?

Emma recognized Nina Blakley, the Tony award–winning actress. She moved with a grace and elegance that spoke of someone who'd trained for the stage. She was as tall as Emma was short, probably close to six feet, and she appeared to be in her early fifties, but Emma knew that if she'd won a Tony award in the sixties, she had to be a decade older than that. The minute Emma and Jenny appeared, Nina got to her feet and crossed the room, arm outstretched to take Emma's hand.

"It's a pleasure to make your acquaintance, Emma," she said in a smooth, controlled voice that didn't reveal a hint of Texas accent even though Emma knew she'd been born and bred in the Lone Star State.

"The pleasure is all mine," Emma said, craning her neck upward.

Nina held her hand a moment and gazed into her eyes. "Anyone who has the courage to kick that tyrant

Scott Miller in the family jewels when he tries that casting-couch crap is forever on my favorite person list."

"I have to tell you," Emma said, "it wasn't the smartest move I ever made on Broadway." She furrowed her brow. "Come to think of it, it was the only move I ever made on Broadway. Blew my big chance before it ever got started."

"Oh, nonsense." Nina patted her hand. "You're a legend around here. Come meet the members of my quilting club and your devoted fans."

Feeling more pleased than she should about that comment—after all, she didn't want to be infamous for sending a handsy Broadway director to the hospital to have a testicle removed—Emma tried to keep up as Nina introduced her to the members of the quilting bee.

"This is Patsy Cross," Nina started with the first woman seated on the left. "She's on the city council and runs the Teal Peacock, it's the most adorable little curio shop just off the square."

Patsy looked to be in her late fifties. She had short blond hair that feathered attractively around her face. A pair of reading glasses rode the end of her nose, and she studied Emma like a high court judge sizing up a defendant. "You used to live in Twilight."

"For a year. When I was fourteen. My f . . . fa . . . father"—she stumbled over the word—"worked at the nuke plant in Glen Rose." She managed to avoid adding, "Your Honor," but the phrase sat on the end of her tongue.

Patsy nodded. "I thought I remembered you. That makes you one of us."

Emma wasn't sure what made her one of them. The

fact that Patsy remembered her, or that she'd once lived in Twilight. Either way, she felt that dangerous sense of delight again.

Patsy leaned over the section of quilt in front of her and went back to her stitching. The women clustered around a quilt that was rolled like a scroll around two wooden rods mounted on metal stands. The quilt was pulled taut between the two poles—spaced four feet apart—and even in its unfinished state, it was stunning. The pattern was intricate, the stitches precise, the colors complementary.

"It's called a double wedding ring," Nina explained, catching the direction of Emma's gaze. "We're making it for Patsy's nephew, Jesse. He's getting married to Flynn MacGregor next month."

That meant nothing to Emma, but she smiled like it did. "Congratulations."

"This wedding was a long time coming," Patsy said. "Jesse and Flynn were high school sweethearts who took a long, tortuous road to romance."

"Not everyone realizes they're destined when they first meet," said the round-faced woman sitting next to Patsy.

She was forty-ish, with a ready smile. The T-shirt she had on bore the photographs of five adorable kids, and along with the unflattering mom jeans she wore, told Emma the woman was a busy mother who didn't have the time or inclination for stylish dressing. She reached out a hand to shake Emma's. "I'm Belinda Murphey. Jenny and Sam's aunt on their mother's side and the local matchmaker."

"Jenny told me about you."

"I specialize in reuniting long-lost loves." Belinda beamed. "I married my own high school sweetheart, and I've successfully matched over a hundred happy couples."

"Um . . . that's nice."

Belinda cocked her head, eyed Emma's bare ring finger. "Are you in a relationship?"

"Don't let her pressure you," said the thin, sharp-nosed woman positioned just to the side of one of the metal stands. She was around the same age as Patsy Cross. "Belinda's a love addict. She can't help herself. Whenever she meets a single person, she feels duty-bound to fix them up."

"Oh," Emma said, taken aback by this woman's frankness. She was still attractive at sixty and she styled her blond hair long and straight in a modern cut. She wore a miniskirt that wasn't age appropriate, but she did have a nice pair of toned, shapely legs to show off. Emma instantly liked her and hoped she would have as much chutzpah when she was this woman's age.

"Name's Raylene, by the way. Raylene Pringle."

"Pringle? Like the potato chips?"

Raylene pointed a finger at her. "If you laugh, I'll hold it against you."

"She will too," Belinda said.

Patsy laughed.

Raylene glared.

Belinda waved a hand. "Pay those two no mind. They have history."

"And yet they're in the same quilting club?" Emma commented.

"We're in a knitting club together as well," Patsy said.

"No kidding?" Emma didn't know what to make of the dynamics between these two.

"I hate her like a sister." Raylene grinned and reached over to hug Patsy's neck.

"You smell like booze." Patsy sniffed.

"One glass. I had one glass of red wine. Dr. Longoria said it's perfectly okay for me to have one glass of red wine a night. Right, Terri?" Raylene winked at the youngest woman in the group, who was sitting directly opposite her.

"Terri's husband is chief of staff at Twilight General," Belinda explained.

Terri raised a hand. "Hi, Emma. Yes, my husband, Ted, is the big cheese over at the hospital and I run Hot Legs Gym. Drop by sometimes. I'll give you a free pass to check out the facilities."

"That's nice of you." Emma tracked her gaze over Terri. She was six or seven years older than Emma, with beautiful caramel-colored skin and dark brown hair cut pixie-style.

"We want you to feel welcome in Twilight," Terri said.

"I already do," Emma assured her. Too welcome. That was the problem. She already felt as if they had too many expectations of her. Expectations she was sure she couldn't fill. Honestly, she felt overwhelmed. "Thanks to Jenny."

"But that was after she had a bit of a scare," Jenny said, settling her arm around Emma's shoulder as if they were old friends. In New York, people didn't get this chummy this fast, and it made her a bit leery. "Patches herded her to Sam's house from the bus stop."

"I'm afraid of dogs," Emma confessed.

"That darn Border collie," said the elderly woman sitting to Terri's right. "He once herded three of Clinton Trainer's cows *into* my backyard garden. They wiped out my entire crop of black-eyed peas. Those fat little Herefords love black-eyed peas."

"Okay." Quilting bees and Hereford cows and black-eyed peas and close-knit friendships were so far out of Emma's sphere of experience, she had no idea how to comment on that.

"Oh, I forgot to say, I'm Dotty Mae Densmore." The elderly woman smiled. "And I remember you, although I'm sure you don't remember me. You used to wash my windows for spending money."

Emma remembered that. Her father—er, Rex—hadn't given her an allowance, but all the little old ladies in Twilight had been very nice about finding chores for her to do for a dollar or two. Things had been far different when Rex had moved her to Houston after the quiet, friendliness of Twilight. "I remember."

"Dotty Mae was the first female manager of Montgomery Ward's," Raylene said. "And if you're ever in the mood for peppermint schnapps, she carries a flask of it in her purse."

"You didn't have to tell her that." Dotty Mae glowered at Raylene.

Raylene stuck out her hand toward Dotty Mae. "I'd like a shot right now. Hand it over."

Terri cleared her throat.

"What?" Raylene said.

"One glass of red wine a night, that's what Ted told you."

Raylene made a face. "Oh, go eat a bucket of worms."

Emma raised an eyebrow.

"Terri won ten thousand dollars on that reality show *Fear Nothing* for eating a bucket of earth-worms," Belinda supplied. "Raylene won't let her live it down."

"No schnapps." Terri pointed a finger.

Raylene blew out her breath in exasperation. "Fine. But how come Dotty Mae gets to drink it?"

"For one thing, she's not one of Ted's patients. For another thing, she's eighty-five. When you're eighty-five I'll let you have schnapps."

"Ladies, we still have one member to introduce," Nina said. Nina seemed so out of place with the colloquial women, Emma couldn't help wondering why she'd left Broadway at the height of her popularity to run a small regional theater. To her it made no sense. "Emma, our most patient member is Marva Bullock."

The forty-something, dark-skinned woman with impressive cornrow braids sat sandwiched between Raylene and Dotty Mae. She smiled warmly at her, and Emma felt a flicker of recognition. "You were my freshman algebra teacher."

"I was," Marva said. "I was wondering if you'd remember me."

"I was miserable at math, but you were so patient with me, taking time to tutor me after school." Emma didn't forget people who'd taken special attention with her. She'd had very little of that. "Thank you. Because of you, I got a solid grounding in algebra that I know I never would have gotten otherwise."

Marva looked pleased. "That's sweet of you to say."

"Not sweet at all. I mean it. Do you still teach?"

"I'm the principal of Twilight High now."

Jenny, who, to Emma's amazement, had managed

to stay silent during the introductions, tapped Terri on the shoulder. "Wanna help me with the refreshments?"

"Sure, sure," Terri said, poking the needle she'd been sewing with into a partially quilted square of fabric. She got up and followed Jenny over to the kitchen area in the far corner of the room.

"Have a seat." Nina waved at Terri's vacated chair.

Emma sat. She couldn't help wondering why she'd been dragged to the quilting club social.

"I imagine you're trying to sort out who we are and just why in the heck we've brought you to Twilight," Nina said.

Emma nodded. "I am."

"We've got a very special project planned and you're the key to its success." Nina folded her hands in her lap. The other ladies sewed industriously, letting her have center stage. From the kitchen area came the sound of platters clanking and ice cubes clinking together. "We're hoping you'll be on board."

What choice did she have? She was flat broke with nowhere to live, her acting career and reputation were in tatters, but for some reason, these women were offering her a second chance. "I'm listening."

"Let me explain how this all came to pass." Nina cleared her throat. "As you might recall from when you lived in Twilight, every year the town has a big Founder's Day celebration during the week of Thanksgiving."

"Vaguely." She hadn't participated much in the local events when she'd lived here. She'd been more the rebel-without-a-cause type.

"It's one of the town's biggest events." Nina reached up to pat a hair that wasn't out of place.

"In a town that loves its eventful celebrations," Belinda added.

"Every year we put on a play reenacting how the town was founded," Nina said.

"This is about the legend of the sweetheart lovers?" Emma asked.

"Exactly."

"Jon Grant and Rebekka Nash were childhood sweethearts in Missouri when the Civil War hit. Jon's family was on the side of the North. Rebekka's family, who were originally from Georgia, aligned themselves with the South. Sadly, the lovers' allegiance to their families tore their love asunder. Jon joined the Union Army, and Rebekka's family fled to Texas. Fifteen long years passed, but Rebekka never married because she never stopped loving Jon, even though she didn't even know if he'd survived the war."

Everyone was listening to her, even though Emma figured they'd all heard the story a million times, but Nina had the kind of vocal control that commanded attention and wove a hypnotic spell.

"Jon was injured during the War Between the States and he was promoted to colonel. He stayed in the army, and in 1875 he was sent to oversee the fort being built along the Brazos to quell Indian uprisings. He arrived on Thanksgiving Day and stopped at the river to water his horse. It was getting dusky." Nina lowered her voice. "Twilight settling. His horse nickered. Jon looked up. At first, he thought he was seeing a ghost." Nina paused.

No one spoke a word.

"There stood his flame-haired Rebekka on the other side of the river, looking just as beautiful as ever. She'd gone out to check her fishing lines with her beloved

Border collie, Rebel, at her side. Rebel started barking. Rebekka's breath stilled as she recognized the love of her life. His face was scarred and the years had sprinkled his hair with gray, but Rebekka didn't care. Jon had come back to her.

"Immediately, Jon jumped into the water and swam to the other side of the river. The minute they looked into each other's eyes, it was as if fifteen years fell away. He took her in his arms and kissed her with all the passionate longing he had in him. They couldn't believe they'd found each other again after all this time. They were married at the very spot where they were reunited, and the town of Twilight sprang up around that fort. The fort is gone now, but the town of Twilight remains, its roots forever entwined with the concept of true and lasting love."

Everyone sighed happily and sat back in her chair.

"So every year, this is the skit we put on," Nina said.

"From the reaction of this group, I'm guessing the skit is one of the highlights of the week."

"Oh, it is. It's performed on Thanksgiving Day. The playhouse is always packed to the rafters," Belinda said. "We have to turn people away. It's been an annual tradition started by Nina in 1975 on Twilight's centennial celebration, the year after she first took over running the Twilight Playhouse."

"An amazing accomplishment," Emma told Nina.

A humble smile tipped Nina's lips. "Thank you, but I can't claim a perfect record at the helm."

"What do you mean?"

"Last year, Nina canceled the skit," Belinda whispered.

"How come?" Emma looked from Nina to Belinda.

"The actress who'd been playing Rebekka was sent to Iraq," Nina said. "To honor her, I decided to skip a year. I just couldn't see replacing her. She was killed by an IED while delivering medicine to an orphanage."

"It was Sam's wife, Valerie." Belinda made a noise of regret. "She looked so much like Rebekka with those coppery locks. Just like yours."

Valerie was a saint. A true war hero. How could she ever measure up to a woman like that? Emma reached up to run a hand through her hair. "That's why you hired me? Because I have red hair like Rebekka and Valerie?"

"It's not the main reason," Nina said, "but it made us feel like you were destined for the part."

Emma frowned. "How long have you been planning this?"

"Since Belinda brought the tabloids to the last quilting club meeting," Jenny said, coming over to where they all were sitting, a tray of cookies and fruit in her hands. Terri followed behind her with a tray of drinks—coffee, iced teas, canned sodas.

"Once we saw the headlines, we knew what you were going through in Manhattan," Nina said. "I know how tough it can be." She moistened her lips. "I know what Scott Miller's capable of."

There was a story in there somewhere. Emma wondered if Nina would ever share it with her. "Were you the reason Miller dropped the sexual assault charges against me?"

"I might have made a phone call or two," Nina admitted.

Emma was flabbergasted. "I can't thank you enough. I so appreciate that. But why would you intervene for me?"

Nina leaned over and touched her arm. "Honey, you're one of us and we look after our own."

Unexpected tears pressed against the backs of her eyes. This much, she had suspected. Her memories of Twilight being a happy, loving place were real. She'd thought she'd just romanticized the town because of Sam, but she had not. These women were sincere. They wanted to help her.

"So what does this all have to do with quilting?" Emma asked, pushing aside the maudlin feelings mucking around inside her. If she was indeed going to have that career she always wanted, she couldn't get too attached to this town, these people.

"After Valerie was killed," Nina went on, "we started thinking about all the other soldiers from Twilight who'd been killed or maimed over the years, going all the way back to Colonel Jon Grant and how the Civil War almost cost him the love of his life."

"So we went looking through history." Marva pulled her needle through the quilt.

"And what we found was a great tradition of quilting during wartime," Dotty Mae said. "When the troops were called out, the women in Twilight pulled out their quilting frames."

"Twilight lost two soldiers during the Spanish-American War," Raylene picked up the story. "Terri, did you bring the pictures?"

"I did." Terri dug around in her sewing bag and produced a photo album. She flipped it open to a page with grainy, faded, old black and white photos of two young men in uniform, and below it was a color snapshot of a quilt that featured a map of Cuba. She slipped the album into Emma's hands. "This picture is of a replica quilt, but the community came together to quilt this pattern. It was displayed on the north wall inside the courthouse for several years to honor the lives snuffed out too young. Flip the page."

Emma obeyed. This one featured many more young men peering out from the photographs clearly taken during World War I. There were many quilts as well, one made for each casualty of war. She flipped the pages, past WWII and Korea and Vietnam, until she came to the last page, which had pictures of four servicemen in desert fatigues and one red-haired woman in uniform. The only woman in the entire book.

Sam's wife. Valerie. She was very pretty, but she had a serious, no-nonsense look about her. As if she carried the weight of the world on her shoulders.

There were no pictures of quilts on this page. Emma assumed the club was in the process of making quilts for this war.

"In total, since Twilight was founded in 1875," Nina said, "two hundred and sixty-four servicemen and women were killed in combat. Another three hundred and ten were wounded. Six were MIA presumed dead, and one, our own Sheriff Hondo Crouch, was a prisoner of war in Cambodia for three years."

"Wow," Emma said. It seemed like a lot for a town of just under six thousand, even if it did span more than a hundred years.

"This year, we want to expand the play to include skits from all the war eras, focusing particularly on the people who perpetuated the spirit of the town legend."

"How romantic."

"I've written the skits," Nina said, "and we've cast the male lead."

"We're going to make quilts for the backdrops," Nina said. "Each skit will have a quilt made honoring the era."

"That's ambitious."

"It is, but the quilting club is up for the challenge. We'll have seven vignettes. The original skit about Jon and Rebekka and then six additional skits for each war where Twilight lost a serviceman—Spanish-American, WWI, WWII, Korea, Vietnam, and Iraq. When the play is over, we're going to auction off the quilts, and all the money we raise goes to benefit our men and women in uniform."

Emma glanced around at the women who looked so earnest and eager. "But it's only nine weeks until Thanksgiving."

"We can make a quilt in a week," Patsy said. "We've done it before."

"Seven in a row?" Emma asked.

"It'll be a first for us," Belinda admitted, "but we're up for it. We have two extra weeks as cushions."

"The big question now . . ." Nina grinned. "Can you sew?"

"Sew?" Emma blinked. "You want *me* to quilt?"

"If you have some basic sewing skills we can teach you to quilt. You don't have to worry about choosing the fabric or designing the quilt, we'll do all that," Nina said. "But it would be wonderful to claim you had a hand in creating them."

"Well, I was a freshman at Twilight High—"

"And we require home economics for all freshmen, boys and girls," Marva said gleefully, "so you did get a well-rounded education from us."

"But I haven't so much as sewn on a button in years."

"It's like having sex," Raylene piped up. "Once you know how, you never forget."

"I did make an A in home ec." Emma couldn't resist bragging even though she knew it was going to get her sucked into making quilts.

"Excellent." Nina clapped her hands together. "We'll rehearse during the day and at night we quilt. Be at the theater at nine o'clock tomorrow morning. Now that's settled, let's take a refreshment break."

The women were up and out of their chairs, each coming over one by one to clasp Emma in a warm hug and tell her how excited they were to have her in Twilight. Her chest tightened and her nose burned. It was the first time she'd ever felt like she was really part of a loving community.

And it scared the living hell out of her.

CHAPTER SIX

*Give a woman a quilt and you warm her for the
winter. Teach a woman to quilt and you warm her
soul for life.*
—Terri Longoria, owner of Hot Legs Gym and member of
the True Love Quilting Club

Later that same evening, Sam was watering Valerie's
vegetable garden in the backyard when he heard splash-
ing coming from Jenny's pool. Could it be Emma taking
a late night dip? He turned off the water spigot, then
went to the back fence. He tried to peek through the gaps
in the wooden slats, but the red honeysuckle his sister
had planted on her side of the fence obscured his view.
He glanced around for something to stand on that would
hold his weight and spied the picnic bench. He dragged it
over next to the fence and stepped up on the bench.

Indeed, Emma was there in Jenny's backyard, stepping out of the pool, her hair plastered wetly down her
back. It shone like polished cooper in the moonlight,
water sluicing down her body clad so provocatively in
a white bikini.

Rationally, he knew she kept in shape. She was an actress. Regular workouts and healthy eating were a necessity in her line of work. But he did not expect her to look like she'd stepped from the pages of *Playboy*. She was curvy in all the right places, but there wasn't an ounce of fat on her. She was lean and taut and . . . well . . . he'd never seen anything so incredible outside of a girlie magazine.

His brain shot urgent messages throughout his body. He forced himself to breathe normally, even though he had an overwhelming urge to pant. But he possessed zero control over his eyes. His gaze roved over her, grazing from top to bottom, ending with the perusal of her bare toes painted deep scarlet. He exhaled and took the return trip back up her slender ankles to her shapely calves. He suppressed the urge to vault the fence, grab her around the waist, and pull her against his chest.

She sauntered over to a lounge chair. She was strangely leggy for a woman so petite, and when she bent to snag the colorful beach towel flung over the arm of the chair, giving him an unobstructed view of the most spectacular rump on the planet, a pang of pure lust grabbed hold of him.

He must have made some kind of noise, because instantly her head came up like that of a cautious doe in the forest, and she swiftly whipped the towel around her. "Take a picture, Peeping Tom," she shouted, "it'll last longer . . ." She spun toward the fence, glaring. "Oh . . . it's you."

Sam felt his cheeks heat. Why hadn't he jumped down off the picnic bench before she spied him? Now he felt like a total idiot.

A knowing grin twitched at the corners of her lips. "Did you just growl at me?"

He shook his head, lied, "No."

She sauntered toward the fence, holding the towel securely around her body. "You were spying?"

"No." What the hell? He wasn't kidding anyone. She'd caught him red-handed.

"No?" She sank her hands on her hips, and the movement caused her breasts to lift.

"Yeah, okay. I was spying on you. Would it be crude to say 'nice ass'?"

"Very crude." She stepped closer, narrowed her eyes. "But thanks."

Sam didn't know what to say. Every nerve ending in his body throbbed. The caveman in him—the one that had made the nice-ass comment—wanted to rip down the fence with his bare hands to get to her.

They stood looking at each other, Sam peering down over the fence, Emma with her head tilted upward. The moment seemed to stretch into forever—hot and full of yearning.

"Was there something else you wanted to say besides the nice-ass thing?"

"Um . . ." He couldn't think with her standing there, water dripping off her. Even though she had the towel wrapped around her now, the way she'd looked bending over that lounge chair was permanently embedded in his brain. "No."

"Okay then, I'm just gonna go on into the Merry Cherub." She turned to go.

"Wait."

She stopped beside a naked cherub birdbath, her bare toes curling into the St. Augustine grass. "Yes?"

Great, now say something brilliant. But what? He stared at her, his throat muscles paralyzed.

She stared right back, all saucy and bold. Scrappy little thing. She reminded him of a Jack Russell terrier, impulsive, determined, and intense. He'd always had a fondness for Jack Russell terriers even though they could be quite challenging to handle. Emma's green eyes glimmered in the fading sunlight, compelling as the ocean on a storm-tossed day.

Something inside Sam shifted. A level of awareness he'd never quite felt before. If he'd been on her side of the fence, there was not a doubt in his mind that he would have kissed her. He noticed every detail of her face. The faint dusting of freckles sprinkled across the bridge of her nose. How her eyelashes were almost the same color as her hair. How her hairline dipped down into a pretty little V shape in the middle of her forehead. Widow's peak, he thought it was called.

Silence spun out between them.

Her cheeks flushed, enhancing her peaches and cream complexion. She looked like one of Jenny's cherubs—pink and soft and sweet. Still, she did not look away. She had a vulnerable, innocent air about her, but Emma knew how to take care of herself. She wasn't aggressive. (In the same situation, Valerie might have just climbed the fence and kissed him.) But neither was she skittish. She didn't turn, she didn't run, she just stood there, looking, waiting, unabashedly curious. She wouldn't make the first move, but she wouldn't mind a bit if he did.

And how he wanted to make that move.

But Sam knew he couldn't act on his desires. Emma was in town for only a short while, and he had Charlie to think about. Not to mention his own well-being.

He knew he had the potential to fall so deep in love with her he could never climb out of it. But Emma wasn't the kind of woman you could spend your life with. He'd always known that about her. She had big dreams, and he was a small-town guy who loved his small-town life. She was blazing a path to stardom, and he wouldn't stand in her way.

"You know what I was thinking?" Sam asked.

Emma stroked the bald head of the naked cherub. "That Jenny really should rethink the whole angel theme?"

"Besides that." He grinned.

"What?"

"That it's good to have you home."

"That's very sweet of you, Sam."

Sweet.

The damn word that had haunted him all his life. He didn't want Emma thinking of him as sweet. Kittens were sweet. Cotton candy was sweet. Watering your dead wife's vegetable garden was sweet. He gritted his teeth. Was that how she saw him? Completely harmless?

He had an impulse to push his hair back off his forehead and show his scar. It was a move of the ego, designed to let her know that he'd done dangerous things and that he wasn't as sweet as she might think. It was vain, it was cheesy machismo, and he did it anyway.

Her gaze went to his forehead just as he'd known it would. Her lashes lowered for a moment, and then she looked him straight in the eyes. He tried to figure out what she was thinking, but the woman was an actress, and the slight smile on her face hid whatever might be going on inside her head.

"Cool scar," she said, then turned and walked into the house, leaving him feeling foolishly puffed up with pride. No one had ever told him his scar was cool before.

After a hearty breakfast of steel-cut oatmeal topped with brown sugar, walnuts, and sliced bananas served in a bowl patterned with frolicking angels, Emma arrived at the Twilight Playhouse the following morning at eight-thirty. She stepped into the darkened lobby, but saw a light on at the end of the hall. The door stood open, and Emma walked over.

"Good morning." Nina smiled in greeting from behind an antique rolltop desk that looked like it could have been built at the same time as the theater. "How did you sleep?"

"Great."

"Jenny put you in the pink room?"

"She did. It's . . . um . . . very pink and angelic."

"Part of the charm of small-town life." Nina's eyes danced. "Twilight is very different from Manhattan."

"You can say that a hundred times and never be wrong."

"How long have you lived in the city?"

"Twelve years." Emma shook her head, unable to believe it.

"You lasted a lot longer than I did."

"With none of your success."

"You underestimate yourself," Nina said. "You might not have yet managed a Broadway debut, but I did my research. I read reviews of your off-Broadway work. The critics were highly complimentary."

"Yeah, that and five bucks will get you a Venti Mocha Latte at Starbucks."

"The entertainment industry functions primarily on luck and timing, true, but you've got talent. You care about craft. You're a true artist. I can tell."

Emma had never been all that comfortable with praise. "Throw in another five bucks and you can get a croissant with that latte," she quipped.

"You've kept your sense of humor. That's positive."

"It's either that or take a header off the Brooklyn Bridge."

"They appreciate you here. I have no doubt you're going to blow their socks off."

Emma grinned. "And with that I can treat a friend to a latte and croissant as well."

"I understand the feelings of desperation that go on in your head when you're faced with such stiff competition. When I was a struggling actress," she murmured, "I did a lot of things I'm not proud of."

Emma wanted to ask her what those things were, but she restrained herself. It was none of her business. "I've seen some crazy things," she admitted. "My roommate Cara slept with a guy who was a janitor at the Ed Sullivan Theater. She got him to sneak her onto the set and they taped a segment of her as if she was being interviewed on *Letterman*. She sent the demo around, and believe it or not, she got a couple of auditions out of the deal. Oftentimes it doesn't have to really be celebrity, it just has to look like it. Another actress I know stole her best friend's union card to get a part."

"You never did anything like that?"

Emma notched up her chin. "I might be desperate, but I'm not a cheater. Besides, you always get found out in the end."

Nina stared at a spot on the wall above Emma's head, a wistful look on her face. "Yes, you do," she whispered, "yes, you do."

The temptation to pry was great, but Emma restrained herself. If Nina had something to tell her, she'd do it in her own time.

"Before we start rehearsal," Nina said, "I need to tell you something about the man who's going to be playing your love interest."

"Okay." Emma sat down in the chair across from Nina's desk.

"I believe in giving people second chances."

"Which explains why I'm here?"

"It does, but I also derive pleasure in proving the naysayers wrong. I don't like the way the media has treated you. Turning Scott Miller into the victim and you into the villain."

"How do you know the reports aren't right? That I assaulted Miller because he refused to give me the part?"

That enigmatic look crossed Nina's face again. "Anyone who really knows Miller understands that's utter crap."

"Hmm." Emma slid to the edge of the plush leather chair so her feet would touch the floor. "Hiring me has almost as much to do with getting even with Miller for something as giving me a second chance?"

Nina canted her head, held up both hands. "It would please me immensely if this role led to revitalizing your career. Both because you deserve it and because Miller needs to be shown up for the tyrant he is."

Emma laughed. "How on earth is a role in a small-town play going to do all that?"

"Now you're underestimating me, Emma. We're

going to have to work on your pessimism. Anyway, let's get back to your leading man and the fact that I believe in second chances." Nina drummed her fingers on the desk. "Beau Trainer will be playing Colonel Jon Grant and all the other leading male roles in the skit."

"I remember Beau. He was the most popular guy in high school. I didn't know he was an actor."

"He's not, but he's got natural acting chops. He put on an act for his entire life. Pretending to be something he wasn't in order to please other people."

"Okay."

"The reason I'm telling you all this is because some people don't believe Beau deserves a second chance. I happen to think they're wrong, but you might hear some grumbling or be expected to take sides. I'd prefer if you remained neutral on this issue."

"Why is he on everyone's shit list?"

"Beau used to be our interim sheriff. He was appointed after his father had a stroke. But then he did some bad things and he was forced to resign his post."

"What kind of bad things?" Fascinated, she leaned forward, instantly intrigued.

"He blew up the old Twilight Bridge and burned down that building on the other side of the courthouse. Perhaps you noticed? It used to house a motorcycle shop and yarn store, but the fire was accidental."

Emma remembered that bridge. She and Sam used to swan dive off it into the Brazos just upriver from Lake Twilight. "No kidding."

"In his defense, the bridge was falling in."

"He didn't want to go through the proper channels of having the bridge condemned?"

"It was a little more complicated than that."

"Why did he do it?"

"Why does any man act like a fool? For the love of a woman."

"I take it she wasn't impressed."

Nina shook her head. "Flynn MacGregor was in love with her high school sweetheart, Jesse Calloway, who'd recently got released from prison. Flynn was engaged to Beau, but then found out he'd framed Jesse because he was jealous. Long story."

"Jesse is Patsy Cross's nephew?"

"That's right."

"And you think Beau is worth taking a chance on?"

"Beau is a complicated guy. He earned a Purple Heart in Iraq. His act of bravery saved the lives of his platoon, and he acted with no concern for his own safety. He was gravely wounded in the incident. And now he's very contrite about what he did, but some people aren't quick to forgive, and understandably so. He did betray public trust and lost his job. He plea bargained and got probation. But he's a good man at heart and he's really struggling with how he damaged his life. He needs help rebuilding his reputation, and Sam and I are about the only people in town who didn't turn their backs on him."

"Wow." It didn't surprise her to hear that Sam hadn't forsaken Beau. The Sam she remembered was nonjudgmental, diplomatic, open-minded, and empathic.

"I just thought you should know right up front."

"Thanks for telling me."

So everything wasn't all merry cherubs and comfy quilts and town square "howdies" in Twilight. Good to know some people had dark, torturous secrets. It made Emma feel more normal, and very curious about what other mysteries and secrets might skulk in this town.

"Here he is now," Nina said as the outer door to the theater creaked open.

The Beau Trainer she vaguely remembered had grown into a tall, straight-shouldered man who said very little to her beyond hello. She wondered what it was like to have messed up so badly that the majority of the town turned against you, and she decided that if he was truly contrite, he had a pretty big cross to bear. She imagined how tough it must be to walk down the street with your head held high when you knew people were mumbling about you behind your back.

Beau was a particular kind of rugged-Texas good-looking, of the Dennis Quaid, Patrick Swayze, Tommy Lee Jones ilk, but he was nowhere near as handsome as Sam—who, if it weren't for the scar pitted deep into his forehead, was drop-dead gorgeous. Beau had a nose that was slightly too big for his face and a hard, unyielding chin. In that chin, Emma saw the things that had orchestrated his downfall—stubbornness, anger, pride. But his dark, soulful eyes belied the chin. In those eyes lurked a man tormented by the demons who'd driven him to violate his moral code. She felt at once sympathy and wariness.

"Well then," Nina said with forced cheeriness. "Let's get started."

She led Emma and Beau into the main part of the playhouse, flipping on switches as they went. Replicas of period chandeliers and wall sconces lighted the auditorium. One look around told Emma little had changed in the five-hundred-seat theater since it was first built in 1886. The white stone walls were exposed. The white-painted doors, molding, and balcony rails were original, and the authentic needlepoint seats evoked a bygone era.

There was a plaque on the wall at the entrance proclaiming that, along with the whole town square, the Twilight Playhouse was listed in the National Register of Historic Places. A second plaque declared it a charter member of the League of Historic American Theatres.

And then there was the legend.

Rumor had it that John Wilkes Booth was not hunted down and killed for assassinating President Lincoln. There was even evidence to suggest that he came to Twilight under the alias John St. Helen, and if that was true, he'd performed Shakespeare at the Twilight Playhouse. Emma cast a glance at Beau, who was standing beside her, staring at the stage. Perhaps Nina was continuing the theater's reputation of providing redemption for bad boys.

Along with the John Wilkes Booth legend came a ghost. Several people swore there was a resident ghost who could be heard at odd times, pacing the balcony. Those who claimed to have seen him said he wore a long-sleeved white shirt, dark pants, and tall, heavy boots.

The musty smell of history transported Emma back in time. Not to the nineteenth century, but to her childhood. She was fourteen again, sneaking in through the side exit with Sam, climbing up the stage steps, kissing in the overhead loft. The memory sent a sweet shiver running through her. This was where she'd first whispered to Sam her aspirations of becoming an actress, of being a star. This place was where he first kissed her; where she'd first fallen in love with both a boy and a dream.

Nina climbed the stage steps, her heels echoing smartly against the old wood. She disappeared from sight for a few minutes. Emma slid a look over at Beau and discovered him staring at her. Tension filled the space between them.

"She tell you about the bridge and the motorcycle shop?" he asked in a deep, rumbly voice.

"She tell you about the guy I half castrated?"

His grin was unexpected. "She did."

And with that, the awkwardness between Emma and her leading man vanished.

The curtains opened and Nina reappeared, carrying three scripts. They joined her onstage. She passed scripts to Beau and Emma, and kept one. "You two are going to carry the play. Most of the extras will be played by acting students from Tarleton State University in Stephenville. We have some locals, but the bulk of it rests on your shoulders. Let's run lines."

Before they could get started, a quick knock sounded on the side door and it opened to reveal Sam's housekeeper, Maddie, with Patches trotting beside her.

"Come on in." Nina waved Maddie up onstage.

Sam's housekeeper climbed the steps.

Patches bounded ahead of her, headed straight for Emma, his head lowered, his eyes trained on her feet, his lips curled back, revealing a flash of deadly white teeth.

A high keening sound escaped Emma's lips and she stumbled backward, desperate to get away from the dog, terrified she was going to trip and fall and he'd be on her, ripping her throat out before anyone could stop him.

"Stand your ground," Maddie said.

But fear had a strong hold on her. Emma spun around, heading for the stairs that led to the loft, but it was as if the Border collie read her mind. Faster than she could breathe, he whipped around in front of her and seemed to give her a wicked, doggy smirk that said, *Go ahead, make my day.*

He slunk toward her, his intense blue eyes never looking away, never blinking.

Dread built a dam in her throat. She took an uneasy step backward, raised her palms in a defensive gesture. Every muscle in her body tensed, on alert. All she could think about was how much it was going to hurt when he sank his teeth into her tender flesh. Fear cleaved through her, axe-sharp as all her concentration narrowed on that black and white dog.

Snap out of it. This is important. Think tough-minded thoughts. You're Joan of Arc, Madam Curie, Maria von Trapp. Nothing stands in your way. She tried to convince herself, but her usual mantras weren't working.

"Patches," Maddie said sharply. "Leave it."

The dog looked from Emma to Maddie and back again. He took another step toward Emma.

"Leave it!" Maddie commanded. "Come."

Reluctantly, Patches turned away from her and sidled over to Sam's housekeeper, but he never took his stare off Emma.

"I'm sorry." Maddie yanked a leash from her pocket. "He doesn't obey me the way he does Sam. The dog has a one-track mind. When he focuses on something, he's focused."

Just my luck, he's focused on me like I'm a red-headed pork chop.

Emma inched away from the dog.

Patches snarled.

Emma stopped in her tracks, blood chugging restlessly against her eardrums. "Back off, Cujo," she said, bravely raising her chin in a desperate bid to overcome her rubbery knees.

"She's shaking," Beau said. "Nina, Emma is really scared of the dog."

"Emma?" Nina sounded very far away, even though she was in touching distance. "Are you all right?"

She opened her mouth to speak but no words came out. Was this how Sam's son, Charlie, felt? Rendered speechless by high anxiety? Empathy washed through her. Poor little kid.

Come on, push through this. "I'm fine," she lied.

Maddie marched over and clipped the leash to Patches's collar. "It's okay, I've got him."

Nina put a hand around Emma's shoulders. "Let's go sit down."

Numbly, she nodded and allowed Nina to lead her off the stage to the auditorium seating, while Maddie took Patches outside. Beau shrank back behind the stage curtain, presumably waiting in the wings. Emma collapsed into the chair, closed her eyes, and drew in a deep breath.

Nina sat beside her. "I understand what you're going through."

"You do?"

"I used to have a dread fear of bees. When I was a little girl about six years old, I climbed in a peach tree, and just as I reached for that juicy peach, dozens of stinging insects swarmed my face."

"Omigosh that must have been horrible."

"They stung me everywhere. On the eyelids, up in

my nose, inside my ears. Stingy with their peaches, those bees."

That made Emma laugh, which was clearly Nina's intent.

"I found out I was quite allergic to them and my throat started closing up. My parents rushed me to the emergency room and they were told that if they hadn't gotten me there when they did, I would have died."

"That must have been terrifying."

"It's the primary memory of my childhood. After that episode, I developed a paralyzing fear of bees. I wouldn't even touch honey. I was convinced they'd come after me because I liked honey in my tea." Nina smiled. "I'm guessing that something equivalent must have happened between you and dogs."

"Yes, but nothing like that."

"I let that fear run my life for many years. Once, when I was doing Shakespeare in the Park—*A Midsummer Night's Dream*—a bee started flying around the lighting. In a panic, I went running off the stage. I got fired for unprofessional behavior."

"That was harsh."

"Well," Nina said, and patted Emma's hand, "not every director is as understanding as I am."

"Thank you."

"But this phobia is something you need to address. It's holding you back. Not only professionally, but personally. Whenever we let fear take hold of us, we give up our power."

"I take it you're no longer afraid of bees."

"Not in the least."

"And honey?" She grinned.

"Drink it in my tea every morning."

"How did you conquer your fear?"

"That night after I was fired, I did some soul searching and realized I'd let my past experiences with bees dominate my current frame of mind. So I sought out a bee expert and learned as much as I could. Then I auditioned for a role in a movie featuring a female beekeeper and got it."

"I saw that. *Never Too Sweet*. You were great. No one would ever guess you were afraid of bees."

"Thank you. I'm pretty proud of that role, if I do say so myself. Also, I always carry an EpiPen around with me." She reached in her pocket and pulled out a syringe preloaded with epinephrine. "I'm forewarned and forearmed."

"What if I can't do it?" she asked, feeling like a big weenie even as she said it. If Nina could get over a fear that had the potential to kill her, she could darn well get over her dogaphobia.

"You can do it. You have to do it. Jon and Rebekka's meeting hinges on the Border collie. A dog has to be in the play."

"So it's either me or the dog?"

Nina slid the EpiPen back into her pocket. "Let's not assume the worst. I'm more than confident you can learn to love dogs. Or at least work with them."

"But how?"

"We'll contact Sam. He knows more about animals than anyone else in town. He'll know what to do with you."

CHAPTER SEVEN

Quilters create history.
—Rebekka Nash, historical figure and inspiration for the
True Love Quilting Club

"Dr. Cheek, there's a Miss Emma Parks here to see you."

Sam was getting ready to perform surgery on a six-month-old Great Dane who'd swallowed a tennis ball. He was washing up at the stainless-steel surgical sink, vigorously scrubbing his fingernails with a Betadine solution. At the mention of Emma's name, his head went up and a bolus of pure heat shot through his bloodstream. His receptionist, Delia, stood at the doorway behind the red line painted on the floor.

By disposition Delia Franklin was a determined girl who took her work seriously. He'd hired her right out of high school—she'd been valedictorian of her class—and she'd worked for him since he'd opened up his practice. She'd grown up in one of the run-down trailer park communities on the unsavory side of the Brazos, and she possessed a deep yearning to do better than her loutish parents. To help her achieve her goal, he was paying for her basic courses at the community college in the neighboring town of Weatherford.

"I told her that you were about to go into surgery, but she says it's really important."

Curiosity got the better of him. What did Emma want? "Show her back, Delia."

"Really?"

"Really."

"You've never allowed anyone back here that's not an employee."

"First time for everything," he said, raking the scrub brush down his arm in a methodical pattern.

"Okay." She sounded dubious and disappeared.

A minute later she returned with Emma trailing behind her. "You can stand here and talk to him," Delia said, "but do not cross the red line."

"Got it." Emma nodded. "Thanks."

Delia folded her arms over her chest and eyed Emma distrustfully.

"You can leave us alone, Delia," Sam said.

Delia had an expression on her face that told him she thought he was making a big mistake by letting this big-city interloper intrude on their territory, but she turned and slowly drifted away.

Sam ran his soapy arms underneath the water faucet controlled by an automatic sensor eye. "What's up?"

"I desperately need your help," Emma said.

He liked the sound of that. Was it stupid to like the fact that she needed him? "Okay."

"I'm in trouble and apparently you're the only one in town who can save me."

"What? Did you swallow a tennis ball?"

"Excuse me?"

He waved a hand. "Inside joke. I'm about to operate on a Great Dane who swallowed a tennis ball."

"The tennis ball swallowing I've managed to avoid."

"Then what's got you tied up in knots?"

"Mental ropes. I'm going to lose my job if I can't get over my fear of dogs."

"Nina said she was going to fire you?" He raised his arms up, elbows held over the sink so the water could drain down off them.

"Not in so many words, but her implication was clear."

"Then I guess we better get you over your fear."

"You'll help me?" The sound of her relief filled the small room.

"I'll help you."

"Thanks, thank you so much. So, um . . . how do we go about this?"

Sam stepped away from the sink, his arms still raised, and headed for the suite where his surgical assistant waited to gown and glove him up after his scrub. He put his back to the door of the suite to enter butt first, but paused before he pushed the door open. "We can start by having you come into surgery with me."

"Insanity, thy name is Samuel Cheek."

"Played a little Shakespeare, did you?"

"Every actor does."

"I'm not joking, come into surgery with me."

She eyed him nervously. "You mean it?"

"What better place to start than with an unconscious dog."

"You gotta point, Doc."

"Delia," he called out.

His receptionist popped back into the room. "You bellowed?"

"Show Emma how to do a scrub and get her gowned up. She's coming in to observe."

"Seriously?" Delia looked at him like he'd lost his mind and looked at Emma like she'd caused it.

"Seriously," he confirmed, and disappeared into the surgical suite where his nurse was waiting to gown and glove him. A jovial mood settled over him, and he wasn't quite sure why, but he felt like smiling.

By the time Emma edged into the surgical suite, her eyes growing larger as she checked out her new environment, he had already started the incision. She wore a surgical mask, and all he could see of her face were those wide green eyes the same color as Charlie's.

He cocked his head at his nurse, who was regulating the flow of anesthesia to the dog. "Linda, this is Emma. She has a fear of dogs so I invited her to see Scooby Doo at his most vulnerable."

"Welcome, Emma," Linda said.

"His name is Scooby Doo?" Emma asked.

"Some people aren't terribly original." Sam reached for the forceps Linda offered that he didn't even have to ask for. She'd worked for him since he started his practice and they'd fallen into a comfortable rhythm. "How are you at the sight of blood?"

"I'm good if I channel a medical character."

"What does that mean?"

"Like right now I'm pretending I'm Meredith from *Grey's Anatomy*. She's tough and spunky. Nothing freaks her out. Well, at least nothing gory. Relationships freak her out. She's not very good at relationships."

"I've never seen the show," he said.

"That's too bad. It's really great. A little soap opera–ish at times, but still the romance sizzles. What shows do you watch?"

"Anything on Animal Planet."

"Ah, that makes sense."

"Emma's an actress," Sam explained to Linda. "She's playing Rebekka Nash in the Founder's Day play."

Linda eyed Emma with admiration. "Impressive. What shows might I have seen you in?"

"She's a Broadway actress," Sam said as he carefully probed Scooby Doo for the tennis ball.

"That's not really true. I never made it to Broadway. I have a few off-off Broadway productions under my belt and I was in several commercials."

"Really? Which ones?"

"I played the big toe in a commercial for an athlete's foot ointment. I was the only toe with speaking lines," Emma said proudly.

"I've seen that one," Linda exclaimed. "That was you?"

"Five of us were smashed together inside this goofy foot costume. We wore harnesses and dangled from this overhead rack."

"I bet it was fun." Linda handed Sam a retractor.

"Fun? Not really. We all ended up at the chiropractor afterward."

"Ouch."

"But the residuals I get on that commercial were worth the pain. It's the most lucrative bit of acting I've ever done. Seems the more you're willing to humiliate yourself, the better it pays."

He envisioned Emma in New York, struggling in a cutthroat business in a cutthroat town to make her mark. How complicated her world must be. A stark contrast to his life here in Twilight. She was so full of energy and courage. She was so much bigger than this place. He thought of all the things he admired about her—how quick she was with a flip quip, how she was drawn to things that were intense and out of the ordinary, how she could see the beauty in things other people would easily overlook. Her courage and resilience took his breath. She was one of a kind. He'd never known anyone like her.

"So if you're Meredith Grey," Linda mused, "does that make Sam McDreamy? He's got the hair for it."

"Mac who?" Sam asked, alarmed to find that Emma and his nurse were ogling him speculatively.

"Or McSteamy," Emma added.

"Who?"

"Nah," Linda said. "He's Finn the veterinarian. Honest, kind, steady, true blue. Just like Sam. Meredith was too screwed up for Finn anyway. He needed a woman with less drama in her life."

Sam could feel Emma's gaze on him, but he did not look up from his task. He had no idea what they were talking about, but by comparing him to this Finn character they were making him sound like a Labrador retriever.

"Right," Emma said. "I forgot about Finn. When was he? Season three?"

"I think so," Linda said to her, and then to Sam she said, "Do you need some suction?"

"Yeah, suction would be great." He tried to focus on his task, but couldn't help casting a sidelong look Emma's way.

Emma cocked her head and studied the unconscious dog. "He looks so sad with his paws tied down and that tiny little blood pressure cuff around his fore-arm."

"You can touch his head," Sam said. "Go ahead, reach under the drape and pet him."

She held back.

"He's out cold, and even when he's conscious, Scooby's gentle as a lamb," Sam reassured her.

"He's bigger than me," Emma said, tentatively sliding her hand beneath the green drape that shielded the dog's face from the sterile area. "Ooh, he's so soft. I didn't expect his skin to be so soft."

Sam looked up, met Emma's eyes over the tops of their surgical masks. Her breathing slowed, and he realized they were inhaling and exhaling in an intimate, tandem rhythm, like familiar lovers cuddling after great sex.

He blinked, dropped his gaze, surprised by the direction of his thoughts. He didn't need to be thinking things like this. He'd invited her into the surgical suite to help ease her fear of dogs, nothing more. Maybe it was because she looked so mysterious behind that mask. Maybe it was because she was the first girl he'd ever kissed. Hell, maybe it was simply because he'd been a long time without sex. Whatever the reason, he needed to get his head in the game, keep his focus on his job. Scooby's life was at stake here.

"Got the tennis ball," he gloated, and dropped the neon yellow tennis ball into the stainless-steel basin Linda extended toward him.

"Um . . ." Emma made a soft noise.

Sam looked to her again. Saw that her face was deathly pale and she was swaying on her feet. "Hey, hey," he yelled at her because he was scared she would hit the ground and he couldn't get to her without breaking the sterile field. "No fainting. You're Meredith, remember. Would Meredith faint?"

She shook her head and swallowed visibly.

"Don't lock your knees," he guided her. "Step back to the wall and slowly slide down it."

Somehow, she managed to follow his instructions and end up on the floor, arms clasped around her knees, shaking from head to toe.

And it practically killed Sam that he couldn't go over to wrap his arms tightly around her and tell her everything was going to be all right.

"I feel like a giant dork, getting all fainty on you," Emma told Sam fifteen minutes later after he'd finished sewing up Scooby Doo and had come over to help her up off the floor. "I've never fainted before. I'm not a fainter. I don't faint."

"You didn't faint this time either. You acted like a complete professional."

"I did?"

"Meredith Grey couldn't have done any better." He headed for the door. Linda had already taken the Great Dane into the anesthesia recovery area, and Emma followed after him.

"You don't even know who she is."

"Doesn't matter. You know. And apparently she's too emotionally screwed up for Finn the vet, but she's a kickass surgeon." He stripped off his surgical gown, mask, cap, and shoe covers, and then stuffed them in the lidded hamper outside the surgical suite. "Sometimes the toughest people are actually the most vulnerable because they won't let anyone in."

Following Sam's lead, Emma stripped off her scrub gear as well. He made a good point. "Do you think it's weird I pretend to be other people in order to get through tough times?"

"Who am I to judge? Whatever works, works. How you feeling now?"

"Okay." She notched her chin upward.

"The color *is* back in your cheeks."

"So, Scooby Doo. Is he going to make it?"

"Yes, simple tennis ball extraction."

"You do this kind of thing every day?"

"Not every day, but fairly often, yeah. So do you think it helped with your fears?"

"I am feeling better about dogs. Tennis balls, on the other hand . . ." she teased.

He grinned, and she got the happiest feeling inside her stomach. "Are you ready for the next step?"

Emma canted her head. "Next step?"

"From an unconscious dog to conscious ones."

She steeled herself, digging her fingernails into her palms. "Umm . . ."

"They're in kennels," he assured her.

"Oh, well then, okay," she said.

"Any idea why you're so afraid of dogs?" he asked, ushering her down the corridor.

She told him about the terrier that'd possessed a special kind of Charles Bronson vengeful streak toward her. "I swear that dog bit me at least two dozen times during the run of that play."

"And the director just allowed it to happen?"

"It was his dog, and in his eyes Fluffy could do no wrong."

"Fluffy?"

"Some people have no imagination."

His eyes sparkled at her joke. "And no consideration for others apparently."

"When I complained, the director threatened to fire me."

"Does stuff like that go on all the time in your business?"

She rolled her eyes. "You have no idea."

"Doesn't seem worth it to me, working for someone who doesn't consider the health and welfare of his employees."

"Are you kidding me? It was one of the best acting gigs of my career. Other than the commercials, which while lucrative, let's face it, are not great art." She ran a hand through her hair, trying to tame it after it had been stuffed underneath the surgical cap. At the end of the corridor lay a set of double doors. Beyond it, she could hear barking.

"So you were the big toe, huh?" he asked, and she could tell he was trying to distract her.

"Are you making fun of me?"

"Not at all. What were your lines?"

"You *are* making fun of me."

"You're not going to tell me your lines?"

"Yow!" she said, "that's some itch!"

His eyebrows shot up. "What?"

"Those were my lines."

He started to laugh but stopped in the middle, sucking his mirth back up inside him so that it ended up sounding like a snort.

"Don't laugh, those four little words earned me close to twenty grand in residuals last year."

"Yow! That's some scratch!"

"Haha. You're a funny guy."

Sam winked and touched her elbow, briefly, gently, and she recognized it as a calming gesture. He wasn't making fun of her. He was trying to get her to relax.

He opened the double doors and led her into the air-conditioned boarding kennels. The minute he entered, the dogs instantly quieted. It was eerie and spectacularly impressive.

The man had a gift. He made you feel instantly settled whenever he was around, as if no harm could come to you as long as he was there.

Still, a room full of dogs was a room full of dogs.

Emma hauled in a deep breath.

"It's all right," he murmured.

A toffee-colored Yorkie in the first kennel to Emma's right barred her sharp little teeth and let out a growl. Emma jumped, shrank back against the door.

Sam stood patiently, his hand extended. "The best way to get over a fear is to face it. Did you know that G. Gordon Liddy was afraid of rats and to get over his fear he killed one and ate it?"

"Um, no, but thanks for the visual."

"I thought you might appreciate it."

"Was it raw?"

"Huh?"

"The rat that G. Gordon Liddy ate. Was it raw?"

"I'm pretty sure he cooked it."

"Oh." She was disappointed. "The story would have been a lot more dark and morbid if he hadn't cooked it. Cooking it leaks out some of the drama."

"So how about it?" His chocolate brown eyes bathed her in warmth.

"I'm not eating a rat, cooked or otherwise."

"I'm not talking about the rat."

She shifted her weight. "I know."

"Dogs are the most loving creatures on earth."

"You have to say that. You're a vet. You love animals, therefore they love you."

"There might be something to that," he agreed. He moved his hand from her elbow to her shoulder so softly and slowly she barely noticed. She was too busy keeping her eye on that yappy Yorkie. "They sense your fear. You've gotta quell the fear."

She sighed. "I suppose this would be good for my character growth."

"That and the fact if you owned the space around you Patches would stop trying to herd you."

"He sees me as a sheep." Now she was noticing Sam. Yorkie, what Yorkie? He was standing so close she could feel his body heat.

"Luckily, dogs can be easily retrained." His hand was at her neck now.

How had it gotten there? Not that she minded, she was just surprised. "Says you."

"And I am the professional here. You never had pets as a kid?" His fingers kneaded her neck muscles.

Until he started doing that she hadn't realized how tense she was. A soft sigh slipped past her lips. "Nope."

"Remember that rabbit I gave you?"

"Rex wouldn't let me keep it."

"You had it rough." His voice was getting lower, almost hypnotic.

"So what if he didn't love me? He took care of me. Roof over my head. Food in my belly. A lot of people have it much worse." She was almost purring now, she felt her entire body relaxing underneath the magic of his soothing fingers.

Suddenly, the Yorkie stopped yapping.

"That's it," Sam said. "Now you're ready."

"Ready for what?"

"To meet Max."

"Who's Max?"

He dropped his hand. Wah! Her neck felt so lonely with him gone. He crooked a finger and started past the kennels. Emma hesitated.

"Don't tense back up again. Relax. Deep breath."

She took a deep breath and followed him. All the dogs in the kennels were calmly wagging their tails.

"Behold, the power of a tranquil mind."

"You are amazing," she whispered, afraid that if she spoke too loudly it would get the dogs all stirred up again.

In that moment Emma became aware of a curious thing. In his quiet steadiness, Sam was far more powerful than any boisterous, swaggering alpha male could ever hope to be. The fact struck her with blinding clarity. A truth she accepted without question. Who could question the influence he wielded over these animals without lifting a hand or speaking a word?

It was all in the way he carried himself. As if he knew who he was both inside and out. Emma was instantly jealous of his spiritual grace, physical poise, and mental maturity. Then she realized something else just as acute. She had too much emotional baggage for a man like Sam. Meredith Grey and Finn the vet aptly summed up their relationship. He deserved someone who wasn't a shattered vase badly pieced back together with Super Glue.

He led her to the last kennel on the left and opened it up. A slow-moving, droopy-faced hound dog that looked like Duke from *The Beverly Hillbillies* loped out. "Max is a senior citizen," Sam said. "Treat him with respect."

Max sat down at Emma's feet and stared up at her with doleful eyes.

"He wants you to pet him."

She crossed her arms. "Me?"

"Go on, it's all right."

She could do this, right? Nothing to it. People petted dogs all the time. Emma squatted and reached out a hand to scratch Max behind the ear.

He let out a moan.

She jumped, yanking her hand away as if burned. The Yorkie in the cage yelped as if picking up on Emma's tension. A couple of the other dogs barked as a consequence. "What happened? What did I do wrong?"

"Nothing." Sam smiled. "That was old Max moaning with pleasure. Face it, you've got the touch."

Emma wrinkled her forehead. "Are you sure? Maybe he just didn't want me touching him. Maybe he doesn't like me."

"He likes everyone."

"How do you know? He's never met me. Maybe he's got something against short girls from Manhattan."

"Trust me, it was a moan of pleasure."

"Oh, so now you're an expert on pleasure moans?"

Sam's smile grew wry. "Are we still talking about dogs?"

Max's tongue lolled out and he rolled over on his belly. Emma so wanted to avoid this topic of conversation that she reached out and scratched the hound's belly without once thinking about her fear of dogs. Max moaned again. The hair stood up on the back of her neck. His noise sounded like the moan of someone in the throes of a throbbing orgasm.

Emma pulled her hand back and stood up. Max looked devastated that the scratching had stopped.

"Now how could you be afraid of a dog like that?" Sam asked. "He's putty in your hands."

"Okay, so I'm not terribly afraid of Moanful Max. Patches, however, is another story all together."

"Why's that?"

"He intimidates me. The way he stares. Like he wants to take a chunk out of my leg."

"He's a Border collie. He's just focused."

"Yeah, focused on taking a bite out of my leg."

"I think I know what might help you with Patches."

"What's that?"

"If you should see him in action."

"Believe me, I've seen enough of Patches in action."

Sam struggled to suppress a grin. "You've been on the receiving end. It would help you to work with him. He'll bond with you as his partner and stop trying to herd you."

"And how do you propose to make that happen?"

"Attend a herding dog exhibition with me."

She made a face. It sounded intimidating. Then again, it was a good excuse to spend more time with Sam.

You shouldn't be spending time with him. You know it's a dumb thing to do. These feelings you still have for him are damn dangerous.

"When is this herding thingy?"

"October 2, a week from Saturday."

She paused, conflicted. Hanging out with Sam meant hanging out with animals. They were a package deal. Plus, she really had no choice. Patches was an essential part of the play. She had to learn how to work with him. "Okay, I'll go."

"I don't want to force you."

"No, I'll do it. Who knows? It might be fun."

"You say that like there's no way in hell it could be fun."

"You *are* proposing taking me to a place filled with dogs. Dogs with sharp pointy teeth. Dogs who jump on you—"

"Not these dogs. They're highly trained."

"Okay then, dogs that try to herd you."

"Not if you don't act like a sheep."

"Easy for you to say, I'm the one who's sheepish in the eyes of a Border collie."

"We're going to change all that."

"Clearly you've got more confidence in me than I do."

"Woman," Sam said, "you moved to New York City all on your own when you were just eighteen years old. If you can do that, then you can conquer this fear. I'll pick you up at eight A.M. on Saturday next, and come prepared to amaze yourself."

Chapter Eight

Starting a new quilt is like falling in love for the first time all over again.
—Patsy Cross, Twilight town councilwoman and member of the True Love Quilting Club

That evening, after fully embarrassing herself in the theater by her terrified reaction to Patches, then almost fainting at Sam's clinic, and finally by looking completely incompetent at the quilting club by repeatedly poking a sewing needle into her own thumb, Emma escaped to the lush backyard of the Merry Cherub after the majority of the B&B guests had retired to their rooms for the night. It was ten P.M. A huge white full moon hung in the sky, casting a silvery glow bright enough to read her script by.

She spread a beach towel over the lawn and lay back to speak her lines. "May God go with you, my beloved Jon, and keep you safe as you fight this horror of a war," she said in Rebekka Nash's soft Southern drawl.

She then read Jon's line in a straight monotone just

to get it out of the way so she could immerse herself in Rebekka's next line. It was difficult reading lines by herself, but she didn't want to impose on anyone to help her. She was eager to memorize at least the first few pages for tomorrow's rehearsal to redeem herself for today's poor performance. Nina was paying ten thousand dollars for a professional stage actress, and Emma was determined to make this the performance of a lifetime.

And if nothing else, being in Twilight gave the opportunity for Emma to fully concentrate on her craft. In Manhattan, the fierce competition consumed so much of her thoughts she hadn't been able to fully relax and just enjoy what she did best. She felt wildly liberated. No pressure, no distractions, no professional jealousy, just acting at its purest.

"Take this, my love . . ." She paused, pantomimed passing an imaginary Jon a pretend lace handkerchief. ". . . and keep it tucked in your breast pocket, close to your heart."

"Each night I will extract it from my pocket, press it to my nose, and dream of you," came a masculine voice from the other side of the tall wooden backyard fence.

Startled, Emma's pulse hip-hopped. She fumbled the script and almost tumbled from her lawn chair. "Sam?"

His face appeared over the top of the fence. "Nay, no Sam here. It is I, my fair Rebekka, your true love Jon," he teased.

"You know the lines?"

"Just the Jon and Rebekka skit. I used to run lines with Valerie. I heard Nina had written two more acts to the play."

"She did," Emma confirmed. "Were you out working in your garden again?"

"Full moon is the best time for garden work."

"Spoken like a true farmer."

"Keep going."

"What?"

He waved at her script. "Keep going. I'll run lines with you at least through the first act. If you want me to help after that, you'll need to bring me a script."

"You know the whole act?"

"Yes."

"Wow, you *were* a great husband."

"You know me. I don't do anything halfway."

"This is great. I really appreciate you doing this for me."

"No problem," he said, his voice carrying over the wooden fence to curl seductively around her ears. He had such a great voice. "Actually, I'm pretty good at multitasking. Saying lines with you will make the weeding go faster. Besides, it'll give me something to look forward to."

That pleased her far more than it should. "You're offering to do this every night?"

"Until you've got those lines memorized."

"Is it weird that we're doing this through the back fence? Do you want to come over here?"

"I've got to keep an ear out for Charlie."

"What about Maddie?"

"She sleeps like the dead; besides, he's my responsibility. She's my live-in housekeeper, not Charlie's nanny."

"I could come over there."

He paused a moment, then said, "Um . . . I don't really want the whole town speculating on our relationship. You start coming over here late every night and the next thing you know, the community will be taking bets on our wedding date."

"You're serious?"

"This is Twilight, remember. The denizens like nothing better than sticking their noses in other people's business. Unless it's making bets on what other people are doing."

"I guess I'd forgotten about all that."

"It's not always a bad thing. The fact that people look out for each other is the reason we don't have to lock our doors."

"I think it's nice, even the nosy-gossipy-taking-bets-on-you parts."

"Twilight is a special place." His heartfelt words settled on the breeze.

They fell silent for a moment, Emma on one side of the fence, Sam on the other. Within touching distance if the wall hadn't been between them.

Sam cleared his throat. "We should get started." He pointed over his shoulder with a thumb. "I'm going back to hoeing."

"Yes, yes." Emma opened her script. Moths circled in the glow of the streetlamp slanting illumination into both yards and giving her just enough light to read by.

"I've loved you since we were kids," Sam said.

For one crazy split second she thought Sam was talking to her, and then feeling rather stupid, she realized he was quoting from the script.

"I'll love you for always." Emma shuffled off her own emotions and slipped under the skin of Rebekka Nash. She got up and began to pace the plush St. Augustine lawn the length of the fence. "Don't go getting yourself killed in the war, you hear me?"

"I'll come back to you. I'm making a vow right now, right here, in front of God."

"Jon." Emma whimpered low in her throat, working hard to approximate the distress Rebekka must have been feeling.

"Do you have any idea how beautiful you look in the moonlight? How your hair glows like a fiery flame?"

Emma's cheeks heated and she had to remind herself she was Rebekka and Sam was Jon. She was grateful for the fence between them. She didn't want him knowing he'd made her blush.

They went on like that, reading the script aloud. Sam read it straight, while Emma embellished her reading with meaning and emotion as she dug deeper into Rebekka's psyche. Time spun away into the crisp night air and they were caught up in the romantic love story of Twilight's past. Through dialogue, Emma could feel how much Jon and Rebekka had loved each other.

"Well," Sam said after they'd finished the first act. "I better head on inside. By the time I shower and get ready for bed it'll be almost midnight. I've got an early surgery tomorrow."

"Someone else's pooch swallow a tennis ball?"

"No, just run-of-the-mill neutering."

"Thanks again, Sam, and you have a good night." She closed her script, headed for the B&B.

"Is it true?" he called out.

She paused and walked back to the fence. "What's that?"

"Delia told me some big-shot producer tried to play grab-ass with you up in New York and you showed him how we do things down in Texas."

"That's one way of putting it." She chuckled.

"Then he claimed you were the instigator and filed sexual assault charges against you?"

"He did," Emma admitted. "He took it kind of personally that I caused him to lose a testicle."

"He deserved it," Sam said vehemently. "I only wish I could have been there to bust him in the chops for you."

"That would have been great. Then you could have joined me in the pokey."

"They arrested you?"

"Yep, they put me in jail and everything."

Sam uttered a curse word so colorful it made her eyes widen. Not because she found it shocking, but simply because she'd never heard Sam use it.

"I don't know what would have happened if Nina hadn't intervened. I still don't know why she did that."

"Anyway," he said, "I just wanted to tell you it's nice to have you back again, for however long you're here."

"It's nice—if somewhat different—to be back in Twilight. I missed it more than I realized."

"Good night, Trixie Lynn," he murmured, "and welcome home."

Home.

It sounded so good. But she wasn't going to fool herself into thinking she belonged here. She knew she did not. She'd lived here for one short year of her life. That didn't make it home.

She pressed her ear against the fence, listening to the sound of Sam's footsteps climbing his back steps. She heard the back door creak open, then shut closed. "Good night to you, Sam Cheek. Sweet dreams."

Then, battling an unwanted nostalgia, she picked up her script and went to bed with visions of Jon Grant and Rebekka Nash swirling in her head.

The next week and a half passed in a blur of activity. By day the Twilight Playhouse bustled with activity as the cast (mostly drama students from Tarleton who eagerly worked for free) rehearsed and the crew (mostly local tradesmen volunteering their time) built sets. By evening Emma quilted with the True Love Quilting Club, learning far more about the art of quilting than she ever dreamed possible. And by the dark of late night, she read her lines through the backyard fence with Sam.

It surprised Emma how much she looked forward to the nightly quilting bees. The women of the True Love Quilting Club were warm, funny, accepting, and generous. They filled her in on all the town news— who was in the hospital with what disease, who was pregnant, who was getting married, who was getting divorced, who'd passed away. They were wise and witty and warm. They teased and argued and debated and celebrated. They were good listeners too, encouraging Emma to tell them about New York as they labored over the quilts. Nina seemed particularly hungry to hear stories of the theater. Asking about the plays she'd seen, the people she knew.

Within a matter of days Emma felt as if she'd been living in Twilight her entire life, as if the past twelve years in Manhattan were nothing but a faraway dream. They made her feel comfortable and safe, which was saying a lot about them. But feeling comfortable made her uneasy, which was saying a lot about her. She'd suffered many losses in life, had struggled hard with little reward. She didn't trust comfortable. It was really just chaos lurking beneath a smiling face. Sooner or later it would all be taken away. Getting too comfortable here was a big mistake and she knew it, but when they smiled at her, she was like a cold, wet kitten to a warm, dry hearth.

They taught her how to quilt. Not just how to sew, but how to create. She learned that basically a quilt was nothing more than a bunch of squares called blocks all sewn together and that each block had three layers. The top layer was the pretty pattern, the inside layer was the padding that made the quilt soft, and then there was the quilt back. But they were also true quilt artists, going beyond the traditional quilts to make contemporary art. The idea was to start with the traditional quilt and gradually get more intricate and complex as the world they lived in (and the wars Twilight had fought in) grew more intricate and complex. They started first on the quilt featuring the War Between the States and the subsequent reunion of the first sweetheart lovers, Jon and Rebekka.

"How's the play shaping up?" Belinda asked Nina and Emma the Friday after their second week of rehearsal.

"We're finding our sea legs," Nina said at the same moment Emma enthused, "I love it."

Finding our sea legs? What did that mean? It sounded like Nina didn't think the rehearsals were going as well as could be expected. That surprised Emma because she'd found herself easily slipping under the skin of Rebekka Nash. She'd done a little research on the first lady of Twilight and discovered that she and Rebekka had a lot in common. They'd both been only children and they were redheads. Rebekka had lost her mother at a young age and she'd been raised by an emotionally distant father. *That* strummed a chord in Emma.

Rebekka had been an unusual woman for her time, preferring to stay single instead of settling for a man she did not love. Tough and strong-minded, she had a career, making chic sunbonnets that she sold in Fort Worth, and she had several avocations—singing in the church choir, raising award-winning roses, and training herding dogs for the local sheep farmers.

Belinda raised an eyebrow. "Problems?"

"Emma's conquering her fear of dogs," Nina said. "We still haven't introduced Patches back into the mix, but Sam is taking Emma to a dog herding exhibition tomorrow. We have high hopes that Emma and Patches can learn to work together."

"Oh." Belinda's eyes lit up. "So you and Sam, huh?"

"Nothing's going on there," Emma rushed to assure her. "He and Patches are just helping me to overcome my . . . er . . . nervousness around dogs."

"Um-hmm." Belinda nodded as if she knew a big secret.

"So Nina, how's it working out with Beau?" Terry asked, pulling the quilting thread through her block of the quilt.

Everyone else stopped sewing and looked over at Nina. There was a bit of drama Emma didn't fully understand. She'd learned Beau had been much beloved as sheriff until he'd violated the town's trust. Some people sided with Nina, believing he should be forgiven. Others thought he should have been run out of town. The quilting club was split right down the middle on the issue. Nina, Belinda, Marva, and Jenny came down on the side of forgiveness. Patsy, Terry, Raylene, and Dotty Mae favored exile.

"He's doing great," Nina said, a warning tone in her voice. "I'm really impressed with his progress."

"What do you think of him, Emma?" Terry asked.

"He seems nice," she hedged. She wasn't about to take sides on an issue that had nothing to do with her. Beau had been easy to work with and he was a pretty good actor for an amateur.

"Here's the important question," Raylene said. "How does he kiss?"

"Raylene!" Marva scolded.

"What? I'm just saying what everyone else was thinking." Raylene tossed her head.

"We haven't rehearsed the kissing," Emma said.

"No? Well, that's a letdown. So who has some good gossip?" Raylene asked.

Everyone shook her head.

"No one? Seriously? Nothing?"

"G.C. passed a kidney stone," Marva said.

"Eeh." Raylene plugged her ears. "That's a case of too much information. Besides, it's not gossip."

"I heard that passing a kidney stone is quite painful," Jenny said.

"I'm sure it is," Marva said. "He was pacing around the house, clutching his side for two days, but then he had the gall to compare it to childbirth. As if!"

"Actually," Terri said, "Ted says that in the pain department it's pretty equivalent."

Raylene rolled her eyes. "Another man's opinion. What we need to confirm this is a woman who had passed kidney stones and given birth. Anyone?"

No one spoke up.

"So G.C.'s kidney stones are the best we can do?" Belinda asked. "Ladies, we've sunk to an all-time low."

"You're the one who reads the *National Enquirer*. Anything interesting in there since you read about Emma?"

"Not particularly. Madonna's adopting another kid from some foreign country."

"That one's a publicity hog," Raylene said.

"Now, now," Marva chided. "You don't know what's in her heart."

"Am I the only one bold enough to say what everyone else is thinking? Why do I have to keep being the lightning rod?" Raylene groused.

" 'Cause you do it so well." Nina stretched her neck from side to side, working out the quilting kinks.

The group fell silent for a moment, everyone stitching on the quilt. Even in spite of the teasing and arguing, or maybe because of it, Emma could tell how much these women loved and depended on each other. It made her feel unexpectedly sad.

"How's Jimmy?" Marva asked Patsy.

Jenny leaned over to whisper in Emma's ear, "Jimmy is Patsy's husband. He has Alzheimer's so bad she had to put him in a home. Such a shame."

"Jimmy's the same." Patsy sighed. "Yesterday he called me by his sister's name. That's actually an improvement. The time before, he accused me of being a spy for the CIA."

"Anything new with Hondo?" Raylene asked.

The whole group sort of froze in mid-stitch.

"Sheriff Hondo Crouch," Jenny whispered to Emma, "was Patsy's high school sweetheart, but things didn't work out for them. Lots of dark, brooding history. But she's still in love with him."

"Jennifer Cheek Cantrell, I am sitting right here and you don't whisper very quietly," Patsy scolded. "And for your information I am *not* in love with Hondo Crouch."

Raylene snorted. "Yeah, and I don't have a bottle of airplane-sized vodka in my purse."

Patsy and Raylene glared at each other, and everyone slid to the edge of her chair, on the verge of running for cover in case World War III broke out right there in the fellowship hall of the Methodist church.

Haughtily, Patsy lifted her chin up, narrowed a look at Raylene that could have killed her if she didn't have such a tough hide, and said, "Out of respect for our servicemen and women, I'm going to ignore that. This quilt needs to get made."

"Well, it's true, Patsy, you know you've loved that man since you were seventeen." Raylene's voice softened.

Patsy's bottom lip quivered. She ducked her head and stared at the block of quilt in front of her. "Are we going to quilt or not?"

Everyone went to quilting, and for a long time, no one said anything. Dotty Mae was the first one to break the silence. "Did anyone else see the article in *Quilters' Monthly* about the woman who was making quilts for the local nursing homes and ended up finding her long-lost mother living in one?"

"What happened?" Marva threaded her needle.

"Turns out the mother had gotten some kind of amnesia years ago and someone found her wandering dazed and confused along the highway," Dotty Mae continued. "The state didn't know what to do with her, so they called her Jane Doe and stuffed her in a nursing home. It was supposed to be a heartwarming story because the mother had been the one to teach her daughter how to quilt, and now quilts had brought them back together again, but I thought it was real sad. Here that poor girl was thinking all these years that her mother just up and ran out on her. Come to find out they'd been living in the same city all along."

Emma sat staring at the midnight blue star she was quilting, and a sudden thought occurred to her. What if something like that had happened to her mother? What if right now Sylvie was lying in some nursing home confused and forgotten? The idea of it made her gut tighten.

Why should you worry about Sylvie? She didn't worry about leaving you confused and forgotten when she went off to Hollywood with Cadillac Man.

Maybe not, but a bad case of amnesia would explain why she'd never contacted Emma again. Never sent letters, never called. Then there was the other alternative. Sylvie was dead. Maybe Cadillac Man had killed her and cut her body into pieces and stuffed her into his trunk. A Cadillac trunk was big enough to accommodate a dead body.

Yeah, right, you wish you had a decent explanation for being abandoned by your mother. Traumatic amnesia. Dramatic dismemberment.

The real truth was probably a lot more mundane. Sylvie didn't give a shit. And yet, stupid hope flickered. Maybe, just maybe, her mother was out there somewhere needing her.

"That doesn't make any sense," Terri argued. "Surely the media covered Jane Doe's disappearance. How come the daughter didn't hear about it?"

"It was a big city. Atlanta, I think, and the girl and her mother had had a big fight about her going to Europe with a boyfriend. The girl left and that's when something bad happened to the mother, they still don't know what caused the amnesia. Wanna know how the girl first recognized her mama after all those years?"

"How?" Belinda asked.

"Through a quilt she had on her bed. The woman and her mother had made that quilt together when the woman was just a teenager."

"I don't see how that can happen these days, what with fingerprintin' and DNA testing and all," Raylene said. "I mean they make you give your thumbprint to get your driver's license. You're on file *somewhere*. The government don't want you wanderin' around unidentified."

Patsy held up a hand like a stop sign. "Don't get going with Earl's crazy conspiracy theory stuff."

"Well it doesn't matter whether it makes sense or not," Dotty Mae said. "It's the way it happened. She fell through the cracks. People fall through the cracks all the time. Somebody drops the ball, doesn't do their job, and *wham*, you're stuck in a nursing home with no name, waiting for your long-lost daughter to come and find you."

"At least she had her quilt," Jenny said.

"Yes," they all commented in unison, and nodded their heads as if having a quilt made up for everything.

Chapter Nine

Next to dogs, quilts are a woman's best friend.
—Delia Franklin, Dr. Sam Cheek's receptionist

Emma dreaded the sheepdog herding trials.

Come prepared to amaze yourself, Sam had said. In between the playacting and the quilting, the thought had circled Emma's brain for the last ten days. Easy for Sam to say. He had no idea just how dogs struck terror in her heart.

On the other hand, he was right. She did need to conquer this fear if she wanted to be in this play. She'd tried to convince Nina to cut the Border collie from the script, but Nina wasn't budging. Rebekka had raised and trained sheepdogs. Rebel's role was essential. It was historically accurate. Emma simply had to deal with it.

Fine, great, okay. She could do this. Emma drew in a deep breath and gave herself a pep talk in front of the mirror in the pink VIP bathroom at the Merry Cherub. All around her, angels looked on. She could almost hear the theme from *Rocky* being played on a chorus of harps.

She finished her makeup and dressed simply in blue jeans; a baby-doll, teal T-shirt—emblazoned with the slogan "Everything's Better at Twilight"—that she'd bought at the Teal Peacock; and a pair of sneakers. She pulled her hair back in a ponytail. Today she was playing girl-next-door, plucky and brave. That's how she would survive this day. By acting the part.

A few minutes before eight, she clamored down the stairs and headed for the kitchen, her mind on one of Jenny's delicious banana muffins, only to find Sam sitting with his sister at the kitchen table. *Ulp.* He was here already and she hadn't finished psyching herself up for the meeting.

And he was looking damn good in faded blue jeans and a long-sleeved blue chambray shirt. He had on cowboy boots, and Patches lay at his feet. The minute Emma walked into the room, the dog raised his head.

Sam made a soft *shhtt* noise and the Border collie immediately lowered his head.

Awesome. What she wouldn't give for that kind of control.

"Hey," she said.

"Morning." He grinned at her.

"Um . . . you're early."

"Jenny told me she'd made banana nut muffins. They're my favorite."

"Have a seat, Emma," Jenny said, getting up from the table. "I'll get you a cup of coffee."

"Shouldn't we be going?" Emma asked Sam. Sitting here sharing breakfast did not seem like a good idea when she was trying hard not to have the hots for this guy. Seriously, come on, who wouldn't have the hots for him? With those dark eyes and those full lips and those earlobes just made for nibbling.

Stop it!

"I'll put your coffee in a travel mug," Jenny called over her shoulder. "You're going to come back a changed woman."

"How can you be so sure?" Emma said, snatching up a banana nut muffin from the basket on the table. They were still warm.

"When it comes to animals, Sam's got the magic touch. You're going to be amazed at yourself." Jenny returned and handed her two travel mugs. "The orange one is Sam's. Decaf, black, no sugar. The green one is yours. Fully loaded—caffeine, three sugars, a tablespoon of heavy cream."

"Thank you."

"No wonder you're so nervous all the time," Sam said. "Drinking that muck."

"I have a fast metabolism," Emma said. "I need it to keep me going."

"Needing it isn't healthy."

"Ah, don't tell me you're the caffeine police."

"I'll cut you some slack today," he teased, "seeing as how you're about to eat a rat."

"What?" Jenny looked startled. "Eeew."

Sam smiled at Emma, and she grinned back at their private joke. "Figure of speech," Sam explained to his sister. "You ready to go, Trixie Lynn?"

Growing up, she'd hated the name Trixie Lynn, but when Sam said it, well, it sounded kind of good. With coffee cups and muffins in hand, they went out the door. Patches immediately circled around beside Emma, and she shied behind Sam.

"No," he said, "don't shrink away. Let him know who is boss."

"He already knows he is."

Sam balanced his muffin on the top of his travel mug and slapped his left outer thigh twice. "Heel."

Patches ducked his head and trotted over to Sam's left side.

"You make it look so easy."

"By the end of the day, you'll be doing it too."

She took her sunglasses from her purse and slipped them on.

"Optimistic fellow."

Sam just laughed. They walked around the back of the Jeep, and Sam opened the rear door so Patches could jump in. Then he followed Emma around to the passenger side and he opened her door too.

"Bucking for white knight of the year?"

"Huh?"

"You don't have to open my door for me. I've been doing it all by my little ol' self for years. And look, I have hands, not paws. Opposable thumbs make all kinds of things possible."

He looked taken aback. "What?"

"You're totally patronizing me."

"By opening the door?"

Okay, she officially sounded insane. What was the matter with her?

"Let me get this straight," he said. "You're insulted by the fact I held the door open for you?"

"I'm not helpless."

"I never said you were. I was just taught it was good manners to hold a door open for a lady."

"Yeah, in 1300 A.D." She slid into the seat. Why was she picking a fight with him? Honestly, she loved having her door opened for her. It made her feel protected and safe and . . . She knew the world was not a safe place and it was stupid to let your guard down or believe that someone else would take care of you, have your back.

"You're *mad* at me?"

"Not mad exactly."

He slammed the door, glowered, and stalked around the front of the Jeep to get in behind the wheel. He started to put the key in the ignition, but stopped halfway there. "Oh, wait, maybe I'm patronizing you by assuming I should drive." He held out the key to her. "You want to drive?"

"No."

"I don't get it. If I open the door for you, I'm being a chauvinistic lunkhead."

"I never said that."

His gaze tracked over her. "You implied it."

She had no response for that. She *had* implied it.

"But you don't think it's chauvinistic for me to get behind the wheel without asking you if you'd like to drive."

"That's right." She calmly snapped her seat belt in place, trying to pretend she didn't notice how intimate it felt inside the front seat of the Jeep with him.

"Why? What's the difference?"

"Because I don't know how to drive."

He whipped his head around to stare at her. "You don't how to drive?"

"I've lived in Manhattan for almost half my life."

"Why didn't you learn before you went to New York?"

"Why do I have to justify this to you?"

"I've never known anyone over the age of sixteen who didn't know how to drive."

"Then you've just had your horizons broadened. News flash, there's an entire world outside of Twilight."

"It's not the world I live in."

"You've got that right," she mumbled.

"What was that?" He cocked his head as if he were hard of hearing, but she knew he'd heard her. "You say something you want to say louder?"

"Oh, look." She pointed out the window. "Cows."

"Hey!"

"What?"

"We were having a discussion and you threw in the Herefords," he said, not letting her get away with a thing. The Jeep bumped over train tracks as they turned off Highway 377 onto the Farm to Market Road that led to Cleburne.

"Herefords? Is that what they're called? What makes them Herefords?"

"They're red and white and have curly hair. You're trying to distract me."

"Is it working?" She peeked over at him. He was frowning, his hands clinging tight to the steering wheel perfectly at ten and two. That was Sam. Traditional, rooted. She remembered that he was a Taurus. It made sense if you believed in astrology, which she wasn't sure she did, but in his case the Taurus characteristics seemed to apply—stable, conservative, reliable, home-loving.

"No it's not working. Let's hash this out."

"Do we have to?"

"You brought it up."

"And now I'm bringing it down." She smiled, hoping he'd let it go.

"What's wrong with the world I live in?" he persisted.

Emma sighed. How had she gotten sucked into this conversation? "You're not letting this go, are you?"

"Bulldog, bone, me." With each word he smacked his palm against the dashboard for emphasis.

"And that means . . . ?"

"I'm not letting this go."

Emma was slow to respond. She was busy staring at the way his jeans pulled across his muscular thighs. How dumb was this? Lusting after a man she was in the process of pissing off. "There's nothing wrong with the world you live in. It's all lollipops and rainbows and merry cherubs."

"Excuse me?" he growled.

Speaking of dumb, it wasn't particularly smart the way her body responded to his low, deep Texas drawl. Her nerve endings sensitized, as if he was slowly trailing calloused fingertips over her skin. All kinds of unwanted—okay, she did want them, but she shouldn't—urges washed over her. She wished he would pull the car over on the side of the road with nothing around them but ranchland, kill the engine, pull her across the seat, and kiss her until she couldn't breathe. She wanted to kiss him back so ferociously that *he* couldn't breathe either.

"I lost my wife in a war. My six-year-old hasn't spoken since his mother's death. When I was sixteen, I was mauled by a mountain lion and scarred for life. You call those things lollipops and rainbows and merry cherubs?"

She felt ashamed of herself. Why hadn't she just kept her mouth shut? What was it that made her say stupid things she didn't even mean?

"Wait a minute." Sam snapped his fingers. "I might be slow on the uptake, but I get what this is."

"What what is?"

"Why you're deliberately trying to pick a fight."

"Who me? I'm too impetuous to do anything deliberately."

"That's what you'd like everyone to think, but it's not true. You're trying to get out of this dog herding thing so you don't have to face your fears. Well, it's not going to work."

"You got me," she said, letting him think that was the reason she was being so difficult. It was better than his learning the truth. That she was really stirring up an argument not because she was scared of dogs but because she was scared of her feelings for him.

"Time to start facing those fears," he said, and turned off the main road.

Sam slowed as they drove over a cattle guard and on past through a wrought-iron gate proclaiming that this was the Triple C Ranch. Other vehicles were turning in as well and parking out in a field. Beyond the field a perimeter had been set up. There were small flocks of sheep housed inside numerous portable pens. The minute Patches smelled sheep, he started whining and pacing circles in the back of the Jeep.

Border collies were everywhere, a virtual sea of black and white.

"You okay?" Sam asked.

"Um . . . no."

He reached across the seat to squeeze her shoulder. She looked into his soulful dark eyes and felt fear of a wholly different kind. The pulse at the hollow of her throat fluttered wildly and her hands trembled. She rolled them into fists, sank her nails into the flesh of her palms.

"You can do this. Remember, you went to Manhattan all by yourself when you were eighteen. That took an incredible amount of guts."

"Yeah and look how well that turned out."

"What do you mean? You made a home there for twelve years. You did great."

"Little do you know I was hocking the last thing of value I owned in order to get the money to take an acting class from some guru, who was probably just a scam artist, in a desperate attempt to jumpstart my flagging career, and that was *before* the Scott Miller fiasco."

"What did you pawn?"

"My mother's star brooch."

"Emma, no."

"Yes."

"But that meant so much to you. It was the only thing you had of your mother's. It was a symbol of your dreams."

She shrugged. "I told you I was rock bottom."

"Well, to me, that just proved how damn courageous you really are."

"I can't . . . I don't . . ."

"You can and you do," he said firmly but gently. "Now come on. Let's do this."

She gulped, undid her seat belt, and hopped out of the Jeep before he could come around to her side and be chivalrous again. She met him at the back of the Jeep. He had a leash in his hand and he passed it to her. Then he took a thin wooden crook from the back.

"You look like Little Bo Peep." She chuckled.

"Don't laugh. You'll be using it today."

"I will?"

"Yep, but for now, you're going to snap the leash clasp onto Patches's collar," Sam said.

"What if he snaps my neck?"

"He's not going to hurt you. Just remember he is interested in one thing and one thing only. Those sheep. This is what he was born to do. He loves doing his job more than anything on earth."

"So he's an exemplary employee," she said, trying to keep things light so she didn't cringe at the sound of dogs barking.

"He is at that." Sam smiled. "Once you have the leash on his collar, and he's calm, I'll open the door. He can't get out until he's calm."

"And I'm supposed to be the one to calm him?"

"Yes."

"How do I do that?" Nervously she nibbled her bottom lip.

He reached up to place his index finger to her lip. His skin tasted slightly salty. "By not exhibiting any anxiety. Stop biting your lip."

"But I *am* anxious."

"You can't let Patches know it. Animals sense your emotional state. So take a deep breath."

She did.

"Hold it. That's good."

Air buoyed her chest. She noticed Sam noticed.

"Now let it out slowly."

She hissed out her breath.

"Now let yourself go loose. Shake your body all over, like you're a dog shaking off water."

She got into it. Jumping and shaking, flinging off the tension, wriggling her arms, shuffling her feet, rotating her neck like a boxer getting ready to climb into the ring. It felt like an acting exercise.

"That's right. Shake it off." He was so patient with

her. "Don't be fearful. But don't be aggressive either. Be calm and assertive. Claim your space. You are the alpha dog."

"You sound like the Dog Whisperer."

"Hey, Cesar Millan is famous for a reason. He knows what he's talking about."

"Got it. Calm, assertive, claim my space."

"Ready?"

"As I'll ever be."

Sam opened the back of the hatch of the Jeep. Patches looked ready to leap out. "He's not calm enough yet."

"What do I do?"

"Tell him to sit."

"Sit," Emma said.

Patches just looked at her.

"He's not sitting."

"Don't complain like a big sister tattling on her little brother, take charge."

"Is this your way of saying you have sibling issues with Jenny?"

"Stop avoiding the situation."

"Okay, all right." She drew in another deep breath. She was an actress. She could do this. "Sit," she commanded.

Patches sat.

"Oh! Oh! He did it."

Patches immediately hopped back up.

"He hopped back up. Why did he hop back up?"

"No high-pitched vocals with inflection. That gets him excited."

"Sorry, sorry," she whispered.

"Try it again."

"Sit."

Patches sat.

She leaned in and snapped the leash to his collar. "This is amazing," she whispered to Sam.

"It's not that impressive. Most dogs know how to sit. Just wait until you see him with the sheep."

The event she'd been dreading suddenly didn't seem so bad.

"Now tell him it's okay to get down."

"Get down," she said.

Patches jumped from the Jeep to the dusty ground and then looked from Emma to Sam.

"He's questioning your authority," Sam said. "Tell him, 'Watch me.'"

"Watch me," she commanded.

Patches immediately swung his gaze to Emma.

"Praise him."

"Good boy."

"Now let's head on over to the registration table. Don't let him pull you. Normally he walks well on a leash, but he's not used to you and he'll probably try to take over. He just needs to know you're in control. Keep your shoulders back and your head held high and your grip loose. If you pull on the leash, he'll feel your tension and it will make him tense."

"This dog thing is complicated."

"Not really. You stay relaxed and in control, then he stays relaxed and in control."

"That relaxed-and-in-control thing?"

"Yeah?"

"That's the hard, complicated part. I'm more of a cat person."

"Because cats couldn't give a good damn whether you're anxious or relaxed."

"Exactly."

"But dogs offer something cats cannot."

"They fetch."

"Yes, but that's not what I was thinking about. They give unconditional love."

"They're dogs, they can't feel love."

"Clearly, you've never owned a dog."

True enough. Throughout the exchange Patches had sat at their feet, the whole time his eyes trained on Sam's face.

"We can argue about this later. Come on." He put his hand to her back as if to guide her, but he didn't touch her.

It didn't matter. She could still feel the surge of sexual energy jumping from him to her and back again, an invisible force as solid as a steel band. All these years she'd tried to put him out of her mind. Tried to forget how much she'd loved him with the kind of passion known only to teenagers. But now, the feelings were back in a hot rush of memory, drowning her in wistful longing.

No, no. She would not, could not allow these emotions to gain a foothold. What was past was past. He had a life in Twilight and she did not. Her destiny lay elsewhere. And yet, no matter how much her mind argued, her body burned.

"This way."

To Emma's surprise, Patches followed at her side, but he kept looking up at her.

"He keeps looking up at me. Why does he keep looking up at me?"

"He's trying to get a read on what you want him to do. Just proceed ahead. Don't look at him, don't tense up. Just walk with confidence."

It was unnerving having a dog walking so close to her. A couple of times his tail brushed her leg, and that made her draw in a gulp of air. When another dog passed very close to them, she tensed and immediately felt the leash tighten.

"Easy, easy," Sam soothed, resting a hand on her shoulder. "Remember, he feels everything you feel."

Emma forced herself to relax, and the leash loosened.

"No fear," he whispered. "That's the key."

He'd proven his point. After they checked in at the registration desk and got their entry number, they went to stand beside a white wooden perimeter fence where the other entrants were lined up. A lush green rolling pasture stretched out in front of them. A tight herd of eight black-faced sheep grazed in the middle of the field. The early October sun was moderate, the breeze cool. A good morning for herding sheep.

As the first Border collie and her handler took their places at the starting point, Sam explained what was going on, filling her in on the terminology and the commands the handler issued to his dog. He spoke with authority and confidence. Sam loved all animals, but she could tell he had a special affinity for dogs in general and Border collies in particular.

Emma had to admit that, in spite of her fears, she was enjoying being with him out here. She watched him roll up the sleeves of his button-down, cowboy-style shirt to reveal muscular forearms sprinkled with dark brown hair and lean against the fence railing, his body nimble and marvelously sculpted. He turned his head to look over at her, his eyes welcoming, his smile gentle. A light breeze ruffled his hair, giving her a silvery glimpse of his scar. She caught the aroma of him, a sexy combination of male pheromones, sandalwood soap, and spray starch.

He kept talking about the dogs and sheepherding, but she wasn't listening to the words. She was hypnotized by the sound of his voice, helpless against the tide of desire his soft, deep rumble stirred inside her. He was earthy, uncomplicated, genuine—so different from the status-seeking, social-climbing men she'd dated in New York.

"We're up next."

"Huh?" Emma blinked and forced her attention back on the sheepherding exhibition.

"You're going out there with us."

"Me?" She slid a sidelong glance at Patches. "And him?"

"If you're involved in the herding, he'll see you as a handler."

"Instead of a sheep."

Sam grinned. "Exactly."

"They're going to allow me out there with you?"

"If this were the finals, no, but this is just a friendly exhibition. You're fine."

"Next at the post," said the announcer over a bullhorn. "Dr. Sam Cheek, accompanied by Emma Parks and his dog, Patches."

"Here, you take the crook." He handed her his staff and pulled a slender whistle from his shirt pocket. "Follow me."

He led her down the grassy slope to where a small wooden platform had been erected. Patches followed at his side. Sam waved for Emma to step up on the platform beside him. Patches scanned the sheep gathered in a clump about five hundred yards away from where they stood.

Sam blew into the whistle. Emma didn't hear a sound, but Patches was off like a shot, running to the far left. "This is called the outrun," he told her. "Patches is running out to the sheep to gather them prior to bringing them to us."

When Patches had reached the maximum extent of his outrun, he approached the sheep to move them forward.

"His first contact with the sheep is called the lift," Sam explained. "He's going to start moving them to us. This is an important step because it gives the sheep their first impression of Patches."

"I remember my first impression of Patches." Emma chuckled. "He made sure I did some high stepping."

Sam blew on the whistle again. Patches came up behind the sheep, guiding them through two white panels erected in the field between the post and the place where Patches had first come upon the sheep.

"This part of the course is called the fetch, when he brings the sheep straight down the centerline of the course to us," he explained.

She noticed the way he kept saying "us" instead of "me." It made her feel odd in a nice way. Like he considered them a real team. Unnerved, she shielded her eyes with her hand and watched as Patches guided the sheep around the post.

Sam touched the whistle to his lips, blew twice more. Patches took the sheep away from them now, herding them through a triangular course bound by pairs of panels. "This is called the drive. He's going to take them through the cross drive panels."

Patches moved like a professional athlete and he never took his eyes off the sheep.

Another blow on the whistle from Sam. "He's going to take them to the shedding ring. Now it's our turn to get really involved. Keep your crook handy. Let's move." He started trotting the distance to the shedding ring.

Emma kept up, jogging beside him, her sneakers sinking into the plush pasture grass. "What's happening?"

"We have to work with Patches in order to separate the sheep into two groups. You'll use the crook to help guide the sheep where you want them to go."

"What if I screw up?"

"You won't screw up."

"But what if I do?"

"You won't," he reiterated firmly. "Just stay focused on the sheep."

Easy for him to say. He was born to this life.

Hey, you're an actress. Pretend you were born to this life. You're a sheepherder. This is second nature to you.

Patches heard the sound of Sam's whistle even if Emma could not. The Border collie immediately went into action, cutting between three sheep and the remainder of the group.

While Patches was dealing with those three sheep, the rest of the herd tried to turn to follow the cut-off trio. Instinctively, Emma reached out with the crook to encourage them to stay back. With a bleat of surprise, they turned in unison, trotting off in the opposite direction from where Patches guided his batch.

"Excellent work," Sam said. "Now comes the single shedding."

They reunited the two groups of sheep and then this time, while Sam whistled instructions to Patches, Emma and the dog isolated one specific sheep from the herd. Then once that task was complete, they returned them all to the starting pen.

The crowd applauded.

Along with pride, Emma experienced a keen sense of accomplishment. "That was fun," she told Sam as they walked off the field with Patches beside them. The dog looked the way Emma felt. Happy. Satisfied at a job well done.

"I told you that you wouldn't screw up." Sam rested an arm over her shoulder and cocked a sidelong grin.

An acute sensation of sexual attraction cut through her. Sam possessed an irresistible blend of quiet confidence, kindhearted generosity, and masculine protectiveness.

He guided her toward the spectator fence; the crowd shifted, letting them through as the next handler and his dog went for the post. "Would you like to grab something to drink while we wait for the scores?" He nodded toward the refreshment stands that had been set up near the registration table.

It was hot work. And standing this close to Sam made her feel even hotter.

They took Patches over to the watering trough set out for the animals, then stepped to the refreshment stands, where Sam bought two bottles of water that had been submerged in a tub of ice water. He lifted the cold bottle to the back of his neck and let out a soft groan. Her toes curled in response to the sound.

"Aah, that feels good."

Emma took a long swallow of her drink. It trickled wetly all the way down.

"So are you feeling less shaky around Patches?" he asked.

"Surprisingly enough, yes."

"I knew you would." He met her gaze and winked. "You've got a lot of courage, Emma."

They stood very close together, off to one side of the refreshment stand, away from the crowd. A line of large pecan trees behind them offered shade from the sun. The irises of his eyes were intense and deeply brown, like cocoa beans steeped in black tea. *You've got a lot of courage,* he'd said, and as long as he was looking at her like that, she needed all the courage she could muster.

After finishing their water, they wandered back to the stands. All the seats were taken, so they stood in the back, watching the remainder of the trials.

"We have the results of the trials," the announcer said several minutes later and rattled off the times, starting with the longest times first. He called out the third place finishers and then second place. "And in first place, we have Dr. Sam Cheek, his assistant Emma Parks, and their dog Patches."

Their dog. In that split second, she realized they'd won.

"We won?" Emma shrieked.

Sam nodded. "I told you that you were going to amaze yourself." He sounded so proud of her. And his voice was husky too, as if something had abraded his throat.

"We won!" Without thinking, she launched herself at him. He caught her, spun her around. Emma locked her legs around Sam's waist and ensnared her arms around his neck. A thrill coursed through her. Beside them, Patches picked up on the jubilant mood and turned in excited circles. "We won!"

"We did." His eyes were so inviting, his smile so big, Emma couldn't help herself. The next thing she knew, she was kissing him.

CHAPTER TEN

*No matter how well planned, the finished quilt will
always take you by surprise.*
—Marva Bullock, principal of Twilight High and member
of the True Love Quilting Club

Sam tightened his arms around Emma, turning what
she'd meant to be nothing more than a quick kiss of
victory into something scorching hot and weighted
with hidden meaning.

He held her tightly around the waist with one
arm, and with the other, reached up to splay his palm
against the back of her head, holding her still while
he explored her mouth. He tasted far earthier than
she remembered. Like great wine, he'd improved with
age. His lips were firm against hers. Firm and hot and
wholly masculine. Emma melted into him.

The electricity sparking between them had not de-
creased with time, but rather had heightened in intensity. Kissing him felt like a gathering storm filled with
tornadoes.

She tried to break the kiss, but damn him, he wouldn't

let her. Instead he pressed harder, plunging deep. She'd forgotten just how erotic kissing could be.

Emma felt Sam's erection. She pulled back, her eyes wide. "Are you . . . is that . . . ?"

"I'm sorry—" He started to apologize, but broke it off, with a daring gleam in his eyes. A gleam she'd never seen before. "No, I'm not sorry. You turn me on like a faucet, woman, and I'm not ashamed of that."

"Wow, Sam, I never suspected you'd be so unabashed about your sexuality," she teased, but secretly her blood churned.

"Normally, I wouldn't be," he said. "But when it comes to you, Trixie Lynn, I have zero control."

Trixie Lynn. On anyone else's lips her old name would have sounded clunky, hillbilly. But when Sam said Trixie Lynn, it sounded like a Mozart melody full of complex notes and rich chords, plucking away at memories.

He kissed her again, apparently not caring that there were people around. That anyone could be watching. This was not the Sam she remembered. Not at all. Swept away, impulsive, heedless of consequences. She was the one thinking of backing off after her impulsive ambush, but she could not. She was kissing her first love all over again and it was wild and fresh and exciting.

No, no. She had to stop this. If she let this continue, things would only end badly. Emma wriggled in his arms, dropping her legs, sliding down the length of his body until her feet hit soft earth. She looked up at him, her chest rising and falling in tight, fast movements. She pressed the heel of her hand against his breastbone, staving him off. "No, you're right. I'm the one who's sorry. I never meant to start something.

I was just excited and . . . never mind. This wasn't meant to happen."

He ran both hands over her upper arms to her shoulders and stared into her eyes. Emma's knees quaked, but she hauled in a deep breath to fortify herself.

Simultaneously, they reached for each other again. "Emma," he murmured.

"Sam," she answered.

He dipped his head.

She raised her chin.

Another shock went through her, more powerful than before, shoving her heart into overdrive. He kissed her over and over again, lengthy improper kisses, all slick tension and piquant spice. She delighted at the feel of his clean-shaven jaw against her chin, reveled in his tongue's urgent inquiry.

Sam? Acting indecently in front of his friends, neighbors, clients, and colleagues. She had done this to him. Brought him down to her level.

And it felt wickedly delicious.

She reached up and cupped both sides of his face in her palms. His skin felt so masculine beneath her fingertips. She didn't know if she was trying to break the kiss or deepen it.

He didn't miss a beat, clearly taking her gesture to mean she wanted more. He increased the tempo, and from somewhere deep dredged up even more heat until she felt as if she was swimming in the fire of his soul.

Emma dropped her hands from his face and encircled his waist, pressing herself against the invigorating landscape of his hard body. Never had she experienced such craving. Such mindless, rushing need.

With one hand, he cupped her buttocks and pulled

her closer to him. He'd gone from simply stiff to marble-slab hard. Swept away on the rising tide of passion, Emma panted, curled her fingers around his belt. If they hadn't been out in a field in the middle of the day surrounded by people, she would have ripped his clothes off and made love to him right then. Right there.

Stupid.

It was stupid and she knew it, but Emma couldn't stop herself from straining against him. A riot of sensation rolled through her. Her muscles tightened. Her body grew slick and moist in the places where it counted. No dessert had ever tasted so sweet. No scent had ever smelled so intoxicating. No melody had ever sounded so alluring as the sound of their hungry lips.

The heavy coil that had settled low in her belly squeezed, sending ever-widening spirals of contractions radiating throughout her pelvis. Her nerve endings begged for release. This was what she'd dreamed of in the middle of the night, in her most secret fantasies, in the place where she hid her desires from herself. Reunion with Sam. Joined to him in every way possible. Fused. Welded. Linked.

And from the feel of it, he'd been having a few midnight dreams of his own if one kiss could unravel him as completely as it was unraveling her. She'd kissed all kinds of men in all kinds of places. A punk rocker backstage at a Metallica concert. A fast-track executive atop the Empire State Building. A minor celebrity on a roller coaster ride at Coney Island. But there was nothing . . . absolutely nothing . . . that compared to kissing her high school sweetheart in a lush field at sheepdog herding trials, for the first time in sixteen years.

A sudden panic swept through her. What was she doing? This couldn't happen. She was trying to rebuild her shattered career and Sam had a child to raise, a life to lead. She could promise him nothing beyond a few weeks of great sex, and he deserved so much more than that.

She pulled back at the same moment Patches whined and stuck his nose between their legs, trying to nudge them apart.

"Someone's jealous," Sam said lightly, but she could see the turbulence in his heavy-lidded dark eyes, in his flushed cheeks and forehead. He was as concerned by what had just happened as she was. Maybe more so. He had more to lose than she did.

"Yeah." Her voice sounded husky.

"One more for the road?" An eyebrow went up.

She shook her head, no, this was wrong. But damn her, she whispered, "One more for the road."

He snagged her mouth again. This time he was fully, one hundred percent the leader. She slumped against him, helpless to resist the intense, deliberate pressure of his lips against hers.

Scent, taste, and sweet-hot rhythmic caressing yanked all her senses into one focused direction. Closer to Sam. She shuddered against him, gave a feral moan. The blast was so potent she couldn't keep up with her own rampaging heartbeat.

Could a woman have an orgasm from a kiss? It seemed so unlikely, and yet she could swear she was on the verge of tumbling over that sweet abyss.

"There," he murmured, breaking the kiss. His lips were shiny, wet. "That should give you something to think about."

Then he stepped back, whistled to Patches, and turned for the Jeep. Leaving Emma feeling dazed, confused, and wildly, impossibly elated. Just what kind of game was this man playing?

Sam could have kicked his own ass. What in the hell had he been thinking? Kissing her like that and in front of everyone he knew. No doubt about it. The Twilight grapevine would be buzzing tonight.

That's just it. You weren't thinking.

He had never behaved like this. Never. Impulsive. Irrational. Out-of-control.

Um, what about when you were fourteen?

Okay, fine. He hadn't acted like this since he was fourteen and the first time Emma—Trixie Lynn then—had blown into his life like gale force winds and turned him upside down.

Now she was back and doing it all over again.

So what was he going to do about it?

He sneaked a glance over at her. She sat on the passenger side of his Jeep singing along with Faith Hill on the radio, nodding her head in time to the music. The sight twisted him up inside. She was so expressive. So spontaneous. So alive. Beside her, he felt like a total dullard, mired in his ways, anchored to the earth.

Sam remembered her at fourteen. How she had a big imagination and loved playacting. She frequently got into trouble for making up stories and telling lies. What people hadn't realized was that she had slipped under the skin of a pretend person, had burrowed into an imaginary world so deeply she'd forgotten the world she was really in. No one had truly appreciated how creative she was. She used to round up the neighborhood kids and announce she was putting on a play. She'd make costumes and design sets. He'd always refused to act in the plays. He'd been too quiet and introspective for that. But he'd eagerly made the sets. He'd wanted to please her, even back then. He'd never known anyone so colorful, original, and exciting. She brought him to life in a way no one else ever had.

"I want to thank you for today. It was wonderful. I feel completely relaxed around Patches now that I fully understand him," Emma said.

"You're welcome." Suddenly, he felt a terrible need to run time backward to undo the kissing, to erase the intimacy they'd just shared. He wasn't ready for this, didn't know how to handle it. Something had shifted. In his mind, in his heart, and the sensations alarmed him.

"You know what?" she said.

He shook his head, increased his speed, eager to get her back home, and then get to his clinic so he could escape into his work and get away from these disturbing feelings bouncing around inside him.

"I think I'm going to take you up on your offer to teach me how to drive."

Had he offered to teach her how to drive? He didn't remember that. "Um," he said. "I don't know if my Jeep is the best vehicle for you to learn on. It's got manual transmission. I'm sure Jenny wouldn't mind teaching you how to drive in her Mazda."

"But wouldn't it be better to learn on a manual? I mean after that an automatic has got to be a piece of cake."

"I suppose that's true."

"Unless you're nervous about letting me get behind the wheel of your Jeep."

"Well of course I'm nervous. You don't know how to drive."

"Don't worry, I promise not to hit anything big." She smiled brightly. "So how about tomorrow? It's Sunday. You don't have to work."

He should have made an excuse. Come up with a good reason why he couldn't teach her how to drive, but he was just so damn charmed by her buoyant effervescence that he couldn't say no. "All right," he heard himself say. "Does tomorrow afternoon at two P.M. work for you?"

That same afternoon Emma found herself at loose ends. She couldn't stop thinking about Sam. She could still smell the grassy field, still taste him on her tongue. In an attempt to distract herself, she wandered the town square and ended up at Hot Legs Gym. But even half an hour on the StairMaster couldn't chase her errant thoughts off Sam.

On her way out of the gym, she bumped into Beau Trainer. He stood in the doorway, looking at once uncertain and determined.

"There you are," he said. "I've been looking all over town for you."

She canted her head at her leading man. "What's up?"

He ducked his head, splayed a palm at the nape of his neck. "I was wondering if you weren't doing anything . . ."

Oh my gosh, he was going to ask her out. She hadn't seen this coming.

"I know you're really busy helping Nina and the other ladies make those quilts and I know this is your day off but—"

"Beau," she interrupted. "I'm really flattered but I've learned the hard way that it's better not to date the person you're working with. Acting has a way of stirring up emotions that aren't really real and—"

"Wait a minute." Beau held his hand up like a stop sign. "You thought I was asking you out? I'm sorry, I'm handling this badly."

Now she felt like an egotistical jerk.

"Not that I wouldn't mind asking you out," he rushed to say, "but anyone with half a brain can see you only have eyes for Sam."

Oh, this was just getting worse by the second. She figured it was better to let his comment slide instead of denying it.

"What I wanted to ask you was if you'd mind doing an extra rehearsal with me. I'm having a difficult time with the last act of this play. You're so accomplished and I just want to be decent enough not to make you look bad up there come opening day." He looked deadly earnest.

Emma thought about what Nina had told her about Beau. How this play was his redemption. It meant a lot to him, and it wasn't as if she had anything else going on this afternoon. Plus, whenever she was acting, she was in another world. That transcendence was the thing she loved the most about her craft. How practicing it could sweep her away to another time, another place. "Sure," she agreed, shrugged casually.

"Really?" A surprised smile inched across his face. "Would right now be okay? I've already asked Nina if I could use the playhouse for additional rehearsals and she gave me a key."

"All right," she agreed.

For the next three hours, she and Beau comman-
deered the theater stage. He was an apt pupil, soaking
up everything she had to teach him, and she found
herself enjoying the role of instructor.

"You really love acting," Beau noted following their
fourth run-through of the last act. He grabbed two
bottles of water from the backstage fridge and tossed
one to Emma. "The craft I mean, not just the acco-
lades that come with it. You love acting even if you're
not in New York or Hollywood. Just as Nina does."

His words gave her pause. The cravings for stardom had always driven her. Not so much for fortune,
although having money would be nice. Not so much
for fame, simply for fame's sake. Rather, she wanted
to be known for her skills, for her ability to make
the audience believe she was someone else entirely.
To create a world they could all inhabit together, if
only for a little while. She was convinced that if she
was just good enough at her craft, fortune and fame
would eventually be hers. And along with the notori-
ety and money would come the feeling of being special, of being wanted, that she had never experienced
as a child. This core belief had pushed her relentlessly
for twelve long years. To have Beau point out that she
loved acting simply for the joy of acting was a bit of a
revelation.

"I don't know about that," she hedged. "My focus
on success is the one thing that's kept me slugging it
out when more talented actors than I have given up the
game. I don't give myself the option of failure."

"Would you give up acting if you knew there was
no chance you'd ever make it big?" He took a long
swallow of water, studied her with an intensity she
found unnerving. What was he getting at?

She laughed, but didn't find anything humorous. "You know, that crossroad is staring me in the face right now. After what happened in New York, Twilight could very well be my last stop on the trail to oblivion."

An intense, faraway look came into Beau's eyes, as if he was staring into the future and found his prospects bleak. Or maybe he was peering into the past, regretting some road not taken. It was a look that sent an unexpected shiver slipping down Emma's spine.

"Don't make the same mistake I did," he muttered darkly, his voice heavy as a thundercloud. "Don't let the thing you love most slip through your fingers."

A lump of emotion hardened in her throat, and she wondered if he was talking about the woman he'd lost or his career as sheriff. She wanted to ask, but the twisted expression on his face halted her.

In the pursuit of her career, she'd stretched the limits of her abilities, wandered beyond the scope of her talent any number of times. She'd stumbled into desolation, lost her true identity in the hubbub of Manhattan, until she wasn't sure who she really was anymore.

But the journey had been among the deepest pleasures of her life. The stage, the lights, the audiences, the utter magic of performance. She had seen herself as brave and determined. A tough young woman with a never-give-up attitude, ready to fight to the death for her dream. Fight on in spite of all the heartache and rejection and disappointment. Putting one foot in front of the other. Every single morning, standing in front of the mirror mouthing affirmations. Never doubting that one day, one day . . .

But the fire wasn't the same now. It had transmuted from the ego of achievement to the humbleness of offering. She wanted to share her gifts with others. That was her main desire. Not riches and fame beyond her wildest imagination. This realization was new territory, and it made her doubt that she had ever really been certain of anything.

"Don't." Beau softened his voice, and in that softness she felt the jagged shards of violent sorrow. "Don't lose the soul of who you are, because the abyss is black as hell."

For the rest of the day, Sam could think of nothing except Emma. Animals came and went through the clinic, and his mind barely registered what his body was doing. He did exams and gave injections and wrote out prescriptions, and he didn't remember any of it. The only thing that felt real to him was the lingering imprint of Emma's mouth against his.

Even afterward, following dinner and bedtime stories with Charlie, he couldn't stop smelling her watermelon and Ivory soap scent; couldn't stop feeling her soft skin beneath his calloused fingertips.

In bed, under the covers, the picture of her sweet freckled face flashed vividly against the screen of his eyelids until, finally, he threw back the covers and got out of bed to pace the length of his bedroom floor in his underwear. Minutes later, he threw open the closet door to reveal his clothes occupying one half of the space; Valerie's dresses, pants, and blouses hung in the other.

He thought about Charlie. About Aunt Belinda's opinion that he wasn't going to be able to move forward until he let go of the past. And most of all, about what had happened between him and Emma at the sheepdog herding trials.

He clasped his hands behind him. Back and forth in front of the closet he paced. Back and forth. Several big cardboard boxes that had once held veterinary supplies lay open and empty on his king-sized bed.

And he paced some more.

Occasionally, he'd glance over and see an article of Valerie's clothing, and a memory would flash through his head. The peach-colored silk top and black slacks she'd had on for their first official date. The purple dress he'd bought her, but she'd worn only once because she said it was too colorful for her tastes. The navy blue skirt and blouse set she'd purchased for his baby sister's graduation from Texas Tech. The modest beige dress she'd worn for their no-frills wedding at city hall. And then there were her Army uniforms. Pressed and wrapped in plastic, hanging in the corner as if they were just waiting for her to come put them on.

Everything about Valerie had been simple, understated, sensible. Their relationship had been like that too—mild, pleasant, uneventful. Until she'd been sent to Iraq. Odd that their life together was more defined by her absence than by her presence. He'd become a widower at twenty-nine. A single father. His roles carved out by Valerie's death.

He accepted those roles without complaint. He'd known what he was letting himself in for when he'd married her, and he didn't regret it, but sometimes he couldn't help wondering how different his life would have been if he hadn't chosen this path. This past year had been the hardest of his life, and yet he'd survived.

But Trixie Lynn had breezed back into town, making him wonder if mere survival was enough.

Pausing in mid-pace, he hauled in a deep breath and stepped into the closet. Then slowly, carefully, piece by piece, he took down Valerie's clothes and packed them away in the boxes.

It was nearing dawn by the time he finished and he'd been through a myriad of emotions—sadness, nostalgia, regret, guilt, reproach, loneliness, melancholia. Now he knew why he'd avoided this task. He hadn't wanted to muck around in the memories. But it had to be done. Aunt Belinda was right. Valerie wasn't coming back. Someone might as well get some use from her things.

And in the end, when it was all over, a surprising lightness washed over him. Like whenever you've been through a long illness and then one day your fever breaks and you know you're going to pull through. That's how he felt now. A sense of weary relief.

"Good-bye, Val," he murmured as he taped up the boxes. "I'll never forget you and the sacrifices you made. You know I'll take care of Charlie like he was my own flesh and blood."

Then with that, he carried the boxes out into the hallway, went to bed, and slept until Maddie called him down for breakfast.

CHAPTER ELEVEN

Not all quilts are created equal.
—Emma Parks, newest member of the
True Love Quilting Club

Sam was napping on the couch when the doorbell rang a few minutes before two that next afternoon, jerking him to an upright position. He'd fallen asleep watching the Dallas Cowboys get their tails beaten by the Washington Redskins. Charlie was halfway across the floor to the front door, leaving behind the LEGOs he'd been playing with, scattered across the living room rug.

He blinked, shook his head to clear it. Charlie already had the door open.

"Hello, Charlie." Emma's voice entered the room, soft as a summertime hug.

Yawning, Sam lumbered to his feet.

Charlie opened the screen door and Emma stepped inside. His son stood looking up at her as if she was the most mesmerizing thing he had ever seen. Sam understood the feeling.

She leaned down, hands placed on her knees, and smiled at him. "Is your daddy here?"

Charlie turned to point at Sam as he ambled over.

Straightening, Emma smiled. She looked vibrant in a red and white striped blouse and flouncy red skirt that hit her mid-thigh, showing off those spectacular legs. "Hey."

"Hey."

Their eyes met, and the moment seemed to spin away into forever. If Charlie hadn't taken Emma by the hand and pulled her across the threshold, Sam had no idea how long they would have stood there staring at each other.

"Boy have you got a strong grip," Emma said to Charlie. "Can I see those muscles?"

Grinning, his son flexed his biceps for her. She reached out and squeezed his skinny little arm. "My gosh, what strong muscles you have."

Charlie looked inordinately pleased.

"Ready for my driving lessons, Teach?" Emma asked.

Charlie cocked his head and looked from Emma to Sam.

"I'm teaching Emma how to drive," Sam explained. "I know you'd like to come but Emma needs to concentrate on driving."

"Yeah," she said. "You wouldn't want to be in the car if I crashed it, would you?"

Charlie shook his head vehemently.

Emma slapped her palm over her mouth and her eyes widened. "Omigosh, I didn't mean . . . I didn't think . . ."

Sam shook his head and frowned, silently warning her to not make things worse by continuing to babble.

"Emma was just kidding, she's not going to crash the car."

Charlie didn't seem convinced. Luckily, Emma kept quiet.

"I tell you what, you go take out the garbage for Maddie and when we get back we'll all go for ice cream. How does that sound?"

Dubiously, Charlie nodded.

"Good boy." Sam lightly swatted his behind. "Now go on in the kitchen."

Once Charlie was out of earshot, Emma sank back against the door. "Sam, I am so sorry," she whispered. "I totally forgot about how his real father died. Me and my big mouth."

"Just drop it, okay. Let's not make a thing of it."

She looked grateful and embarrassed. She reached up to push a strand of hair from her forehead, and the numerous silver bracelets at her wrist jangled jauntily. Even her jewelry was too jovial for Sam's life.

"Mm, are you going to be driving in those shoes?" He looked down at the sassy red slippers with tiny heels that she had on. Mules, he thought they were called, but he had no idea why.

"Sure, why not?"

"They don't seem all that sturdy."

"They're fine." She waved a hand and the bracelets jangled again.

They looked dangerous to him, but everything about her looked dangerous. Those daring green eyes. That gorgeous mop of red hair. Those rosebud lips just begging to be kissed.

"Keys?" She held out her hand.

Reluctantly, Sam tugged his keys from the pocket of his jeans and dropped them into her upturned palm.

How had he gotten himself into this? It wasn't so much that he didn't want to teach her how to drive. Because, come on, it was a crying shame that a thirty-year-old woman had never mastered the skill. It wasn't that he was afraid she'd wreck the Jeep. It was a Jeep after all—rough, tough, and built to take a licking, and he wasn't about to let her drive over thirty-five miles an hour. Rather, it was the fact that he was going to have to be in close confines with her, smelling the sweet scent of her cologne, watching her shapely legs pump the clutch, hearing her soft little gasps of surprise when something didn't go the way she expected.

"Come on." She jangled the keys. "Last one to the Jeep has to buy the ice cream." She turned and vaulted for the door.

The kid in him who'd grown up with three brothers and two sisters couldn't resist the thrown gauntlet. He took off after her, his stride eating up the ground he'd lost until they were sprinting neck and neck across the thick St. Augustine lawn to his bright yellow Jeep parked at the curb.

They reached the Jeep at precisely the same moment.

"Guess it's gonna have to be Dutch treat," he said.

"You cheated."

"How's that?"

"You've got longer legs."

"Take it up with God." He grinned.

She trotted around to the driver's side door. "Okay, now how do I get in this thing?"

He came to stand beside her. He'd forgotten how petite she was. Next to the Jeep, which had come equipped with a lift kit, she looked delicate and fragile. "Step on the running board." He patted the metal bar running along the side of the Jeep.

She swung open the door, climbed on the running board, bounced up into the seat. "Wow, I love the vantage point from up here. This is gonna be fun. Hurry up and get in, I can't wait to get started."

Sam got in on the passenger side and buckled his seat belt. He wasn't sure he was ready for this.

"Okay, what do I do first?" She turned toward him, the hem of her skirt riding seductively up her thigh. He tried not to look, but he couldn't help himself.

"You don't know?"

"If I knew what to do, why would I ask?"

"You're kidding, right?"

"What part of 'I don't know how to drive' is confusing you?"

"You didn't take driver's ed in high school?"

She shook her head. "Rex wouldn't shell out the cash."

"Do you ever see him?"

She squirmed, and he could tell she really wanted to change the topic. He knew how devastated she'd been when she'd learned Rex Parks wasn't her father. "Not in several years. He remarried, and I'm happy that he found someone finally. We exchange Christmas cards, talk on the phone once a year."

"You sound like you've made peace with the situation."

"What are you gonna do?" She shrugged. "So about this driving thing . . ."

"Key in the ignition."

"Oh, right." She fumbled with the keys.

"It's the one with the thick round head."

She found the key he was referring to and slipped

it in the ignition and grasped the steering wheel with both hands. "Now what?"

"Put your left foot on the clutch."

"Which one is the clutch?" She looked down at the floorboard, and a sheaf of shimmery copper hair fell across the side of her face. Sam's fingers itched to reach out and push it back behind her ear.

"The one in the middle. Put it all the way to the floor."

She complied. "It's harder to mash than I thought it would be. What's next?"

"Make sure it's in neutral."

"How do I do that?"

"It's the N on the gearshift."

"What's the gearshift?"

"This." Sam touched the gearshift at the same time Emma said, "Oh," and reached for it.

Their fingers touched on the knob, and instantly, they both drew back. Pinpricks of awareness shot up his arm.

"Oh," she said again.

"Go ahead, put it in neutral." He nodded, trying to sound cool and unaffected while he rounded up his scattered thoughts, which were running along the lines of: *Wonder what it would feel like if her hands were on* my *gearshift?* Sam shook his head, shook off the thoughts. Or tried to. They clung to his mind with the tenacity of a grass burr.

She slid it into neutral. "Next?"

"Turn the key and start the engine."

"Gotcha," she crowed triumphantly. "Now what?"

"Slowly ease off the clutch at the same time you give it some gas."

She peeked down at the floorboard again. "The accelerator is on the right?"

"Yes, and the brake is the one on the left. Remember that."

Audibly, she sucked in air. "Here goes nothing." Slowly she eased off the clutch and pressed down on the accelerator. To Sam's amazement, the car didn't immediately die. Instead it idled to life.

"Good job."

She beamed as if he'd told her she'd just been nominated for an Academy Award. "What's next?"

"Press down on the clutch again and then ease it into first gear as you give it more gas and—"

She popped the clutch, jammed it into first gear, and hit the accelerator all at the same time. The Jeep shot forward. "Look at me! I'm driving."

"Don't get ahead of yourself."

"Oh crap, I'm driving, I'm driving! What do I do now?"

"Get out of the middle of the street. Stay on the right side of the road, this isn't England."

"Man, you just touch it and it goes all over the place."

Up the street a car was backing out into the road, the driver clearly not looking behind him.

Not trusting Emma to steer out of the way in time, Sam leaned over to grab the wheel. His upper arm grazed her breast.

"Ohh," she exclaimed. Her warm breath burned the side of his cheek.

His heart galloped, and Sam guided the Jeep to the far side of the street, narrowly missing the car that had kept on backing out.

"Yipes," she whispered, "that was a close one."

He pulled away, settling into his seat, getting as far from her as the close confines would allow. "Both hands on the wheel at all times. And always be on guard for the other guy."

"Thank you," she chirped, and rolled her fingers tightly around the steering wheel. "But I probably could have handled that myself."

"Maybe."

"You don't have much confidence in me."

"Eyes on the road."

She sped up and the engine revved.

His shoulder muscles bunched. "Put it in second gear, but remember to press in the clutch first. If you don't, the car will—"

The Jeep sputtered, died.

"Oops, sorry. Let's try this again." She got it started and they were going again, cruising slowly through the neighborhood. "Remember the time I stole Rex's car?"

"I do. You drove it into a ditch. That's what worries me."

"I haven't been behind the wheel of a car since then."

"Now I'm really worried. Take a left at this next street."

"Where are we going?"

"You're the one who's driving."

"Yeah, but you told me to turn left, why am I turning left?"

"To avoid the tourist traffic heading from Ruby Street to 377."

"Oh, good idea."

"Put on your blinker!"

"Where is it?"

"Here." He showed her.

She peeked into the rearview mirror. "Good thing there was nobody behind us, huh?"

"Good thing," he echoed as his blood slipped swiftly through his veins.

They drove in silence for a few minutes. Emma was getting the feel of it. As long as she went slow and straight, she wasn't doing too badly.

"I know where I'd like to go."

"Where's that?"

"To see the old Twilight Bridge."

"Beau blew it up."

"I know. I want to see what the river looks like without the bridge there."

It was a good choice, get out of town, away from the traffic and pedestrians and stop signs. "Okay, then make another left and you'll hit Highway 51 to the river."

"Can we turn off the AC and roll the windows down? I want to feel the wind in my hair."

"Sure," he said, but cringed the whole time she was rolling her window down. That left her with only one hand on the wheel.

"Woo-hoo! That feels great. Jeeps are cool. So high and bouncy." She bounced in the seat for effect.

"Both hands—"

"I know, I know, on the wheel. Yes, master."

"Safety first."

"And look there's fun, a distant second. Bye, fun."

He laughed. How could he not?

"Now that's a sound I like to hear."

"What else do you like?" he asked, charmed, his eyes transfixed on her windblown hair whipping against her long, slender neck.

"You mean besides piña coladas and getting caught in the rain?"

Delighted, he laughed again. Back in high school the local skating rink had played that song endlessly, and he and Emma had both agreed they hated the tune with a passion.

"You remembered," she said.

"Hey, the skating rink is still there and they're *still* playing that song. I took Charlie there for a birthday party recently. When I heard it, I thought of you."

"Our *anti-song*," she said in a faux romancy voice, and grinned.

Then in unison they started singing the lyrics they'd invented for the song, starting with, "We hate piña coladas . . ." They remembered every word of their made-up song as if they'd been singing the cockeyed duet for years.

When they were finished, they laughed together, and vulnerability cut through him like a knife. Quickly, Sam squelched the mood. "Okay, slow down here and take the next right. You're going to have to downshift."

She took the exit, and a few minutes later they were at the river where the bridge used to be. It looked odd now, the bare water without the familiar span reaching across to the boat ramp on the other side.

"Whoa, slow down," he cautioned, and almost had a heart attack when she drove right to the river's edge, braking just in time before the front tires hit the water.

"Woman," he croaked. "I don't know if you're gutsy as hell or just damn crazy."

"Thought you could use some serious shaking up." She grinned and hopped out of the Jeep.

"My hair's gonna turn white overnight," he muttered, put on the parking brake, and got out to follow her.

A hint of autumn was in the air, although it would be a couple more weeks before the leaves started to turn, unless they had an early freeze. But already the shadows were growing longer as the days shortened. Emma spread her arms wide, threw her head back, and inhaled a deep breath. "Ah." She sighed. "Don't you just love the smell of the river?"

"I suppose I don't think about it much." He didn't get down to the river very often. Once in a while when his family kidnapped him from his clinic, forced him down to their summer house for a barbecue.

"Come on," she said, stripping off her cute little red shoes and heading into the water. "Let's go wading."

"Be careful," he called as she plunged in. "That sandbar isn't very wide and—"

Before he got the words out of his mouth Emma just disappeared, swallowed up by the water.

"Shit!" Sam exclaimed, and flung himself in after her, cowboy boots and all. He dived down, his heart pounding.

Emma bobbed to the top of the water, laughing and treading water. He came up sputtering beside her and swiping the water from his face with a palm. "It's not funny," he yelled. "Stop laughing. I thought you got pulled down by an undertow."

"Nope, just stepped off the sandbar. Hey, the water is really deep right there. Why didn't you tell me?"

"I was trying to tell you before you dived in so impulsively."

"Oh well," she said, swimming back to the river's edge. "No harm done."

"But harm could have been done," he scolded, "lots of harm. You could have drowned."

"But I didn't," she said impishly, pulling herself to shore.

Sam got out and collapsed on the ground beside her. "My pulse is racing. You scared the hell out of me."

"BS. Let me feel." She sat up beside him, splayed her palm over his chest.

Her touch was electric, sending bolts of awareness shooting throughout his body. He looked into her eyes, green as the sea, her face encircled by coppery wet curls. Sam did not plan what happened next. He was simply compelled by biology to act.

Who's being impulsive now?

The thought flashed through his mind, but in the heat of the moment, it was washed away by a torrent of hormones.

His blood hummed, his brain sizzled. He sat up, reached out, spanned her waist with both hands, and pulled her into his lap. Beneath that soaking wet, red and white blouse her glorious breasts mashed into his chest and her soft, damp skin branded his flesh. The scent of her, always that dangerous watermelon shampoo and Ivory soap scent, inflamed his senses. Instantly, he had a hard-on. Never mind that he was wet to the bone. Didn't he always get an erection whenever he was around her? It was damn embarrassing how little control he had over himself.

She didn't move, just sat snugged in his lap studying him. Their noses were almost touching.

His hand slipped down her back to cup her butt, and what a heavenly ass it was. His palm seemed made for cupping her. His fingers had a mind of their own; they trailed lower. Still, she didn't wriggle away, but she did inhale sharply while her gaze stayed hooked on his face.

She caught her bottom lip up between her teeth and her cheeks pinkened prettily as she shifted forward ever so slightly.

The sounds of the motorboats cruising up to the boat ramp on the other side of the river faded from his ears. He forgot they were soaking wet and sitting on the banks of the Brazos River. He was aware of nothing except her mesmerizing green eyes.

"Your hand is on my ass," she whispered.

"It is," he confessed.

"I'm wet."

"I noticed."

"You're hard."

"I noticed that too."

"This is a problem."

"It's one of the main reasons you don't go running off half-cocked. It can result in unintended consequences."

"Pun intended?" She arched one copper-colored brow.

"Not really."

"You don't do anything on impulse?"

"I pulled you into my lap, didn't I?"

"Ah, but you stopped short of a kiss."

"Are you asking me to kiss you?"

"Not asking, no."

"Hoping?"

Her breathing was so shallow she was almost panting. "Praying."

Blindly, without purposeful thought, Sam trailed his fingertips over the nape of her neck and leaned his head down to kiss the throbbing pulse at the hollow of her throat. Her silky skin softened beneath his mouth, and a tight little moan escaped her lips.

His hand crept from her neck and down the hollow of her throat to her breast, heaving with each inhalation of air. A simple but lingering touch that escalated the erotic intimacy between them.

Sam could not fully comprehend the hold Emma had over him. She made him want to chuck all his values and restraint and just do what felt good. He was a lost soul, bested by her lips. He could think of nothing else but being melded with her in any way that he could.

She rocked her pelvis against him, lithe and graceful.

Blood surged through his body, pouring out from his heart and pooling into his crotch, setting his erection in stone. He closed his eyes, grappling for some semblance of control, but it was nowhere to be found.

He kissed her again, his clashing tongue hot against hers, tasting the vibrant flavor of her, absorbing her brilliant warmth.

She shivered in response, a tremor quaking through her slender body. He pulled his lips from hers and ran his tongue over the outside of her ear, and she shuddered even harder.

Her quick intake of breath, low and excited, in the vast openness of water and sky, ignited his own need, sending it shooting to flaming heights.

She lightly bit his chin.

The feel of her teeth against his skin rocketed a searing heat to all his erogenous zones, and he groaned. God, she was one helluva woman, dragging him out on a limb with her.

Sam's lips found hers again and as they kissed, he raised a hand to her breasts. Her nipples poked through the material of her lacy bra.

His thumb brushed against her hard little nipple, and she responded by sliding her bottom against his lap. The feel of her sweet little ass against the leg of his jeans made him crazy.

When he bent his head to gently suck at her nipple through her shirt, she gasped and ran her fingers through his hair, clutched his head close to her bosom.

This wasn't good enough. He had to touch her bare skin or go insane.

Sliding his hand up underneath her shirt, he unhooked her bra from behind and set her breasts free. She moved against him, hot and fiery. No way could he resist the mounting pleasure, or the sweet little sound slipping past her lips. Desire consumed his body, snatched his soul.

"Sam," she murmured, and rocked restlessly.

He couldn't believe he was with her. Sixteen years vanished in the ethereal stream of time, and here was Steady Sam with the most audacious girl in the freshman class. He'd wondered then, as he wondered now, how on earth had he managed that feat?

You're falling in love with her all over again.

It was true but he didn't know how to stop it. Didn't want to stop it even though he knew he was headed down a treacherous path. With a fierce growl, he pushed aside her blouse, exposing one of those perky breasts. Pure lust shot through him as he bent his head to draw her hard-beaded nipple into his mouth.

She let out a gasp. "Oh, oh."

He teased her nipple with his teeth, biting down on it so softly. She gasped again and ground her pelvis against his. Her legs straddled his lap, and the crotch of her panties rested against the bulging zipper of his jeans.

Never in his life had he made out with a woman in the open like this. Any moment someone could drive up. Hell, someone could motor by on the river and catch a glimpse of them through the trees, but Sam couldn't bring himself to care, which was completely out of character. He knew he just had to have more. To have her in his arms again was nothing short of a miracle, and he couldn't help thinking it was all an erotic wet dream.

He pulsed with need for her. Awestruck, he suckled her tender nipple, extracting more exquisite sounds of pleasure from Emma's sweet lips. How he wanted her, ached for her, craved her. But he shouldn't do this. Not only were they in a public place, but he knew this relationship couldn't lead where his heart wanted it to go. Emma was bound for bigger things. He couldn't expect her to be happy in a place like Twilight. At least not for long. And he couldn't be happy anywhere else. Besides, he wasn't free to make decisions based on whims of the heart. He had a son, and that changed everything.

But even as he told himself these things, his body wasn't listening. He had to kiss her again, practicality be damned. He tugged her shirt down over her swollen breasts and captured her lips. She kissed him back with a passion that rocked him to his core. He kissed her until he couldn't breathe, and when, finally, he was forced to come up for air, she made a soft noise of disappointment.

The late afternoon sunlight fell through the leaves of the sheltering elm trees overhead, sending a cool breeze over their damp skin. He felt goose bumps rise on her arms and realized he had plenty of goose bumps of his own, none of them related to wet clothes and breezy air.

"You're shivering," he said. "We better get you warmed up, dried off."

"You're wet too, Doc."

They looked at each other, sexual tension throbbing between them, an intense, undeniable force.

Emma leaned in for another kiss, but he cupped her face in his palms and shook his head. Then he wrapped his hands around her waist and lifted her off him.

"What's happening, Sam?" she whispered.

He had to fist his hands to keep from kissing her again. He wanted her so badly. His masculine urges were all-consuming, numbing his conscience, short-circuiting his brain. *Take her, take her, take her.* A wicked, primal chant rang in his ears. He had to get away from her or do something irrevocable.

Emma, however, had a mind of her own.

The kiss she planted on his lips was as full of life as she was—energetic, spontaneous, generous. She kissed as she did everything, putting all her heart and soul into it. Intensity exuded from her mouth, lighting a brushfire inside him. She threaded her fingers through his hair, held him still while her eager little tongue went searching. She tasted so damn delicious.

He let it go on for much longer than he should have; he was going to get hurt, no two ways about it. Sam broke the kiss. "We gotta stop. I should never have started this."

"No," she agreed, nodding.

"You're on a path to the stars and I'm just Steady Sam, forever in Twilight. I can't keep up with you, Trixie Lynn. You're out of my league."

"I'm not and I'd take you right here, right now, Sam Cheek, but I don't want to cause you any more pain. You've suffered enough."

"You've done some suffering of your own, sweetheart."

"If I thought an affair with you would cure our aches instead of complicate them . . ."

"I know. I want it too, but there's too much at stake." Sam cringed. He hated the way that sounded, as if she wasn't worth the risk. "I'm sorry, that came out wrong. What I meant was—"

"No, no." She held up her palms. "I get it. I really do. I have very little impulse control, so this is me, uncomplicating your life." Emma hooked her bra, adjusted her blouse, got to her feet, and started for the Jeep, her clothes clinging wetly to her small, slender frame.

She looked so forlorn. Watching her walk away ripped Sam's heart from his chest. But she was right. It was better to stop this before it ever really got started.

The question was, why did he feel as if he was making the biggest mistake of his life?

CHAPTER TWELVE

Quilts are like people. No two are exactly alike.
—Maddie Gunnison, Dr. Sam Cheek's housekeeper

The conversation on the drive back to Sam's house rested exclusively on driving dos and don'ts. The awkwardness between them hung heavily inside the confines of that little yellow Jeep. Emma didn't know what to say to break the tension, didn't know if she should even try.

Everything was such a mess between them. She wanted him so badly she couldn't think straight, and it seemed he felt the same way about her, but they both knew the potential for hurt was huge. Their values were just too different. The things they wanted in life were polar opposites. She wished she could ignore that reality, but every time she looked at him, she saw it. The small-town family man who was happy with his life. He didn't yearn for more the way she did. He had no desire to make his mark on the outside world. No driving need to be special. As long as he took care of Charlie and had animals to tend, Sam was content.

It wasn't an indictment of him. In fact, she was jealous that he could be satisfied with such simplicity. She wished she was hardwired differently. That she could be less ambitious, less determined to succeed at all cost, but it was in her blood. She had no idea how to settle for less than the dreams that drove her with an unrelenting fire.

"What in the world happened to you two?" Maddie asked the minute they walked through the back door and into the mudroom.

"Long story," Sam said chivalrously, not getting into the details of her stupidity.

"I decided to go wading on the sandbar where the old Twilight Bridge used to be and fell in. Sam jumped in to save me from drowning without any concern for his own safety."

"That's our Sam," Maddie said. "Hero through and through."

Sam's cheeks reddened. "You weren't drowning."

"You didn't know that."

Maddie made a clucking noise. "Well, you were gone so long I was about to call Hondo to go look for you."

Emma felt her own cheeks heat as she thought about what the sheriff might have come upon if the housekeeper had called him out to search for them.

"You went in with your boots on?" Maddie stared at Sam's wet cowboy boots.

"When you're jumping into the river to save someone's life, it's customary not to take time to strip off your boots," Sam drawled.

"Don't move." Maddie pointed a finger. "Either one of you, until I can put some paper bags down for you to walk on. I just mopped the kitchen floor."

Emma jerked her thumb over her shoulder. "I'm going to go on back to the B&B, Maddie, and get out of your hair."

"Hold it right there, little missy." Maddie shook her index finger.

"What is it?"

"You promised that napping child upstairs you'd take him for ice cream when you got back." She shifted her gaze to Sam. "And while I don't approve of ice cream before dinner, you did promise him. He's been waiting two hours for you to return, and he's going to get his ice cream come hell or high water."

"Sam can take him," Emma said. The last thing she wanted was to spend more time with Sam and Charlie in a cute ice cream shop in their cozy little town.

"He's expecting you to go too."

"How do you know?" Emma asked.

"He drew this." Maddie stepped from the mud-room into the kitchen, and removed a crayon drawing attached to the refrigerator with a magnet. She came back and handed it to Emma.

The drawing consisted of three stick figures. A dad, a mom, and a little boy eating ice cream. The mom had a mass of curly red hair.

Emma's chest tightened, and tears pushed at the backs of her eyes. Charlie missed his mother so damn much he couldn't bring himself to speak, but the picture said it all. "That's not a picture of me."

"Yes it is," Maddie said, and Emma could see tears misting the other woman's eyes as well. "Look what she's wearing."

The mother in Charlie's drawing was wearing an outfit identical to the one Emma had on—red skirt, red and white striped blouse, red shoes.

Her heart cracked wide open, then. This was all the more reason not to go eat ice cream with them. Charlie was getting attached to her. She shot a desperate look at Sam and saw the same concerns on his face.

"Maybe it would be best if Emma did go on back to—" Sam started but didn't get to finish because Charlie came charging into the mudroom, a huge grin on his face. He stopped when he saw they were wet and canted his head.

"We fell into the river," Sam explained.

Charlie spied the drawing Maddie held and pointed to it.

"Yes, we're still going for ice cream. We just have to put on some dry clothes first."

Charlie nodded.

Emma resigned herself to ice cream. "I'll pop over to the B&B and change."

"You don't want to go traipsing through the B&B soaking wet," Maddie pointed out. "Sunday afternoon is when all the tourists are checking out. I'll find something here for you to wear."

She wanted to argue but Maddie had already disappeared. She came back with dry clothes for both Sam and Emma and paper bags to put down on the floor. Sam peeled off his boots in the mudroom while Emma followed the brown paper bag trail that Maddie made leading to the downstairs bathroom.

Once she was alone in the bathroom with the door shut, she shucked off her wet things, took a quick rinse-off shower, and dressed in the bright purple dress with a fitted bodice and flouncy hemline that skimmed just above her knees. It molded to her body as if it had been made for her. She loved it—the color, the fit, the soft cottony material.

She knew at once the dress must have belonged to Valerie. It would never fit someone as tall and big-boned as Maddie.

Immediately, she wanted to take it off. Not because it had belonged to a dead woman, but because she was already sinking too deeply into Valerie's old life. The longer she stayed, the harder it would be to shake off this town, that little boy, and the man she now realized she'd never stopped loving.

The line at Rinky-Tink's old-fashioned ice cream parlor extended out the door; most of the patrons were tourists on this Sunday afternoon. It was easy to distinguish the locals from the tourists. The tourists had on fanny packs and walked with slow, loping gaits as they browsed store windows. They wore sunshades, festive straw hats, or visors, and they smelled of coconut-scented sunscreen after a day spent boating on the lake.

Charlie was impatient with the wait, wiggling like a worm and hanging on the metal bars set up to keep people in an orderly queue. Several times, Sam had to rest a restraining hand on his shoulder to hold him in check.

"Waiting gets boring, huh?" Emma said to him.

Charlie nodded so vigorously his glasses slipped to the end of his nose and he used his thumb to push them back up.

"I'm gonna get coffee ice cream," Emma said. "Do you want some?"

Sam should have known her favorite would be something cosmopolitan and different. No plain vanilla for Trixie Lynn.

Charlie made a "yuck" face.

"What kind do you like?" she asked the boy.

He pointed at the large wooden sandwich sign posted just inside the door with all the flavors listed on it and numbered.

Emma looked over. "There's a lot of flavors there. How am I supposed to know which one you want?"

He held up eight fingers.

"Ah," she said. "Rocky road. I should have known that was your favorite. All little boys like rocky road."

Charlie nodded again.

To distract him from the long wait, Emma started telling him a story about a little boy who was made out of rocky road ice cream. As she spoke, Sam found himself mesmerized. Her voice was so compelling, honed, he was sure, by years of acting lessons and stage plays. Her story spun out into the ice cream parlor, and soon several other kids had gathered around to listen.

"Your wife is a really good storyteller," one of the lady tourists waiting behind them said. "She could make a living doing it."

"Thank you," Sam said, not bothering to explain she wasn't his wife. There was no reason to go into that.

But his gaze ensnared Emma's, and for a split second he saw a look on her face that he couldn't describe— part sadness, part delight, part raw vulnerability—and it made him catch his breath. Was she imagining what it would be like to be his wife? He sure was wondering what it would be like to be her husband.

Well, stop it. You have no business imagining that.

Emma gave him a shy smile and then ducked her head, continuing her story to Charlie and the other children hanging on her every word.

Thirty minutes later their turn at the ice cream counter came. "One scoop of coffee ice cream in a . . ." Sam looked over at Emma.

"Cup," she supplied.

"A scoop of strawberry on a waffle cone, and a scoop of rocky road . . ." Sam paused again as Charlie tugged on his pants leg. "What is it, champ?"

Charlie held up two fingers.

"You want two scoops?"

He nodded.

"Maddie will have my hide if I give you two scoops. You won't eat your dinner."

Charlie pressed his palms together in a gesture of entreaty. The look in his eyes said, *Please, please.*

When he'd stopped talking, Charlie had gotten really expressive with his eyes. "You promise to eat your dinner if I get you two scoops?" Sam asked, knowing that more than likely he'd have to finish it.

Charlie nodded again.

"Okay," he told the girl behind the counter. "Make that rocky road cone a double."

The girl scooped up the ice cream, handed the orders out to Emma and Charlie while Sam reached in his wallet and pulled out a ten. "Keep the change."

They headed for a table near the front window that a family of four had just vacated. Charlie stumbled over his shoelace that had come untied. Top heavy with two scoops of rocky road, his cone flipped over the side of his little hand and fell top down on the floor. Sam saw it all unfolding but couldn't do a thing to stop it.

"Aww," a couple of patrons said in unison.

A shocked expression crossed Charlie's face, and it was quickly replaced by a look of utter heartbreak.

He'd waited all afternoon for this cone, and in an instant, it was lost. His son hovered on the verge of bursting into tears, his bottom lip trembling.

"I'll get you another one," Sam said.

Simultaneously, he and Emma swung their gazes to stare at the line that was even longer now than it had been when they'd first arrived.

"No need," Emma said brightly, and crouched beside Charlie. "Only that first scoop touched the floor. The second scoop and the cone are fine. Hand me a couple of napkins, Sam."

And as quick as that, she saved the day, separated the two scoops of ice cream, handing Charlie the one that was still clean, scooping the other off the floor with the napkins and tossing it in the trash. Charlie grinned and went to licking.

"Whew," Sam said. "Smooth move. You saved the day."

Sam couldn't help thinking that Valerie would probably have scolded Charlie for not watching where he was going, and she certainly wouldn't have let Sam get him two scoops of ice cream, especially before dinner. And germ-obsessed as she was, Valerie would have had a heart attack over Emma's maneuver. But Emma had a valid point. The ice cream that hadn't touched the floor was perfectly good. Disaster averted.

"Do you need a wipe for your hands?" asked the lady tourist who'd assumed Emma was his wife, and produced a moistened towelette from her purse.

Emma smiled and rose to her feet, rubbing her sticky fingers with the wipe.

"You're a natural-born mother," the woman enthused. "You're so at ease with your son."

"Thank you," she said, looking embarrassed.

The woman went on her way, and Emma sat down to join Sam and Charlie at the table. The woman was right, Emma was a natural with kids. Probably because she was so bubbly and adventuresome herself, just like a kid.

"You ever think about having one of your own?" he asked.

"What? Me have a kid?"

"Yeah."

"*Nooo*," she said it like he'd suggested she climb Mount Everest.

"Why not?" he asked, not knowing why he was grilling her, but doing it all the same.

"It's really difficult to be a good mother and have an acting career, and I'm a firm believer that kids should come first. Why do you think so many actresses wait until they're in their late thirties or forties to start a family?"

"Do you think you'll want one when you're forty?"

"Honestly, I don't think that far into the future. I'm just trying to make it day by day."

He could look at her and see it was true. She was spontaneous, impulsive, free-spirited, the kind of person who lived in the moment. And while he supposed it was a gift to be able to exist solely in the here and now, he didn't understand it. He was a planner, a plotter. He had to know how things were going to line up. Without a plan, Sam didn't make a move. If he went on vacation, he had all the stops mapped out, right down to the gas stations. He didn't go anywhere without reservations and a backup contingency plan.

Charlie, who was sitting beside Emma and across from Sam, reached out and lightly patted her hand. His little face was smeared with chocolate. She turned to look at his son, and in that moment, he saw a flash of tenderness in her eyes so strong and true, he had to agree with the tourist lady. Emma was a natural-born mother whether she knew it or not.

"What is it, Charlie?" she murmured.

Charlie wiggled himself around on his knees and leaned over to kiss her softly on the cheek.

A tear-jerking mix of surprised delight and wistful longing crossed her face. "Why Charlie," she said. "What a sweet kiss. Thank you."

And then she kissed his cheek in return.

Charlie beamed as if the sun had come out after weeks of being trapped inside by rainy weather.

Sam's gut contracted; a cold sweat broke out on his forehead as his heart ripped right in two. This was bad. This was really bad. His six-year-old son was falling in love with a woman who could never be his surrogate mother.

"I'll bring this dress back over to you tomorrow," Emma said when Sam let her out of the Jeep in front of the Merry Cherub.

"Don't bother," he said. "I'd already boxed it up for Goodwill and Maddie dug it out. It looks good on you. Keep it."

"It was Valerie's."

"Yes."

They didn't say anything, just looked at each other. Sam was finally boxing up his dead wife's things and giving them away? It was a good sign. He was moving on at last. She felt happy for him.

"Well then." Emma held up a palm. "Good night."

"Good night," he said in return, mildly, blandly, with no inflection, no emotion behind the words.

"Are we on for next Sunday for more driving lessons?"

He looked like he wanted to say no, but then imperceptibly nodded. "Same time?"

"Sure."

"Okay then."

"And the line readings?"

He hesitated.

"I understand if you don't have time . . ." she rushed to say before he could turn her down. "I've imposed on you too much as it is. You're a busy guy—"

"I'll be working in the garden on Tuesday evening if that's convenient for you. Just holler at me over the back fence."

"Yes, great, sure, thanks." She raised a hand, then turned and hurried into the B&B, her pulse thumping crazily and she had no idea why.

Luckily, Jenny was occupied with checking in guests when Emma went inside and she didn't have to stop and chat. She just raised her hand in greeting and headed for the stairs.

Once she was in her room, she closed the door and sank against it, willing her erratic heart to calm down. Why was she signing up for more driving lessons with Sam and begging him to read lines with her? She knew she was sliding in deep, and the more she was around him, the more it was going to hurt when she left.

Emma stepped into the bathroom. She looked at her reflection in the mirror, saw the imprint of tiny chocolate lips on her cheek where Charlie had kissed her. Her heart, already reeling, lurched, stumbled.

"It's too late," she whispered to her reflection and reached up to touch her cheek. "You've stepped off the sandbar into a deep, deep undertow."

Unnerved, she turned on the water, splashed her face, washed off Charlie's sticky, rocky road kiss. She wasn't the only one in trouble. The little boy was getting as attached to her as she was to him.

"It's just because you remind him of his mother," she told herself. "The hair color, the short stature, and you were wearing his mother's dress. That's all it is. Transference."

But no matter how she tried to rationalize it, guilt continued to nibble at her. She wished there was something she could do for the boy. Some way to connect him to his mother. She unzipped the dress and slipped out of it, the bright purple cotton material pooling to the floor at her feet.

The True Love Quilting Club sometimes used scraps of clothing in the quilts they made to pay tribute to loved ones. Emma picked up Valerie's dress. Sam didn't want it back and she certainly wasn't going to wear it again. What if she used it to make a quilt?

A special quilt for Charlie, in honor of his beautiful mother who'd given up her life for her country.

Almost a week had gone by and nothing changed, at least not on the outside. Every night after Charlie was in bed, Sam would go outside, sink into the lawn chair, the script to the Founder's Day play in his lap, a glass of iced tea resting on the picnic table, and wait for Emma to come outside so they could read lines together. But on the inside, something was happening to Sam. Something that stirred him up, inflamed his soul.

Since that day on the banks of the Brazos River where he'd lost his self-control, Sam had been troubled, both by his lack of restraint and by his stark need for Emma. He feared that if he didn't stop hanging around with her, he was going to do something that could never be undone.

And yet he'd been unable to stop himself from coming out here every night, losing sleep to stay up until the wee hours running lines with her. It was only through the words of the characters they were reenacting that Sam could tell Emma how he really felt about her.

Dammit, but acting was a sorry substitute for the real thing, and yet he didn't dare let her know what was going on inside his heart.

It wouldn't change anything if you told her.

He knew that as surely as he knew his own name, so he held his tongue, kept his feelings to himself, and read those romantic lines of love.

But on this Friday night, as he heard the back door to the Merry Cherub open and close and the soft padding of Emma's footsteps on the soft grass, dissatisfaction swelled against his chest. He didn't want to read lines. He didn't want to sit here passively while the woman he wanted, needed, waited just beyond that fence.

He threw down the script, got up, began to pace. Tonight they were supposed to read the last skit in the play. The one Nina had written in honor of Valerie.

A brushing noise came from the other side of the fence, and he could see Emma standing there as vividly as if there were no barrier between them, fluffing the pages of her script. "I'm leaving for Iraq tomorrow, Sam, and I want you to make me a promise."

At the sound of Emma speaking words so eerily similar to the ones Val had actually spoken, something unraveled inside him.

"Anything, my love," he spoke the lines, although he had not said that to Val. What he'd really said was, "I'm listening."

"I want you to promise me that if anything happens to me over there you'll move on. Marry again. Give Charlie a new family."

"Nothing's going to happen to you."

"Please, Sam, just promise me."

He couldn't read the next line. The words hung in his throat. His feelings were a fiery jumble, his needs, his desires eating him up inside.

"Sam?"

He didn't say anything. A sledgehammer of doubt, fear, regret, and shame squatted on his chest.

"Are you all right?"

"Fine," he finally managed.

"All right. Now where were we—"

"Wait," he said.

"Yes?"

"I do want to stop. This skit is bringing back painful memories." He pressed a palm to his head and was surprised to find sweat beaded there in spite of the cool evening breeze. He expected her to acquiesce, to excuse him and let him off the hook.

She did not. "No."

"No?" Taken aback, he stopped pacing. He could hear her ragged breathing from the other side of the fence.

"You need to see this through. Not for me, but for you."

"What are you talking about?"

"Valerie. Her death. You getting over it."

"I've gotten over it."

"Have you?"

"Yes."

"Then let's read the lines."

"I don't want to read the lines." Irritation ripped through him.

"It's not healthy, the way you're hiding out."

"I am *not* hiding out." Irritation turned to ire.

"Everybody in this town kid-gloves you," she said.

"What in the hell does that mean?" he snapped.

"I get why they do it. You're a great guy and no one wants to hurt you, but Sam, you seriously need your cage rattled. People—your family, this town—they let you get away with hiding out."

"I'm not hiding out," he reiterated, knotting his hands into fists.

"Okay, maybe hiding out isn't the right term, but you play it too safe. Life is a smorgasbord and you choose to eat bologna sandwiches every day."

"I like bologna sandwiches."

"You could like other things too. You don't know because you're too afraid or too set in your ways to give it a try."

"I'm warning you, woman, you're pissing me off."

"Good," she said. "You need your feathers ruffled. "You've had it too easy."

He hardened his jaw. "My wife died."

"And you're the only one who's ever lost someone? Wise up. We're all walking wounded. Me? From what I've heard about her, I think Valerie would kick your ass for hiding out."

"Excuse me, you didn't know her and you don't know me."

"Yes I do, Sam Cheek. I do know you."

"You knew me once. For a year. When we were kids. Don't assume you know me."

They were having their first fight with a wall between them. What a flippin' metaphor for how withdrawn he'd become. He wasn't even fighting with her face-to-face. She was right. He *was* hiding from life.

She wanted to see him rattled and ruffled, then, by God, he'd show her. Sam stalked to the gate separating his backyard from his sister's B&B and yanked it open.

Emma stood there, so tiny and yet so fierce, staring up at him, her spine drawn up, her chest thrust out, her chin defiant. He stepped toward her, the back gate slamming shut behind him. She didn't flinch, didn't back up.

Sam didn't hesitate, didn't consider the consequences. He simply reacted to the hormones crashing around inside him and the vulnerable look in her sea green eyes. Emma was full of brass bravado, but she was scared of what she'd provoked in him, he could see it on her face.

He grabbed her around the waist, pulled her up on her tiptoes, and planted a punishing kiss on her lips. He kissed her roughly, demandingly, and he might have gone on kissing her that way for the rest of the night if guilt hadn't started knocking on the back of his brain. He was taking his anger and frustration out on her.

Stop it.

He sat her down on the ground. "There," he said, "does that feel like a man who's hiding out?"

A trembling hand rose to her lips and her eyes grew wider. "No," she admitted.

They stood looking at each other in the darkness, the damp night air seeping through their skin.

"What is wrong with you?" she asked.

"What is wrong with me?" His pulse quickened. "You want to know what is wrong with me?"

She jutted out her chin. "Yeah."

"You," he said. "You're what's wrong with me. You've turned me inside out and I don't know how to deal with it."

"Maybe we should stop reading lines together. Stop the driving lessons."

"I think that's a very good idea."

Her face told him she didn't really want to stop and, dammit, neither did he. But this . . . this . . . well, he couldn't deal with it.

"Why did you really marry Valerie?" she asked softly. "Was it just because you felt sorry for her and Charlie?"

The question caught him by surprise. "You really want to know?"

She nodded.

Sam suddenly felt like a balloon that had been leaked of its air, flat, empty. "I married her because she wasn't you, all right? Because I knew she wouldn't leave. She had no aspirations beyond being a great mother, a good nurse." He snorted. "But as it turns out she was more like you than I imagined. She did leave me and she never came back."

"I came back," Emma whispered.

"Yes," he said, "you came back to taunt me, haunt me, but then you'll be gone again. Flying away to the stars."

"Sam . . ." She looked utterly miserable.

"Can you deny it?"

"No."

"I thought not," he said, then pivoted on his heels and walked away.

Chapter Thirteen

This quilt smells like my mommy.
—Six-year-old Charlie Martin Cheek

The next two weeks passed uneventfully. The air grew cooler and the leaves on the trees changed colors, bathing the countryside in a panorama of yellow, red, orange, and brown. The extra time she'd spent rehearsing with Beau paid off. His performance had improved markedly. She'd gotten over her fear of acting alongside Patches. Things were going well on the stage, even though Emma was no longer reading lines with Sam. While it was a relief not to murmur lines of love to each other through the fence, she had to admit she missed it. Knowing he was there, steady as a rock, something she could truly count on. She'd replaced that nightly routine with another—using Jenny's sewing machine to make a purple patchwork quilt for Charlie from pieces of his mother's cut-up dress.

On the quilting club front, everything was running on schedule. They were planning the fifth one tonight, the one honoring Korean War veterans. Emma's fingertips, which had once been sore and sensitive, were now toughly calloused. She was amazed at the beauty and artistry of the quilts that emerged from their work. They fairly vibrated with the themes of duty, honor, and sacrifice. It made her proud to be supporting the troops in some small way, and for once she truly understood what patriotism was about, and the big-hearted women of the True Love Quilting Club were her teachers.

Beyond the horror that was New York City on September 11, 2001, Emma hadn't given much thought to the troops overseas. She hadn't known anyone directly involved in the war effort. At times, she felt ashamed of herself. That she put so much of her mental energy into acting out fantasies when there were people dying in battle far from home.

In her life, the war took on added dimension and she understood for the first time that the families of the soldiers and airmen and sailors were just as brave. They were the silent heroes rarely honored. They went on with their daily routines scared witless for the men and women they loved, holding it all together in the face of adversity. And when they spoke of loved ones killed so far from home, she felt the sharp, biting edge of their grief.

In light of such bravery, she felt inconsequential, her acting talent paling in comparison. She did the only thing she knew to do. That was to listen and observe; to internalize their sacrifice and courage so that when she got up onstage she could tell their stories through her facial expression, tone of voice, body language.

She used everything and it changed her.

On a Friday, October 22, more than a month after she'd come to Twilight, Emma arrived at the church a little early to find that Nina was the only one there. She was sitting at the quilting frame, her head bowed and her shoulders moving as if she was quietly sobbing.

Impulse urged Emma to slip back out the door and pretend she'd seen nothing, but something pushed her across the floor toward the other actress. "Nina," she murmured, "are you all right?"

Nina's head came up. She straightened her spine, swiped at her face with the back of her hand, and forced a smile. "Fine, fine. I'm fine."

"Are you sure?"

The older woman's eyes met hers, and for a flash of a second she saw a hurt so deep it made Emma's heart ache. "Can I get you anything?" she offered. "A cold drink?"

"No thank you."

"You sure there's nothing you want to talk about?" Emma sat down across from her in one of the chairs ringing the quilting frame.

Nina looked like she was about to confess something, and Emma couldn't help wondering if it had anything to do with the reason the older actress had rescued her from Scott Miller and brought her back to Twilight.

She didn't know why she felt this, but the idea burrowed inside her.

But before Nina could say anything, Raylene came breezing in, her hair, which was usually teased big, lying flat against her head. She had a lit cigarette dangling from her mouth and a fifth of vodka tucked under her arm. "Don't either one of you tell me I can't smoke in here." She glowered. "I've had a damn shitty day."

Emma raised her palms in a gesture of surrender.

"Give me a hit off that." Nina held out her hand. "My day hasn't exactly been peaches and cream."

Raylene's eyes rounded in surprise, but she passed her lipstick-stained cigarette to Nina, who took a long drag off it. "I haven't smoked in forty years," she mumbled through a haze of smoke.

"Well here, give it back," Raylene said. "You don't need to take that up again."

Nina coughed, handed it back. "Thank you, I feel better."

Raylene took the cigarette over to the kitchenette and doused it with water from the faucet before flicking the butt in the trash can. Just then the door opened. Patsy, Marva, Dotty Mae, and Terri walked in, hands loaded with quilting supplies.

Patsy sniffed the air. "Who's been smoking in here?"

Nina looked guilty.

Raylene raised a hand. "Who do you think?"

"Should have known," Patsy groused.

"Don't mess with me, Cross. I've had a bad day." Raylene narrowed her eyes as if gunning for a fight.

"Don't you two start," Marva said, playing peacemaker.

"Well, join the club. Mine was a pisser as well. Jimmy fell out of bed at the home and broke his hip. They took him over to Twilight General."

"Ted's doing surgery on him as we speak," Terri added.

"Ouch! I'm sorry to hear that." Raylene grabbed a stack of Styrofoam cups and brought them back to the quilting frame, along with the bottle of vodka still tucked under her arm.

Patsy shrugged, but her face looked haggard. "What are you gonna do?" she asked rhetorically.

Jenny and Belinda showed up then, completing the circle. Jenny carried a plate of her homemade chocolate chip cookies.

"Sorry I'm late," Belinda said, looking flustered. "I got called into the principal's office at the middle school. Kameron got into a fight and it's looking like he started it. Harvey and I were having a set-to with him. Am I raising a bully?"

"He's just going through a phase," Dotty Mae assured Belinda. "It's hard being a twelve-year-old boy."

"And I just got back from the doctor's office," Jenny said glumly. "Once again, I'm *not* pregnant."

"Oh honey," Marva patted her shoulder. "It'll happen. You're still plenty young."

"I'm thirty-four. Not so young anymore. The doctor says if it doesn't happen within the next six months we should consider in vitro, but we don't have the money for that."

"Sounds like everyone's having a bad day," Raylene said, and plopped into her chair. "And I've got the cure." She held up the vodka bottle and the Styrofoam cups. "Who's up for a drinking game?"

Emma figured everyone would shoot down Raylene's idea, but to her surprise, Patsy sat beside Raylene and propped an arm on her shoulder. "What kind of drinking game?"

"It's called I Never. Ever heard of it?"

"I have," Emma said.

"Well of course you have, Miss New York City," Raylene popped off.

"I've heard of it too," Jenny said. "I saw it on *Lost*.

Sawyer and Kate played it around the campfire. Actually it was a really good episode. I'm in."

"Ooh, that *was* a good episode." Terri nodded. "It really ratcheted up the sexual tension between Kate and Sawyer. I'm in."

"So explain the game to the rest of us," Marva said. "My day wasn't all lollipops and rainbows either. Just found out the government is eyeing the land my daddy left me out past Crescent. They want to take it away under eminent domain for that new expressway loop they're building around Fort Worth."

"Rat bastards," Raylene spat. "Anyway," she said, pouring vodka into the nine cups she'd lined up on the edge of the quilting frame. "Here's how the game works. You start off with 'I never . . . ,' then you tell us something you've never done. If any of you *have* done it, you take a drink. If you haven't done it, you don't drink. For example, I never kicked a man in the balls so hard that he had to have a testicle removed. Emma would have to take a drink, but none of the rest of us would unless they *had* kicked a man in the balls so hard that he'd had a testicle removed."

"So it's like a liquid lie detector," Dotty Mae said.

"Something like that." Raylene passed out the cups. "Y'all ready?"

"Past ready," Patsy said. "Who starts?"

"I'll start," Terri said, "and then we can go clockwise around the circle. I've never played a drinking game."

Emma, Jenny, Dotty Mae, and Raylene all took a drink.

"Dammit," Patsy said. "Ask something you know I've done, Belinda, so I can take a drink."

"I've never been in love with a Vietnam War veteran," Belinda said.

Patsy took a big swallow of vodka. "Thanks for that."

"Your turn," Belinda said to Emma.

Emma looked across the table at Nina. She didn't know why she said what she said, it just popped from her mouth. "I've never had an affair with a Broadway producer."

Nina met Emma's stare and brought the cup to her lips.

"Hmm," Marva said. "My turn? I don't know what to ask."

"Make it something provocative," Raylene goaded.

"Okay, here goes. I've never been skinny-dipping," Marva said.

"And you live in a lake town?" Dotty Mae clucked her tongue. "For shame."

"I'm modest," Marva said. "There's nothing wrong with that."

Everyone but Marva drank. Emma had drunk twice now, and a smooth, pleasant feeling floated over her.

Now it was Jenny's turn. She looked balefully at the group. "I've never been pregnant."

Everyone except Emma took a drink. Even Nina. As far as Emma knew, Nina didn't have any children. Had she lost a baby?

"I've never had a one-night stand," Dotty Mae said.

Raylene took a drink, looked around the table at everyone else who wasn't drinking. "Come on! You have to tell the truth."

No one else drank.

"Okay, so apparently I'm the only slut in the room."

"Hey, this game was your idea," Terri said. "Don't get your nose out of joint."

"In my defense," Raylene huffed. "I *was* a Dallas Cowboys cheerleader. Things got a little blurry back in the seventies."

"It's okay." Patsy patted Raylene on the shoulder. "We love you anyway, slut puppy."

"Your turn," Dotty Mae said to Nina.

"I never cheated on my husband in order to further my career." Nina raised her cup, met Emma's gaze again. Emma saw that same haunted vulnerability in the older woman's eyes that she'd seen when she'd walked into the church. Had Nina been married? She didn't know about that.

"Dammit, y'all are picking on me," Raylene groused and took another drink. "Just for the record, Lance was already cheating on me."

"Lance was her first husband," Belinda explained to Emma. "He was a football player and an asshole."

Dotty Mae took a drink as well.

Everyone stared at her goggle-eyed.

"What?" Dotty Mae said defensively. How do you think I made it as the first woman manager of Montgomery Ward?"

Belinda shook her head, made a noise of disapproval.

"Don't judge." Dotty Mae waved a finger. "I had two boys to support, no money in the bank, and Stuart was dying of pancreatic cancer. Sometimes a woman just has to do what a woman has to do."

"No one's judging you," Nina said, then she tilted back her head and downed the entire contents of her cup.

"Well," Raylene said, "whaddya know about that?"

* * *

Emma finished Charlie's quilt on Sunday. She and Sam hadn't spoken since their odd fight. She'd been so busy with rehearsals that she hadn't seen him except to occasionally catch a glimpse of him on the square. Every time she did, her heart revved, even though she kept telling herself that Sam's influence in her life had drawn to a natural close.

But that didn't stop her from wrapping the small purple quilt in a box and tying it up with a blue bow. This was about Charlie, not the complicated issues between her and Sam. At three that afternoon, she climbed Sam's porch steps and knocked on his door.

Sam opened the door, looking drop-dead-delicious in tan cargo pants and a green and white Dallas Stars T-shirt. His face remained expressionless, but she saw the flicker of welcome in his eyes.

"May I come in?" she asked.

Sam moved aside, and Charlie came running into the foyer, grinning.

Emma stepped over the threshold and followed Sam into the living room. He waved at the couch and she sat down. He took the recliner positioned across from her, perched on the edge of his seat, and leaned forward, elbows resting on his knees. "What's up?"

"I have a gift for Charlie."

"That was nice of you." His voice was even, devoid of emotion.

Charlie crawled up onto the couch beside Emma, and she smelled the sweaty scent of little boy. She set the box in his lap, then immediately had qualms about the gift. He was a kid. He was probably expecting a toy, not a quilt. Anxiety bit into her. What had she been thinking? It was a dumb idea.

"It's not any big thing," she added as he untied the bow.

He was a meticulous kid. Not tearing into the box, but rather going slowly, taking his time. Just like his father on that score. Emma glanced over to see Sam studying her.

Charlie lifted the lid and stared down at the quilt.

He hates it. How stupid to think a kid would like a quilt.

Charlie took the quilt from the box, his green eyes solemn. He held it up to his face and took a deep breath.

Emma nibbled her bottom lip. "Do you like it?"

The boy lowered the quilt and stared off as if looking at a memory. Or a ghost. He raised the quilt to his nose again and took another sniff.

"I made it myself," she said.

"From Valerie's dress," Sam murmured.

For the first time, it occurred to her that he might not appreciate her cutting up Valerie's dress to make the quilt. "Was that okay?"

"I gave it to you to do as you wish." His eyes were as enigmatic as his son's. "Give Emma a hug for working so hard to make you a quilt," Sam prompted Charlie.

Emma glanced back at Charlie, her heart a tight knot in her throat.

A single tear glistened at the corner of Charlie's right eye, but he just kept sitting there. He made no move to hug her as his father had directed.

Oh dear. He was upset with her. Misery pushed against her breastbone. Why had she done it? What had she been thinking?

"Charlie," Sam admonished. "Give Emma a hug."

The boy opened his mouth as if to protest, but he

hadn't spoken a word since his mother's death over a year ago. His little fingers curled tightly around the quilt, bunching it up.

"It's okay, Sam, he doesn't have to hug me if he doesn't want to," Emma said.

"Go on," Sam urged. "Emma put in a lot of hard work on that quilt. She made it just for you."

"He's a kid, he doesn't get that. No worries. I understand." Emma stood up.

"No, Charlie needs to learn it's good manners to thank someone when they give you a gift."

Charlie took another deep breath, his small chest expanding on a big gulp of air. Then, in a raspy voice that sounded like a rusty hinge creaking open in an old barn, he whispered, "This quilt smells like my mommy."

Emma's mouth fell open. Was she hearing things? Or had Charlie just spoken? Stunned, she raised her gaze to meet Sam's.

He looked as gobsmacked as she felt. "Did he just . . . ?"

"I think he just did." Emma grinned.

She could tell Sam wanted to grab Charlie in his arms, spin him around the room, and holler in triumph, because she wanted to do exactly the same thing. But neither one of them wanted to startle the boy. If they made too big a deal of it, he might stop talking.

"Did you say something, son?" Sam sank down on his knees in front of Charlie and put his arm on the boy's shoulder.

Charlie looked at his dad, pressed the quilt to his nose once more, and then his words came out in a pell-mell rush. "This smells just like my mommy.

How come it smells like my mommy? Is she here?" He glanced around the room. "Where is my mommy?"

Emma's heart cracked. The child looked so vulnerable with his big, sad eyes brimming with confusion behind the thick-lensed glasses, and she knew immediately she'd committed a monumental mistake by making the quilt from his mother's clothes. Remorse had her pressing a hand to her mouth. How could she have been so stupid?

Sam slipped his arm around the boy's waist. "Charlie," he said softly, "you talked."

Charlie thrust out his chest and cocked his head. A pensive expression crossed his face as if he was considering what Sam had said. Finally, he nodded.

"You know your mommy is gone, right? We've talked about this."

He nodded and said haltingly, "She . . . went to . . . live with . . . angels."

"That's right."

"But not Aunt Jenny's angels?" He turned his head in the direction of the Merry Cherub.

Maddie was standing in the doorway, her hands clasped over her mouth, her eyes brimming with tears. Emma felt tears of her own pushing at the backs of her eyes.

"No," Sam said.

"But this *smells* like my mommy."

"That's because Emma made the quilt out of your mommy's purple dress. The dress still had mommy's smell on it. Emma made the quilt just for you to have something you can always remember your mommy by," Sam patiently explained.

Charlie thought about this a moment. "Oh."

A plethora of emotions sent goose bumps spreading over Emma's arms. She was responsible for getting Charlie's hopes up and then dashing them. She could feel the little guy's disappointment, and it killed her soul. But because of the quilt she'd made him, he'd spoken for the first time in over a year.

Maddie could contain herself no longer. She rushed into the room, scooped Charlie into her arms. "You talked! You talked!"

"Uh-huh."

She spun him around in circles. Patches got into the mood, doing some spinning of his own. "What's your name?"

"Charlie Martin Cheek."

Maddie laughed joyfully. "How old are you?"

"Six years old."

"What's my name?"

"Maddie."

"Why didn't you talk before now?"

Charlie shrugged, still holding tight to the purple quilt.

"Who cares, right? It doesn't matter. Not at all. I'm making your favorite meal for supper," Maddie declared.

"Hot dogs?" Charlie asked.

"With macaroni and cheese from the box, just the way you like it."

Patches barked as if to say he concurred.

Emma looked over at Sam, mixed emotions swimming in his eyes as well. Would he reproach her for the quilt? She deserved a rebuke for not thinking this thing through. She had no idea Charlie would have such a strong reaction to the quilt.

"May I see you out on the back porch?" Sam asked.

Oh no, here it comes. Bracing herself for a strong tongue-lashing, she stepped out onto the porch. "Sam, I am so—" she began, but her words were nipped off.

Sam pulled her into his arms, tugged her to the back of the porch so they couldn't be seen from the kitchen window, and captured her mouth in a rough, demanding kiss.

As kisses went, well, it was the best damn kiss she'd ever gotten. A girl could get drunk off kisses like that.

He wrapped his arms tightly around her waist, tilted his head to deepen the kiss, his beard stubble brushing lightly against her chin. Emma melted, opening her mouth, letting him have full run of the place. *Go, Sammy, go.*

A mockingbird in the backyard mimosa tree sang to them. A slight breeze ruffled her hair. When she breathed she smelled the scent of garden—ripening squash and onions and turnips. And Sam. He smelled like the earth, rich and loamy and alive.

He kissed her as if it was his life's mission, as if this was what he'd been put on earth to do. His body pressed hard and hot against hers. Emma's blood pounded restlessly in her ears. She reached up and threaded her arms around his neck, savoring the kiss, forgetting for a moment where they were and how they'd gotten to this point.

"Thank you." He breathed, breaking off the kiss and resting his forehead against hers. She could feel the uneven ridges of his scar against her skin. "Thank you."

"I thought you'd be mad."

"Why on earth would you think that?"

"I cut up Valerie's dress."

"You got Charlie to talk." His hands were shaking slightly as he ran his palms over her upper arms. "You're a miracle worker. You're amazing."

"I also brought up a painful memory."

"He's talking . . ." Sam paused. She could hear the emotions clogging his throat. "My son is talking again and it's all because of you."

His dark eyes drilled into hers, shining with the feverish light. She felt a similar fever slip through her veins, heating her from the inside out.

"Do you have any idea what you've accomplished? I've dragged him to doctor after doctor, grief counselor after grief counselor, therapist after therapist. None of their techniques or suggestions or medications helped. Nothing worked. Until you."

He made her sound like a saint. "I'm not a saint."

"In my eyes you are." He stepped back, reached down, took her hand in his, and gazed deeply into her eyes as if he never wanted to stop. Although she was probably projecting that onto him, because *she* never wanted to stop. "Listen, I've gotta call people, tell everyone what's happened. Go show Charlie off to my family."

"Of course." She nodded. "I understand completely."

"I still can't believe it." He grinned and planted another quick kiss on her lips. She'd never seen him look so giddy, so trouble-free. It warmed her heart. "You're awesome, amazing."

"You already covered that."

"Can't say it enough. Look, we're going to have to go out and celebrate big-time. My treat. Charlie's grandparents on his father's side are coming up from Florida next weekend and they want to take Charlie camping. How about you and me drive to Fort Worth for dinner? Someplace really nice."

"I'd love to go celebrate with you, Sam, but it's fine with me to stay here in Twilight. We can just go to the Funny Farm."

"That'll be good enough for you?" he asked hopefully.

"Why would you think otherwise?"

"You're from the city. You're used to nice restaurants and fine dining."

Emma laughed. "The ideas you have about struggling actresses in the city. We're going to have to have a long talk."

"Saturday night. For the eight o'clock seating at the Funny Farm. I'll register with the hostess station."

"I'll meet you there."

"It's a date."

He had a date with Emma. A real date, an official date. Their first date, Sam realized. Sixteen years after he first kissed her.

Was it dumb? Most likely. Did he care? Not at this point. In fact, he couldn't remember when he'd been so happy. Emma had gotten Charlie to talk and they had a date. Hell, he was even whistling that silly piña colada song.

Maddie was as excited as he was. She burned up the phone lines calling everyone she knew to tell them that Charlie had started talking again.

Sam tucked his son in the Jeep and took him around town, showing off with an unabashed fatherly pride. He drove over to his aunt Belinda's on the other side of town.

"Hi, Kimmie, Kameron, Karmie, Kyle, and Kevin," Charlie greeted his cousins, who were all playing Statues on the front lawn. That was quite a tongue twister even for someone who hadn't gone mute for over a year, and Charlie didn't miss a syllable.

His cousins converged on him, asking him a million questions while Aunt Belinda came running down off the porch. "Did I just hear Charlie speak? Sam, was he talking?"

Charlie raised one hand; his other hand clutched the purple quilt. "Hi, Auntie Belinda."

"Oh, oh, my sweet boy!" Belinda grabbed him up in her arms, swung him around. She squeezed him tight and dropped kisses on his face. He wriggled in her arms.

"Go on," she said to him, "go play Statues with your cousins." To Sam she said, "I love games that cause them to stay still for half a second. Come up on the porch."

Charlie went to join in the game, quilt in tow, and Sam followed Belinda up onto the porch.

"What happened?" she asked, plopping down into her rocking chair.

Sam took the one beside her. "Emma happened."

Belinda smiled. "How'd she do it?"

"She didn't tell you about the quilt?"

Belinda shook her head.

He nodded in Charlie's direction. "She made it from one of Valerie's dresses."

"That was so sweet of her."

"Charlie said, 'This quilt smells like my mommy.'"

Belinda's eyes swam with tears, and Sam had to look away to keep his own eyes from misting up. "She's quite a woman, that Emma."

"Don't I know it," Sam said. "But she's far more than I can ever hang on to."

"When it's meant to be, Sam, it's meant to be."

"I wish I could share your optimism."

"Give her some time to figure out what she really wants."

"Emma already knows what she wants. She's known since she was fourteen years old."

Belinda studied him a long moment. "I do believe she does."

"She'll get it too."

"I have no doubt." She reached over and patted his knee. "Have you told your mama about Charlie?"

"Not yet."

She stood up, held out her hand to him. "Come on," she said, "let's go call her. This news is gonna make her year."

CHAPTER FOURTEEN

If you've got the blues, need quick comfort,
and you're out of vodka, a quilt will
tide you over in a pinch.
—Raylene Pringle, owner of the Horny Toad Tavern and
member of the True Love Quilting Club

By Saturday night, Emma was a nervous wreck. She couldn't decide what to wear that would strike just the right note for her date with Sam. Finally, she ended up going with simplicity. A crisp, pink, button-down linen shirt that served as a jacket over a sleeveless white silk tee, blue jeans, and a pair of new cowgirl boots the same color blue as her jeans. The plan was to meet Sam at the Funny Farm.

The family-style restaurant did not take reservations. Because the home-style cooking was so popular and the place was usually wall-to-wall on the weekends, you had to come early in person to sign up for one of the nightly seating times. Sam had called to tell her he'd gone over at four when the hostess stand had opened and put them down for the eight P.M. seating.

She discovered that when you arrived, you waited in line outside while the restaurant emptied of the customers from the previous seating. Then the hostess rang a large dinner bell mounted on a streetlamp outside the restaurant, announcing it was time to enter the building. It created a relaxed, festive atmosphere as the street filled up with people. It was a great opportunity to gab with visiting tourists and fellow denizens of Twilight.

She got in line and glanced around just in time to see Sam ambling up Cobalt Avenue toward the square. He looked lean and lanky in an outfit much like hers—starched blue jeans, white Western-style shirt with silver snaps instead of buttons, and polished, chocolate-colored cowboy boots. He didn't wear a Stetson or a baseball cap emblazoned with a sports team like most of the men in the crowd. His hair was neatly combed down over his scar, and it looked slightly damp, as if he'd just gotten out of the shower and hadn't bothered with a blow-dryer.

He spied her and raised a hand in greeting.

Immediately she felt herself go breathless. God, he was handsome. It wasn't lost on her that several of the women in line turned to look at him as he stepped from the street to the sidewalk. She had a powerful urge to snatch their hair out by the roots. The ferocity of her jealousy startled her.

Sam gave her a slow, knowing grin, as if he could read her mind.

"What are you smirking about?" she asked as he came to a stop beside her.

"I'm not smirking," he denied, and smirked even bigger. "I'm just appreciating the way those jeans hug your behind."

The hostess clanged the dinner bell as if she was calling in hungry field hands. Waitresses in uniforms designed to resemble straitjackets, minus the arms-tied-behind-their-back feature, opened the wide double doors. The crowd poured inside as the waitresses passed out cards with color-coded seat assignments. The Funny Farm was new to Emma. It hadn't been there when she'd lived in Twilight before.

"How many in your party?" the waitress asked.

Sam held up two fingers.

The waitress handed him a pair of red cards with roosters printed on them. "You're upstairs."

"Thanks."

Inside, the walls of the restaurant were covered with farming equipment and memorabilia—an old horse-drawn plow, a glass butter mold, a shiny silver milk bucket, a couple of black-handled pitchforks.

Sam reached out and took Emma's hand, disconcerting her. She didn't pull back. She felt out of her element, and she had to remind herself to enjoy the ride but stay emotionally detached. He led her up the stairs to the section painted red and decorated with everything poultry—hens and chicks and roosters and eggs. He held out her chair for her and she sank down, looping the strap of her purse around the chair.

He walked around the table and took the seat opposite her.

"So," she said, unrolling the silverware from the napkin, and then settling the napkin in her lap. "So."

"At a loss for words?" His smirk was back and he lifted an eyebrow.

"Yes," she admitted. "This place is—"

"Rustic."

"I was going to say quaint, but rustic applies as well."

"Tourists love the Funny Farm."

"I can see that." Emma nodded at a family sitting near them. Mom, Dad, sister, two brothers. They had sunburned noses and windblown hair, as if they'd spent the day on the lake, and they all wore identical T-shirts that said: "I've Done Time at the Funny Farm."

Sam's grin widened.

"Whimsical," she said.

"That's Twilight."

"I'm amazed by how much the town hasn't changed. It feels like I've stepped back in time thirty years."

"We're not that backward."

She held up both palms. "Hey, it's a good thing. I like Twilight."

He cocked his head, angled her a speculative look. She was so aware of him—his size, his scent, his sinew and bones. She thought about that afternoon in the theater loft when they'd stared up at the stars together, and she gulped. She felt the movement slide all the way down her throat, leaving her feeling parched and restless.

"Yes," the waitress was saying to the twinsy family, "we do serve fried pickles."

Emma wrinkled her nose. "Fried pickles?"

"Don't knock it till you've tried it."

She shifted her legs, felt her knees brush against Sam's underneath the table. Oops. Quickly, she moved her legs away, but her gaze went straight to his face. Had he felt that? Did he think she'd touched him on purpose? Should she apologize for bumping into him or just let it go? "Should we order some?" she asked. "Fried pickles, I mean."

"Are you kidding? They're disgusting."

Dammit, she couldn't stop staring at him, couldn't stop watching his angular lips open and close as he spoke. "But you said—"

"I was merely making a point."

"That being?"

"You shouldn't make judgments until all the facts are in. Even then, you should be careful, there are always unknown factors."

She propped an elbow on the arm of her chair. "Not everyone can be as studied and controlled as you. Some of us just like to make our mistakes and get it over with."

"But if you took time to ponder, you might not make so many mistakes."

"Sometimes pondering can be a mistake in and of itself. For example, say a runaway truck was speeding toward you. Me, I'd just get out of the way. You'd stand there pondering and more than likely get squashed." *What are you doing? Why are you acting like such a goofball? You're on a date with Sam. You shouldn't be dreaming up whacky what-if scenarios.*

"That's a bad example," he said.

"How so?"

"For one thing, what caused the truck to be runaway?"

"I don't know. The driver forgot to engage the brake?"

"If the driver forgot to engage the brakes, how come it's speeding and not just simply rolling back?"

"It's on a very steep hill."

"And the driver forgot to engage the brakes?"

"That's right."

"Then he's either intoxicated or a total dumbass and deserves to be sued."

"What happened to the pondering and withholding judgment? You've already sued the guy. What if he was really distracted? What if his kid was sick?"

"It's not a real guy, it's just a hypothetical situation you cooked up."

"So you agree?"

He looked confused. "About what?"

"I would have leaped to safety and you'd be a pancake."

"I agree to no such thing."

"Look, in the time it took for you to analyze and question me, you could have jumped to safety."

"Except for the fact there is no stupid, drunken driver with a sick kid, no runaway truck."

"But there could be."

"You've got some kind of imagination. You know that?"

"So I've been told."

"What'll y'all have to drink?" asked the perky waitress who sashayed up to their table. She had her hair pulled back with a red kerchief and wore a red gingham apron over her short-skirted uniform. She looked like a milkmaid, which Emma supposed was the idea.

"I'll have iced tea," Sam said.

"Nothing alcoholic?" Emma asked.

Sam shook his head. "I don't drink much."

"Ah, but this is Saturday night and a special occasion."

He shrugged. "Okay. I'll have a beer, whatever you've got on tap."

"And for you, ma'am?" The waitress stood poised.

"I'll have the same."

"Gotcha. Two beers coming right up."

Sam gazed into Emma's eyes as if he could see straight through to her soul. Unnerved, she moistened her lips, but the dryness hung on. Where was the waitress with that beer?

Quick, think of something to say.

"So," she said, picking up her menu. "What's good here?"

"I always get the roast beef. Charlie likes the chicken-fried steak."

The waitress returned with their beers and took their food orders and they tried again for light conversation, but the mood felt awkward. This wasn't the way she'd wanted their first date to go.

He reached across the table, touched her hand. "I want to thank you for more than just getting Charlie to talk."

"Oh?" she said lightly, her pulse fluttering as he looked into her eyes.

"You've helped me to see that I was holding myself back, and by holding myself back, I was holding Charlie back as well. I've decided it's time to stretch the dimensions of my world."

"That's wonderful," she said.

"You make me feel alive in a way I haven't felt in a long time."

You do the same for me.

And then just like that the awkwardness passed and they connected with a click. He was changing her, she realized, in ways too unsettling to examine. She was getting too close to him, and she knew it, but she couldn't think of how to stop. She'd tried staying away and that hadn't worked at all.

Their meal arrived, and as they ate, they talked. About their childhood, their pasts. She told Sam funny stories about New York. He matched them with tales from the life of a small-town veterinarian. She found herself telling him things she'd never told anyone. About her doubts and fears. About the loneliness she tried so hard to keep hidden.

Sam let her talk. He stroked her knuckles with his fingers, but he didn't offer any commentary.

And yet, the more she revealed to him, the more her chest tightened with tension. She was deeply drawn to him, but in that path lay danger. The closer she got, the more her independence slipped away. She was going to get hurt. She knew it, but couldn't help the fall.

So when he said, "Would you like to go somewhere after dinner?" she answered, "I never thought you'd ask."

The parking lot of the Horny Toad Tavern was packed with pickup trucks, SUVs, and a car or two. Sam parked the Jeep under the vapor lamp. After dinner, they'd walked back to his house to pick it up. He hadn't set foot in the tavern since his college days, and even then, he hadn't been much of a partyer. He'd simply gone along with his brothers and friends. He rarely drank. He didn't care for the taste of liquor or the way it made him feel, so he would order a beer and nurse it all night. He quickly figured out his friends asked him along so he could be their designated driver. That was okay with Sam. Just as long as no one expected him to be the life of the party. He left the spotlight to those who enjoyed it. Like Emma.

Except tonight. She seemed determined to drag him into the spotlight with her. The minute they walked through the door, her hips started twitching in time to the music. Over on the dance floor boots were scooting to the live band playing "Little Miss Honky Tonk." She turned, took his hand, and started walking backward to the dance floor.

He pulled his hand back, held up his palms. "Whoa," he said. "I'm going to need a little loosening up before you can convince me to get out there and make a fool of myself."

She canted her head and looked as if she might argue with him, but then she nodded. "You need foreplay before the floor play."

"I wouldn't put it like that . . ." He couldn't help grinning.

"I would." She grinned back. "Come on. Let's go see if we can find a table."

He scanned the room, but the place was packed. "Maybe we should come back another time when it's not so crowded."

"I'm not letting you off the hook that easily, Doc. Oh, look." She pointed. "It's some of the women from the quilting club and they're waving us over."

Sam groaned.

Emma nudged him with an elbow. "Don't be such a grumpy old hermit. Socializing will do you a world of good."

"In what universe?" he muttered under his breath.

"In my universe," she said, and took his hand again.

Feeling like a dinghy being towed by a flashy speedboat, he followed her to the big table in the corner near the pool tables, where the women were already shifting to make a space for them.

"Hey, Emma, hey, Sam," the group—consisting of his aunt Belinda, his sister Jenny, Terri Longoria, and Dotty Mae Densmore—greeted them.

"Hey, everybody." Emma plunked down and patted the seat of the empty chair beside her.

"Evenin', ladies," Sam said, and eased down beside Emma. "Where are your menfolk?"

"Girls' night out," Terry said. "Ted's on call."

"Harvey's watching the kids." Belinda took a pull of her strawberry daiquiri.

"Dean's holding down the fort at the B&B." Jenny raked a hand through her hair.

"Whatcha all up to?" asked Dotty Mae.

"We're out on the town celebrating Charlie's accomplishment," Emma said.

"Why, isn't that nice," Belinda said. "You *are* going to take Emma for a spin around the dance floor, aren't you, Sam?"

"I am," Sam surprised himself by saying.

"Well, lookee here." Raylene Pringle sashayed over. She came up behind Sam and rested a hand on his shoulder. "I haven't seen you in the Horny Toad since that time your brother Ben broke up with his girlfriend, got drunk, and punched a hole in my Wurlitzer with his bare fist."

"That was almost ten years ago," Jenny said.

Raylene tapped her temple with an index finger. "I got a good memory and I've been known to hold a grudge, especially when it costs me money. So what'll you have?"

"You waitin' tables tonight, Raylene?" Terri asked.

Raylene rolled her eyes. "That Holloway girl we hired called in sick, but I heard through the grapevine she's preggers by one of the Townsends. Those boys are pure rascals."

"That they are." Dotty Mae nodded.

"I'll have a beer," Sam said. He wasn't much on gossip. "And Emma will have a . . ." He paused, looked at her.

"Beer?" Emma said. "I thought you were going to live a little."

"For me this is living a little."

"How 'bout a margarita," Raylene said. "They're not too sweet the way Sonny makes them."

Emma rubbed his arm. "Come on, let down your guard a little. It's okay to let loose once in a while. Charlie's with his grandparents, Maddie's out of town. For one night you have no one to answer to. You deserve to have a little fun."

Sam looked over at Emma. Her eyes glowed with a devilish light. Copper-colored curls bounced around her shoulders when she turned her head, giving her a pert, girl-next-door appearance. The pink linen blouse she wore complemented her peaches and cream complexion. And the gloss she'd applied made her lips look wet and shiny. God, she was gorgeous.

"I'll have one of those margaritas, Raylene." Emma held his gaze, visually daring him to go for it.

What the hell? If he was going to get out on that dance floor, maybe being halfway lit wasn't such a bad idea. Sam didn't look away. "Bring me one too."

"I'll be right back." Raylene sauntered off.

Emma smiled at him, and it felt like the sun had finally come out after a long winter storm.

The whole table hooted their approval.

"I don't know what magic you've worked on him." Jenny raised both thumbs in the air. "But anyone who can get my little brother out of the house and the animal clinic gets my vote."

"I'm not that entrenched," Sam protested.

"The hell you're not." Jenny wagged her head.

"Okay, so I'm a stick-in-the-mud. But I'm out now and I'm ordering margaritas and"—he cast a glance over his shoulder—"contemplating line dancing. So I don't want to hear more lip from anyone. Got it?"

"Yes sir." Jenny saluted him with a smirk.

Emma stacked her hands on the table in front of her and leaned forward, unwittingly exposing her cleavage. "So have you guys hit the dance floor yet?"

Sam just happened to be looking down at just the right time. He didn't intend to ogle, but hell, a man would have to be stone-cold numb beneath the waist not to notice a pair of tits like that. Round and firm and ripe like Texas peaches in mid-July.

He lounged back in his chair to get a better view and couldn't help grinning to himself. He had to admit, he liked the way she made him feel. Lusty. Alive.

"Here you are. Two margaritas on the rocks." Raylene slid the drinks in front of Sam and Emma. "You wanna start a tab?"

"I think one will be enough for me." Sam pulled a twenty from his pocket and handed it to Raylene.

"Yes," Jenny said. "Heaven forbid, Sam have two drinks."

"What? Do you want me to get drunk?"

"Might be interesting. I've never seen you drunk." His sister stuck out her tongue at him.

"That's because I've never been drunk."

"Seriously?" Emma swung her head around to take his measure.

"It's not my style."

"Here's to Sam having a style all his own," Emma said, and lifted her glass.

"To Sam," everyone else chimed in, and they all clinked glasses.

Except for Sam. He was embarrassed. "How perverse is this?" he asked. "Drinking to sobriety?"

"Come on," Emma egged him on. "Take a sip."

He took a sip of the lime-flavored drink. It packed a wallop. "How big was that tequila jigger, Raylene?"

"Big enough, cowboy." Raylene patted him on the head. "Let me know if you change your mind about wanting another."

"You women are ganging up on me," he said as the liquid slid smoothly down his throat. "One big sister is bad enough—"

"It's what happens when you crash girls' night out." Jenny winked.

"You ready for that dance now?" Emma asked. "It's beginning to look like the lesser of two evils."

"You got a point." Sam took another swig of the margarita to help fortify himself.

"Could I just scooch out?" Belinda asked, getting to her feet.

"Sure, sure." Sam scooted back his chair, and after Belinda slipped by him and disappeared into the crowd, he got to his feet and held out his hand to Emma. "May I have this dance?"

"I thought you'd never ask." She sank her delicate little hand into his, and he felt like a hulking oaf. She was so petite. Just as they reached the dance floor the song ended. He caught a glimpse of Belinda whispering something to a band member. What was his aunt up to? He got the answer to his question a second later. Belinda couldn't help herself. Matchmaking was in her DNA. He should have been irritated. Normally, he would have been irritated. Instead, he was touched, and for the life of him, he didn't know why.

"We're gonna mix things up, folks," said the lead guitarist. "This one's a waltz, and it's going out to all you couples out there who ended up with your high school sweethearts and still love 'em."

"Oops," Emma said, "maybe we should sit this one out." She turned to head back to her seat as people shifted, some going to the dance floor, others stepping away.

"Whoa." Sam snagged her elbow. "You aren't running out on me now. You asked for a dance, I'm giving you a dance."

"But this is a waltz."

"And?"

"It's dedicated to lovers."

"And?"

"We're not lovers."

"No, but we were once high school sweethearts."

"Not really. We were more friends than anything else, until . . . well . . . you know."

"Yeah." He lowered his eyelids and his voice. "I know."

The pulse at the hollow of her neck fluttered fast and she ducked her head, tugged against his grip. "Let's wait for something livelier."

"You've been poking at me to get out and live a little, and just when I'm ready to do that, you get cold feet and try to take off on me."

"A waltz is intimate."

"And what's wrong with that?"

The column of her throat moved as she swallowed.

The band started up the opening strains of "Waltz Across Texas." At the sound of the unofficial honky-tonk anthem of Texas, even more people got up and headed for the dance floor. Belinda had requested a good one. As the man at the mike sang the lyrics, Sam swept Emma into his arms. It was a song about a man who got his storybook ending with the starry-eyed woman he loved, and all he wanted to do was waltz her across Texas.

He looked down into Emma's eyes, and emotions slammed into him in such rapid succession he couldn't sort them—melancholia, exhilaration, apprehension, hope, and raw sexual attraction. He seized on that last one. It seemed safest. It was basic, understandable. The other feelings were just too damn risky to entertain.

It had to be the tequila making him feel so sentimental. The tequila and the music and the feel of Emma in his arms. He'd learned to waltz with her in his mind, secretly hoping that one day, some way, he would waltz with her, and now that that day had come, he couldn't believe it or trust in it.

The Horny Toad Tavern was filled with what could have been and what would never be between them. But for this precious moment in time, they were together. Waltzing. Time shifted beneath their feet. They were caught in a glorious time warp, fourteen-year-old sweethearts too young to explore their passion, now all grown up and reunited if only for a whisper of a moment. They were at once earnest kids and wary adults.

A dozen different emotions flitted across Emma's

face, mirroring what was going on inside Sam's head. For one brief second he could have sworn he saw a mist of tears in her eyes, but she blinked and it was gone.

They swayed to the music, their gazes welded. She sighed, and the bittersweet sound seeped through Sam, ripping any last remaining threads of his sobriety. Never mind the tequila. This intoxication came from the scent of Emma in his nostrils, the feel of her soft body pressed against him.

And then she did something that unwound him completely. She rested her head against his shoulder, buried her face in his neck.

His heart pounded. He tightened his arm around her waist. In that moment, she owned him. He felt it. The sharp throb of sexual energy bubbled up inside him. The music strummed, vibrating the air, pulsating through their bodies as they moved together in flawless harmony.

"Sam," she murmured, her mouth brushing against the bare flesh of his collarbone.

The sweet sound of her voice, so vulnerable and tender, shivered through him. He lowered his head, gently kissed her forehead. They waltzed around the other dancers, gliding underneath the revolving crystal sphere overhead. Someone had lowered the main lights when the waltz began, and it cast silvery slants of light over them, bathing the moment in longing and faux starlight.

Her tight, compact body was melded against his. Sam could feel every curve, every angle, making him want things he had no business wanting. There was chemistry between them. A blind man could see it. But, dammit, they weren't right for each other no matter how badly he might want it to be so. They wanted different things from life, and he had responsibilities he could not deny.

"Emma." He half whispered, half groaned her name.

She pulled back and looked into his face, studying him as if seeking answers to an unspoken question. Her green eyes were both innocent and worldly. Her thick copper-colored hair rolled down her shoulders, chaotic as a waterfall. The look she gave him arrowed straight through his heart and stopped his breathing.

He blinked, dazed, even as a piece of him hummed with the gift of holding her in his arms. He stared into her and she stared into him and Sam just felt wiped out.

Around them couples waltzed, the sound of boots sliding across the cement floor creating its own kind of sibilant harmony, surrounding them in a cocoon of music.

Waltzing, waltzing, waltzing.

The yeasty smell of beer and the acrid twang of burnt popcorn mingled with the odor of stale cigarette smoke and ladies' perfumes. On his tongue, in his mouth was the taste of tequila and the sharp flavor of the past.

Emma looked up at him, splayed a palm over his heart, her eyes wide and curious. His pulse quickened. He felt as shaken as a James Bond martini.

Then the song ended and the band announced they were taking a break.

Leaving Emma and Sam standing in the middle of the dance floor in a long, awkward moment as fantasy vanished and reality returned.

Chapter Fifteen

Best hangover cure? Two aspirin, one gallon of water, and a soft quilt to crawl under while you sleep it off.
—Earl Pringle, owner and proprietor of the Horny Toad Tavern

The expression in Emma's eyes had Sam's gut in knots. Hell, what had he done? Why had he agreed to come to the Horny Toad? Why had he drunk a margarita? Why had he waltzed her across Texas? He was in trouble, treading on shaky ground.

Shit. How had he gotten here? He stared at her and wished the evening had never happened. *As long as you're wishing, why not wish she'd never come back to town at all?*

That thought made him feel even worse. Who was he kidding? From the moment he'd seen her standing on his front porch, all those old teenage fantasies had come rushing back with the intrusion of a Sherman tank.

She took a step back, jerked a thumb in the direction of the ladies' room. "I'm gonna . . . you know . . ."

He nodded, smiled like everything was just dandy, and jammed his hands into his pockets. She was everything he shouldn't want, but as he watched her back pockets sway as she walked away, his body burned for her.

This wasn't good. Not good at all. He shouldn't be throbbing like one gigantic exposed nerve. He was a professional, an animal doctor, a dad. He had too much to lose. He forced himself to stop looking at her, turned and headed for their table. The ladies from the quilting club had dispersed and he found himself sitting alone. He took a long pull of his margarita in a vain attempt to quell the fire burning inside him.

"Check out the ass on that redhead," laughed an oversized man in coveralls and a straw cowboy hat standing at a nearby pool table. He was leaning on his pool cue, waiting his turn to shoot.

"Where?" asked his skinny companion. The guy had a ponytail that hung to his back and so many tattoos on his forearm, it looked like he was wearing a long-sleeved shirt.

"She just left the dance floor all by her lonesome."

"You know her? I ain't never seen her in here before."

"Looks like she could use some company."

"I'd like to break her over like a shotgun." The string bean sniggered. "That's what I'd like to do."

"You gotta wonder on a redhead like that does the carpet match the drapes?"

The two cretins smirked and made suggestive motions with their hands.

That was all the provocation Sam needed to say something to the redneck assholes. It wasn't like him. He was accustomed to tempering his anger with prudence and holding his tongue in the heat of the moment, but he couldn't allow them to say such things about Emma. He fisted his hands, clenched his jaw.

At that very moment, Emma walked past the pool table on her return from the ladies' room.

The skinny guy whistled, and the beefy one reached out and slapped her on the rump.

Sam saw red. Literally. The bar blurred into a crimson glow. Heat rushed up his neck, the veins at his temple pounded. Rage surged through him as fast and overpowering as a flash flood. He'd never experienced anything so all-consuming. He heard someone snort like a bull and realized it was he. Blindly he jumped up from his chair, pushing aside tables, knocking over glasses and beer bottles in a blind rush to get to her.

He clamped a hand on Coveralls's shoulder. Up close the guy was the size of a Clydesdale. "Apologize to the lady," Sam ground out through clenched teeth.

"Piss off," snarled Coveralls while his squirrely little buddy sniggered and jumped around, swinging his pool cue like a hillbilly ninja.

The guy might be big, but he was drunk. Sam saw the punch coming long before Coveralls swung.

Sam ducked and simultaneously planted his fist in Coveralls's gut. He might be a pacifist at heart, but he'd grown up with three brothers. He knew how to fight.

"Ooph." Coveralls's knees bobbled.

Crack!

Sam heard the sound first, tasted blood second, felt the blast of pain third. He jerked his head around to see the ponytailed, tattooed string bean wielding the pool cue now broken in two.

"That'll teach ya," the guy said in a nasally voice. "That'll teach ya."

Sam wadded up his fist to swing at the guy, but the distraction had given Coveralls just enough time to recover. He launched himself at Sam, punching hard.

It was two against one, but Sam was holding his own, that is until their friends jumped in. How come he hadn't realized they had friends?

"Take it outside, take it outside," Earl Pringle was standing on the bar hollering.

The side door opened and people went spilling into the parking lot. Someone shoved Sam. Sam shoved back, but he couldn't fight the flow of bodies. They were outside, the tepid night breeze blowing over his skin. Stars dotted the sky but he had no chance to notice them. He was in his first bar brawl. People were pushing and hitting and gouging and cussing. The air smelled like beer and engine exhaust. The taste of blood trickled down the back of his throat.

Someone was walking on the hood of a pickup truck in cowboy boots, *clomp, clomp, clomp*. A woman shrieked.

Where was Emma? Was she okay?

He turned his head, scanning for her, but in the melee of arms and legs coming at him, he couldn't see. Where was she? In his effort to find her, he failed to duck when Coveralls's meaty fist crashed into his face.

His head spun. His ears rang. His eye hurt like a son of a bitch.

"Stop hitting him, you giant jackass!" a woman hollered.

Emma.

He tried to glance around again, but between his blurry vision and his rubbery legs, his brain was having a really tough time getting any messages through.

Somebody, he didn't see who but he suspected it was the weasely guy with the ponytail, punched him hard in the stomach.

All the air left his body. His legs went out from under him and everything turned soupy black.

Sam lay groaning softly in the glass-strewn parking lot of the Horny Toad Tavern, blood sliding down his forehead and pooling in the ridges of his old scar. The thugs who'd beaten him had packed into the pickup bed of a Ford F–150. The zigzagging red taillights winked away in the darkness. The rest of the crowd had dispersed as well.

Emma knelt beside him, her heart wrenching in her chest. He'd gotten clobbered fighting for her honor. "Sam, Sam, can you hear me?"

He didn't answer.

Gently she slapped his cheeks in an attempt to rouse him from his stupor. "Sam? Sam? Speak to me. Please speak to me. Are you okay?"

"Honey, you better get him out of here," said Raylene from the open doorway of the bar. "Earl's called the cops, and unless you wanna go through a lot of rigmarole it's best to be gone by the time they show up."

As if to punctuate her statement, the wail of police sirens rent the night.

"Come on, Sam, you gotta wake up. We gotta get out of here unless you want to spend the night in the pokey. Look at me, Sam."

"Huh?" He shook his head and pried his eyes open, or at least one of them. His gaze seemed fuzzy and out of focus. He wasn't looking at her and he kept blinking. Crap, this was bad.

"Sam." She grasped his chin in her hand. "Do you know who I am?"

"Trissy Lynn," he slurred.

Punch drunk. The man was punch drunk.

"I like that blousss," he said, reaching up to latch a finger at the neck of her T-shirt. "It shows off your boobies."

"What?" Emma looked down and saw that yes indeed, bent over the way she was, he had an excellent view of her cleavage. She quickly buttoned up the pink blouse she was wearing over the tee.

"Awww, don't put 'em away on my account."

She snapped her fingers. "Come on. You've gotta concentrate. We have to get you to the Jeep before the cops show up."

"Okay, okay, concentrating." He furrowed his brow. "Ow, that hurts."

The sirens wailed closer.

"Come on, hurry, I'll help you up."

"You are sooo pretty," he murmured.

"I'm just going to lever you up off the ground with my shoulder," Emma said.

"Hang on honey, I'll help you." Raylene minced over in her stilettos.

"What happened to Terri and Belinda and Jenny?" she asked Raylene.

"They went home before the fightin' even started. I could kick Earl's behind for calling the cops. I mean sure, I wouldn't care if those other two assholes got thrown in jail, but I don't want to see Sam in trouble."

Then to Sam she said, "Listen to me, Sam Cheek, you gotta get with the program. Little Bit here and I ain't that strong. You're gonna have to help us."

Sam shook his head vigorously as if to clear it. "I'm up, I've got it." He struggled to his knees.

Raylene took one arm, Emma took the other, and they tugged him to a standing position. He swayed on his feet and put a hand to his forehead.

"Are you dizzy?" Emma asked.

"It's passing."

"Take him home, give him a big glass of water, clean him up, and put him to bed," Raylene advised.

"Shouldn't I get him to a doctor?"

Raylene stood on tiptoes, eyed the cut on Sam's head. "Flesh wound. I've seen worse."

"He could have a concussion."

"Do you know where you are, Sam?" Raylene asked.

Sam slid Emma a chiding look. "Somewhere I shouldn't be."

"What your mama's maiden name?"

"Guthery."

"How old were you when you lost your virginity?"

"Raylene!"

"What?" Raylene shrugged. "Don't get your panties in a bunch. I know it wasn't with you, Emma. He's not gonna be giving away any secrets."

"Eighteen," Sam answered. "My freshman year in college. Her name was Molly Hampton."

"All you Cheek boys were late bloomers." Raylene eyed Sam. "But bloom you did."

"What does this have to do with anything?" Emma snorted.

"He remembers the important stuff." Raylene patted his shoulder. "He's fine."

The sirens shrilled louder the closer they drew.

Raylene trotted over to the passenger side of Sam's Jeep and flung the door open. "Y'all better go *now.*"

Emma slipped an arm around his waist. "Come on, I'll hold you steady."

Sam laughed then. It was a short, abbreviated sound. "Remind me not to do that," he said. "Makes my head hurt worse."

Somehow they managed to get him into the Jeep and out of the parking lot before the cops came pulling up. In the rearview mirror, Emma saw Raylene waving down the patrol officers.

"Whew." She breathed. "That was a close call."

"Are we having fun yet?" Sam asked.

She slid a glance over him. "Hey, don't blame me. No one told you to punch the big guy in coveralls."

Sam rested his head against the window. "He slapped you on the ass."

"You make a habit out of this knight-in-shining-armor thing?"

"Only when it comes to you, Trixie Lynn."

That pleased her more than it should have. These feelings she had for Sam were getting more complicated by the minute and she didn't know how to combat them.

Who says you have to combat them? Go with the flow.

"I could have handled Coveralls, I *am* from Manhattan, but thanks for intervening." She smiled at him. "It was sweet."

"Sweet?" he growled. "Is that how you see me?"

"There's nothing wrong with sweet."

"Women go crazy for the bad boys, not for *sweet* guys."

"Valerie didn't."

He made an odd noise.

Emma turned her head to look at him. "What?"

"It wasn't like that with Valerie and me."

"What do you mean?"

He shrugged. "I guess you could say it was marriage of comfort. She was a good person and she had Charlie, and after her husband was killed, she had no one to look after her."

"So you just volunteered?"

"Not exactly. I mean we were friends and one day I came over to fix her dishwasher and she cooked me dinner and we drank a couple of beers and we ended up in bed together, and while the earth didn't shatter, it was pleasant enough and we both realized that we shared the same values and that we wanted the same things in life, so we started dating. Then when the Army called Val up, she had no one to leave Charlie with. Jeff's parents are in their eighties, so I asked her to marry me and adopted Charlie."

"I suppose people get married for far worse reasons."

"What about you?"

"What about me?" She kept her eyes trained on the road. She was still a novice driver.

"You ever been married?"

"No."

"Ever been engaged?"

"Not even close." She braked at the stoplight in front of the Albertsons even though there wasn't another car on the road at this time of night.

"Why not? Afraid of commitment?"

"I didn't want a relationship to derail my career. In

retrospect I can see that was shortsighted since I have no career."

"You have a career. You've been in sixteen plays and—"

"All off-off-Broadway. And how do you know that?"

"The power of Google."

"You Googled me?"

"Does that upset you?"

It pleased the hell out of her. "No, I'm just surprised that you took the time."

"Now why would that surprise you?"

She darted a quick glance his way before hitting the accelerator again when the light turned green. "I thought you had better things to do. You're a busy guy."

"We make time for the things that interest us."

"I interest you?"

Sam snorted. "I just got my head beaned over you, what do you think?"

"I didn't ask you to do that."

"What? You wanted Coveralls's hands all over your ass?"

"No, I didn't need rescuing."

"I'm sorry, Emma, I'm not going to stand by while the woman I—" Abruptly, he broke off.

Suddenly, she was desperate to hear him finish his thought. Her ramshackle heart lurched. "What?"

"While some guy disrespects the woman I'm with," he finished.

Somehow she didn't think that was what he'd originally intended on saying. "You know what your problem is?"

"I didn't realize I had a problem."

"You've got blood drying on your temple, I'd say that's a problem."

"Okay, fine. What's my problem?"

"You've got a Sir Galahad complex."

He turned in his seat. "And you know this how, Dr. Freud?"

She could feel the heat of his gaze as she studied her profile. "It was Sam to the rescue when Valerie needed a man in her life, and when Coveralls grabbed my ass, you immediately stepped in."

"I was just doing what any self-respecting man would."

"Take care of the womenfolk?"

"If they need taking care of yeah, what's so wrong with that?"

Emma blew out her breath. "I knew Twilight was thirty years behind the times, but I had no idea you were too."

"If being modern means standing by when you could have helped someone, then I'm proud to be archaic."

She didn't even know why she was arguing with him. In all honesty she was glad he jumped in when the beefy guy in coveralls went after her. She didn't like that Sam had gotten hurt, but a part of her thrilled to the fact that he had fought for her honor. His chivalry made her feel safe, protected.

It occurred to her then why she was acting so testy when she should be thanking him profusely. She couldn't dare get used to feeling this way. It would be too hard when she had to go back into the real world and fend for herself again.

"Do you know what your problem is?" he asked.

"I don't know how to keep my mouth shut?"

His smile was wry. "There is that, but I'm referring to your independent streak."

"What about my independent streak?"

"Once in a while, you have to let other people help you. No one is an island. We all need someone to help us through the tough times."

"Gee, what pillow did you see with that homily embroidered on it?"

He laughed. "Valerie patchworked it into a quilt."

She parked the Jeep in his driveway and they went inside. "Come on," she said. "Let's get you cleaned up."

"I can handle it from here."

"No, no. It cuts both ways. You got hurt fighting for my honor. That means I get to doctor you up."

"All right," he conceded. "I'll let you play nurse-maid if you have your heart set on it. I'll go get the first aid kit. Help yourself to something to drink."

"You want anything?"

"Tall glass of water."

He headed upstairs while Emma wandered into the kitchen to make two glasses of iced water. When she turned around, he was standing in the doorway, first aid kit in hand. She took one look at him—blood matting his hair to the scar on his forehead, his dark eyes not just looking at her but staring *into* her—and her heartstrings tugged. She was treading on shaky ground here. Emotional quicksand of the most dangerous kind.

His eyes told her things that his pride and his caution could not let him say out loud. When he stepped across the linoleum to gently cup her cheek in the palm of his hand, his tenderness rocked her to the core. He was trying so hard, struggling with his inability to express what he was really feeling. From a man like Sam, that simple gesture meant so much.

Then the look vanished from his eyes and he moved away from her, setting the first aid kit on the table, going over to a kitchen chair, turning it around, plunking down in it backward. He sat with the back of the chair flush with his chest, his arms folded over the top.

"Where's Patches?" she asked, opening up the first aid kit.

"Backyard. I don't like leaving him cooped up in the house when I'm not home."

"Should we let him in?"

"You're feeling completely comfortable around him now?"

"Thanks to you." She retrieved a package of gauze and a bottle of hydrogen peroxide from the kit.

"We can let him stay out awhile longer," Sam said. "I'll bring him in after I walk you home."

Home.

The sound of the word stirred something sentimental inside her. *Don't go all sappy on me. Twilight isn't your home. Your main goal is to do well in this play, get your reputation back, and get back to New York ASAP.* To chase the thoughts away, she concentrated on soaking the gauze with peroxide.

Gently, she leaned over to dab Sam's wound.

He hissed in a breath.

"Sorry, sorry, I'm trying to be as gentle as I can."

"It's okay. Just cold."

Methodically, she washed away the blood and struggled not to notice the tingle that shot through her nipples when her breasts accidentally brushed against his shoulder. She ignored the feel of his warm breath on her skin. She denied the swell of his finely muscled biceps and disregarded the raspy sound of his breathing.

"You're going to have quite the shiner, but at least your eye isn't swelling shut."

"I'll live."

Emma brushed back the hair on his forehead and slid her fingers over his skin, washing the old scar.

He flinched.

"Did I hurt you?"

"No. I just . . . I suppose it's vain, but I hate for you to see my scar."

"You're sensitive about it."

He grunted. "Dumb."

"Not dumb. I get it."

"I didn't have many dates in high school because of it," he said. "It looked really raw for years."

"It's why you grew your hair long."

"Yeah."

"It must have been a lot to deal with."

"Other people carry much worse burdens. Take Beau for instance."

"I wish I could have been here for you. It wouldn't have bothered me one bit."

"I know," he said softly, and she could tell he meant it. "It's probably a good thing you left when you did. As hot and heavy as we were getting, we'd have gotten into big trouble."

"Oh, you think so?"

"Emma, I dreamed about you every night for months. The kind of hot and horny dreams only a teenage boy can dream."

"Aww," she teased. "You telling me you've passed your peak?"

"I've still got some life left in me."

"Yeah, I felt some of that life on the dance floor. Not too shabby, Dr. Cheek." Emma tilted her head, trying to get a better glimpse of the wound on his head. Gently, she took clean, dry gauze and patted it dry. "I don't think you're going to need stitches. It looks like it's stopped bleeding."

Sam shifted, turning around in the chair. He slipped an arm around Emma's waist and pulled her down into his lap. Her back was to him, her legs straddling his.

"Oops, what's this all about?"

"What do you think?" he asked, and brushed his exploring lips against the curve of her neck.

She shivered against the sensual promise.

He nibbled lightly at her skin, and when he found the spot that made her squirm, he deepened the pressure. She leaned her head back against his shoulder, giving his tongue free access to the erogenous zone she hadn't even known was there.

While his tongue was busy with her neck, his sly hand was creeping up underneath her blouse, his calloused palm skimming up over the smooth, flat skin of her belly, headed north.

She hooked her feet around his legs, pushed back into him harder. She should tell him to stop. Tell him that they really needed to think this thing through, but the sensations zinging through her dulled her mind and sharpened her nerve endings. She tingled from head to toe, and a sweet heaviness pooled low and deep inside her.

His fingers kept skating, up and around the band of her lacy bra. The next thing she knew her bra was undone and his fingers were caressing one of her nipples. Instantly, it hardened into a tight little bud of longing.

"Emma," he whispered, his breath hot on her neck. Sam shifted her in his lap until she was facing him. He stared into her eyes. "Damn, but you are beautiful."

"I'm not. I'm really rather ordinary—"

"Don't contradict me, Trixie Lynn. You've always been beyond gorgeous to me."

"And I never could figure out why," she whispered, addicted to peering into his cocoa-colored eyes.

"You've got the cutest little nose." He kissed the tip of it.

"Ah, so you're hot for my nose."

"And your lips. When it seems like every actress on television is going for that bee-stung look, you've got the sweetest cupid's-bow shape. Delicate, delicious."

"You think so?" she murmured.

"I know so." His eyes were focused on her lips, his lashes lowered to half mast. "And your body." He tightened his arm around his waist. "Don't even get me started."

She touched the tip of her tongue to her lips. "You think I'm sexy?"

"I want you so badly I can't breathe."

Hypnotized, she let him swallow her up with his eyes. "Sam."

"Em." He kissed her again, harder this time, more demanding. "But this isn't smart."

"Nope," she agreed, and brought her lips back to his.

"There's Charlie to consider."

"Of course."

"And you don't want to do anything to derail your career."

Right now the last thing on her mind was her career. She fisted the material of his shirt in one hand, hanging on to him like she was riding a wild bronco.

He splayed one hand to the nape of her neck, holding her solidly in place while he took his time, searched her mouth with his.

Instant heat flared through her, bathing her body with an incredible throbbing warmth. Sensation upon sensation built inside her, layer by layer.

Finally, he pulled his lips from hers, lifted her from his lap, and settled her on the floor. A soft sound of protest escaped her lips. Why was he stopping? She didn't want him to stop. All she wanted was to kiss him, touch him, taste him, smell him, make love to him all night long, never mind how stupid it might be. She couldn't control her desires any longer. They'd been dancing around this moment for weeks, and she wanted him.

Now.

He stood and reached for her hand. To walk her home? She tried to quell her disappointment, but she felt what she felt.

Then he surprised her completely by pulling her toward the staircase instead of the front door. Her heart started a restless pounding and her blood surged. This was it.

The moment she'd waited sixteen years for.

CHAPTER SIXTEEN

*There's nothing sexier than Emma stretched out
naked on my quilt.*
—Veterinarian Dr. Sam Cheek

He led her upstairs and she followed. Once in his bed-room, he flicked on a lamp with a soft, low-watt bulb. Her head was so stuffed with lust she didn't notice anything in the room beyond the king-sized bed sitting in the middle.

Uncharacteristically, she held back. "Are we sure—"

"Yes."

"It can't be for keeps," she said.

She didn't want to say it. She wanted it to be for keeps, but in her heart, she knew she couldn't give Sam what he needed, couldn't promise him what he deserved. If they were going to do this, he had to know up front it wasn't going to lead anywhere.

"I've got my eyes wide open." He pulled her to him.

Emma's hands were cupped between his chest and hers. "You've been drinking."

"I'm not that drunk."

"A beer at dinner, a margarita at the bar. You're not used to drinking . . ."

"I promise you're not taking advantage of me."

"And here I was thinking you were easy prey."

He kissed the top of her head, his hands moving to unbutton the pink shirt she wore over the white tee, slip it off her shoulders and let it drop to the floor. Then he cupped her chin in his palm and raised her face up to his. He peered deeply into her eyes. "I've wanted to do this for weeks."

"What took you so long?" she whispered.

"Fear."

"Of what?"

"Not being able to stop once I got a taste of you."

"What changed your mind?"

"I couldn't resist you a minute more," he said. "Arms up."

"What?"

"Your arms. Raise them over your head."

"Oh." She raised her arms, and he took the hem of her T-shirt in his hands and slowly pulled it up over her head, along with the bra that he'd unhooked while she sat in his lap in the kitchen. He bent to plant warm, moist kisses on her bare skin, kisses on her belly, the tops of her breasts, the hollow of her throat.

She stood before him, feeling suddenly shy. The look in his eyes was hot and hungry. If they took this step, there was no going back.

He stepped back to stare at her in the soft glow from the lamp. "You're more beautiful than I ever dreamed."

A heated flush swept up her body, and she covered her bare breasts with her folded arms.

"Don't hide from me, sweetheart." He dipped his head to kiss her.

His lips fired a fresh urgency inside her and she grabbed the front of his shirt. Laughing, he helped her strip it off. She splayed her palms over his rippled muscles, her fingers tracking the delineated lines, and she took joy in caressing his exquisitely muscled body.

"Hmm," he said, "your touch feels good."

Her fingers tangled in the springy dark hairs sprinkled over his chest. She tugged on them lightly and he pulled her closer, his arms tightening around her waist. As he did, she slid her hands around his back, checking out those amazing muscles as well. Everything about him electrified her—the feel of his hard planes and angles, the tangy smell of his skin, the heated taste of his mouth, the sounds of his masculine pleasure.

She could feel his erection straining hard against the zipper of his jeans. She molded her body to his, rocked urgently against him.

"Whoa, whoa," he said, "you're moving too fast. We've waited sixteen years for this moment and I want to savor every second."

"I don't think I can stand to wait any longer," she protested. "I want you. Need you so badly."

"Exactly why we're taking our time."

A disappointed whine escaped her throat.

"Soon enough, sweetheart. Soon enough." He turned away, leaving her bereft, and walked over to the stereo system she just now noticed sat on a shelf on the other side of the room. He picked up a remote, punched some buttons. The soft sounds of classical music filled the room. She couldn't help thinking that he and Valerie had made love to this music.

"Um, do you have a radio?"

"Not a fan of classical music?"

"I'd like something a little sexier. Satellite radio has a love song channel."

He handed her the remote. "Be my guest."

She fiddled with the buttons and found the station she was looking for. "Unchained Melody" was playing.

"Good choice," he said, and swept her into his arms again.

His kiss took her breath. She wanted to keep on kissing him and kissing him and kissing him. She'd been thinking they could make love, have an affair, and then she could just walk away. Go back to her life sated but unscathed. She was beginning to see that was impossible. If she did this with Sam, no matter where she went, no matter who she eventually ended up with, she was never going to be the same again. The realization clobbered her like a clout to the head. Her body tensed.

Sam must have sensed the change in her; he pulled back, looked into her eyes. "What is it? What's wrong?"

"I'm scared," she confessed.

"Me too."

"Maybe we shouldn't . . ."

"Shh." He placed a finger over her lips. "You're the one who's always telling me to take a chance, take a risk. Well, now here I am. Ready to risk everything for one glorious night with you. Don't back out on me now, Emma. Not when I need you most." This was a switch. Sam confessing he needed someone when he was usually the one being needed. "Just relax and know that you're completely safe with me."

"You're safe with me too," she said.

"I know." He kissed the top of her forehead and reached for the snap of her jeans.

Leisurely, he kissed his way down her face as, simultaneously, his fingers eased her zipper down. Kisses landed on her forehead, the tip of her nose, lips, chin, the underside of her throat. Down he went, sinking to his knees. His mouth roved over her breasts, gently playing with first one nipple and then the other, rolling them around on his tongue.

Her body stiffened, and, careful of his wounds, she threaded her fingers through his hair to keep from toppling over. With painstaking slowness he edged her jeans down her hips at the same time. It seemed to take him forever, and all the way, his wicked tongue kept licking little flames of heat all across her bare belly.

Her sex throbbed, begging him to hurry up and get down there.

When finally, *finally*, her jeans were around her ankles, he shifted to one side so she could kick them off.

Then he reached for her panties and began peeling them down, but suddenly stopped cold. "Emma!" He sucked in a breath. "What in the hell happened?"

She blinked down at him. "What do you mean?"

"You're . . . you're not . . ." He rocked back on his heels, splayed a palm to the nape of his neck, and looked absolutely shocked. "You've got absolutely no hair down there."

Emma laughed. "Stop it."

"Stop what?"

"You're pulling my leg, right?"

"About what?"

"You've never been with a woman who's had a Brazilian?"

"I'm hoping you're not talking about a Brazilian lover."

"I know Twilight is behind the times, but this is just sad."

"What is it?"

"Hot wax."

"Hot wax?" he repeated.

"They smear the wax on." She motioned toward her crotch. "Then they rip the hair off."

"Like in the movie *The 40-Year-Old Virgin* where the guy gets his chest waxed?"

"Yes, except it's . . . you know . . . down there."

Sam bit down on his knuckles. "God, but that must hurt like a bastard."

"You get used to it."

"How? You'd think no one would go back after the first time."

"The results are worth the pain, plus it helps to have a couple of glasses of wine before you go for your appointment. The more you do it, the less it hurts."

"And you just let strangers pour hot wax on you and yank it off?"

Emma cocked her head. "You've honestly never heard of a Brazilian?"

"Other than the people native to Brazil, no. It doesn't make me a freak. In fact . . ." He eyed the slick V at the apex of her thighs. "If you want to talk freaky . . ."

"I did not come here to be insulted. I'm leaving. Where's my clothes?" Emma pretended to be mad.

"You're not leaving."

"You bet I am, buster. You're making fun of my muff!"

"Hey, hey." He reached out to her. "I'm sorry. I didn't mean to make fun of you."

"That would sound a lot more convincing if you weren't smiling."

He tried to flatten his lips, but the corners kept tipping up.

Her nostrils flared. "Go on, admit it, your conventional sensibilities are insulted by my sleek, slick look."

"It's not that my sensibilities are insulted. You just caught me by surprise. I had an image in my head of what you looked like down there and I was expecting . . . well . . . I am a veterinarian. I like petting furry things."

"Well, I'm an actress and I live in New York, and among my peer group, au naturel down there just doesn't cut it."

"You could try going native while you're in Twilight. You've got a different peer group now."

"FYI, Terri Longoria has a technician who does bikini waxing at her gym."

"No?" Sam shook his head. "You mean there are women running around Twilight looking just like you?"

"Well, maybe not just like me. Most people just go for the bikini line, or a landing strip, not a full Brazilian."

"Landing strip?"

"You know, a little strip of hair about this long." She measured it off. "Like a landing strip. Don't you watch porn?"

"No, I'm a father. I can't have stuff like that in the house."

"Seriously?"

"Hmm." He scratched his head. "I guess I'm behind the times."

"Are you imagining all the women in Twilight with bare muffs?"

"Not all of them." Sam grinned. "But pretty much everyone under forty."

"What happened to petting furry things?"

"You did tell me I need to open myself up to new experiences." He reached for her. "Tell you what, I'm willing to plunge in with gusto and embrace this Brazilian thing if you'll stay the night."

Who could turn down an offer like that? Especially when the look in his eyes was one of pure lust. Whether Sam was willing to admit it or not, the novelty of her bare anatomy was turning him on.

"I just realized there's something else we haven't discussed," she said.

"Safe sex."

"Yeah."

"Do you have a condom?"

He shook his head. "But I can run down to Walgreens. They're open all night."

"I have one in my purse."

"Why didn't you just say so? I'll go get your purse." He darted for the door.

"Come back without those pants on," she called after him.

In the silence that followed in his wake, Emma took a deep breath. They'd had time to cool down. This was her opportunity to get dressed and get out of here before she did something that could not be reversed.

But she didn't want to go. Every fiber of her being wanted Sam. She'd thought about this moment—well, okay, minus the coitus interruptus with the Brazilian thing and the condom—since she was fourteen. Honestly, he was the ideal of masculinity she'd carried around in her head. Her expectations were through the roof. What if sex with Sam couldn't live up to her fantasy?

He came bursting back in the room, a little breathless, as if he'd run the whole way, buck naked.

Emma's mouth dropped open. He far exceeded any daydream. His bare tight butt flexed as he stalked toward her, the pale skin contrasting with his tanned legs. Spellbound, Emma could not wrench her gaze away.

He was magnificent. She'd never been with such a well-endowed man. She would remember his body for the rest of her life.

She shot a gaze to his face.

He grinned. Clearly, he knew he had a fabulous package. But it wasn't just this great butt and impressive penis that had her heart slamming into her chest wall. He was so handsome. She had no idea how he'd stayed unattached after Valerie's death. His dreamy brown eyes balanced his angular jaw and prominent cheekbones. His hair shone black as oil in the muted lamplight. The shaggy length suited his steady, nurturing nature. Veterinarian, father, gardener, a man who knew how to use both his heart and his hands.

"Emma," he said.

"Sam," she whispered.

They kissed again, even hotter than before. Sam cupped her breasts in his warm palms. Her nipples beaded hard beneath his hands, and he thumbed them ever so slightly. And they exhaled at the same time, breathing out each other's air.

She thought he was trembling, but then realized it was she.

"Sweetheart," he murmured, "are you okay?"

"I don't think my legs are going to hold me up."

"I'm feeling just as shaky," he admitted. "Let's lie down on the bed."

He threw back the quilt and climbed up on the bed, pulling her with him. They lay on their sides looking into each other's eyes. He reached out and planed his palm over the curve of her hip. "Tell me what you like, Em, I want to please you."

"I like the way you're touching me right now."

"How much pressure?"

"Velvet soft," she said.

"It's a starting point." He reached out, and with extraordinarily light strokes ran his fingertips across her belly.

Goose bumps spread over her arms.

His calloused hand contrasted erotically with her soft skin. He traced her body with his fingertips and blazed kisses with his mouth. Tenderly and thoughtfully he kissed the pulse leaping at her collarbone. Then he took tiny succulent nibbles over the length of her throat.

She tried to wriggle closer to him, she wanted to get in on the action, but he held her pinned. "My turn first," he said.

"No fair."

"You'll get your chance to pay me back."

His mouth journeyed south to her breasts now swollen with urgent need. His tongue flicked out to lick over one nipple, while his thumb achingly rubbed the other straining bud. His thigh tightened against her leg, and his penis hardened to pure, smooth steel.

"Sam . . ." she whispered his name on a sigh. She loved saying his name. "Sam."

"Mmm," he murmured, the sound vibrating erotically against her achy flesh.

He slid his hand slowly over her pubis, fully checking out her Brazilian.

She giggled until he settled directly on her most sensitive spot. His lips closed around the tiny throbbing head of her cleft while his fingers slipped into her wet entrance. In a matter of seconds, she was calling his name in a long, keening moan. Her body was locked in a surge of pleasure that rose higher and higher with each heated flick of his sinful tongue.

It was too much, she couldn't take it anymore. She grasped his hair to tug him away, but he reached up and manacled her wrists with his hands. Holding her pinned, driving her mad with desire.

His tongue laved her sensitive skin as he suckled her deeply. She writhed against him, trying to push her body into his, needing more at the very same time she felt utterly weak and exhausted. Barbed ribbons of fevered sensation unfurled straight to her throbbing sex. Her inner muscles contracted, quivered.

"Yes," she hissed as he moved his mouth back and forth in a steady, unrelenting strum. "Yes, yes, yes!"

Sam worked magic with his fingers, his tongue, leading her into alien terrain. He lifted her up to a place she'd never known existed. She loved the adventure of him. Between what he was doing to her and her own vivid, artistic responsiveness, Emma's senses short-circuited. She smelled sounds—she caught a whiff of chiming bells. Tasted shapes—a basket of circles spilled into her mouth. And heard colors—their sex noises echoed strawberry red.

Synesthesia. They used such imagination exercises in her acting classes, but she'd never actually experienced it.

Was this some kind of bizarre dream?

But this wasn't a dream. This new sensory awareness of him awoke something inside her, and all the old failures and disappointments fell away. He pushed Emma past her knowledge of herself. She had never before been so physically possessed. His movements shook her world. The walls of the room seemed to ripple. Everything moved and changed with her consciousness, her emotions flowing in a hundred different directions.

She rode his tongue, navigating the swell of pleasure and desire and discovery, and she experienced a sense of safety that she'd never felt before.

A bittersweet longing seized her as she realized this feeling could not last. She bit down on her lip, dismissing the wistful sadness. This was enough. A sweet slice of delight. She didn't do commitment. Had no role model for how a loving relationship operated. There was nothing to get sentimental over. They were simply having a good time. They'd both acknowledged that up front.

He kept going and going and going. The man had stamina, no doubt about it. The friction was maddening, his carnal tongue stealing away her worries until she was left whimpering and throbbing on the precipice edge.

And then everything splintered, shattering tight and hard as her orgasm broke in herky-jerky jolts.

"Emma," he whispered.

"Uh-huh?" she managed to murmur weakly.

"Don't think we're done yet."

She roused herself, propped up on her elbows to gaze at him through heavily lidded eyes.

His erection burgeoned rigid, darkening as capillaries filled to capacity. Amazed, she reached out to trace her finger over his velvety head and heard his sharp intake of breath.

He looked into her eyes, and simultaneously, they were in each other's arms, kissing, groaning, caressing. Hands and lips and tongues were everywhere. Sam pushed her back against the pillows, nudged her knees wide open with his leg. She tilted her hips up. He looked down into her eyes and eased into her.

She inhaled on a sigh as his long, thick heat glided inside her body. She grasped his shoulders, pressing her fingers into his skin.

He held her gaze. "I don't want to hurt you. I'm so big and you're so small."

"You're not hurting me."

"I'm not all the way in."

There was more? Impossible. "I can handle it," she said.

He pushed against her, and she felt her body shift to accommodate his size. He watched her face, sensitive to her nuances.

Now, with him deep in her moist wetness, she felt every twitch of his muscle. He lit her up inside. She had no thoughts beyond wanting him deeper, thrust completely to the hilt inside her.

"More," she said. "I want it all."

"Em," he whispered, then gave her what she craved.

She wrapped her legs around his waist and rocked him into her. Her fingers gripped his buttocks. Her turn to own him. Her turn for control.

Tumult.

Everything was urgent and desperate and frenzied. She felt like her heart encompassed the entire universe. Need. Such need. To find, to press, to soothe, to fly free.

They came together like twin shooting stars falling across the sky. Saturated, she could not tell where he began and she ended. No division. No separation. No room for anything else. Their oneness banged through their whole bodies, encompassed every cell.

She teemed with ecstasy. It felt spiky and robust and brilliant. Her second orgasm of the night ripped through her, a five-alarm blaze burning her to a crisp. She was warm and gooey and completely scorched and she loved it.

When it was over and they'd floated back to reality, Emma lay panting in his arms, the total obliteration of their joining redefining everything she ever thought she knew about sex.

He shifted her into his arms, and she turned her face into his chest. She felt utterly womanly and sweetly raw. "I've never felt anything like that, Em."

She heard his voice rumble through his chest. "Me either," she confessed.

"I'll never forget the first time we met. Even then, I knew you were special," Sam said. "You know why I hung out with you?"

"Because I was a live wire who shook up your safe little world?"

He grinned. "That wasn't my take on the situation."

Emma wriggled her eyebrows. "No?"

"I saw you taking a lot of daring chances and figured somebody better pull you back before you hurt yourself or got into serious trouble."

"Oh yeah?" She reached out to trace a fingertip down the length of his nose. "Like what?"

"What about that time you graffitied the old Twilight Bridge? If I hadn't served as lookout you would have gotten arrested by Sheriff Clinton Trainer."

"Please." Emma rolled her eyes. "I could have gotten away from him without you being there. It was a total thrill for you. You'd never stayed out that late in your life."

"Yeah, and I was grounded for two weeks because I missed curfew."

"The life of an outlaw comes with consequences," she teased.

"Then there was the time you tried to catch a copperhead."

"Hey, I was from the city, how was I to know it was a poisonous snake?"

"And what about the time you 'borrowed' your father's car and went joyriding and drove it into a ditch."

"There wasn't much joy to it," she grumbled. "You lectured me far more than Rex did. I was a lonely kid just acting out."

"I know," Sam said softly, then pulled her closer to him and kissed the tip of her nose.

"How pathetic was I?"

"Not pathetic at all. Every kid longs to be loved."

Powerful feelings pushed at her. Scary feelings. If she wasn't careful she was going to get hurt and get hurt big. Shoving away all thoughts of love and home and family, she sat up beside him, smiled big, and said, "Wanna go again?"

CHAPTER SEVENTEEN

A quilt by any other name wouldn't be the same.
—Hollywood actress Emma Parks

What in the hell was he going to do?

He'd told her this was nothing but fun and games, but he'd lied through his teeth, and now he was going to have to deal with the consequences. At the time, he would have said anything to get her into bed. He craved her that much.

But the rational Sam, with his brain temporarily drained of lust, knew that making love to her only made the cravings worse, not better. She couldn't be his, no matter how much he might want it to be so. He had a child to think of. A life here in Twilight. A family who loved him. A community he served.

And Emma had her dreams of stardom, and he knew if she remained unfettered she would achieve her goals. She had the drive and determination to make her big dreams a reality. She didn't need any complications, and he was a huge complication.

He wouldn't stand in her way. Those dreams had

sustained her for years. He wasn't about to be the one to put a kink in her plans. He had only one choice open to him. Pretend that tonight hadn't meant anything beyond stupendous sex.

Sam reached across the bed, felt the warm, small shape of her underneath the quilts. He turned onto his side, propped himself up on his elbow, and stared down at her.

The moonlight streaming in through the open curtains cast her sleeping features in a soft glow. His breathing grew shallow, and his eyes drank her in. He couldn't believe it. Here he was with Trixie Lynn after all these years.

Don't count on this feeling. You can't keep her. Enjoy it for what it is and then just let her go.

But Sam didn't know if he could do that. He'd never been casual about sex, and he'd been with only three women in his entire life. Molly Hampton in college, Valerie, and now Emma. He took relationships seriously. He wasn't a one-night-stand kind of guy. It simply wasn't the way he was hardwired. He wasn't prudish, he just cared about women too much to treat them like sex objects. He knew he was a rare male in that regard. His friends and brothers teased him about it, but he was who he was.

Steady Sam.

God, how boring. What did she see in him? Why was she here? She was smart, sharp, witty, daring, gorgeous. She could have any man she wanted. Why him?

Sam pushed a hank of hair from his eyes, and his chest tightened as he studied his sleeping beauty. He loved her so much it hurt to breathe. He knew he couldn't keep her, and the realization made this moment all the more precious.

But he didn't regret making love to her. Being here with her was one of the most joyous events in his life.

He trailed his hand along her body, learning the slope of her shoulders, memorizing the arc of her breast, her taut flat stomach, the sweet triangle she'd removed of hair. He smiled into the darkness. Proud of her courage and spirit. She had such spirit.

"Sam," she whispered his name like a prayer. "Sam, Sam, Sam."

She was a warm quilt, opening her arms, welcoming him to her bosom.

He was damned. He could not stay away from her life force, her vitality. He sought her lips and branded her with his kiss. She made a soft noise of approval and snuggled closer.

His mouth found her nipple and she shivered beneath his lips. She tasted so good. This felt so right, and yet at the same time, he felt as if he'd stepped off the sandbar, and gotten pulled down by the undertow of emotions. But he couldn't stop, wouldn't turn back no matter how hard he tried.

She moaned softly, arched her back. His erection hardened. He pulled her closer, ran his hand down her spine, tickling her skin with his fingertips.

"Mmm." She sighed into his hair.

His hand drifted from her back to the round smoothness of her sweet butt. Imperative need sprang up in him, the force of his desire unabated by the sex they'd just had. Need he could not deny.

Shifting his kiss to her lips, he stroked one palm along her buttocks, the other over her belly. Then lower to that bare area above her thighs.

Her eyes were open. He felt the heat of her stare. He opened his own eyes and peered into her, felt something monumental. She was his woman. If only for tonight.

His fingers tiptoed downward and she opened her legs to him. He smiled at her, and her eyes widened as he found her warm, wet entry.

"Sam," she whispered again.

"Emma."

"Is it really you? Are we really here?"

"It's real, sweetheart."

"I thought I'd dreamed you, Twilight, all of this."

"Nope." He kissed her forehead. "No dream."

"You mean," she said, "if I were to do this . . ." She wriggled away from him, but just so she could push him on his back and straddle his waist. "You wouldn't disappear?"

He spread his palms. "Still here."

She dipped her head, and her lips took possession of his. He opened his mouth and met her tongue with eager enthusiasm. Impishly, she slid her palms up his arms to his wrist, then encircled them with her fingers and pinned his hands over his head.

Slowly, she eased herself down over his erection.

He hissed in a desperate breath. "Emma."

She moved over him, her soft body warm and relaxed. How amazing it felt to be inside her. He was lost, washed away in the whirlpool of her mesmerizing eyes.

Her copper curls tumbled about her shoulders. Her green eyes glistened with fire as fierce as his. Her mouth was puffy from his rough kisses. He'd worked her over fully and she was coming back for more.

They played and teased until primal need consumed them. They slung pillows, mussed sheets, and thumped the headboard. Sighing and groaning, they consumed each other in the heat of their desire.

"With you," she whispered, "the future is today. Tomorrow is too late."

What did that mean? What do you mean? He wanted to ask her but his brain was too clogged with testosterone. He was on a mission, driven, driven, driven to find that trigger that would spring a dual release. Him, her, both of them together.

She was on all fours in the middle of the mattress now, slanting him a look over her shoulder as he grasped her around the waist with one hand and gently used the other to toy with her breast. He spread her legs wider and eased his rock-hard cock into her.

"Make me come, Sammy," she said, her husky voice filled with passion. "Make me come again."

He couldn't hold back any longer, he thrust deep inside her and she moaned in pleasure with each thrust.

"Yes," she hissed, "yes, Sam, yes," and pushed her bottom up against him. "That's it."

Deeper and faster and harder until they were both flying. His breath was a freight train in his lungs.

"Ooh, I'm coming, Sam, I'm coming," she cried.

He felt it welling up inside him. The incredible primitive force overtook him, spilled from him.

Both their bodies jerked in unison, and, shuddering, they collapsed together on the mattress that somehow in the fray had lost its sheets.

He pulled her to him, curled his body around hers, kissed her tenderly on the nape of the neck, and then he nibbled on her ear, his palm skimming over her stomach.

Emma reached behind her, tucked her hand behind his butt, pulled him closer, keeping him inside her as long as she could.

"Thank you, sweetheart," he whispered, "thank you, thank you, thank you."

They dozed again and woke just before dawn. Opening their eyes at the same time and finding themselves face-to-face.

"Morning, sunshine." He smiled at her.

"I'm the happiest squirrel in the whole U.S.A," she said, singing another one of the ubiquitous skating rink songs they'd perverted.

"Songwriters must really hate us."

"I could lie here all day staring at you," she said. "But I gotta pee."

"Me too."

"Bathroom, brush teeth, shower, breakfast," Emma said. "In that order."

"Race you."

After a shower together where they lazily played and kissed and cuddled and teased, they wandered hand-in-hand to the kitchen. Sam wore his pajama bottoms, Emma wore his pajama top. It was so big on her petite little frame that the hem reached almost to her knees.

"You look adorable," he said as he opened the refrigerator and took out a carton of eggs.

"So do you." She grinned.

"Can you watch the bacon while I feed the critters?" he asked.

"Will do."

He stepped out onto the back porch, cool morning air seeping in. She rolled up the sleeve of his sleep shirt, scrambled eggs and flipped bacon. Within minutes delicious breakfast smells filled the room. She loved being able to cook for him and decided she'd whip up some pancakes as well.

She heard the back door creep open. "Coffee's ready," she called over her shoulder. "But none of that decaf mess, and if you want any, you're going to have to come over here and give me a kiss for it. I don't work for free."

"Okay," said a feminine voice. "But I'd really rather just pay for a cup."

Emma yelped in surprise and spun around, bacon fork in hand.

There, looking not much different than she had sixteen years ago, stood Sam's mother.

"M . . . Ma . . . Mrs. Cheek," she stammered.

"Trixie Lynn Parks," Lois Cheek said.

"Mom!" Sam exclaimed, darting in the back door. "What are you doing here?"

It turned out Sam's parents had just gotten back in town from their two-month RV road trip, and were unaware that Charlie had gone to spend the weekend with his other grandparents. Sam's mother had come over, unable to wait to see for herself that her grandson was talking again. She handled the fact that she'd caught her son and his lover half naked in the kitchen with unruffled aplomb.

"I didn't mean to interrupt your breakfast," Lois Cheek said, avoiding Emma's gaze. "Just wanted to let you know we were back in town and our annual Halloween party is still on for tonight. Trixie Lynn, will you be attending with Sam?"

"Um . . . um . . . yeah, sure," she'd said.

"Good, I'll expect you around seven then." With that, she'd turned and walked out the door.

Now they were standing on his mother's front porch. Sam was dressed as a cowboy, Emma as static cling.

"Lame costume," she said to him. "The only change you had to make to your regular wardrobe was to put on a cowboy hat."

"And the lariat," he said, tossing the rope around her and pulling her to him. "Don't forget the lariat."

He leaned down for a quick kiss. Her heart hopped at the brush of his lips against hers. *Easy. You're falling too hard, girl.*

The door opened before he had a chance to deepen the kiss, and a billow of fog rolled out followed by Frankenstein. "Monster Mash" was playing in the background.

"Son." Frankenstein clapped Sam on the back.

"Dad, you remember Trixie Lynn."

"It's Em—"

"Trixie Lynn, welcome." Frankenstein, aka Sam's dad, Bill Cheek, shook her hand. His eyes twinkled as he surveyed the socks Velcroed to her sweat suit. "Static cling?"

"See," she told Sam. "He guessed it right off the bat."

"And you're Wyatt Earp again." Bill Cheek shook his head. "What's this, five years in a row now?"

"I don't have everyone else's imagination."

"You better get inside," Bill said. "I see a fresh round of trick-or-treaters coming up the walk. There's punch in the kitchen, and your mother is making a fresh batch of popcorn balls."

Sam took Emma's hand and led her through the dry ice fog and into the living room. Immediately, her senses were assaulted with the sights, smells, and sounds of a lively party.

There were bowls of candy everywhere and all kinds of kitschy Halloween novelties. Motion-activated skeletons danced. Banshees howled. An automated werewolf sang "Werewolves of London." Cobwebs dangled from ceilings. Chains creaked. A replica coffin in the middle of the living room served as the buffet table laden with ghoulish treats—peeled grapes that stood in for eyeballs, spaghetti that masqueraded as worms, a small watermelon carved up to look like a brain. People milled around in all manner of costumes from the ubiquitous Darth Vader to over-the-top vamp tramps to circus clowns to Disney princesses. Not so dissimilar from backstage at a play. This was right up Emma's alley.

"I wish I'd had more time to come up with a better costume," she whispered to Sam.

"You're loving this, aren't you?"

"Absolutely." She grinned.

Sam reintroduced her to his brothers. Ben, the oldest, wore a three-piece suit.

"CEO?" Emma guessed.

Ben turned around to show her a pillow strapped to his behind painted yellow and black.

"I get it." She laughed. "A corporate drone."

Sam's second oldest brother Mac was dressed as a banana, and his cute girlfriend, Coco, was a chocolate chip cookie.

Jenny and Dean were Raggedy Ann and Andy.

Emma met Sam's baby sister, Katie, whom she remembered as once having a penchant for Barbie dolls.

Katie was dressed as a 1970s stewardess in go-go boots, a straight blond wig, and a miniskirt. "Coffee, tea or me," she teased.

And Sam's younger brother, Joe, looked like a California surfer dude with his wavy golden hair, tanned skin, and straight white teeth. He put her in mind of Matthew McConaughey—leanly muscular, charming, devil-may-care. He wore green surgical scrubs and a stethoscope, and he tried to give her one of those complicated handshakes that Emma fumbled miserably.

"I have a feeling you and Sam have the same minimalist outlook on costumes," she said.

"Yep." Joe nodded and slanted her a lady-killer grin. "Where do you think I got the scrubs?"

"He's a klepto, that one," Sam said. "You better keep your eye on him."

"Speaking of, can I steal my big brother for a minute?" Joe asked Emma.

"What did I tell you?" Sam grinned and punched Joe lightly on the shoulder. "Watch yourself. He can coax a snake out of its skin."

"Emma!" Sam's mother called and waved her over. Lois was dressed as Lily Munster with a long black wig and a glowing shroud of a gown. "There you are. I'm sorry I called you Trixie Lynn before. Jenny tells me you changed your name."

"It's okay."

"Would you mind helping me in the kitchen with the popcorn balls? The trick-or-treaters love them and we're about to run out."

"Sure, sure." She waved good-bye to Sam as Joe pulled him in one direction and Lois Cheek led her in another.

His parents had updated their kitchen since the last time she'd been in it. But of course, that was sixteen years ago. The countertops were granite now, instead of tile. All the appliances were stainless steel and the walls were a popular shade of fawn, where they'd once been sunshine yellow.

"I like what you've done with the kitchen," she commented.

"Bill got a nice severance package when he took early retirement. We redid the kitchen, bought the RV." She tossed a package of popcorn at her. "You pop the corn. I'll cook the candy syrup."

Emma didn't mind helping but she wondered why Lois hadn't recruited one of her daughters. She measured out the popcorn oil and put it in the kettle to heat before adding the popcorn.

"I've been getting reports about you from my sister, Belinda."

"We're in the quilting club together."

"I heard. I also heard about the quilt you made Charlie, and I could tell from the minute I laid eyes on Sam that Charlie wasn't the only one you've charmed."

Emma didn't know what to say to that, so she concentrated on shaking the kettle so the popcorn wouldn't burn.

"I want to thank you for bringing my son out of his shell," Lois said. "I've never seen him so lively. He's smiling, teasing, winking. I even heard him whistling. He was always a guarded boy, and that was one of the reasons I wasn't thrilled with his marriage to Valerie."

"Oh?" Emma raised her eyebrows.

"It wasn't that I didn't like her or that she wasn't a

good person. She was. But they were too much alike. Both of them cautious to the point of letting life pass them by."

"If Valerie was so cautious, why did she join the reserves?"

"To pay her way through nursing school. Honestly, she never thought she'd get called up."

"She probably could have gotten out of it, since she was sole support of her son."

Lois shook her head. "Valerie wasn't like that. As I said, she and Sam were two peas in a pod. When she gave her word—just like with Sam—you knew it was golden."

"You said their similar personalities was one of the reasons why you weren't thrilled with his marriage to Valerie," Emma ventured even though she realized she was treading on dangerous ground. Did she really want to know all the answers to her questions about Sam's marriage? Why was she getting more entrenched in his life when she would be leaving soon? It wasn't fair to either one of them. Nor to Charlie, who was getting more attached to her every time she saw him. "What were the other reasons?"

"Valerie was six years older and she was done having children. I thought Sam deserved to have a child of his own."

"Charlie is his."

"I know that and you couldn't ask for a better father. But I wish he could experience the joy of bringing his biological child into the world. There's nothing like it, especially when you're married to your true love. And I know that while he and Valerie did love each other in their way, it wasn't the deep, passionate love he deserves. Valerie didn't challenge him to try new things.

They never argued. It was eerie weird. Every married couple argues."

Emma thought of all the arguments she and Sam had had since she'd come back to Twilight.

"A soul mate helps you change and grow, pushes you to be a better person. Sam and Valerie weren't soul mates. It hurt my heart to see him settle for less." Lois paused in stirring the candy syrup and cocked her head toward Emma. "I always thought he really married her because she looked a little like you. Petite, red-haired, great pair of legs."

Emma didn't know what to say to that so she changed the subject. "I think the popcorn is ready."

"Yes, you're good for him."

"Thank you," she said. "Sam is good for me too."

"I know, but you worry me, Emma."

Goose bumps went up her spine. What was she talking about? "Shall I put the popcorn in a bowl?"

Lois handed her a big plastic bowl. "I think it's great you've put a spring in Sam's step, and I don't know how we can repay you for getting Charlie to talk again. But you're not a forever kind of girl, are you, Emma?"

Emma dumped the popcorn in the bowl; steam rose up between her and Sam's mother.

"Sam needs—no, he deserves—someone who can commit her all to him, and we both know you can't do that."

Oh shit. What was she supposed to say? Emma gulped.

"As long as he knows you're just having fun, well, that's okay. Does he know you're just having fun? That this thing between you can never be serious?"

Silently, Emma nodded. A roaring sound rushed through her ears. "He knows."

"That's good," Lois chirped brightly. "Because if you break his heart, I will never, ever forgive you."

Emma didn't tell Sam what his mother had said, because in her heart, she knew Lois Cheek was right. She couldn't honestly give Sam the kind of commitment he so richly deserved. Even if she wasn't hell-bent on succeeding in acting, she had no role model for how a real wife was supposed to act. She'd grown up motherless and more or less alone. All she knew about family life was when she imitated it on the stage.

She went back to work on Monday still feeling unsettled, only to find Nina in the theater singing a ditty from *The Sound of Music* and dancing across the stage like a giddy teenager in love. Such frivolity on the normally elegant older woman took Emma aback. The same feeling of apprehension she'd experienced in Lois Cheek's kitchen washed over her again. "Nina, are you okay?"

"Emma." Nina waved her up onstage. "Come here, I have great news."

Leery, Emma approached. The last time she'd gotten great news it had landed her in jail. "What's wrong?"

Nina laughed gaily. "Wrong? There's nothing wrong. In fact, everything is very right."

"Okay." Emma folded her arms across her chest.

Nina walked over and cupped a hand to her cheek. "Smile," she murmured. "It's a beautiful day."

"So about this news . . . ?"

Nina looked around. They were alone in the theater so far, but the other actors and crew would be arriving soon. "Let's go across the street for a walk in Sweetheart Park."

"Um, all right."

They left the theater to stroll the park, still adorned with Halloween decorations from the holiday weekend. Workers would be along today to replace the ghosts with pilgrims, the goblins with turkeys. The hay bales and pumpkins would stay. Early morning dew glistened in the grass, and Emma snuggled deeper into her sweater.

"My ex-husband, Malcolm Talmadge is coming here on Thanksgiving Day. To see the play."

"*The* Malcolm Talmadge? The head of Shooting Star Studios?"

"Yes."

"Seriously?"

"Seriously."

A chill of excitement traced over Emma. They walked past a pond. Four white swans glided gracefully past.

"I've got a confession to make," Nina said.

"A confession?"

"I haven't been completely honest with you about why I brought you here, and you deserve to know the truth."

Hmm, she wasn't surprised. She'd suspected all along that Nina had ulterior motives.

"You thought Twilight was your last stop, your only hope for redemption. Didn't you?"

Emma jammed her hands into her pockets. "Yes."

"What you didn't understand was that you were *my* last chance at redemption." Nina stopped beside the Sweetheart Tree and motioned at the bench underneath. "Shall we sit?"

"Is it that bad that I need to be sitting down?"

Nina smiled. "Not for you. My knees are the shaky ones."

Nina sat down, leaving Emma with little choice except to sit beside her. A long moment stretched between them, and a faraway look came into Nina's eyes. Finally, she said softly, "Last year, I was diagnosed with stage two breast cancer."

Emma inhaled sharply. "I'm so sorry to hear that."

"It could have been much worse, but I had to undergo both chemotherapy and radiation treatments. The women in this town were wonderful—Patsy, Marva, Terri, Raylene, Belinda, Dotty Mae. They rallied around me. Took care of me. Made me whole again. But it was while I was going through this process that I realized I'd never forgiven myself for something terrible I'd done. And I didn't want to die without making amends."

Her words sent a shiver of sympathy through Emma. "This is why you believe so deeply in giving people second chances."

Nina tilted her head. "It is." She paused, took a deep breath of the morning air that smelled like pumpkins and the scent of yeast bread from the Twilight Bakery. Overhead a pair of mockingbirds called to each other, batting a melody of songs back and forth across the park.

"Malcolm and I were childhood sweethearts who shared the same dream. He was a playwright. I was an actress. We married and moved to Manhattan together, shared a tiny, grungy apartment in SoHo. We struggled to feed ourselves, but there were parties all the time, people in and out of the apartment. We stayed up late, but got up early to hit the pavement looking for work. You know how it is. We were young and in love, full of hope and ambition. It was the best time of my life."

Emma waited for her to go on, watched a leaf the color of her hair drift down from a tree across the way.

"Then I met Scott Miller. He was young, yes, but he was already a director. His father had money. Scott was Ivy League, powerful, rich. He could have any woman he wanted. Actresses threw themselves at him, but not me. I didn't care. I was desperately in love with Malcolm."

"I have a bad feeling about where this story is headed."

Nina patted Emma's knee. "Of course you do. You lived it. Anyway, one afternoon following an audition, Scott cornered me backstage and propositioned me. If I'd become his mistress, then he'd give me a part that would make me a star. I turned him down. He kept after me. The more I spurned him, the more he pursued me. Malcolm and I were so broke. Although Malcolm had written an amazing script, he couldn't get anyone to take a look at it. You know how brutal it can be trying to get attention in Manhattan. You can understand the things people are driven to do for their careers. The values that get compromised along the way."

Emma nodded. Boy, did she ever understand that.

"Scott is brilliant at figuring out other people's weaknesses and targeting them. He knew I wouldn't sleep with him to further my career, but he realized Malcolm was my Achilles' heel. He upped the ante. Sleep with him and not only would he give me the starring role in his next production, but his next production would be Malcolm's play."

"*Firelight*," Emma guessed.

"Yes. Scott loves the power. He likes making people grovel and dance to his tune." Nina tightened her jaw. "God help me, but I did it for Malcolm, and he never knew how he got his big break. At least not in the beginning."

"I can't imagine what that was like. Agreeing to have an affair with Scott Miller in order to help your husband achieve his dreams. It was a huge sacrifice."

"Don't paint me out to be altruistic," Nina said. "I got my piece of the pie. *Firelight* went on to earn me a Tony award and it's grossed both Malcolm and me millions over the years."

"So what happened with your marriage?"

Nina smoothed her skirt with a palm. "I got pregnant."

"Oh, gosh." Emma splayed a palm to her chest.

"I had to tell Malcolm the truth. I didn't know whose baby it was." She took a deep breath and told the rest of the story in a rush. "When I could no longer avoid it, I finally told him the truth. He was shattered by my betrayal and he asked for a divorce. When I told Miller I was pregnant, he fired me. I fled New York, came back to Twilight, and that's when I had the miscarriage. That day you caught me crying in the church? If he had lived, that would have been the baby's birthday."

Emma touched the other woman's shoulder. "Oh, Nina, I'm so sorry."

"I didn't even realize I was waiting for a chance to make things right with Malcolm until I heard about what happened to you with Miller. I must confess, bringing you here was twofold. I did want to help you after you'd been devastated by that tyrant, but I also wanted to find peace with my past. I wrote Malcolm a long letter. It was the first time I'd contacted him since losing the baby. I told him about you, how talented you were. About how Miller was treating you. About Twilight and the play. About my breast cancer. And I asked for his forgiveness. I'd kept up with what he was doing over the years. Watched his career skyrocket as he turned from writer to director to producer. I knew he'd lost his wife to cancer. That his only child, a son, enlisted in the Army and came back from overseas so traumatized he ended up taking his own life."

"How sad," Emma said.

Nina nodded. "Tragic."

A school bus lumbered by. A man on a motorcycle tooted his horn. Nina waved a hand in greeting. "I didn't hear back from Malcolm. I took it as a sign he wasn't going to forgive me."

They sat there, not talking, the town coming awake around them. Emma didn't know what to think about the bombshell Nina had just dropped.

"But then he called me last night," she said, and a happy smile curled her lips. "He'd been out of the country and hadn't received my letter until just now. He wants to meet you and Beau. He's pulled some strings, and a crew from *Entertainment Tonight* is coming out to cover the story of you, our quilt making, and the charity auction for our troops."

"And you and Malcolm?"

Her smile widened. "We talked for hours. It was like forty years just fell away. Unbelievably, the love was still there. I think . . ." She paused. Her lips trembled. "I think we rekindled a spark."

"Nina, that's amazing." Emma squeezed her hand.

"It's amazing for you as well. If Malcolm likes your

performance, and I'm certain he will, there very well could be a part for you in one of his movies."

"You mean it?"

Nina nodded. "But we've still got a lot of work ahead of us."

"I'm up to the challenge."

"No distractions?"

"What do you mean?"

"You and Sam."

Emma said, "I've always been focused on my career."

"And that hasn't changed?"

She thought of Sam and how much she loved him. Thought of how his mother had warned her off. Thought of all the issues that lay between them. Thought of how he truly did deserve a woman who could give him her all. She swallowed, pushed back the part of her that wanted so much to be that woman, and said softly, "Nothing's changed."

CHAPTER EIGHTEEN

The quilting must go on.
—Nina Blakley, ex-wife of movie mogul
Malcolm Talmadge

When Emma told Sam about Malcolm Talmadge, he wrapped her in a big bear hug and whispered, "This is it. Everything you've wanted is about to come true."

Not everything.

She looked at him sadly. By following her dreams and achieving the one major thing she'd set out in life to do, she would be losing Sam. Her gut wrenched as her heart split in two.

"Hey," he said, and chucked her lightly under the chin. "Why the glum face? This is cause for celebration."

"I'm going to miss you," she whispered.

"No you won't. Once you get to Hollywood, start making friends, you'll forget all about me."

She squeezed him tightly. "I will never, *ever* forget about you, Sam Cheek."

They savored the three weeks that followed, both

of them knowing this was their last hurrah. They treasured each moment they shared, acutely aware of how bittersweet and fragile it all was. They agreed that while they could handle the temporariness of their relationship, Charlie could not. So they limited his exposure to Emma. Each evening, after Sam put his son to bed, he would slip over to the Merry Cherub and spend his night making love to Emma, arising at dawn to slip back home to be at the breakfast table when his son awoke.

During the day, Emma kept her mind honed on the work, and never had she wrung from herself such a commanding performance. Twelve long years of toil and sacrifice were finally coming to fruition. The thought of it took her breath. At long last, success hovered just inches from her fingers. All she had to do was reach out and grab it.

She tried not to dwell on what she was going to lose, but instead, stayed focused on each precious second they shared, enjoying the beautiful fantasy of those soft autumn nights. She set about learning everything she could about Sam and committed it to memory. The way he brushed his hair down over his scar, his favorite foods, his easy way with animals and children. She admired his patience and calm demeanor, but also the way he stood up for the underdog, even if it meant letting go of some of that calm patience.

Save for not letting her get too close to Charlie, he let her into his world without reservation. He introduced her to his friends, of whom she was surprised to discover he had many. She'd thought he was too insular for that many intimate contacts. Then again, that was Twilight and he'd grown up here. Everyone knew him, respected him, and came to him for pet care advice. He didn't put expectations on people and he didn't judge them. He let them be who they were meant to be. Sam was a live-and-let-live kind of guy, and everyone loved him for it.

With Emma, he was adventuresome in a way he wasn't with others. In bed, he eagerly took to role playing with her and they had fun. More fun than she'd ever had. It went beyond sex into true intimacy. A physical bond forged between deep friends.

"We'll always be friends," he told her one evening just a few days before Thanksgiving. They were lying naked on her bed, snuggled beneath a beautiful wedding ring quilt. He reached out a hand to gently stroke her cheek, his eyes gleaming in the muted light from the pink angel lamp on the bedside table. "Even if we marry other people. No one can ever take that away from us."

"I've opened up to you in a way I've never opened up to anyone," she confessed.

"I know," he said, and kissed the tip of her nose. "And thank you for that precious gift."

"You'll never be far from my heart."

"Nor you from mine."

Then he made love to her, slow and tender, all night long.

Thanksgiving Day turned out to be one of those not uncommon autumn days in North Texas where the temperature suddenly notched up to the high seventies. Kids shed their jackets in favor of short sleeves and abandoned the Macy's parade on TV for sandlot baseball. Mothers raised kitchen windows to grab a bit of springlike weather while toiling over the upcoming feasts. Fathers dug boxes from attics, getting a jumpstart on decorating their yards for Christmas.

After a restless night of going over and over her lines in her head, Emma woke to the smell of roasting turkey mingled with the scent of bacon. The sound of Christmas music wafted up the floorboards. "Jingle Bells," she recognized, and threw back the covers. The Merry Cherub was booked for the holiday weekend. Emma heard numerous footsteps outside her door as guests flocked downstairs for breakfast.

Emma did some yoga stretches, and then showered. The dining room was packed, and besides, she was too nervous for a sit-down meal. She greeted Jenny good morning, grabbed black coffee and a muffin, and went over to the Twilight Playhouse to get ready for the play. This was the event she'd been working toward for the past nine weeks.

She found several members of the True Love Quilting Club working with the stage crew to get the quilts strung up on battens and counterweighted ropes for use as backdrops. More grips were loading in other sets and props. The place pulsed with activity. The college students hired as extras frantically rehearsed lines. Nina prowled the control booth, going over final instructions with the sound and lighting technicians. The costume designer and her assistant sorted through costumes, while the prop man ticked off the items in his catalogue, making sure every prop needed for the play was present and accounted for.

Putting on the play was a team endeavor, and Emma was grateful for the behind-the-scenes crew who made her look good. They were the unsung heroes of any successful stage production, and she took the opportunity to stop by and tell each one how much she appreciated his or her contribution.

Nina came down out of the control booth and waved Emma over. "Malcolm's here. He wants to meet you."

Oh gosh. Was she ready for this? Emma raised a hand to her hair. "I'm not in makeup, I haven't done my hair—"

"Malcolm understands about all that. He just wants to meet the girl who had the balls—sorry for the pun—to stand up to Scott Miller."

Nina turned and waved to a silver-haired man in the booth. "Come on." She took Emma's hand and led her up the steps to introduce her to her ex-husband.

"Malcolm, this is Emma Parks. Emma, this is Malcolm Talmadge, head of Shooting Star Studios."

It hit her then. The importance of this moment. She was meeting one of the most influential men in Hollywood. And yet he looked so normal. Like he could be anyone's grandfather. He had an affable smile, keen blue eyes, and a small paunch that slightly hung over the waistband of his jeans. If it wasn't for the Vacheron Constantin at his wrist—that made Scott Miller's Rolex look like a dime store trinket— no one would guess he was a billionaire accustomed to rubbing shoulders with royalty, celebrities, and VIPs. The way he gave her his complete attention made Emma feel like a VIP.

"I know you're going to be very impressed with her performance, Malcolm," Nina went on. "For the life of me I can't figure out why Hollywood isn't beating a path to her door."

"Perhaps all that will be rectified today." Malcolm smiled warmly. "It's my great pleasure to meet you, Emma. If you've earned Nina's seal of approval, I have no doubt I'm in for a treat. She has high standards. And . . ." He flicked a gaze to Nina. "I can't tell you both how impressed I am with your tribute to our soldiers overseas. The quilts are visually stunning and I . . ." Malcolm paused and swallowed visibly as if struggling to control some intense emotions.

"Malcolm's son was in Afghanistan," Nina murmured.

"There was no reason for him to enlist," Malcolm said. "He was my son. He had all the privileges that money could buy, but he insisted the war effort needed people from all walks of life. He wanted to do his part, and I was so proud of him."A dark look of heavy sadness crossed Malcolm's face, and Emma remembered what Nina had told her about his son.

"My son, Brian couldn't deal with what he saw over there, what he was forced to do. He was always a sensitive boy, and he came home a shattered shell of a man. I tried to help him but I was ill-equipped in spite of all my money . . ." Malcolm shook his head. "He ended up . . . I lost him." His voice cracked, fractured into a sharp sound of grief.

"Oh sir, I'm so sorry." Emma's heart wrenched. "I can't imagine what you went through."

He forced a smile, and she could see him purposefully putting his emotions on the shelf. "Please," he said, "you must call me Malcolm."

"Malcolm." She nodded.

"My son's death was the worst thing that ever happened to me, but because of it I got involved in the war effort. It's become the driving focus in my life for the last few years, and I like to think I've helped a few people along the way."

Nina touched a hand to his shoulder. "Malcolm is being modest. He spearheaded an entire campaign that's resulted in a change in military policy about treating post-traumatic stress disorder. So many of the young men and women returning from the Middle East weren't getting the help they needed to deal with what they experienced over there. Their families can't understand what they're going through and they feel isolated, cut off. Malcolm is determined to change all that. He's got a film in production dealing with just that."

Sympathy fisted inside Emma. So many people had been touched by the war. Far more people than she'd expected. When she'd first come to Twilight, her main motivations had been self-interest—money and a desperate last chance to redeem her career. But somewhere between rehearsing the play and making the quilts and listening to the stories of women who lived in Twilight and dating Sam and getting to know Charlie, all that had changed. The only thing that concerned her now was giving a performance that was truly worthy of the men and women in uniform who had sacrificed so much for their country.

"But enough of sad talk." Malcolm waved his hand. "Today is a day of honoring, recognizing, and celebrating those who have fought to keep our country free."

"I want you to meet our leading man, Beau Trainer," Nina said, linking her arm through Malcolm's. "He was in Iraq and had an ugly case of PTSD himself. He made some bad choices, did some regrettable things, but this play is *his* chance at redemption."

Malcolm's face looked animated. "I *would* like to meet him."

Nina looked around at the busy theater, and then glanced back at Emma. "Have you seen Beau?"

"Not since yesterday's rehearsal."

"I'm just going to go into my office and give him a call. Proceed with what you were doing, Emma."

"It was nice meeting you," Malcolm said.

"It was an honor for me, sir."

Nina escorted Malcolm in the direction of her office, leaving Emma to prep for the biggest role of her life. She still couldn't believe that a Hollywood movie executive was going to be watching her performance. It was every dream she'd ever dreamed come true.

And yet it didn't bring the instant joy she'd always anticipated. Maybe she'd learned to take the emotional roller coaster in stride. Or maybe it was because she'd begun to have a life that wasn't based solely on her identity as an actress. She was a quilter now and she'd formed bonds with influential women in the community. She'd learned to drive a car and herd sheep. And she'd gotten a mute boy to speak when no one else could.

She had accomplished a lot in a short amount of time, and it had changed her. What had once seemed like the ultimate human endeavor was simply just another career, glamorous maybe, but it didn't define who you were deep inside. Once upon a time, she'd felt that if she wasn't an actress, she wasn't anything. Now, she knew that wasn't true. She was so much more than just a performer. She was no longer defined solely by her work.

"Ready for your stage face?" asked the makeup

artist, who stood with a soft-bristled brush in her hand and a pot of powdered rouge.

"Yes."

Emma followed her backstage, and while the woman applied her makeup, she mentally went over the lines she knew by heart. After the makeup came the hair-styling, and then she donned the Rebekka Nash costume. When she looked into the mirror, she *was* the plucky pioneer woman who believed so deeply in the man she loved that she spurned all other suitors.

The bustle of the theater had reached fever pitch. The grips were tripping over one another in their hurry. The young acting students were looking a little green around the gills as stage fright kicked in. With her script and blocking book in her hand, Nina went over last-minute details.

The performance started at noon. It was just before eleven, but people had already started lining up outside the ticket office.

Nina rushed over. "Where is Beau?"

"I thought you were going to call him."

Nina bit down on her bottom lip. "I did. He didn't answer. I've left a dozen messages. I put the True Love quilters on his tail. Terri was going around to his apartment and I sent Patsy up to his parents' house. Raylene's gone down to see if he's sousing it up at the Horny Toad. All I've got to say is that he better be lying dead in a ditch because if he stands me up after I went out on a limb for him . . ." She left her threat unfinished, but wadded up her fist.

Immediately, Emma understood her anxiety and frustration. Here they were putting on a tribute to the soldiers of Twilight, and one of those soldiers who'd been given the male lead in the play hadn't shown up. Then there was Malcolm Talmadge and the crew from *Entertainment Tonight.* Emma realized Nina had as much stake in the outcome of this play as she did.

"Where's Malcolm?" she asked.

"He went to meet with the crew from *Entertainment Tonight.* They just got into town."

"Does he know Beau is AWOL?"

"Not yet. We need a contingency plan."

"In case he doesn't show."

She nodded curtly. "We have that young understudy from Tarleton, but honestly, he's dreadful. I was so sure Beau would come through for me, and having a soldier in the role was the angle Malcolm used to lure the media here. That and your appeal as the plucky young woman who put Scott Miller in his place."

"I'm still here. Still gossip-worthy."

Nina managed a small smile. "Thanks for trying to cheer me up. I guess as unappealing as it is, we'll just have to go with the understudy."

Raylene and Patsy came hustling down the aisle to where Nina and Emma stood off to one side of the stage.

"He's not at the Horny Toad," Raylene said.

"And Beau's parents haven't seen him in a week," Patsy added.

"Don't give up hope," Emma said. "Beau might still appear. He knows how important this play is to the whole town."

"I wouldn't hold my breath on that," said Terri, who'd come bounding up to them, her face flushed.

"I hate to ask." Nina shifted the script in her hand and pressed a hand to her stomach.

"His landlord said he moved out last night. The apartment is empty."

Nina slapped her forehead with a palm. "Son of a bitch."

Emma had never heard the older woman curse, and it sent apprehensive shivers down her spine.

"Hey you," Nina said to one of the cast members who was milling about. "Go find Toby, tell him it's his big moment and I need to see him right away. Beau's a no-show."

The guy darted off to find Toby.

"It's all going to work out fine, Nina," Patsy soothed. "You'll pull it off, you always do."

Nina shook her head. "I've got more at stake than usual." Then she told them about Malcolm and the crew from *Entertainment Tonight.*

"This is your Malcolm?" Patsy said.

Nina nodded.

"Are we talking rekindled romance?" Terri asked.

"Or just hot sex?" Raylene added.

Everyone glared at her.

"What?" Raylene raised her palms. "I'm just saying not everyone has to fall madly in love. Sometimes sex is good enough."

The lanky cast member sprinted toward them. "Nina, Toby's sick."

"What do you mean he's sick? He can't be sick. He's the understudy, and the lead actor has flaked on us," Nina exclaimed. "He *must* go on. He's just got butterflies."

"He's blowing chunks all over the bathroom floor and clutching his abdomen. He looks just like my brother looked when he had to have his appendix out."

"Crap. Take me to him," Nina said.

The young man led the way and everyone followed. They found Toby, the understudy, swaying on his feet in the hallway, his face blanched of all color.

Terri laid a palm on his forehead. "He's burning up. I'll call Ted and have him meet us at the hospital. You guys go on with the play."

Terri and the lanky kid helped Toby out the side exit.

Nina shoved her script in Patsy's hands and plastered her palms over her ears. "I don't want to hear this. I'm not hearing this."

"Denial doesn't solve the problem," Raylene observed.

Nina took a deep breath, drew herself up tall. "Okay, let me think. Let's pretend for a minute that there's not a Hollywood camera crew in town. Let's pretend that I haven't just reconnected with the love of my life and he's here to see my young protégée perform the role she was born to perform. Let's take that pressure out of the equation."

"Okay," everyone said in unison, including the stagehands who'd been eavesdropping.

"What are our options?" Nina asked.

"Shut down the production," someone called out.

"Keep trying to get hold of Beau," Patsy offered.

"Find someone else to play the part."

"There." Nina snapped her fingers. "That one. That's the answer. But no one else knows the entire script, except for me and Emma and her understudy."

"You could play Jon Grant, Nina," Raylene offered. "Put on a guy's uniform and a wig. You're tall and you've got a deep voice. I don't know how Emma feels about kissing you, and yeah, it'll be a bit lezzy, but hey . . ."

"Raylene!" everyone shouted.

"Okay, okay, forgive me for thinking outside the box."

Just then the side door opened.

Sam and Charlie and Patches stepped into the theater, and Emma suddenly got a mad idea.

Sam smiled at Emma, even though he was getting weird vibes from everyone. Something beyond the normal chaos of putting on a play was going on here. Sam had come backstage to drop off Patches before he took Charlie to hang out with his folks during the play. He'd decided the play wouldn't be appropriate for a six-year-old, but his son had insisted on at least wishing Emma good luck.

"Could we see you a minute?" he asked Emma after he'd handed Patches over to the professional dog wrangler that Nina had hired. "There's something Charlie wants to tell you."

Looking grateful for a reprieve from whatever was going on around her, Emma came over to them. Sam's gaze hung on hers and his heart skipped. He put a hand on Charlie's shoulder.

She squatted in front of Charlie. "What did you want to tell me?"

Charlie tilted his head up and gave her a dazzling grin. "Break a leg."

It was still a joy to hear his son's voice. He couldn't thank Emma enough for making that happen.

"But I don't really want you to break a leg," he whispered, and darted an anxious glance at Emma's legs. "Daddy says that's sumpin' you're s'posta say 'cause it means good luck."

"That's so sweet of you." She held her arms open wide. "Can I have a hug?"

Charlie wrapped his arms around her and squeezed her tight.

"Well, we don't want to get in your way." Sam placed a hand on his son's head. "We just wanted to wish you good luck. The play is going to be great, I just know it." He gave her a wink and thumbs-up.

"Ha!" Raylene snorted. "Proving you're not the least bit psychic."

Nina eyed Sam speculatively. It made him nervous. "Emma, didn't you tell me that Sam had been reading lines with you?"

"Yes."

"How well do you know the play?" Nina asked Sam.

He chuckled. "I could recite the thing backward. Emma is such a perfectionist that—"

Nina grabbed Sam by the hand and tugged him into the theater, jostling the words out of him. "You're a bit shorter than Beau, but that's actually a good thing. The kiss scenes between Beau and Emma were problematic because of their extreme height differences. You're much more suited to her petite size."

"Um, thanks, I think."

"His costumes will be long on you, but I'm betting Leandra can baste them up right quick."

"Wait a minute." Sam held up his hands. "I don't like the way this conversation is going."

Nina pressed her palms together in a gesture of supplication. "Please, you've got to help us. Beau has disappeared and Terri just rushed our understudy to the hospital. There's no one else who knows the lines."

"Beau's disappeared?"

"He took off. Moved out of his apartment. No one's seen him."

Sam blew out his breath. "He'd not been the same since he came back from Iraq."

"It's my fault. I shouldn't have taken a chance on him. I thought—" Nina stopped herself. "Never mind that. What's done is done. What we need now is a new leading man."

Sam shook his head. "I'm not an actor. I'm not comfortable in the spotlight."

Nina leaned in close and whispered, "Look, I'm not asking for me. I've had my run. This is for Valerie and all the other soldiers who've fought for Twilight. This is for your hometown. But most of all this is for Emma. This is her big chance. She's damn good, Sam."

"I know it."

"She's been unlucky in the past, but now her luck has changed."

"Because you took a chance on her," he said.

She looked him squarely in her eyes. "Right, and now you're the only one who can help her get to her destiny."

Sam looked over at Emma and his heart wrenched. More than anything in the world, what he wanted for her was happiness, and if that meant giving her a shot at Hollywood, that was what he'd do. Never mind that he disliked the spotlight, that he knew nothing about acting. Emma needed him, and he wasn't about to let her down.

"Okay," he said. "Tell me what to do."

Chapter Nineteen

Quilt my name in the stars.
—Sylvie Douglas Parks Rodriquez Cleary, failed mother,
wife, and actress

Knowing she was going onstage with an untested leading man had Emma's stomach in knots. Sam wasn't an actor, and while he might know the lines, he didn't know any of the moves. How was she expected to pull off a performance good enough to wow Malcolm Talmadge? She paced. She fretted. She wrung her hands.

Then just before the curtain was about to go up, Sam—wearing the costume of Colonel Jon Grant—looked over at her and said, "You, Emma Parks, are going to nail this. You've always been destined for stardom."

In that moment, an invincible calm settled over her, and she felt as if she could do anything.

For the next hour and a half, she performed as she'd never performed before. Sam followed her lead, flawlessly reciting his lines. Emma took the passion she felt for him and channeled it through her body, using the power of their bond to express all the emotions of the characters she portrayed. But the most poignant moment of all was when she played Valerie and Sam played himself. As she looked into his eyes and told him good-bye, the tears that ran down her cheeks were honest and true.

And when it was over, the crowd was on their feet in wild applause and the cast had to take three curtain calls before the audience finally began to disperse.

Buoyed on a high unlike anything she'd ever experienced, the next few hours passed in a blur as she accepted congratulations, dined on the Thanksgiving feast hosted on the town square by the Funny Farm restaurant, and participated in the charity event auctioning off the quilts to support America's servicemen and women.

She was interviewed by *Entertainment Tonight*, but she hardly remembered any of it. What stuck in her mind most was the way Sam stood waiting in the wings. He let her have the spotlight, never getting in the way, but whenever she looked up, there he was, giving her a smile of encouragement, letting her know he supported her no matter what.

At the end of the eventful day, Nina and Malcolm Talmadge cornered her for a talk.

"You're every bit as talented as Nina said you were," Malcolm said. "Even more so, I suspect, since you were working under the handicap of having your leading man take off on you."

"Thank you, sir."

"Malcolm," he corrected gently. "I understand you've been working very hard over the last few months, and I was wondering if your work ethic might allow you to jump right into a new project."

Nina was grinning from ear to ear. Emma's blood pumped so hard she could scarcely breathe.

"I have a film that's currently in production, with Matt Damon in the lead role as a war vet who discovers he can't go home again. The actress slated to play his younger sister has just checked into drug rehab and won't be able to complete the project. Luckily, we haven't yet started filming any of her scenes. The part is fairly small, but very pivotal to the movie. Can you do it?"

"I . . . I'd . . . I need to talk to my agent of course, but yes, yes!"

"Excellent. Let me call your agent and we'll get all the details ironed out. I'll also tell *Entertainment Tonight* that you were discovered right here in Twilight and I'm predicting big things for you. I'm sure they'd like to interview you again for a second segment on *ET.*"

Nina congratulated her with a hug, then she and Malcolm went off together, leaving Emma standing on the courthouse lawn, stunned by the turn of events.

She looked up, and there was Sam. "Did you hear?"

"I heard." He smiled. "I told you."

"I'm numb."

"You've worked so hard and so long it's going to take you a bit to get used to your newfound fame. But it'll sink in once you're in Hollywood."

"I can't even think."

"Before you take off on your grand new life, I've got something for you." Sam had a look in his dark eyes that turned Emma's stomach inside out. She didn't really know what the look meant, but to her it said he thought she didn't belong here, no matter how much he might wish she did.

"You got me a going-away present?" Her heart felt goopy.

"I did." He pulled a palm-sized white box wrapped with a red ribbon from the pocket of his jacket.

She fumbled the box as she took it from him, almost dropping it for no good reason other than her hands were shaking. Why were her hands shaking? *Bette Davis.* She slipped into the persona of that hard-edged actress who never let sentimentality get in the way of what needed to be done, and immediately her hands stilled. Blowing out her breath, she undid the ribbon and lifted the lid.

There, nestled in tissue paper, lay her mother's star brooch.

She'd tried to get it back, but Hagzilla told her she'd sold it.

She gazed up at him in wonderment. "Sam, how did you get this?"

"Most pawnshops are putting their inventory online these days. I took a stab at it and did a global search for 'star-shaped emerald brooch' and it just popped up."

"Lucky."

"Or fated." His eyes crinkled along with his smile.

"How much did it cost you?" She was certain Hagzilla had made him pay through the nose to reclaim it.

"Don't worry about that." He took it from her hand and pinned it to her jacket. "There." He smiled softly. "No 'gonna be' to it. You, Emma Parks, are a star."

Life in L.A. was a whirlwind. The minute her feet touched down at LAX, she was off and running. She had a lot to learn about the movie business, and Malcolm appointed her an assistant to help her navigate the pitfalls. She was so busy she didn't even have time to drop Sam an e-mail or text message. Maybe it was for the best. Breaking off all contact, rather than trying to hang on to something that would only cause them both pain.

She quickly learned it was much different from New York. And being on a movie set was much more grueling (and at times more boring) than she expected. People were nice, but she found she couldn't always trust the niceness. At least in Manhattan, you knew where you stood. People called it as they saw it. Here, you had to try and guess at motives. She didn't like that. And after letting down her guard in Twilight, where what you saw was what you got, it was doubly hard to get her emotional shield back up.

She was grateful that Sam had taught her how to drive, but she hated the traffic. And what was with the darn sun? It shone constantly. She found herself homesick for a little inclement weather.

A few days after she arrived, she stopped by the supermarket to pick up a few groceries and ran into her old roommate Jill Freeman, the one who'd put in the good word for her with Master X.

"Emma!" Jill squealed at her over the avocados. "I heard you'd moved to L.A."

They embraced in the middle of the store.

"God, let me have a look at you." Jill stepped back. "You're radiant."

"And you're gorgeous. What a tan."

"Congrats on landing that part in Malcolm Talmadge's latest." Jill clapped her right hand against her left palm in soft applause. "Especially after that crap you suffered through with Scott Miller."

"Thanks."

"This business, huh?" Jill shook her head. "Remember how naïve we were when we first started? You have this dream of what you want and it seems so magical, that if you achieve it, somehow everything will be perfect after that." Jill's laugh was harsh.

"Did something happen?" Emma asked, concerned for her friend.

"They're canceling *Coeds*."

"I hate to hear that," Emma said, and meant it. "But you'll get something else."

Jill shook her head again. "I don't think I want something else."

"What are you saying? You're quitting acting?"

"This life isn't real, Em. It changes you, and not in a good way. I don't know who I am anymore. I've lost myself. All this time I've been pretending to be someone else and I realize I don't even know who I am anymore. You dumbly think money will solve everything. That if you just get that next part everything will be great. But it's not. There's no peak to the mountain. You're never satisfied. And fame isn't what it's cracked up to be. It gets to be a real drag. Everyone loves you when you're a success, but when you hit the skids, they're all gone. So you run and run and run trying to keep up, but after a while, you just want to get off the treadmill. I don't want to wake up one day, forty years old, without a husband and kids because I put my life on hold. Do you know what I mean?" Jill paused, hauled in a deep breath, and looked her straight in the eyes. "No, of course not. You're flying high right now. You haven't hit the wall yet. Forgive me. I don't mean to be a buzzkill. Don't listen to me. Enjoy the good times while they last."

Jill's words struck her like nothing else could have because they echoed Emma's own fears about her choices.

Shrug it off. Jill is just down about her canceled series. She'll be singing a different tune as soon as she gets a new gig.

They hugged again and promised to keep in touch, but for the rest of the day, Emma couldn't shake the sadness that settled in her bones. All she could think about was what she'd left behind in Twilight, and she couldn't help wondering if her sacrifices were worth it.

The dachshund was a biter.

Every time Sam tried to examine the short-legged dog, it latched on to his hand with sharp little teeth.

"Oh dear, oh dear, oh dear," exclaimed the pooch's owner as she forcefully wrung her hands. "I'm *so* sorry, Dr. Cheek. Prissy is *so* high-strung."

It ain't Prissy who's high-strung. "Ms. Applebaum—"

"*Miss* Applebaum," she emphasized, and fluttered her eyelashes at him. "I'm not married. And please, call me Tara."

He raked a gaze over the woman, seeing her for the first time. Actually, she was quite pretty, with long dark hair, big brown eyes, and dimples in both cheeks. Her body wasn't bad either. Nice boobs, long legs, but Sam didn't feel even a whisper of sexual interest. She wasn't Emma.

He narrowed his eyes. "Did my aunt Belinda send you?"

"Aunt Belinda?" She looked confused.

"What brought you into my office today?"

"I told you, Prissy hasn't been eating and her tummy

is getting so big. I'm scared she's got an intestinal obstruction."

"And that's it? You have no hidden agenda?"

"Well . . ." She straightened, sent him a dazzling smile. "I did hear that your girlfriend left town and I was thinking—"

"I'm sure you're a very nice person," he interrupted. "But I've got no room in my life for romance."

Tara pushed her bangs from her eyes. "Still hung up on her, huh?"

"You heard?"

"It's all over Twilight—"

The dachshund bit him again.

"That's it," he said, "I've had enough."

"What?"

He bared his teeth at Prissy, who backed down and whimpered. "That's right pooch, I've got teeth too. No more of this biting nonsense." Then to Tara he said, "Prissy's pregnant."

"But that can't be, I never let her out."

"She's not spayed."

"No but—"

"She's pregnant," he said. "Congratulations. Now if you'll excuse me, I have someone I need to speak to."

"Okay," Tara blinked and gathered up Prissy.

Sam stripped off his exam gloves and stalked into the front office. "Cancel my appointments," he said to Delia.

"For how long?"

"Indefinitely," he said.

He stalked over to the Twilight Playhouse to find Nina rehearsing the nativity scene with the fifth graders from Twilight Middle School.

Nina looked up and caught his gaze. "Children, let's take a short break."

The kids dispersed, and she came over to him. "Is something the matter, Sam?"

"I let her slip through my fingers, Nina. I had her and I let her go."

"You didn't want to stop her from going after her dreams, Sam."

"No, I did not. But I could have told her I loved her. I should have told her I loved her, but I didn't."

"You were afraid that if you did, she wouldn't go."

He nodded. "She deserves this chance, but she also deserves to know that I intend on being here for her, no matter what."

"You're going to put your life on hold until Emma decides she's had enough of the limelight?" Nina asked gently.

He pulled a palm down his face. "Yes."

"That's not realistic."

"I know, but it's how I feel. I don't want any other woman. It's always been her from the time I was fourteen years old."

"If you go to her and tell her you love her and then she gives up her career for you, you're always going to feel guilty."

"I know," he said. "That's why I'm ready and willing to move to L.A. to be with her. I'm a vet. I can get a job anywhere. And Charlie, well, it's time he knew there was a world beyond Twilight."

"There's nothing else in the world that could make you leave this town, is there?" Nina asked softly.

"No," he admitted. "But Emma is worth it and I'm going to tell her so. Do you know her schedule? Where she'll be at this evening?"

"She and the rest of the cast are attending a charity event for our troops. Malcolm left for the event this morning."

"You're not going with him?"

Nina waved at the kids horsing around on the stage. "I'm otherwise occupied. Plus, there's some other business Malcolm had to attend to. In fact, if everything works out like he's planning, we might have a solution to your long-distance love affair."

"What do you mean?"

"I can't say anything, just that you might want to hold off on professing your love for a few weeks."

Sam shook his head. "No. I need to see her. I can't wait any longer."

Nina nodded. "Okay, but if you're going to go you'll need a tuxedo and an invitation. I'll arrange for someone to meet you at the airport with both."

Six hours later, after he made arrangements for Charlie to stay with his mother, Sam's plane touched down in L.A. He was met by a driver in a Lincoln Town Car, along with the tuxedo and invitation to the charity event that Nina had promised. He changed in the airport bathroom and they took off for Beverly Hills.

On the plane ride over, he'd mentally rehearsed how he was going to handle this, but by the time the driver pulled up in front of the Ritz-Carlton, he was second-guessing himself. And when he was ushered into the luxurious ballroom packed with celebrities, luminaries, and VIPs, he realized it was the fanciest building he'd ever been in.

A buffet table groaned under the weight of the lavish spread—lobster rolls, beef puff pastry canapés, shrimp tapas; caviar and foie gras and pâté. Off to one side, a harpist played heavenly sounding notes. It made him think of Jenny. His sister loved all things cherubic. Exotic flowers decorated the tables—bird of paradise and plumeria and bougainvillea—their lush scent filling the room.

Waiters carried silver trays laden with champagne flutes throughout the gathering. He noticed their tuxedos looked exactly like his. The plain-Jane rental type. Nothing at all like the expensively tailored tuxes that the other guests wore.

He swallowed hard and tugged at the collar of his tuxedo. The pinch of the Italian leather shoes squeezing his feet reminded him that he didn't fit here, that he was a fish out of water. Hell, if he was being honest, he'd confess this was his first time in a penguin suit.

Except that he had no one with whom to confess. He knew no one. He was completely alone.

Buck up and stop feeling self-conscious. You're here for one reason. Emma.

Sam scanned the room, searching the throng for that familiar flash of copper-colored hair. At last he spied her, up on the podium at the back of the room, standing beside Matt Damon and some other movie stars he recognized. His heart skipped a beat at the sight of her and his mouth went dry.

Sam moved closer, trying to figure out how he was going to get her alone, realizing all the way he'd picked a bad time, a bad place. He should have listened to Nina. He should have waited.

You don't belong here.

Matt Damon leaned over to whisper something to Emma. She laughed. He could hear it from where he stood. The soft sound of her joy.

"Here," snapped a waiter carrying two trays with champagne. "Take one of these, you slacker."

Before Sam could tell him he was a guest, the waiter shoved a tray at him and he stood there like the hired help, while up on the stage, Emma laughed with Matt Damon. She was a star and he was just Steady Sam from Twilight, Texas. Nothing could have been clearer.

That's when he knew for certain that Trixie Lynn was lost to him as surely as Valerie was, and it was time he accepted it. He had to let her go.

Mentally shutting down the emotional pain that stabbed at his heart, he sat the tray down on a nearby table, turned, and walked away.

Emma had never felt so lonely in such a crowded room and she had no idea why.

All her dreams had come true. She was in L.A. at a charity event with Matt Damon. She was eating lavish food and drinking expensive champagne, and on the way inside the event a half-dozen people had asked for her autograph. It was everything she'd ever imagined and yet it did not feel magical.

She thought of what Jill had told her. *This life isn't real, Em.* And in that moment, she realized just how true that was. Tonight she would go home. Back to the apartment Malcolm had rented for her. She'd be alone, surrounded by nothing familiar. Nothing she knew.

Biting down on her bottom lip, she tried to shake off the gloom, but all she could think about was Sam. She wondered what he was doing right now. Probably reading Charlie a bedtime story.

Emma took a deep breath. How she wished she could be there with them.

You could, if you wanted. You could dream a new dream.

The hairs on the nape of her neck lifted, and she had the oddest feeling, as if she was being watched. She raised her head, looked out across the crowd milling around the stage, saw the side exit door open, watched a man in a tuxedo walk out.

Sam, her crazy heart cried as the door closed behind him.

Of course it wasn't Sam. Same height, same build, same color hair, yes, but she knew he was home in Twilight where he belonged.

And she was here alone in L.A., seeing phantom images of the love she'd left behind.

A week after the charity event, Emma was sitting in the makeup chair in the trailer she shared with another actress playing a minor role in the movie, when the door swung open.

Emma and the makeup artist turned their heads.

A gaunt woman, dressed in shabby clothing, stood in the doorway. "Hey, lamb chop, remember me?"

Emma hadn't seen her in twenty-four years, but the minute she looked into the eyes, she recognized her mother. Sylvie Parks—or whatever her name might be now.

The years hadn't been kind. Sylvie appeared thin and worn, like a cotton dress washed too many times. There were deep lines dug in around her eyes, as if she had to keep squinting at the world to hold on to her rose-colored point of view. Her hair was long and unkempt—blond on the ends, graying and brown at the roots. She had a hank of it pulled back from her face by a child's blue barrette, and her teeth were yellowed with nicotine stains. She wore a purple tunic top embroidered with butterflies, a pair of faded jeans, and flip-flops that showed off toes badly in need of a pedicure. On her wrist she wore a pale green plastic bracelet with the word "dream" printed on it in black lettering. She looked like she'd shuffled in from a day at the flea market. Emma wondered how she'd managed to get onto the set.

"Ma . . . Mama?"

So many times over the years she'd envisioned a moment just like this, where she'd made it big and her mother came crawling back begging her forgiveness for leaving her and praising her for having become a star. But now that it was happening, it felt totally surreal, and she wondered if perhaps she was imagining it.

Sylvie stood there assessing her, not saying a word.

Emma had forgotten how much her mother had hurt her. Taking off with the man in the Cadillac, never calling, never writing, never sending a birthday card or a Christmas present. She'd pushed aside memories of those nights she'd cried herself to sleep. How Rex hadn't known how to comfort her or hadn't bothered to make an effort. She'd disconnected from her teenage angst of the hurt, anger, and betrayal that had caused her to lash out in foolish ways, like joyriding in Rex's car and graffitiing the Twilight Bridge.

And yet, in spite of all that, she felt a surprising rush of pity and forgiveness for her mother.

Sylvie opened her arms wide. "Aren't you gonna give your mama a big hug?"

Emma did just that, waving aside the makeup artist who looked ready to call security, sliding from the chair, rushing up to embrace her mother for the first time in over two decades. She smelled the same, like cigarettes and Wind Song cologne and despair. It was a stiff hug, awkward and cool, not like the warm, enveloping embraces she received from the members of the True Love Quilting Club.

In her mind, she'd always imagined there'd be tears at this point, from both of them. But she didn't feel moved to that degree. She felt detached, as if she was standing outside her body watching it all play out with mild curiosity and nothing else. In all honesty, she was appreciative that there was no big emotional fallout. It helped.

Sylvie was the first to step back, and she cocked her head to study Emma. She reached up and fingered a lock of Emma's hair. "Still shiny red."

"Uh-huh."

"I've missed you so much. I love you, Trixie Lynn."

Was she supposed to tell her she loved her back? Once upon a time, she had loved her mother with an undying fierceness. Now? She just felt hollow. "I go by Emma now."

"Of course you do." Her mother nodded. "It sounds more like a movie star name. Can't say I blame you for that. I never wanted to call you Trixie Lynn in the first place, but Rex wanted to name you after his grandmama."

"Funny," she said, "seeing as how Rex wasn't my father."

Sylvie's gaze darted away. "Oh. You found out about that, huh?"

"Who's my real father?"

She shrugged. "I dunno. It was a long time ago. I knew a lot of men before I met Rex."

"You were pregnant with me when he married you and you didn't tell him? How could you do that?"

"Let's not talk about ancient history." Sylvie ironed a palm across Emma's shoulder. "Let's discuss something more pleasant, like you being in the movies. I can't believe it, my own daughter a big star. Who would have thought it would ever happen after you kicked that Broadway producer in the balls."

"You heard about that?"

"I read the tabloids, honey."

"And you're just now coming to see me?"

Sylvie ignored that and prattled on. "I gotta say, ouch! You don't go around kicking a big-time producer in the balls just because he spurns your sexual advances."

Emma was floored. "You believed his story?"

"Well, it *was* in the tabloids."

"He lied. He put the make on *me*, and when I refused to have sex with him to get the part, he got rough. That's when I defended myself."

"You're sure?"

"Are you calling me a liar, Mother?"

Sylvie held up her palms. "No, no. Don't get testy, I was just telling you what I read."

"Well, it was a lie."

"It was in the paper."

"In the tabloids, salacious gossip rags. There is a difference between them and a real paper. If there's a UFO on the cover and the headlines are *Brad Pitt Is an Alien and I'm Having His Out-of-This-World Love Child*, a rational person can sorta figure out it's not true. Then again, I'm betting no one has ever accused you of being rational."

Sylvie tucked her lips together as if to keep from saying what she really wanted to say.

Holding back her opinion, was she? How very noble of her.

"You don't have to be so cruel," Sylvie whispered.

Oh, so now she was the cruel one? That gave her the courage to blurt the question that had been gnawing at the back of her mind for twenty-four years. "Why did you leave me, Mother?"

Sylvie's eyes widened and she looked startled. "I . . . I didn't leave you. I went to follow my bliss, to become an actress."

"And you never once considered that in following your *bliss*"—she spat out the last word—"that you also left me motherless?"

Her mother notched her chin up and slanted a look down her nose. "Everything is not about you."

Emma barked out a sharp laugh. "So tell me, Mother, where did your bliss take you? Were you ever in a movie? Ever been in a stage play? Did you get commercial gigs? Voice any audio books?"

"It's a very difficult business."

"I'm guessing that means the answer to my questions is no."

"I want to talk about something more pleasant."

Anger flared through Emma. Her mother had heard about her through the tabloids. Had known she was in New York after the Scott Miller incident, but her mother hadn't shown up then. When Emma was in trouble and could have used a shoulder to cry on, no Sylvie, but now that Emma had made a success of herself, poof, here was dear old Mom. "What do you want to talk about?"

"Let's talk about your movie."

"Well, I did it. It took me a long time, but here I am." Emma spread her hands to include the dressing room. "I did what you told me to do. I became a star."

Sylvie looked startled. "I never told you to become a star."

Emma drew back. "Of course you did. That's my primary memory of you. You'd chanted over and over again, saying it like a lullaby. Then you gave me this." Emma pulled the star brooch from her purse.

Sylvie made a noise, half grunt, half laugh. "Well, I'll be damned."

"What?" Emma frowned. Had she imagined it? Was it all something she'd concocted in her head because she'd wanted so badly to believe that her mother wanted the best for her?

Sylvie placed her cupped hand against the hollow of her throat. "You thought I was talking to you?"

"Who else would you have been talking to? You used to rock me in your arms and whisper, 'You're gonna be a star, you're gonna be a star, you're gonna be a star.'"

"That was an affirmation."

"And it worked. Whenever I felt down and kicked around by life, I'd just tell myself what you told me all those years ago. 'You're gonna be a star.' It would renew my commitment. The fact that you believed I was capable of being a star kept me going."

"It wasn't an affirmation for *you*." Sylvie laughed, dry and mirthless. "I was repeating it to *myself*."

Before Emma could answer, before she could formulate any kind of a response, a knock sounded on her trailer and an assistant wearing a headset opened the door. "We're ready for you on set, Miss Parks."

"I've got to go," she told Sylvie.

"Um . . . maybe we could have dinner later. There was something I needed to ask you."

"I'm working all day. No time."

"I suppose I deserve the brush-off," Sylvie said. "Leaving you the way I did."

So now she was having a twinge of conscience. Emma snorted. "Have you ever once thought about me in twenty-four years?"

"Sure I did."

"When? When you heard about me on *Entertainment Tonight*?"

Sylvie looked so guilty that Emma knew it was pretty damn close to the truth.

"Let me guess, this thing you needed to ask me. Does it have anything to do with money?"

Sylvie hung her head.

Emma snorted, still holding back the pain thrashing around inside her. She couldn't deal with it now. She had no time to process it. "How much do you need?"

"Ten grand would help a lot."

Ten thousand dollars. The same amount Nina had paid her. Hauling in a steadying breath, she went to the bedroom and retrieved her checkbook. With a shaky hand she wrote her mother a check for ten thousand dollars, tore it out and thrust it at her. "Here," she said. "Take what you really came for."

Her mother stuffed the check in her pocket and mumbled, "Thank you."

"No," Emma said. "Thank *you* for teaching me a very important lesson."

Somehow Emma managed to get through her fourteen-hour day. She played her part and the scenes came out well. She managed to unhitch her mind, at least for the time while she was working, from what her mother had said to her in the trailer that morning. She was professional and proficient. She was, after all, a star, even if she had come to it by repeating affirmations that had never been meant for her.

But once filming wrapped for the day, once she was back in her trailer all alone, lying underneath the quilt that the wonderful, wise women of Twilight had quilted for her and presented to her before she left, all the emotions she'd denied and channeled into her acting came rising up with a vengeance.

All these years, she'd been struggling to live up to her mother's prophecy for her. All she'd ever wanted was to be a star in order to impress her mother and win back her love. All this time she'd thought that her mother had believed in her. Everything she'd ever done had been with this goal in mind. To become a star.

But now she understood how she'd twisted things around in her childish head. How she'd allowed her misguided beliefs to dominate her thinking. Her whole life was built on a bed of lies. Who was she if she wasn't Trixie Lynn Parks turned Emma Parks vying for stardom? What was she if she wasn't striving to be an actress in order to regain her mother's love?

Her impulse was to pick up the phone and call Sam, but it was two in the morning Texas time. Besides, what could he do? Yes, she considered him her best friend in the world, but how could he begin to understand the loneliness, isolation, and betrayal she felt? He had a big, happy, close-knit family. He had his own life to live and he'd made it clear enough that she couldn't give him what he needed.

It was okay. She could get through this. She'd gotten through much worse. In all honesty, she'd lost her mother twenty-four years ago. But today, she'd lost her sense of self.

She tossed and turned. He'd told her she could call him anytime. But did he really mean it?

Emma got up, went to her purse, dug out her cell phone. Then put it back. It was selfish of her to expect him to assuage her fears and worries when she was the one who'd left him. She'd turned her back on Twilight for the glamour of Hollywood.

But she couldn't stem the longing and sadness. She reached for the phone again, flipped it open. She switched it on. Switched it off. Switched it back on again, and then plunked down on the edge of the bed.

Her thumb accidentally brushed against the video feature on camera mode, and it started playing the segment that she'd recorded of Charlie when he and Sam had come to see her off at the airport.

The minute she saw his sweet little face, her heart cracked.

He was smiling at her, big and wide, revealing the priceless gap-toothed grin of a six-year-old. Charlie, the child who'd lost so much, was smiling at *her* like she was someone special. At the time, she hadn't fully appreciated the significance of his smile.

She felt the sting of tears burn the backs of her eyes. She'd been his age when Sylvie had left her. The weight of it still haunted her. Empathy ripped through her, immediately replaced by deep guilt. She'd left him too; no wonder Sam hadn't wanted her to get close to the boy. She wasn't much better than Sylvie. Leaving a boy

and his father, who'd come to care about her, in order
to chase a career.

She'd asked Sylvie how she could just walk away
from her, and yet Emma had done the exact same
thing. She turned off the phone, stuffed it in her purse,
collapsed back on the bed, self-loathing eating a hole
through her.

*You deserve to be alone. You don't deserve to have
a child like Charlie in your life, a man like Sam in your
heart.* In that moment, for the first time, Emma completely understood her mother and how she'd justified
her choices, because the thought was in her own mind.
*If you can't give them what they need from you, then
you better stay far away from them.*

Sylvie wasn't evil. She was just emotionally damaged. Unable to love others the way she loved herself.
It was a genetic defect that apparently Emma had in-
herited.

Grief-stricken, Emma rolled up tight in the special
quilt the True Love Quilting Club had made for her
and softly cried herself to sleep.

CHAPTER TWENTY

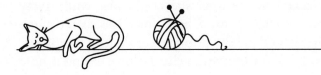

The pattern of a quilt will always lead you back home.
— Quote carved into the Sweetheart Tree, Twilight, Texas

She finished filming her role in Malcolm's film three days before Christmas and caught the first flight back to Texas.

Anxiety had dogged her the whole way home but the closer she got, the more nervous she grew. Heart in her throat, Emma approached the Twilight Playhouse. She was ready to throw herself on the quilting club's mercy and beg them to help her win back Sam. She'd pinned the star brooch to the lapel of her jacket, and she reached up to stroke her fingers over the jewel to bolster her courage.

She paced the sidewalk in front of the playhouse, working up the courage to go inside. The lights flickered on, glowing ghostly in the December fog rolling in off the lake. The square was adorned with twinkling blue and white Christmas lights. A lavishly decorated, twenty-foot-tall tree stood on the courthouse lawn.

Mistletoe and holly were strung from the Dickens-esque streetlamps. Storefronts displayed nativity scenes and Santa with his reindeers. The smell of turkey and cornbread stuffing wafted over from the Funny Farm on the opposite corner. The town in *It's a Wonderful Life* had nothing on Twilight.

Emma wanted to spend the rest of her life here. With friends and neighbors who cared about you, looked in on you. She wanted so badly to belong. Had she waited too late? Had it taken her too long to realize this was where she was meant to be? Would Sam still have her? Could she convince him that she truly no longer wanted fame and fortune? That the dream she'd been dreaming all these years had belonged to her mother, not Emma? That for her, Twilight was the real treasure. That yes, while she loved acting, it was the craft itself she loved, and she didn't have to be in Hollywood or New York to practice it.

Too nervous to prance right in through the front door, she walked around the playhouse to the side entrance, the same entrance where once upon a time she and Sam had sneaked in and found a place to kiss in the loft. Remembering, she ran her fingertips over her lips.

She tried the handle. It wasn't locked. She eased it open slowly and stepped into the short hallway that led into the theater. The sound of voices kept her rooted to the spot as the door whispered closed behind her.

"Thank you so much for helping us set up the nativity scene." She recognized Nina's smooth, cultured voice.

"No problem."

She recognized that voice too. It was Sam. Her heart thumped restlessly, and she almost turned and ran, but then she heard someone else say, "How are you doing, Sam?" in a way that suggested he hadn't been doing well at all.

"I'm fine." He grunted. "Why wouldn't I be?"

Emma dared to shift her position, trying to peek into the theater from this vantage point. All she could see was the backs of two women's heads. One was Patsy. The other was Terri Longoria.

"It's okay to admit you're hurting." That sounded like Marva.

"I'm fine."

"Are you sure?" Patsy asked.

"Sure, I'm sure."

"There's no reason to hold it in."

"I'm not holding it in," Sam growled. "Just because you ladies all buy into the sweetheart myth this town perpetuates doesn't mean I do."

"You're saying you don't believe in the power of that first love?"

"I'm saying it's all in your heads. If you believe it, then it's true for you. If you don't, well . . ."

Emma could almost see his dismissive shrug. Sam was fine. He didn't miss her at all. Hurt rushed over her, immediately pursued by denial. Maybe he was just putting up a brave front. She'd discovered Sam was adept at tamping down his feelings. Or maybe she was just kidding herself that she'd meant more to him than a good time. She turned to leave, grateful she'd overheard the conversation before she made a fool of herself and confessed her undying love for him.

"Frankly," Sam continued, "I think you obsess about this true love stuff. Plus, you feed into each other. I mean, come on, Patsy, everyone knows you're still mooning over Hondo after forty years. Give it up and release yourself from the torture."

Several of the women let out a collective gasp at his audacity in bringing up Patsy's failed romance with the only man she'd ever loved. Emma was amazed by his soliloquy. She'd never heard him string so many words together at once, or be so forthcoming with his opinions.

"But maybe I'm just kidding myself because the alternative is too painful," he said.

The women murmured in agreement.

"I've already lost my one chance at lasting happiness because the woman I've loved since I was fourteen years old can't love me back the way I need for her to love me. So I'm doing my damnedest to forget her, and I'd appreciate it if you'd let me stay surly and bitter for a while."

The murmurs of agreement turned to noises of sympathy.

Emma splayed her palm to her mouth. A chill chased down her spine. Inside that room was a world she so desperately wanted to be a part of. Did she stand a chance?

Spurred by a need to fix everything she'd screwed up, Emma stepped from the darkened hall and into the lighted theater. Sam's back was to her as he set up the manger. He was kneeling on the stage, the members of the quilting club surrounding him as they set out Wise Men, Mary and Joseph, and baby Jesus. No one had yet seen her.

"You guys need any help?" Emma forced the words from her throat.

Slowly, Sam turned his head. He looked at her, but he didn't move, his hands frozen around the wooden leg.

"Yep," she said. "It's me. The bad penny returns."

The True Love Quilting Club stared at her, looked concerned.

Sam said nothing. His face reflected no emotion at all.

Emma's heart took the roller coaster ride to her feet. Fear pleaded with her to run, but she pushed herself forward, moving down the aisle toward the stage. "I'm back for keeps. What do you think about that?"

She raised her chin, looked at the women who'd befriended her—Nina, Patsy, Marva, Terri, Dotty Mae, Raylene, Jenny.

Still, Sam said nothing. Neither did the women.

She'd just put her ass on the line. Committing to a future in Twilight, and no one said a word of welcome. Had she been wrong about them after all? Had she been kidding herself about these women, this community, this man?

Emma tried to think of the appropriate character or actress to channel for this situation, a line from a movie that would break the tension, make it all okay, but her mind went blank. She was on her own.

Gulping, she soldiered on. She'd come this far. She wasn't turning back. If Sam didn't want her, he was going to have to reject her.

"Once upon a time," she said. "I had no doubts. More than anything in the world, I wanted to be a star. I ate and slept and breathed acting. I avoided getting close to people because I didn't want anything to stand in my way of stardom. I was going to do this thing or die trying. I worked and I hoped and I prayed for my dream to come true. Every night before I went to bed I chanted, 'I'm a star, I'm a star, I'm a star.' "

She paused. Sam's face remained unreadable. No one said a word. The silence deafened. If she was making a fool of herself, she wasn't doing it halfway. It was all or nothing.

"But now . . . now I just . . . I'm not sure of anything anymore. Then I got a part in a major motion picture. It was supposed to be fulfilling. *I* was supposed to be fulfilled. It was supposed to make up for all the love I never had as a kid. But I didn't feel in any way fulfilled or loved. Instead, I felt . . . *empty*." She moistened her lips, blinked back against the tears threatening to trickle down her cheeks. "And it was because you weren't there. I couldn't touch you. I couldn't bury my nose against your shirt and smell your puppy dog and spray starch scent. I couldn't hear your voice or see your smile. I missed you so damn much, Sam."

Sam straightened. His face gave away nothing. She had no idea what he was thinking. Whether he'd come down off that stage and gather her to his chest or tell her to leave.

Every muscle in Emma's body tensed. She clenched her jaw, clenched her fists. "I've been so stupid and narrowly focused. So blind to what was right in front of me. I thought being a successful actress would make me feel like a star. It didn't. I thought it would make me feel special. It didn't do that either. The only place I've ever felt special was right here in Twilight with you."

She couldn't stop the tears now. They were streaming down her face. "It might be too little, too late, but I love you, Sam. You've made me whole."

Sam shook his head.

Dear God, he didn't want her anymore. Her heart quivered.

"No?" she whimpered.

"No," he said.

In that moment, her entire world hung in the balance as she felt all her hopes shatter.

"I won't let you give up your dream."

"But I want to give it up."

"And I can't let you make that sacrifice for me."

They stared at each other.

"We can make our way through this," he said. "Maybe if I moved to L.A. with you if that's where you have to be. Or maybe we can live here in the winter and in L.A. when Charlie is out of school."

"Sam . . ." She swallowed. "Are you saying what I think you're saying?"

"I want to be with you no matter where you are, but I can't let you give up your dreams for me. Those dreams are what make you who you are. We can find a compromise."

"So you love me too?" she asked, her heart overflowing with hope.

"Woman," he said gruffly, "don't you know that I've loved you since we were fourteen years old?"

Vaguely, she heard the members of the True Love Quilting Club applauding and cooing, "Awww." She didn't mind. This was, after all, their doing. They'd taught her how to take the pieces of her life and cobble them into a patchwork quilt of love. Because of these wonderful women she'd come to recognize that everyone was a star, each and every one special and unique in his own way.

Sam was striding off the stage as she was flying

up to meet him. He caught her around the waist. She linked her arms behind his neck. He twirled her in a circle, and his mouth came down on hers, urgent and salty.

She wrapped her legs around him as they kissed deep and hard. He carried her up the aisle and out the door. He didn't let her go when they were on the street. He strode purposefully past tourists and locals alike who stared at them with curious interest. Grinning, she clung to him, watching the town square disappear behind them as he headed up Topaz Street to his house.

He marched up the porch. The same porch Patches had herded her onto the day she got off the bus. The bells on the Christmas wreath adorning the front door jingled merrily as he pried it open without putting her down.

"Where's Charlie?" she asked as he carried her over the threshold.

"Spending the night with Belinda and her brood."

"Oh," she said. "What about Maddie?"

"Her sister had surgery, she went to spend the holidays with her."

"I hope it's nothing serious."

"Not too serious. She'll be fine."

"That's good."

He let her slide to her feet and then he pulled her against his chest and dipped his head for another kiss. He threaded both hands through her hair, holding her close. His heated lips melted every last vestige of doubt. He wanted her. He loved her.

After a long moment of teasing her with his maddening tongue, Sam took her hand and guided her upstairs to the bedroom. Frenzied, he tugged at her clothes. She felt just as urgent, plucking at the buttons of his shirt, hungry to have him, fully, completely, totally hers.

"God, how I've missed you, Em," his voice came out heavy, strained. "I need you *now*."

"We don't have to hurry. We've got all night."

"Gotta have you." He tugged her jacket off her shoulders, sent it sailing to the floor on the other side of the bed. "I needed you so bad that two weeks ago I hopped on a plane and flew out to L.A. to see you."

"Why didn't you see me?"

"I did see you. In your element, and then I couldn't bear to let you see me. You were up there on that stage with those movie stars and I—"

"You were at the charity event."

"I was."

"I knew it! I knew you were there."

"What do you mean?"

"I felt you. I looked up and I saw you walking out the door but I couldn't believe it was you." She chuckled. "You came to L.A. for me?"

"I was going to tell you we could find a compromise and then I realized I didn't belong in your world. But that was just my fear talking. If you can come back here, prepared to give it all up for me, then I can get over my fears and let you show me your world."

"Really?" She breathed, twisting the buttons on his shirt.

He kissed her again. "Really."

They looked at each other in the darkness. Her shirt was off, his was unbuttoned. The fire rolled over them again, their self-control evaporated. They finished ripping their clothes off, leaving them scattered in a heap.

He laid her back on the bed, poised his body over hers, rested his weight on his forearms, and looked down into her face. She smiled up at him. His hair fell to one side, revealing his scar.

She reached up to trace it with her fingertips and he didn't flinch. "Beautiful," she whispered, and pressed her lips to the old wound.

And he let her, without pulling away or looking self-conscious. He kneed her thighs apart and she opened her legs, letting him in.

He moaned low in his throat, a wholly masculine sound of pleasure, and sank into her deep and sweet. His eyes were alight with a hot glow, his thrusts long, hard, and slow. He captured her lips, roughly, but lovingly. Their mouths clung as he increased the tempo of their mating.

He pushed harder, faster. Emma raised her hips, egging him on.

"I love you," she whispered fiercely, "more than anyone or anything I have ever known."

His body stiffened, and she wrapped her legs around his waist, pulling him in as deep as he could go. Release claimed them both in that instant and he called out her name in a rough, guttural cry.

Emma awoke sometime later to find herself cradled in the crook of Sam's arm, his hand gently stroking her hair. Her head was nestled against his chest, and she could hear the steady thumping of his heart. Steady Sam. *Her* Steady Sam. The urgency of their previous mating had died down, and in its place was a gentle softness. His fingers massaged her scalp, sending shivers of delight skipping down her spine.

She traced the ridges of his chest with a finger, savoring his taut hardness. His lips touched her temple and he nibbled at her skin. Immediately, her body responded. Her breathing quickened, her body stiffened.

"Relax," he murmured, smoothing his palm over her shoulder, moving his mouth from her temple to her earlobe.

But how could she relax when he was running his other hand over her breasts, lightly playing with her nipples? He shifted, and his mouth followed his hands, his tongue suckling gently on her beaded peaks. And there went those exploring fingers, tracing down her midriff and sliding between her thighs, his masculine fingers finding her feminine moistness and roguishly slipping inside.

Moaning, she encircled his wrist with her fingers, guiding his exploration, showing him exactly how she liked it. He didn't make a misstep. Every stroke took her intensity up a notch. He kissed the underside of her chin, his lips wickedly hot.

Then he turned her on her side and bumped his hip against her butt. He bent her right leg and edged in closer, positioning himself to sink deep inside her from behind.

"Welcome home, Emma," he whispered. "Welcome home."

He moved purposefully, the rhythm easy and languid. She whimpered and pressed against him, urging him to pick up the pace, but he only laughed and went even slower. The tension built slowly. Smooth and silky. She was acutely aware of every breath, every pulse beat. He cupped her buttocks as he slid in and out, in and out, a train chugging up a hill. Building momentum, working up a head of steam.

His hands pulled her helplessly against him. Rocking. Rocking. Soft, mewling sounds escaped her throat, slipped into the darkened room to mingle with his pleasure-induced groans. His mouth burned the back of her neck, hot and erotic, tender and loving, but he never lost the rhythm. Their bodies were joined, fused, perfectly matched. Each movement elicited more delight, more surprise.

Then he rolled onto his back, took her with him, turning her around until she straddled him. Their gazes met and Emma sank into the exciting comfort of his eyes. He locked his hands around her waist, helping her move up and down on his hard, long shaft.

Swept away by intense sensation, she quickened the pace. Sam met her challenge, raising his hips up, digging his heels into the mattress, giving her a ride to end all rides. He kept at it, chasing her pleasure with a devotion that dizzied her head.

Higher and higher he drove her toward climax. The light of love was in his eyes, real and true and forever. She smiled at him, and he laughed a laugh that hugged her soul.

At the peak, she cried his name, a chant, a litany, a prayer of thanksgiving. "Sam, Sam, Sam."

He followed right with her, dropping into the precious abyss, freefalling into the sensuous undertow, going under for the third time and loving every minute of it. Drowning, lost, and yet at the same time found.

He held on to her waist as she flopped forward to bury her face in his neck. She drew in the scent of him, breathed deep. This was the smell of love. They clung to each other, quivering with sensation, breathing deep of life. Sam stroked her, murmured sweet nothings until her heart rate returned to normal and her body had stilled.

"I've never felt so special," she whispered.

"That's because you are special." He lifted her chin, looked deeply into her eyes again. "You're my shining star."

They slept for hours, until Patches pressed his cold nose against Sam's bare calf sticking out from under the covers and whimpered for his breakfast. The midmorning sun seeped in through the curtains, casting a cheery light over the carpet. Everything looked fresh and shiny and new. Sam felt fresh and shiny and new.

Emma lifted her head off the pillow, a sheet crease marking her cheek. She smiled at him and stretched, and the world was absolutely perfect.

He leaned over to kiss her. "Stay here. I'll make you breakfast in bed."

"Don't be silly. I love to cook. I'll whip up an omelet while you feed your menagerie and call to check on Charlie."

"How did you know I was going to do all that?"

"Because you're steady, Sam. A man a woman can always count on." She looked at him with such love in her eyes that hearing himself called steady no longer made him feel predictable and boring.

Steady was a good thing, and Emma made him feel alive in a way no one ever had. He was her anchor and she was his star. He grounded her; she lifted him up.

While the smell of frying bacon and percolating coffee filled the air, Sam fed the animals and then picked up the cordless phone and stepped out onto the front porch to call Belinda. "How's Charlie?"

"He's great. He wants to talk to you. Ever since that boy started talking it's like a dam burst. As if he was saving up everything he had to say and now he's just letting it all out."

"He drove you crazy."

"Absolutely not. I have five kids. I was already crazy." She laughed.

"Listen, could you keep him a little while longer? There's something I need to do and—"

"It's okay," Belinda said. "I heard about Emma."

"I guess this is the part where I apologize for yelling at you for meddling in my life."

"Apology accepted."

"If you hadn't instigated this whole thing and convinced Nina to bring her here . . ."

"Hey, it was touch and go there for a while."

"Thanks."

"You're welcome."

"Belinda . . ." He took a deep breath. "I love her so much." Sam realized he'd grown as chatty as his son. There was a time not so long ago when he would never have been able to confess that to his aunt. But Emma had taught him that expressing yourself could be a good thing.

"I know, Sam," Belinda murmured. "I'm so happy she came home."

"Me too." Sam smiled. "Me too."

After breakfast, as they washed the dishes together, Sam told Emma he had some errands to run, including picking Charlie up from Belinda's. "Take a long hot bath. Relax. Make yourself at home. I'll be back in a couple of hours."

His suggestion sounded heavenly, so once he left,

she went into the bathroom and drew herself a hot bath. Her body was sweetly sore from the night before. She caught a glimpse of her reflection in the bathroom mirror. Her eyes glowed and her hair blazed a burnished copper in the light. She'd never thought of herself as a beautiful woman, but in that moment, her looks pleased her.

"This is what being in love looks like," she whispered, and reached up to trace her image in the mirror. Her pulse skipped. She could hardly believe she was here and that this was happening. Sam had taken her back with open arms. Not only taken her back, but posed a compromise that she'd never thought possible.

The soft feeling in her heart told her she'd come full circle, made the journey back home to her fourteen-year-old self. She'd been lucky enough to end up with the only man she'd ever loved. She'd gone from being an outsider to being a member of the fold. It was all she'd ever really wanted. All her yearning had evaporated. Thanks to Sam and Charlie and the True Love Quilting Club, she was fully sated and blissful.

She slid into the tub, lay back, placed a damp washcloth over her eyes, and let the warm water and clean scent of soap flow over her. She must have dozed off, because a sound in the hallway caused her to jerk upright with a start. "Hello?" she called. "Sam?"

Silence.

"Is anyone out there?" Muscles tensed, she reached for a towel. Had someone broken into the house?

A bumping sound against the door made her smile. Patches. She'd forgotten about the dog. She got out, dried off, and drained the tub. Then she opened the door to find the Border collie lolling on the floor outside the door. He looked up at her with intent eyes. How had she ever been afraid of this beautiful animal? She headed for the bedroom, Patches trotting at her side. She stepped over the threshold and stopped in her tracks. Someone had been in the house.

On the bed lay a silky jade green dress and a pair of matching heels. Her heart caught in her throat. It was exactly like the dress she'd described to Sam when she was fourteen, when she told him what being a star meant to her—parties and fanfare and fine clothes. Beside the dress was an envelope. Emma opened it and read:

Get used to being spoiled. Put on this dress and come to the Twilight Playhouse at noon—Sam.

Excitement pushed against her chest. What was he up to?

It was almost noon now. Hurriedly, she dressed, brushed her hair, and put on some makeup.

The courthouse clock rang its last chime of the lunch hour as she hurried up the steps of the playhouse, her stomach tight with anticipation. She pushed through the door and stepped inside the lobby, expecting to find Sam, but instead she found Nina sitting inside her office with the door open.

"Emma!" Nina waved her over. "Come on in. We've got a lot to discuss."

Tentatively, Emma edged into Nina's office and saw Malcolm sitting on the sofa. "What's up?"

Nina pointed at the chair across from her. "Have a seat."

She frowned in confusion, but sat down and rested her hands in her lap.

"That dress looks beautiful on you," Malcolm noted.

"Thanks. Sam bought it for me."

"He has excellent taste," Nina added, "but I'm sure you already knew that."

Emma nodded, not knowing what else to say.

"I imagine you're wondering why Sam told you to come here."

"Yes."

Nina spread her hands out on the desk. "This is really Malcolm's news. He should be the one to tell you." She turned in her chair. "The floor is yours, honey."

Emma shifted her gaze to Malcolm.

He got to his feet, clasped his hands behind his back. "Even before Nina and I reconnected," he said, "I was growing tired of L.A. I was looking to relocate my movie studio. Several producers have made the switch to British Columbia, and Vancouver was on my possibilities list . . . but then so was Texas. Over the last decade or so, movie making has come of age in the Lone Star State."

"You're moving to Texas?"

"I am. I've bought land near Fort Worth and just finished making all the arrangements. It's a done deal." Malcolm smiled.

"That's wonderful."

"I also hope this means you'll consider working for Shooting Star Studios."

"You're serious?" She could scarcely believe it. With Malcolm's offer, she'd be able to have her cake and eat it too. Live in Twilight with Sam and Charlie and still be able to work for one of the most famous producers in the world.

"I am. You're a great actress, Emma. It would be my honor to continue working with you." He held out his hand.

"I can't thank you enough." Emma shook his hand.

"Don't thank me. Nina was the one who convinced me Texas was the place to be."

Emma swung her gaze to her generous mentor.

Nina stood up and smiled, her eyes misted with joyous tears. "Malcolm has asked me to marry him again."

"That's wonderful! Congratulations, Nina, Malcolm. I'm so happy for you both."

"And we're happy for you and Sam." Malcolm moved to put his arm around Nina's shoulder and draw her close.

Emotion clogged her throat and she thought she might cry. *Joan Crawford*, she thought, trying to stop the tears, *Bette Davis* and . . . oh, what the hell. She was just going to cry and be done with it. She sniffled.

Nina was sniffling too. She reached for a Kleenex, handed one to Emma, took one for herself, and dabbed at her eyes. "Oh," she said, "the adventures we're all going to have."

They talked for a long while, ironing out the details, discussing a future filled with possibilities.

"We'll talk more later," Malcolm said. "Right now, Nina and I have an appointment with a wedding planner."

"Yes, yes, thank you again."

"Stay here a bit if you'd like," Nina invited. "Revel in your well-deserved success. Lock up when you're done." She tossed her the keys.

"Okay." Emma smiled.

Nina and Malcolm left and Emma walked around Nina's office looking at all the playbills tacked to the wall. She could scarcely believe her good fortune. To think she could have it all. Sam, Charlie, Twilight, the quilting club, and acting. Her heart overflowed.

She breathed in deep, taking in the slightly musty smell of the old building. There was so much history here. She grazed her fingers over the stone walls, caressed time beneath her fingertips. A sense of connection quilted her to this place, to this town, to these people. She belonged, fully, wholly, completely.

And she couldn't wait to see Sam. Clearly, he'd been involved in this. She turned to go, Nina's keys in her hand, and headed for the front exit. She opened the door and spied Patches sitting on the sidewalk. He must have followed her over here.

She started to step out, but the Border collie moved toward her.

"Oh, don't start. I'm not afraid of you anymore." Emma moved right. The dog blocked her.

"Patches," she scolded, "let me by."

The dog sat on his haunches.

She moved left.

Immediately, he cut her off.

Emma sighed in exasperation. "What is going on here, dog?"

Patches nosed her foot.

"You don't want me to go forward, nor to the left or the right, where do you want me to go?"

He started intently at the theater door.

"You want me to go back inside?"

He thumped his tail.

She tried to stalk forward, but he went around her. "You're not going to leave me alone until I go back in there, are you?"

Patches cocked his head.

"Great, not only am I talking to a dog, I'm taking

instructions from him as well. Fine, fine, I'm going back in." She opened the door, stepped inside the lobby. "Happy now?"

Patches darted in.

"Okay, we're here. Now what?"

He bumped her knee.

She turned and headed for the theater. The dog stayed right behind her. If she stopped, he'd nudge her. If she went left or right, he cut her off. Obviously, the dog wanted her to go into the theater, but she had no idea why. He bumped her again.

"I'm going, I'm going." She pushed open the heavy wooden double doors leading into the theater, the sound echoing in the emptiness.

The theater itself was dark, but there was a light on over the stage. It had to be in the loft. The place where she and Sam first kissed. She'd better turn it off.

She started down the aisle. Patches followed at her side. Had the dog somehow known the light had been left on? Nah, Border collies were smart, but they weren't *that* smart. Emma climbed up on the stage, Patches with her every step of the way.

After pushing aside the heavy red velvet curtain, she moved to climb the metal stairs leading to the loft.

That's when she heard the giggle.

Someone was up there.

"Hey," she called, rapidly scaling the ladder. "Who's there?"

Another round of giggles.

She poked her head through the opening, and there sat Sam and Charlie, dressed up in tuxedos, looking completely adorable. Sam held a dog whistle in his hand and had a sheepish grin on his face. That explained Patches's behavior.

"What are you guys doing up here?" she asked, stepping onto the loft platform. "And why are you dressed like that?"

"'Cause," Charlie explained, displaying a gap-toothed grin. "We got sumpin' very important to ask you."

She walked over to them. "You do, huh?"

"Yep." He nodded. "Don't we, Dad?"

"That we do," Sam said. "Here." He stood up. "Sit down."

It was Emma's turn to giggle. She sat down in the thin-legged, straight-back wooden chair Sam had vacated. "What are you two up to?"

Sam tucked the dog whistle into the breast pocket of his tux. He looked so handsome that her breath caught. Then from the pocket of his jacket, he withdrew something he kept shielded in his palm.

He went down on one knee.

Emma started shaking all over.

He extended his hand, revealed the black ring box, and cracked it open with his thumb. A beautiful diamond solitaire, nestled in a star-shaped setting with smaller diamonds filling in the points of the star, winked at her in the light.

"Oh!" She splayed a palm over her heart.

"Trixie Lynn Parks, my one true love, who has now bloomed into the beautiful, incomparable Emma, will you marry me?"

Charlie joined his father on his knee. "And will you be my new mommy?" Charlie looked at her with earnest eyes exactly like Sam's.

"Yes, yes," she exclaimed.

She saw Sam's chest fall with a quick exhale of air

as he slipped the ring onto her finger. Saw a wide grin cut across Charlie's face.

Emma jumped to her feet and embraced them both in a tight group hug. Then Sam pressed his lips to her ear and whispered, "I can't wait to spend the rest of my life with you."

EPILOGUE

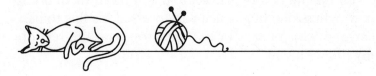

With this ring, I do thee wed.
—Words sewn into the wedding ring quilt gifted to
Dr. Samuel and Emma Cheek on their wedding day,
from the True Love Quilting Club

They got married in the theater on Valentine's Day. The playhouse was packed to overflowing. Half the town of Twilight showed up, it seemed. All of Sam's family was there, and of course everyone from the quilting club, and Malcolm Talmadge.

The man who'd raised her, but couldn't bring himself to love her because she wasn't his daughter by blood, did not come, and neither did her mother. But that was okay. She had Sam and his big, boisterous, colorful family, who teased and argued and loved one another in powerful and generous ways. The Cheeks behaved the way she always imagined a real family behaved, supporting one another through thick and thin, even if they disagreed. They accepted her with open arms and willing hearts.

She asked Sam's father to walk down the aisle with her, and she could have sworn his eyes misted as he gruffly said, "I'd be honored." Sam's brother Ben was his best man, Mac and Joe served as groomsmen. Sam's sister Jenny stood in as maid of honor, while Katie and Maddie were bridesmaids. Lois Cheek took her aside before the ceremony and told her how happy she was for Emma to be her daughter-in-law and gave her full blessing.

Charlie was the ring bearer, and he looked so adorable in his tux with his copper cowlick (the color so much like Emma's own) stubbornly standing up in the back, defying all Maddie's attempts to flatten it. He carried the ring on the pillow as if it was a sacred responsibility, his shoulders as straight as a soldier's, his hands outstretched, each step taken with deliberate thought. The sight of him warmed her to the center of her soul. Emma couldn't wait to mother him. To give him the kind of unconditional love she'd never had as a child.

As Emma moved toward the altar that had been erected onstage, her arm linked with Sam's dad, a sense of complete and utter peace settled over her. And when she looked into Sam's eyes, and he reached for her hand, the entire theater vibrated with the force of their love.

And when Sam said, "I do," and slipped the ring on her finger, Emma fully understood that family didn't always come from whom you were born to, but from those who saw you for who you really were deep inside, past the defenses and the fears and self-doubts, past the mistakes and missteps. Family was where you hung your heart, and hers had gotten sweetly tangled up in Twilight, Texas.

"You may now kiss the bride," exclaimed the minister.

Sam kissed her, cementing their union. Her lips tingled, sending a message of pure joy pulsing throughout her body. Amid loud applause, Sam finally broke the kiss and looked down into her eyes and whispered, "Welcome home."